Praise for Emily Sue Harvey

"A talent to watch."
—Steve Berry, *New York Times* bestselling author

"Emily Sue Harvey captures the humor and heartbreak of Southern Culture."
—Kay Allenbaugh, bestselling author of *Chocolate for a Woman's Soul*

"Emily Sue Harvey has now become a new favorite author for me."
—The Book Tree

"Emily Sue Harvey has a beautiful way with words."
—Peeking Between the Pages

Twilight Time

Twilight Time

Emily Sue Harvey

THE
ST●RY
PLANT

The Story Plant
Studio Digital CT, LLC
P.O. Box 4331
Stamford, CT 06907

Cover design by Barbara Aronica-Buck
Author photo by Vanessa Kauffmann

Print ISBN: 978-1-61188-172-1
E-book ISBN: 978-1-61188-173-8

Visit our website at www.TheStoryPlant.com

First Story Plant Printing: February 2015

Printed in the United States of America

0 9 8 7 6 5 4 3 2 1

I dedicate this book to Father God, who is the author and finisher of my faith, who gave me life, and then granted me a miracle on New Year's Eve, 2012. During a horrific accident, rather than taking me on to Heaven, He left me here to continue work in His earthly kingdom and blessed me with full restoration of mind and limb. I shall ever sing His praises and do His will.

To my husband, Leland Harvey, the most loving, generous, kind, and courageous man I've ever known. You are my hero in every way possible. Thank you for being the iconic man of God, provider and protector for me and our four beautiful children. Your beauty and grace extends to the next generations bearing your DNA. You have always been and will forever be my heart.

To my pastor, the Rev. Jerry Madden, who challenges me weekly to go deeper, deeper, and yet deeper in the faith, a faith that tethers me to the Great I AM.

And finally, I dedicate this book to—and applaud—those who first-hand and courageously face down the terrifying blight of Alzheimer's, as well as the multitude of caregivers who daily do battle for their loved ones who are stricken with dementia, Alzheimer's, or other tragic neurodegenerative diseases, and to Dr. Mary T. Newport, M.D. for sharing her experience and findings on how the brain uses ketones as an alternative fuel. Let us pray together that we may keep our loved ones with us as long as possible and that soon a cure will appear on the horizon.

Acknowledgments

Twilight Time is a set-in-fiction story that is partly based on true life. It is one that changed my course in life's journey. On New Year's Eve, 2012, I experienced a near-death accident. My survival was declared a miracle. My recovery was long and arduous. That voyage provided a model for this book's heroine, Rachel's, struggle through trauma. At the same time, the book's hero, Peter, experiences short-term memory lapses that prove so challenging that, at times, he despairs. *Twilight Time* is upon the couple. Some of the story's drama is pure fiction but the emotions are genuine.

I want to take this opportunity to thank the following "angels" during that post-trauma period of my life:

The medical staffs at both Greenville Memorial Hospital and Roger C. Peace Rehab, who first battled to save my life, and then assist me on my way to full recovery.

So many nurses, aides, and doctors who "dropped by" to simply chat and encourage me will forever remain dear to my heart. You each know who you are.

In particular, ICU nurse Angela, an angel who kept me adrift during those critical first hours, physical therapist Shaun Ison, the mentor who gave me hope, Kristy Wolfe who coaxed my self-sufficiency to life, and beautiful recreational therapist Margie Davis, who showed me I could leave pain and despair behind for long moments during fun "stuff."

Susan Cooper Harvey, my daughter-in-love, who camped out in my hospital room for three weeks and later continued her vigil with hands-on care during my initial home recuperation. Also, thanks to my son, David Harvey, who faithfully looked out for his parents during this interim.

My sister, Patsy Roach, who ventured daily to my house for months to do those things for me that I could not do, and my other sister, Karen Bradley, who stood by, helping when needed.

My brother, Roger Miller, who presented me with a laptop to carry me through long, dark days of mostly bed confinement.

Daughter, Pam McCall and granddaughter, Kristin Smith, who drove up from Charleston on my first day home to treat me to a gourmet meal, the memory of which still lingers tantalizingly. Pam's regular phone calls lifted me during hard times.

My own "Gang:" friends Billie and Bill McGregor, J.C. Bowick and the late Drusilla Childress, my muses for "The Gang," who still to this day lend my life an extra dimension of brightness and humor that gets me through many rough patches. Also Jeff Engst, Tammi Sweatt, Christina Lynch, Jordan Plemmons, Stephanie Hughes, Stephanie Phillips, and Dave Taylor, muses for the staff at Eli's Place, who—in real life—make daily dining with The Gang a true pleasure.

Sheila and Rollie Knoke, close friends who loaned me their amazing Sharon Rose Farm and animal menagerie as the model for my book's own Sugar Hills Farm setting. And yes, it is as amazing as the book describes! Not only that, these two brought hubby and me a wonderful meal during my second week home from the hospital, visiting and engaging and brightening an otherwise dismal time.

Other visiting "angels" bearing delicious cuisine were friends Terry and Mary Lou Montgomery and Jim and Frieda Baird, each blessing us with their goodies, time, prayers, and love.

Kudos to Fire Chief Jesse West and the Startex Fire Department, who got me into my house on my homecoming day (without aid of a ramp).

And to all those who took time to phone, send cards, do Facebook and e-mail posts, and the dozens of family and friends who dropped by to cheer me up—and most of all, those who took time to pray for me, I give you my heartfelt thanks!

Last but certainly not least, as always, I owe a mammoth debt of gratitude to Lou Aronica and Peter Miller, whose belief in me opened doors that ushered in my dream of sharing my heart with wonderful readers. I wish for you both God's richest blessings!

Part One

\|/

*"Heavenly shades of night are falling.
'Tis Twilight Time."*

Prologue

Her holiday traditions are legendary . . . and her twilight dream displays endless tables, bulging beneath her time-honored culinary delights.

Joy evades her.

"I can't believe it," she groans. "Here I am—a Christmas dropout."

Rachel's eyes popped open on that admission. She awoke with a heaviness that defied justification. It was like some invisible entity had invaded her head, manipulating her tear ducts and emotions like a thrill-seeking kid's fingers on a new game.

Peter had earlier kissed her goodbye and left to go check on one of their rental houses with wobbly door knobs and faulty locks.

She remained in bed, pillow propped, staring vacantly at the TV screen. Eartha Kitt's sexy rendition of "Santa Baby" wafting over from Sirius XM's Traditional Holiday Music channel barely grazed her ear-waves.

Music—her sole concession to celebrating Yuletide this year. And even that left her unmoved. This aberration from a heart that channeled, through slender fingertips onto two keyboards—some of the world's most beautiful music and/or words and phrases choreographed to arouse infinite, universal human emotions. Rachel excelled in both music and writing.

Yet her spirit remained flatlined.

No Christmas tree decked Rachel James' holly-less halls this season. Outside in the crisp South Carolina winter, her burgeoning holly bushes' vibrant red berry clusters preened, untouched. Jolly decorations remained hidden away in an upstairs closet.

No walnut fudge or Mounds candy incubated in the fridge, or the dozen other traditional goodies that had accompanied her on her six-plus decade's life journey. Why bother? Her house sat eerily silent and vacant with her family splintered and flung to the four winds.

The Gang was out of town. Sister Gabby and hubby Leon were visiting their children and grandchildren. So were cousin Drusilla and J.C. Gabby had invited Rachel and Peter to come along and celebrate with them all, but Rachel had declined, knowing it would only make her feel worse to see their tight closeness.

Most debilitating was that both a son and daughter were now erased from Rachel and Peter's family portrait. Both gone. No affectionate teasing in the kitchen while whipping up time-honored recipes or the fun of opening gifts as they made family memories.

Traditions were only enjoyable if you had someone to share them with, else they became as empty gongs.

Amber and Jason, both gone.

Jason through death. Amber by choice.

Their absence rang and wailed through her hollow soul today. The PTSD lapses she'd experienced since her accident still hovered, nearly a year later, like the eye of a hurricane, one moment serene, the next spinning her into hellish chasms so deep she wondered if she would make it back up far enough this time to haul herself out.

She'd thought that by now, her emotions would be leveled out.

Wrong.

The past year had been seasoned with spices and flavors utterly at odds with each other: Twilight shadows and rainbows of joy, horror and newly plumbed love, an interval storm-tossed and weathered with unspeakable pain yet incredibly tender.

She'd been jerked about like Raggedy Ann yet had survived each challenge—the likes she'd never have fathomed—by the skin of her teeth.

Hers and Peter's favorite song, "Twilight Time," the sound track of their lives, had taken on diverse connotations. Heavenly shades of lilac falling now kept the gloaming bearable, just barely at times, but she'd made it thus far. Only her faith in God and the fact that Peter needed her propelled her to take that next step, knowing that eventually, this thing called life would snap together with the greater puzzle pieces.

At the moment, however, in the earthly here and now, according to the Captain and Tennille, love was what kept it together.

Oh, she had no fear of death. She'd faced it eyeball to eyeball months earlier and would have succumbed had it not been for Peter and a virtual regiment of angels.

Peter, the love of her life, who'd brought her both agony and ecstasy.

She alone held the key to his happiness or lack thereof.

She alone held the final enigma piece to confirm his existence. He wouldn't come out and say it because he loved her too much. She'd ignored it all these years, but now, she felt his need all the way to her bone marrow.

The purple-colored curtains were slowly falling, to mark the end of day. And her heart heard Peter's heart's cry.

Lord, help her to do the right thing, while there was still time.

Because "Twilight Time" was upon them.

Chapter One

\1/

Eleven months earlier

*"This is the true wine of astonishment: We are not over when
we think we are."*
—Alice Walker

Rachel did not see it coming.

She should have when Peter's sleep pattern veered into restless tosses, twitches, and wild thrashing. That should have jangled an alarm. At such times she would awake with a dread of encountering something potentially volatile and unpredictable, like a fist flailing against skin and bone.

Hers.

But since portent was intangible and the dreaded had dropped off the radar screen, she'd managed, until this morning, to ignore it. Denial and repression dug in. At the same time, Peter's tiny memory lapses had also dug in. But she'd managed so far to kick it all aside as messy clutter strewn across her path.

Besides, Peter had experienced some good nights, when he slept peacefully beside her while nightmare demons slinked off to torment some other inopportune soul.

Her husband had, all his life, been prone to sleep walking and acting out his dreams. His mother, before her poor mind wandered off into the shadowy unknown, told Rachel how, one night during his teens, Peter leaped through a window, providentially open at the time, and crashed atop the screen on the ground. In his dream, he'd been pursued by evil forces. Fortunately, he wasn't seriously wounded, except for his blasted pride.

In his younger days' search for validation, Peter's modesty—most of the time—played peek-a-boo. At times, it disappeared behind fiery temperamental outbursts and at others colored Peter the most giving, nurturing guy ever created. And it was maddening. But at the same time it added to his romantic mystique. Rachel was hopelessly in love with the man.

Decades earlier, a week into their marriage, she awoke one night blinking against blinding light with Peter moving briskly about like a man on a mission. He'd switched on every lamp and overhead bulb in the house.

"What's—what are you doing?" Rachel rasped, propped up on elbows, squinting and bewildered. Fully dressed, down to socks and shoes, Peter shot her an icy glance, never breaking his determined stride, and she wondered if something major had transpired during her slumber. For several moments he continued to hasten about, busy as a behind-schedule construction foreman doing a punch list. Seemingly satisfied with what he had accomplished, he headed vigorously for the front door.

"Peter?" Bafflement husked her voice.

He halted and pivoted to peer at her with a fierce predatory expression on his face.

"What?" he snapped, clearly agitated at her intrusion.

"Where are you going?"

He scowled even deeper. "I'm going to see Rachel," he enunciated, as in, what a stupid question.

Rachel's head reeled with the reality of her dashing groom's detour off the beaten romance path. Still scowling, he walked over to the bed and reached to the bedside table for his car keys and only then did his face change. Something in his eyes flickered, cleared—and in one movement, he collapsed onto the bed where he lay silently for long moments before he spoke.

"I was dreaming that I was going to see you," he murmured feebly, raised forearm covering his face.

"I know." She reached over and switched off the lamp and scrooched back against him to spoon, their usual sleeping position that would remain so for the coming decades. Her love was such that his humiliation was hers and so the incident lay dormant until years later when they could laugh over it. That marked the beginning of dozens of nocturnal goings-on, during which she learned to gently wake Peter and, if he was afoot, lead him back to bed.

This behavior had gradually, until recently, ebbed and floated into misty corners of the past. But in recent months, coinciding with Peter's short-term memory lapses, the night-time incidences began to reoccur, with his dreams growing increasingly confrontational and combative. A few times, Rachel received feeble jabs and misguided punches before rolling deftly away to safety. She'd learned to awaken him when he began to utter garbled speech and his hands and feet started to twitch and flail about, escaping before she became the target in his "fights."

So this morning she awoke around four a.m., restless to resume editing her latest novel before sending the first draft to her publisher. This, she did on occasion when not sleeping well. No use in wasting time, she figured. She crept from their upper-level bed, took a warm bath downstairs, so as not to disturb Peter with the noisy upstairs shower, applied makeup, and went to her ground-level computer. The morning primping ritual not only invigorated her and got her going, but it made her feel prepared for whatever the day offered up.

Rachel spent about an hour and a half editing a passage from the book about an amusing Halloween incident involving a shotgun-toting hero investigating next door's empty house. A suspicious character appeared to be sitting on the back steps. The hero discovered the "intruder" to be a human-shaped shadow cast over the doorsteps. Then when the police arrived a short while later, in response to another neighbor's report of seeing a gun-toting prowler, they all realized that the culprit was the story's hero. All ended well. She finished editing the passage and then realized she was still sleepy.

Yawning and lethargic, she retraced her steps upstairs and found Peter still sawing logs. She crawled in and spooned back against him for more z's.

Rachel immediately drifted off to sleep.

"*Hey! Hey!*" Peter's voice jerked her awake. It was still dusky outside. Just enough light filtered through blinds to bring the furniture into a blur. His arms tightened around her midriff like a conveyer-belt vise. It tautened in rhythm to his garbled, angry utterances. Alarm sluiced through her. She struggled to free herself as Peter's rising incoherent speech pierced the morning's stillness and his arms squeezed tighter and tighter . . .

Rachel's ribs throbbed and her breath grew short.

"Peter!" she cried, desperate and frightened, clawing to wrest his arms loose, which only incited him more. "Please, Peter. Let me go." She pleaded in a voice unfamiliar to her ears, one fraught and horrified.

Frantic.

He laughed; a harsh, ugly burst of sound, and prepared his heft for action, shifting just enough that Rachel slithered free of his arms and poised to roll from the bed onto her feet. He seized her upper arm, large fingers digging into soft tissue.

"Peter!" she screamed. The claws tightened painfully. "Peter! You're hurting me!" She burst into tears, wailing like a child.

Again, that angry huff of laughter. "I'll show you what hurt is," he snarled and as he drew back to hit her, an adrenaline-flight surge burst her up and onto her feet. She bolted for the door, sobbing hysterically.

Rachel never dreamed that she could move so fast. She didn't look back as she snatched open the door to the stair's landing.

All she could think was *escape!* In Peter's warpath dream, she was the enemy and she'd not been able to wake him! The implication twisted and roiled her insides.

With trembling hands she opened the stairwell door, stepped down onto the top step, and turned to quickly jerk the door closed behind her. Demons nipped at her heels.

She yanked hard to shut the door. Her hand slipped from the door knob.

Loss of balance descended in slow motion horror.

Her mind scrambled with thoughts as she toppled: *No, no! Not like this! This can't be happening!*

In the next moment, she was free falling backward down fourteen steep steps.

And Rachel knew as she twisted and hurtled through space.

Was certain.

She was dead.

\\\/

During high school, Peter and Rachel snapped together like Velcro and never looked back. They met at a youth cookout sponsored by Rachel's church, where her father pastored. Though not very religious at that time, Peter came as a guest of his church member buddy, J.C. Johnson, who conveniently dated Rachel's first cousin, Drusilla West.

One look at Rachel and Peter was had. Peter didn't get around to proposing. Didn't have to. Within six months into their junior year, it was a given that as soon as they graduated, they would marry.

They would both get college degrees, Peter's in engineering and Rachel's in journalism. She would one day be a great writer or concert pianist and dazzle the world. He would create colossal, one-of-a-kind structures and become a millionaire by the time he was thirty.

Her romantic mind snatched at phrases from movies and books . . . *love strikes like lightning and cannot be denied . . . it is both beautiful and messy.*

Only much, much later would Rachel see the "messy."

Peter's consistent spin was that he was the one who loved at first glance. "It was like lightning struck me, splitting my chest open and spilling out my heart for everybody to see. But the only one I wanted to see my soul was you, Rachel. Only you." While voicing this, his tone would vibrate with young love's intensity.

It was true. He fell first. And in his own words, "I fell hard."

In the universe's view, the two were total opposites. He was the dangerous-looking guy with his Winston cigarettes rolled up in his T-shirt sleeve (which he soon gave up to please Rachel's pastor father, a wise choice) and she was the girl who loved music and wrote stories and worked on the high school newsletter and yearbook. Ashes and dreams. She was Leo and he was Virgo. Not supposed to meet in this lifetime.

Right?

The powers that be had other ideas. So did Peter. Nobody, but nobody, could surpass Peter when it came to wooing. Only a matter of days passed before the thunderbolt struck her in the same irrevocable way as it had Peter. It turned her inside out and there was no going back to before.

Once the intensity-mist settled, she learned that Peter's dangerous look was—hmmm, *partly* justified. He could be testy when riled but it took a lot to prod him loose from reasoning. He was tender and even a little hesitant at times. A bit shy, she discovered, just enough to add to his appeal. She found his innocence refreshing in the sixties and early seventies, when "anything goes" was the favorite youth entrée.

Character went a long way with Rachel because her pastor dad, Hampton West, was a tough act for any young man to measure up to. Bottom line: Peter's rugged good looks drew gazes, a phenomenon to which he seemed immune—except when those eyes were Rachel's.

His laid-backness and lack of guile sealed it.

They both decreed their marriage a fairy tale. They worked their way through college with help from Rachel's widowed dad but none from Peter's parents, poor folks with other siblings to clothe and feed. This was okay with Peter because his struggles with destitution and alcohol-fueled family disunity had muscled him for skirmishes to come. He'd long ago become the James family Alpha and that defined him in a good way.

Truth was, Peter readily slid into Alpha-mode in any setting. His quiet confidence spelled strength to anybody who spent any time with him.

Their University of South Carolina Upstate college degrees—Rachel's in journalism, minor in music, and his in engineering, minor in psychology—fit them well and they both set out, together, to fulfill their dreams.

\\//

Trauma.

It blindsided Rachel.

Peter's bad dream would forever change her life. Earlier she'd bathed and primped before her extra snooze, something not out of the ordinary. Her pre-dawn writing had also been commonplace. Productive. A great start to a New Year's Eve.

Now, because of one misstep, she found herself fighting for life.

Free-falling backward down fourteen stairs she'd spanned hundreds of times.

The horrific plunge seemed to happen in slow motion and, at the same time, her life zipped past in a blur because death hovered. How many times had she made her way down those same stairs, reciting safety rules, knowing their potential threat?

Today, a dark sinister battle raged for possession of her.

Her body, hurtling through space, was no longer hers.

"Help me, God!" she cried again and again as she ricocheted from step to wall, helplessly twisting and spiraling until finally she heard the impact of her head that brought the spinning descent to an abrupt end.

Crash. Simultaneously, Rachel saw an explosion of light like an atomic blast. She would never forget that vision and its roiling sound. It was exactly like the movies she'd seen of the explosion over Nagasaki on that fateful day that ended WWII.

And then, in that timeless state of nothingness, she hung suspended, body coiled like a python. Slowly, it all settled into a surreal silence.

Pain exploded in her right leg and tightly twisted neck, ratcheted there by the sheetrock wall holding her head captive, stopping just above her eyes. She blinked back the haze. On a primal level she prepared for the sound of breaking bones.

"Help me, Lord. Please help me." Her voice came out weak—strangled.

But, declared her survivor-mind, *I am still breathing.*

Rachel seemed split in two. One detached and watching. The other in a mortal battle.

"*Peter!*" she croaked, praying her cries would reach him. "Peter! Help me!" Each strangled utterance drove home the severity of her wounds.

The pressure on her neck tightened. She listened for the final snap, like the condemned at the guillotine.

Years of her dad's sermons flashed by. "*There's power in that name*" beckoned in neon.

She whispered "*Jesus*" again and again, hanging onto it like a drowning rat to floating split timber.

Peter's dear features zoomed in above her.

"Oh, my God," he cried, face engulfed in shock and desperation. "What happened, honey?"

And Rachel knew. He didn't know what precipitated the accident.

"This is it, Peter," she croaked in a whisper, compelled to say goodbye.

"No!" he shouted.

"This is it," she repeated weakly. He needed to know the end was near.

"No! No, it's not!" Had shock not sheathed her, his vehemence would have startled Rachel. "No, it's not. Here, let me get you free."

His desperate denial somehow penetrated mortality's stranglehold and Rachel felt a familiar emotion slide through her consciousness.

Trust.

Peter would take care of her.

He cupped his hands beneath her head, then gently eased it from the wall. At its release, her neck exploded agony in every direction, like electrical surges, blasting her shoulders and skull.

"Nnnn," she moaned as he laid her carefully on the floor.

"Do you want me to take you to bed?" His need to help throbbed.

"No." she croaked. Talking through a garroted neck was difficult. "Don't move me."

She knew instinctively that was the wise thing to say and knew that Peter would comply without question.

He was already calling 911.

\1/

Within minutes, the ambulance arrived and paramedics braced Rachel's neck and checked her vitals, asking her basic questions to check responses. Then, they deftly scissored and peeled away her favorite black jeans. She'd not removed them when she'd earlier climbed back in bed. The loss caused her a heartbeat's regret, which faded immediately into the more immediate ordeal.

Survival.

Moving her onto the gurney proved problematic because the space at the stairs' bottom was too narrow to accommodate a stretcher's width.

"This isn't what we want to do," one paramedic apologized. "But we have no choice."

As one, several of the squad gingerly lifted and placed her on the gurney's hard, bracing surface, which straight away shot ankle- and leg-trauma indicators to Rachel's brain.

The agony interrupted her concerns of cranial bleeding and a broken neck.

At least, the thought drifted as if from another world, I can *feel.*

Another distraction was intense thirst, such as she'd never known. "Please . . . may I have water?"

"No," replied another paramedic. "You may be rushed to surgery and any liquid in your stomach could make you very sick. Could even back up and choke you."

At least, another consideration scudded through, *you are breathing.*

\١/

Peter glanced at his watch as he sped along behind the EMS ambulance. He knew they were working on Rachel inside the van. Had it only been forty-eight minutes since he'd first heard Rachel's tumble down the stairs? His heart had nearly stopped when he looked down those steep steps and saw her crumpled in a grotesque twist, head wedged in the wall.

Another possibility blitzed him. What if he'd not been home? No way would she have been able to extricate herself from the wall. She'd have died.

Dear God. He swiped a hand over his face and blinked back the image. How had she survived that? How could he live without her?

No! He took a deep breath and expelled it. No, she was going to live. With God's help, he would will it. No way would he let her go. She couldn't die as long as he was there loving her, coaxing her to stay, could she? No. No way.

Only yesterday, they'd planned to celebrate this livelong day.

How quickly plans go awry.

And he wondered, what day is this? *A holiday?* He drew a blasted blank.

On its heels came the flash of anger. Just a tiny spurt. What did it matter anyway? He shook off the annoyance. He was getting older, after all, and little memory bleeps were normal. All his peers would vouch for that.

Mid-morning traffic thickened as they neared Greenville Memorial Hospital, which, the paramedics had insisted, had the best neurology department in the area for "injuries like these." Again, Peter's heart did a dip.

What exactly were those "injuries like these"? She'd looked so pitiful with her head swallowed by that huge neck brace, so helpless as they'd lifted her like a sack of potatoes onto the gurney. So surrendered to her fate. So brave.

Rachel had not changed much from that eighteen-year-old girl he'd married. Not physically. Oh, she was older but she'd been a late bloomer, some told her, growing more beautiful with the passing of years. He agreed. But he was fond of telling her that her beauty was as great on the inside as the outside. How proud he was of her.

Two years older, he'd waited for her to graduate high school while he worked in the Manilowe cotton mill to squirrel away college funds. Her widowed pastor dad, Hamp West, provided the lion's share of Rachel's tuition funds. Her older sister, Gabrielle—Gabby—had forged ahead several years earlier, earning a degree in physical education from USC Upstate.

Peter found a parking space near the Emergency Room entrance and bolted inside in the wake of the gurney carrying the love of his life. He fought back tears as the sight of her—so pale and silent and reconciled—smote him anew.

He rushed to her side and leaned close to smile and hold her cold hand in both of his.

"I love you," he murmured.

"I know," her lips whispered. "Me too.

Chapter Two

\|/

*"Her purse was a weight, ballast; it tethered her to the earth as
her mind floated away."*
—*Ann Lamott*

Mary Rivers Emerson looked out the kitchen window of her
two-story, red-tiled-roof farmhouse, the heart and apex of their
twenty-two acre farm. She watched her son, Mark, scurrying
about doing farm chores alongside her husband, Ralph.

At thirteen, Mark was evolving into a young man. Too
quickly. The thought brought a brush of sadness to her mother's heart. And then, a burst of spritely boyishness propelled his
gangly legs and feet to lope ahead to unfasten the black four-
board fence's gate.

She chuckled with a surge of humor and pride as the boy's
stepfather's big hand reached out to affectionately rub the boy's
shoulder as he shuffled stiffly through the entrance toward the
compound of red barns and shelters that mushroomed from the
rolling, lush green fescue spread that was Sugar Hills Farm. In
Mary's opinion, it was the best danged completely organic farm
in the entire south.

Just as suddenly, Mary blinked back tears, wondering again
what she'd done to deserve what the Almighty had dropped into
her lap. Over thirteen years ago, after fleeing Manilowe in dis-
grace, she'd gotten a fresh start when hired by widower Ralph
Emerson as the bookkeeper at his thriving farm.

She'd never dreamed it would one day be her home.

Being the good church deacon he was, her new boss invited her to his little country church there in upper Oconee County. His only child, Chris, was studying agriculture at Clemson University. He would later disappoint his old dad by embarking upon a military career rather than partnering at Sugar Hills Farm. Ralph still hoped his son would eventually, after spending his youthful idealism and patriotism seeing the world, migrate to farming.

"It's got to be in his wiring somewhere," Ralph insisted, following up with his infectious laughter while posing absurdly in his vintage Oshkosh overalls and brogans.

"He will," Mary would reassure him, knowing it to be true.

After first moving there, Mary had told everyone she was a widow, to cover her evident pregnancy. The outpouring of sympathy had nearly tsunami-ed her with guilt.

Divorced and expecting simultaneously, Mary had been surprised and grateful for Ralph's friendship, which quickly turned to romance, despite her being honest with him from the beginning about her past—except for naming the baby's father. And despite Ralph being twenty years her senior, she fell in love. He was still a handsome, formidable man with his sturdy, firm six-foot-three frame and full white mane.

"You clean up good," she and her son both loved to tease the self-deprecating farmer, who loved the nonsense. His sense of humor went a long way in leveling the romantic dynamics of the May-December match. The other levelers were his compassion, understanding, and, at the very top, his love for Mark.

"There's no need for anyone to know," he'd privately told Mary. "Your past is nobody's business. In a sense you are a widow. Sam Morgan deserted you emotionally and morally. And this baby's paternity is nobody's business either. He'll be mine because he's part of you."

That had always moved her to tears.

He often added, very gently, "When the time is right, the boy needs to know who his father is."

Mary always panicked at the suggestion until Ralph would sensitively backtrack. "The timing is up to you, honey. Entirely up to you."

"Are you sure you want to start over?" Mary had asked more than once, worried that Ralph's optimism might fizzle on up the road, when the newness of marriage wore thin. After all, that had happened before.

"Besides, I miss having a little one underfoot," was his response to her concerns of his re-entering fatherhood. "The empty nest doesn't sit well with me," he'd added for good measure.

That settled it for Mary.

They'd married in her last trimester and no man could have been more attentive and nurturing than Ralph in those final weeks and days. And when little Mark entered the world, Ralph had been there to catch him, laughing his big, boisterous laugh that could turn any gathering into a party. "Just look at that, would you?" he'd crowed, preening, and then turning tearful as the babe was whisked away for cleanup and weighing. He'd hovered protectively until he could gently gather the tiny babe to his wide chest and kiss his downy face as he'd returned to the bed and reverently placed him in Mary's ready arms.

Oh, how thankful Mary was that she'd not aborted this precious life. Her wise mother had counseled her to *please* wait— during the first surge of panic upon learning she was pregnant. "You'll feel differently if you'll just wait and pray," Dot Rivers had insisted and it had proven to be true. The terror subsided when Mary realized that this was one of those things that had— in the long run—"worked together" for her good.

She'd wanted children during her brief marriage to Sam Morgan, but when she pressed, he'd confessed that he'd had a vasectomy before marrying her, saying he wasn't cut out to be a father. Turned out he wasn't cut out to be a husband, either. After only a year, Mary learned of his affairs and filed for divorce.

The church had accepted Mary's widow-status version and approved whole-heartedly Ralph's selfless father role.

At the time, Mary had seen no reason to change her story. Mark's father was—to her—dead.

Today, however, her eyes turned sad as she watched the older man and adolescent boy ambling together through the apple orchard, Ralph's arm slung across Mark's shoulders as the boy gazed trustingly up into the only father's face he'd ever known, soaking up wisdom from a never-ending fountain.

A sudden weakness seized Mary and she made it to the bar just in time before collapsing onto a stool and laying her head on the gray granite surface. Guilt weighed heavily upon her as she fought to maintain consciousness. She groped for the cup of grape juice sitting within reach and quickly drank it. She missed her orange juice but dialysis patients couldn't afford to consume its potassium. Footsteps at the back door tugged at her attention and she fought to compose herself as the two men in her life burst into the kitchen.

"Mom," Mark rushed to plop across from her, eyes alight with excitement. "Hortense had her piglets. Six of 'em!"

Ralph, however, angled her a worried gaze. "You okay, honey?"

She breathed deeply and forced a smile. "I'm okay."

"Well, you don't look okay. You look mighty pale. Did you take your insulin shot?"

Mary nodded tiredly. "I did."

"You're scheduled for dialysis Monday. Think you should call the doctor?" His brow furrowed with concern.

"No. I'm okay since I drank some grape juice."

Next thing she knew, Mark was beside her, draped across her shoulders and hugging her for dear life. "Please be okay, Mama," he murmured against her dark hair as she returned his embrace, bear-hugging his skinny midriff, relishing the texture and outdoorsy smell of him, with the cold air still clinging to him. Even the faint pig-pen odor didn't turn her off. It all blended together in a wonderful boy fragrance.

"I'm fine, darlin' boy," she murmured, squeezing her eyes against rising tears, wishing it were true. But she would protect him as long as possible.

Then Ralph was engulfing both of them in his long, brawny arms. "Your mama's a'gonna be just fine, son," he vowed hoarsely. "You just wait and see."

\1/

Rachel groaned as the ER technician inserted an IV line. One . . . two . . . three pricks before her elusive vein cooperated. You'd think that in the midst of trauma, such a non-critical procedure would not even appear on the pain radar screen. Unfortunately, it did.

Dazed and shivering from shock, Rachel remained conscious. Barely. Medicinal smells hardly registered. Trussed like a mummy, her view from the lofty gurney was limited to a tiled white ceiling with inset overhead lights and the occasional glimpse of anyone tall passing or family leaning in to talk to her.

Like Peter, who, after the technician finished gathering blood samples, hovered close to her face, clasping her free hand in both his big, warm ones. He'd always done that—a nurturing gesture, one of hundreds, because he knew how good the warmth felt to her classically icy hands. It was a genetic thing, cold hands.

How she hated folks to say after shaking her hand, "My! Your hands are cold." As though she could fix it. The thought fluttered eerily then evaporated.

When she complained of being quirky, Peter was fond of saying, "I love everything about you."

Rachel would grin, "Even my cold hands and feet?"

"Even your cold hands and feet."

And they were not just words. Peter lived his declarations.

But it had not always been so.

Today, all that faded into the atmosphere as, on a primitive level, Rachel drank in his love like a perishing kitten nuzzling to nurse.

Perishing . . .

Speaking of which . . . she cut her eyes past Peter's broad shoulder, glimpsing a hospital coat. Peter stepped aside as the female doctor again checked Rachel's vitals.

"Please," Rachel rasped. "May I please have some ice chips to wet my tongue?"

The doctor's compassionate yet resolute smile dashed Rachel's hopes. "I'm sorry. Even a little liquid ingested could cause complications during surgery." Her sympathetic squeeze to Rachel's hand did nothing to assuage the dryness and craving.

Why couldn't they just wet a cloth and dampen her lips, she wondered?

She had, in the past couple of hours, become a wounded beast, shivering and jerking from shock. Trauma reduced one to primal needs and impulses. To beg for water was no longer beneath her. On another level, a higher one, her mind kept a steady conversation going. Was there internal bleeding? Even though she'd survived the initial fall, would this seemingly lack-adaisical delay be the death of her?

If so, the crowded ER had declared her a less valuable victim.

"Why is it so crowded?" she asked her sister, Gabby, who'd rushed in almost as soon as Rachel's arrival. After Peter had called her, she'd left in the middle of a health presentation in Physical Ed class, one she'd once taught at Manilowe High. She had, until her retirement five years earlier, served as the Manilowe High Girls Basketball assistant Coach.

Five years older than Rachel, she'd held that honorable position well past her prime. As retirement had encroached, students and staff alike mourned the inevitable. It was a sad day when Coach Gabby departed those hallowed halls that both sisters had walked, amid much weeping and emotional good-byes.

Gabby's dark salt-and-pepper head vanished for about three minutes then swooped back into overhead view. "It's New Year's Eve and the medical staff is short." She snorted in disgust. Then she leaned in close. "You okay?" The brown eyes softened from their characteristic keenness and Rachel saw the worry. And the love.

It nudged aside the blasted mortality hovering so closely, foaming at the mouth.

Just a little. She could still feel its fetid breath from the chasm below that threatened to swallow her. No. She would not surrender to the pull.

"Yes." Rachel whispered what she willed to be true. She didn't feel like talking but could not, of course, nod. In fact, her aching, trussed-up neck and head were beginning to throb even more.

The basso-thrumming had already revved up in her leg and ankle, which according to Gabby was swelled up like a cantaloupe. Since she could not look down to see for herself, Rachel took Gabby's word as gospel.

Another seizure of shock-chills and jerks coursed through her, and for long minutes she endured the involuntary muscle contractions that, at times, exhausted her even more than the indescribable debilitation already foisted upon her.

"Thank God Daddy's not here to see you like this," Gabby muttered hoarsely and walked away. Rachel knew she wept. Not something her tough sis wanted others to see. Not even her. Especially since Rachel was the underdog of the moment and Gabby's humongous heart could not bear to heap more on her.

And like a feather in the wind, Amber's face flitted past.

Her prodigal daughter whom she hadn't seen in over a year this time. Last time she saw her, the pop-in-and-out Mother's Day visit ended the same as always. Amber and her dad clashed like two wounded grizzlies, neither giving an inch and neither coming out of the fight unscathed. Both had hearts of gold and tongues like razors when provoked. Two peas from the same pod, they both were. Rachel could count on one hand the number of times Amber had visited since her departure some twelve years ago, after her brother Jason's death.

And the only reason being that Amber loved them, despite everything, she still loved her parents and couldn't make the final break. Like her mama, her familial roots ran deep, which was what had provoked her fleeing the nest in the first place. She'd felt betrayed by the two who had always protected that hallowed pantheon of family and, in one tragic season, she'd toppled Peter from his larger-than-life seat atop a milk-white charger, morphing him into a shyster and iconic debauchee whose sleazy sleight of hand had destroyed their home.

Rachel had not gotten off lightly either. Amber had accused her Steel Magnolia mother of being more steel than magnolia in the aftermath of the adulterous interlude that had pushed the James' marriage to the brink of annihilation. Amber had, Rachel realized today, even as she lay so mortally threatened, designated herself to the role of angel recorder of her family's flaws and wars, wars that had stolen the girl's peace and forever (in Amber's own poetic words) shattered her sense of family unity.

Rachel's hope that love would bring her child safely back to them fizzled when Peter grew more resentful as the years passed. Rachel mostly felt regret and maternal disappointment. But never hatred. Peter's sentiments, to her, bordered on just that.

Maybe daddies were just different. That's what Gabby told her.

Through the years, they'd wondered what had happened to the once beautiful girl, now almost thirty years old. The parting had been bitter between Peter and Amber and like a sad death-knell for Rachel. Parental-disillusionment had stolen both parents from Amber.

Today, in Greenville Memorial Hospital, the vision faded as quickly as it appeared.

Everything was surreal. Sounds. Smells. Being.

Peter immediately took up the space left by Gabby and gently gripped Rachel's cold hand, lifting it to his heart as he leaned close and kissed her on the lips.

Tears gathered in those beautiful green eyes.

Rachel closed hers and began to spiral downward. She opened them. She could not allow herself to sink into darkness. She did not trust it. It would devour her.

Pain gnawed at her as another icy spasm sliced through her. Her teeth began to clatter.

Help me. Please help me, God.

\\//

Gabby took Peter's arm and tugged him toward the arrowed-hallway that led to the coffee machine. "C'mon, Peter, let's get some high-test." She read desperation on his shock-dulled features. It was in his eyes and she knew that the stress-confusion he now experienced was symptomatic in his case. "Rachel isn't alone. Drusilla will stay with her while we take a coffee break."

Peter straightened his shoulders and complied, relief palpable. Gabby knew he'd been wound up tighter'n a banjo string all day. Peter, who'd always been a bastion of good old take-charge, now—at times like these—needed a shoulder to lean on. A voice to guide him. And he didn't trust just anybody with that power.

Mostly just Rachel.

And thank the good Lord, he did trust Gabby.

Sometimes.

To a point.

Drusilla was Rachel's first cousin and best friend—alongside Gabby, Rachel always added. Heck, Gabby was glad her sister had someone as loyal as Drusilla at her side that very moment. Drusilla, blonde hair now white, was still pretty in an aging Doris Day kind of way. Her badge of beauty was a big old grin that rarely faded. It lit up any room or crowd. She and both the West girls had always been close, where Gabby was big sister to both, celebrating their extraordinary alliance and, at times, refereeing during disagreements.

Dropping her denimed bottom into a chair felt good as Peter sat down across from her.

The java was pure hospital. But it did land a solid kick.

She looked at Peter, who'd grown silent and was staring blankly across the near-empty hospital cafeteria.

"She's gonna be okay, Peter. Y'hear?" she said, trying to convince herself as well as him.

He blinked and looked at her, shifting to lean elbows on the table. Something of the old Peter sparked and he gave a half smile and a nod. Then, in the next breath, tears gathered and one trickled down his gaunt cheek.

"Don't know what I'll do if she doesn't make it," he said and, face in hands, burst into silent sobs that quaked his body. Tears gathered in Gabby's eyes but she gulped them back. Not the time to cave in.

"Hey! Whoa!" She reached across the small table to give his hand a firm squeeze. "Rachel's not going anywhere, Peter. We've got to stay strong for her. Can't let her see us moping and whining, now can we?" She forced a smile that she knew was monstrous. But Peter's tears would blind him to that. Besides, what she'd said was true. Her baby sister needed them to bolster her right now.

"We can cry later if we have to," she said in her matter-of-fact way.

"Ahh, Gabby. I hate that I ever hurt her." Another tear splashed over and he swiped at it. "She's so good and didn't deserve—"

"Ah ah! None of that." She wagged a finger at him. "That was a long time ago. Let it go."

"Yes, but—"

"No buts, Peter, my boy." Gabby planted her white Reeboks firmly on the floor and hoisted herself up. Her slight limp from last year's hip replacement was almost gone as she rounded the table to take his arm. "Come on. Our girl needs us."

\\ /

Drusilla stood guard beside the gurney when they returned to Rachel's side. Sitting in a chair beside the tall stretcher would lower the visitor considerably and remove them from Rachel's vision range. So most of the time, one of them remained standing, to give her a sense of connection.

And Rachel appreciated the gesture. The hours crept slowly by and the bustle only intensified her needs . . . water . . . pain-killer . . . and she knew that tests were a prerequisite to all else. Time no longer existed. Only corporeal awareness of thirst and pain.

"When will she have a room?" She heard her sister's sharp query to a white-coated passerby.

"When one comes open," was the impersonal reply, fading with the footsteps.

The ER hallway was the hub of emergency activity, both going and coming. Rachel did not react to the sounds. Pain superseded all. Her mind snatched at bits of clatter that turned bizarre. The upside of it all was that her mind still functioned, however spaced out. She was still relatively lucid.

Relatively. The word took on new meaning.

Visions of the fall and the impact's cranial atomic explosion proved invasive at intervals and she kept resisting them. Had to. They endangered her. The bullying was chilling and sinister. She knew instinctively that she could not sustain any more terrorization while dangling from the thin thread that barely tethered her *here*.

Peter now hovered over her, holding her hand in his. It was so warm, his hand. "How do I look?" she whispered and her voice sounded slurred. "Deathly?"

He smiled. "You look beautiful, honey."

"Yes, you do," Gabby chimed in, grinning over Peter's shoulder. "Everybody's talking about how pretty you are." Then she leaned in close to whisper, "You still have makeup on." She winked.

Then Rachel remembered the pre-dawn primping she'd done, never dreaming what lay ahead nor that she'd be seen by so many before the day was done. "Good thing," she rasped and the laughing response was like she'd done a buck-and-wing pratfall.

Actually, she knew that they were looking for signs of normalcy from her when normalcy was the farthest thing from her at that precise time.

"I'm so thirsty," she groaned to Peter, who looked pained.

"I know, honey," he crooned. "I would take this for you if I could."

And Rachel knew that he would if he could. But that's just not the way trauma is done.

Slowly, pressure in her bladder had been building through the hours. Late in the afternoon, Rachel could bear it no longer.

"Gabby, please find a nurse—someone."

Gabby disappeared and returned with a lovely brunette nurse whose name tag said ANGELA. Her face registered surprise when she saw Rachel. "Honey, they haven't done anything for you yet?"

"No," Gabby barked, indignation resonating.

Nurse Angela's nostrils flared delicately and she said, "Well, we'll see about getting the ball in motion."

Within moments, Rachel watched tile ceiling and lights flash past as the gurney wheeled down the ER hallway and into a room, one blessedly quiet. She cut her gaze to take in several nurses moving about—then to Peter and Gabby hovering nearby.

Peter was already bragging to the nurses about his published author wife. Bless his sweet heart. He was her greatest cheerleader in an otherwise lonely world. The iconic hospital gown was all that now stood between her and ogling spectators. Yet, to a usually modest soul, her undignified exposure to the huddled humanity there was, by now, neither here nor there.

Her revealed author-identity sparked up the atmosphere a bit as her audience bombarded Rachel with questions about her books. What information she wasn't able to articulate, Peter filled in. Curiosity and awe reigned.

The diversion's result was that the not-so-pleasant catheterization procedure passed uneventfully.

The tube insertion wasn't as painful as Rachel had anticipated. Another reason for breathing space was that she could move her limbs with no problem, with the exception of her injured right leg. An added plus was that the catheter insertion was a done deal, remaining intact for upcoming surgery. One down.

"Ahhh, thank the good Lord," Rachel murmured as her bladder relieved itself into a plastic bag.

Everyone laughed, giddy with the joy of helping her, Rachel realized.

"You're being taken to X-Ray and then we'll do the other tests right away," Nurse Angela informed her.

Rachel felt a tiny rustle of hope take hold. And gratitude.

When Nurse Angela adjusted Rachel's hospital gown and bedding, she smiled down at her. "You are my Angel," Rachel informed her with not one iota of reservation.

It was true.

Nurse Angela's appearance at that precise time was not happenstance.

\|/

Several weeks earlier, Rachel had researched local physicians specializing in diagnosing and treating dementia and Alzheimer's. Dr. Ringel came highly recommended.

Getting Peter's okay to go ahead was another matter. It was like coaxing a bull into a room full of crystal without a single crash.

Despite his tough veneer, Peter was terrified of pursuing a diagnosis. And Rachel understood. Who wouldn't be? Especially since Peter's two older brothers, a sister, and his mother had succumbed to Alzheimer's ravages. He'd witnessed the decline and deaths of them all. Not a pretty sight.

Now, he too, experienced the onset of those same dreaded symptoms. Rachel began to notice the memory lapses before Peter did; things that others might fail to detect unless they spent considerable lengths of time with him.

"What's today?" was one of the first indications. Rachel had just five minutes earlier told Peter the day was Monday. This wasn't the first time it had happened but was the first time it actually registered. To Rachel, it was like being hit between the eyes with a slingshot rock. A big one.

Her mind screamed *what?*

And for weeks, months, she would snap, "I've already told you. Remember?"

Until poor Peter would mutter, "No, honey, I don't remember."

And she would apologize and pretend that it was her lapse. That maybe she had not told him. And Peter began to emphasize the things he still orchestrated well, like driving his business routes, when he did checks on his real estate holdings and maintenance work.

"I don't have any problem functioning on that level," he insisted. "All folks my age are beginning to forget things."

And that was true. The sixties are notorious for denting brains and bodies. Why, Rachel herself forgot monumental appointments at times and enjoyed watching Peter's relief when she 'fessed up.

They were, for a time, codependents in denial.

Rachel kept quiet most of the time during Peter's discourses on how well he coped with life. Between the lines she heard his silent screams; *"I'm not getting Alzheimer's!"* And it broke her heart.

She even found herself agreeing with those poignant denials.

She prayed that he be spared. And then presumed he would be.

Where did faith end and presumption begin? Or vice versa? For the life of her, she did not know.

Her patience with the lapses thinned and she demanded that he *remember*, for crying out loud. Then she would feel like a worm when confusion pooled in his eyes. The worst times were when he simply climbed into his service truck and disappeared for hours, refusing to answer his phone.

Then she would call herself all kinds of scum for being so callous.

Rachel knew that he carried a revolver in his truck. Had her insensitivity pressed Peter to his breaking point? At such times, Rachel vowed to never again make an issue of his waning recall. And she prayed desperately for God to protect him, both from the dreaded blight and also from himself.

Oh, how she detested the genetic family curse. No words did justice to her hatred.

Nor to the dismay.

As time passed and the incidents increased, Peter himself grew more and more pensive and began to slowly accept that something was going on in his mind. "I have to admit, Rachel, that there are times when my memory fails me."

Rachel would take his hand. "We're in this together, honey. All the way."

"I don't think I'll go into severe Alzheimer's, though. Mother started in her late forties and my siblings much earlier than this." He'd cut his eyes to watch her reaction and Rachel always hid her unrest. Because, by now, she knew that by doing so, she freed him to be honest about his fears.

Other times, despair surfaced with a vengeance. "I'd rather die than go through that," he would hiss through his teeth.

"No," Rachel would try to gather him in her arms. He would resist but as she soothed and reassured him, he would melt against her as a child to his mother. "No more of that, Y'hear? We'll get through this. Together. I'll take care of you."

The appointment with Dr. Ringel was scheduled for January 2.

Two days after Rachel's fall.

Gabby reminded her as she lay motionless in the ER. At least she was inert for the moment, a short interval before another spasm of shock chills struck. "Peter's appointment is in two days," she said to Rachel and took her limp hand in hers. "Bad timing, huh?"

Rachel blinked back confusion. Appointment? She cut her eyes at Gabby.

"The neurologist."

She blinked again and looked away. At that moment, the threat seemed far away.

In another world.

Another time.

\v/

Minutes following the bladder catheterization, Rachel was propelled into a blurred round of tests; MRI, X-Rays, and Cat Scans. After ten hours of ER campout, the pace was dizzying.

The room they put her in was quiet. That in itself was relief. Later she would remember it only in bits and snatches. The neurologist relaying test results . . . *A miracle* . . .*God surely had her head in His hands because she doesn't even have a concussion . . . neck fracture . . . not operable . . . three leg fractures . . . surgery first thing in the a.m.*

Nurse Angela leaned over her, smiling. "Rachel? You can have something to drink and eat now."

Water had never tasted so good. She drank greedily. But the thought of food was not welcome. Yet, on a primal level, Rachel was certain she needed the sustenance for strength.

One thing she knew: she had a battle on her hands.

A fight for her life.

That blasted black blob of mortality hovered, clutched at her, hissed in her ear *"you're mine."*

Rachel refused to give in to it.

She forced down token bites of yogurt and peanut butter crackers, the only available snack at the after-dinner hour.
Besides, someone had just informed her that she would receive
nutrients in her IV.

Another soft voice told her, "I'm inserting some morphine
in your IV for pain."

In moments, she drifted away into blessed nothingness.

Chapter Three

\|/

"I'll tell you something about tough times. They just about kill you, but if you decide to keep working at them, you'll find your way through."
—*Joan Bauer,* Close To Famous

Next time she opened her eyes, it was morning and a green-clad orthopedic surgeon said to her, "You'll have screws in your ankle. You may have nerve damage. Maybe not."

"Don't put metal in me," Rachel slurred. "I'm allergic to it."

"Don't worry. We have newer, improved materials without side effects," he assured her.

Peter's face swooped in, eyes adoring her. Worry lurking in green depths. A kiss and fervent, "I love you."

Drusilla, J.C., and Leon, the rest of The Gang, all followed along murmuring words of encouragement and love.

Gabby telling her, "Hang in there, sis. You're doing great. It'll all be over soon."

What other choice did she have? The gurney rolled her toward surgery.

Then, blackness.

\|/

Mark would forever look back on that homework assignment as pivotal.

This morning, he pushed growing apprehension to the back burner and rushed outside into sunshine and mild, high fifties, South Carolina temperatures and headed to the animal kingdom of Sugar Hills Farm.

There, troubles could not linger.

Mark thought the baby piglets were the cutest things he'd ever seen. Though the pens stank to high heavens, he couldn't resist tiptoeing past Hortense and picking up her smallest one to cuddle, laughing uproariously at the squeals emitted from the tiny pink snout.

"Little Petunia," he murmured before freeing her to scamper away. His habit of naming his favorite animals sometimes troubled his mother because she said they would be sold eventually and he would have to part with them. When he was younger, it had crushed him to lose a pet, but now that he was older and saw how the farm operated, he didn't mind that too much because there were always new litters coming along to replace those departed.

This school holiday morning, he left the north corner and moseyed past the little red farm stand with its white shelves and matching rocking chairs, from which they sold organic produce, eggs, and meats during harvest times.

He thought of how his dad had moved the stand down near the rural highway a while back and operated on the honor system, placing a bucket there into which payment went, alongside a list of posted prices. He was such a good man, one who trusted others to be as honest as him. He taught Mark, by example, that it was more blessed to give than to receive.

"God blesses us with so much plenty," he insisted. "We can't afford not to share. And we need to trust others." And left unsaid was that if a needy one came along, who didn't have money to pay, it was okay to take enough to ease his hunger.

Then they discovered a neighbor—not a needy one—was regularly taking the produce without paying. Sadly, this forced them to move the stand back to its present on-site location. Mark loved his father and learned daily about how good life

4646

could be, both spiritually and emotionally. "It's all about attitude, Mark," was one of his favorite little sermons, as Mark
teasingly called them. But his dad never took offense.

"You shoulda been a preacher," Mark often told him and
the big man would laugh that pealing laugh of his, but Mark
enjoyed seeing him blush.

"Naw. I'm doing exactly what God wanted me to do. You
see, He knew how amazed I am at how things reproduce and
grow. I see the miracle of it all. I can't really call it work, son."

Today, the air was brisk but Mark's work jacket warded off
the cold. He unlatched the gate to the Event Barn area, where
his mama and dad hosted weddings and parties—shucks, just
about any celebration, you name it.

They'd let him throw a party there on his birthday last year
and he'd invited his entire class, who'd entered these portals
with slack-jawed awe. The outside portico was cement floored,
with white colonnades and rich green ferns and white swings
mounted from the ceiling. In warm weather, overhead white
fans swirled lazy, cooling breezes. Mark loved it when in-season
apple blossoms perfumed the air from one side of the farm and
peach blooms from the other. A guy couldn't ask for better, now
could he?

To the side of the Event Barn stood a stone-creation fire pit
with benches, surrounded by multi-shades of shrubbery. There,
his classmates had roasted marshmallows after feasting on hot
dogs and burgers—with Maybelle's home-cooked chili—inside
the rustically elegant barn with its knotty pine walls, marble-like
and acid-stained concrete floor, black wrought-iron chandeliers,
catering alcove, kitchen, and several eye-popping bathrooms.

Even a "Bridal" room graced the structure, used for changing gowns or costumes. His friends had gone on and on about
its impressiveness for days on end, making Mark feel like the
king of the walk.

In his perfect world, Mark had never lost his wonder of the
near-Disney beauty and allure that was Sugar Hills Farm. From
the colorful, arrogant Tom-turkeys now strutting in quartet

before him in the apple orchard beyond the fence, cutting loose in synchronized musical gobbling, to the squealing piglets, the *prrkking* chickens, and the lowing of cattle—and the endless melee of other animals, holding him rapt by their concert of life.

The only thing marring his perfect world was that his birth father had died before ever seeing him. It was something his mom didn't like to discuss. Refused to, actually. He'd tried to sensitively coax information from her but the door was always shut. Even his gramma, Miss Dot, as folks all called her, always told him, "That's something you have to ask your mother."

Mark thought that was kinda funny because his gramma was usually open about everything. He knew his mother had insisted Gramma not talk to him on the subject. And he couldn't help but wonder why.

"Maybe it's just too painful," Gramma usually suggested.

Maybe so.

But *why?*

And of course, his dad Ralph would shrug eloquently and say virtually the same thing. "You'll have to talk to your mom about that. I never knew him."

Now, the fact of having a faceless, virtual-stranger father smacked him broadside. His social studies assignment for tomorrow was a term paper chronicling his family tree, with pertinent information about his parents and grandparents. He would even have to list the cause of death for a deceased parent. That much he knew. His father was dead. But beyond that, his mama was as tight-lipped as a Trappist nun in the throes of quiet. But only on one topic—his father—did she commit to this radical silence.

He'd finished the paper except for the blanks for his biological father's information.

Today, while his dad—the only one he'd ever known—was gone out on the business of distributing the famous Sugar Hills Organic Eggs to grocery stores, Mark decided to approach his mother one more time on the subject of his biological father. Though his stepfather was the best, when his mother became upset, his dad always blocked the source of her distress. In this case, it would be Mark, searching for answers.

Inside, the house was quiet but Maybelle, the cook, had left some delicious-smelling stew warming in the oven. Or it would have smelled great had nervousness not sabotaged Mark's appetite. He shook himself, calling it stupid to be such a wimp.

"Mom," he called, pausing in the den. She must be upstairs resting, which she was doing more and more of these days. He took the winding stairs two at a time. He found her on her bed lying on her back, arm raised over her face, with the blinds closed. His heart skipped a beat because he loved his mother more than anything on earth.

"You okay, Mama?" he asked softly.

Her arm came down. She peered at him and half smiled. "I'm okay. Just tired. Anything wrong?" But he could tell from her voice that everything was not okay. She seemed to be fading before his very eyes and it scared the daylights out of him.

"No, nothing's wrong." *Liar.*

When she patted the space beside her, he sat down on the edge of the bed and she reached for his hand, giving him that warm smile she saved exclusively for him. Should he broach the subject of his late father again? He didn't want to make her feel bad.

She squeezed his hand. "Need to talk?" she asked.

Wasn't that a sign that it was okay? He nodded. "I—I need to know something."

The smile turned to concern. "Okay. Shoot."

He cleared his throat, so nervous he could feel his heart beating in his ears. "How did my dad die? You never told me."

He saw it, the fear that seized her features and dilated her eyes and made her go all rigid. "It's okay, Mama," he said as he rushed to undo her stress. "You don't have to talk about it. It's just—"

He gazed helplessly at her. "It's just that when someone asks me what happened to my dad, I don't know what to say. You know?" His voice trailed off dismally. Disappointment rumbled through him like a locomotive and he felt the sting of tears behind his eyes. "I need the information for an assignment in social studies next Thursday, is all."

But he knew. He didn't have to hear it. He *felt* the door slam shut.

He arose and started from the room, then turned back, "I'm sorry, Mama." His voice broke on her name because he didn't know why he should feel guilty to want to know about his late father. He spun on his heel and dashed from the room, down the stairs, through the house, and slammed out the back door.

With tears streaming down his face, he didn't stop until he reached the peach orchard and plopped down beneath a tree and gave vent to his frustration. What was so freaking unspeakable about his biological father's demise? Was it some horrific accident? Did he get shot in a bank robbery attempt? If so, that's all she had to say. He could handle that. What he couldn't handle was this—this door shut in his face every time he mentioned the man. This deep, dark secret that kept him conjuring up all sorts of bizarre scenarios. Dread curled his insides tighter.

He'd kept a secret journal to deal with his feelings of being shut out. It was just for him, nobody else to read. It was too revealing. He snuffled and wiped his nose with his jacket sleeve. He would have to do what he always did in this particular situation. Pull himself up by the boot strings, as his dad had taught him to do, and then put one foot in front of the other and keep on a'trucking. At least he had a mother and dad to take care of him. Some kids in his school didn't have a great home to go to like he did.

"Mark!" his mother's voice called from the back door. "It's suppertime!"

He knew she wasn't able to cook anymore but she made sure to be the one to call him in to have their family mealtime together. He knew what effort she put into getting out of bed at these times. Whatever her reasons for avoiding the topic of her late husband, Mark knew she loved *him*. He couldn't ask for a better mother. He got to his feet, dusted the seat of his jeans, and began to lope across the orchard toward home.

Nope. In spite of everything, he was one lucky dude.

\|/

Peter felt caged. The OR waiting room was packed and he needed some air. Some space. Sensing it, Gabby said, "Go on, Peter, they said surgery would last at least three hours. Take a breather. I brought a novel to read." She sat in one of dozens of cushioned earth-tone chairs.

J.C. and Leon called out, "Need us, Peter?"

"No," Gabby called back across the waiting room. "He needs some time alone."

"I shouldn't leave—"

"Pssshaw. I'll call you if you're needed." To illustrate, she pulled out her Michael Barton novel and began to read.

Peter strolled to an elevator and, on the ground floor, spied an exit. Outdoors, he discovered a lovely circular oasis, umbrella tables and chairs on a smooth stone floor, wrapped in deep green holly foliage burgeoning with red berries. He slid into one of the chairs and crossed his ankles. He had it to himself.

· Gabby was right. He did need time alone to sort out things.

Despite the chilling temperature, he enjoyed the brisk air and sunshine. That was another opposite in the Peter/Rachel duo. He never got too cold. Rachel got chilled when the temperature dropped below sixty-five. Fact was, he rarely wore more than a light jacket, even in the midst of winter.

Rachel said that South Carolina had very little winter. Even she, with her propensity for feeling cold, rarely wore heavy coats. Without warning, Peter's eyes filled with tears and he began to silently weep. Why Rachel? He looked up into the blue sky and felt the old familiar anger rise.

"Why, God?" he asked, his voice hoarse and guttural.

He'd fought this battle over a long stretch and, at times, felt he was rid of the bitterness. In some ways, he felt liberated. He loved Rachel and knew beyond doubt that she'd forgiven him of his betrayal thirteen years ago. At times, when pain seized him, it seemed to have happened only yesterday. Yet—sometimes in the dark hours before dawn—it seemed ages ago.

And Amber. In the midst of it all, he'd lost Amber. The daughter who'd abandoned them when they needed her. He shook his head, dispelling the disappointment. And anger. Amber had made her decision to leave hearth and home. Now she reaped the rotten harvest of the family schism. He wouldn't waste time grieving her.

This had been a bone of contention between him and Rachel. She never gave up on her oldest child, who was all—in Rachel's estimation—she had left. So the years of Amber's leave-taking had taken a toll on the mother who'd suffered so much.

Peter swallowed back a rush of bitterness and remorse.

Loss of his faith was the greatest pain of all. How could he trust a God who'd allowed the tragedy that would define his life for so many years to come?

Of its own accord, his mind traveled back to that fateful January day when he and their son, thirteen-year-old Jason, buckled up seat belts for their morning trek to school. Amber, sixteen, had a sore throat and fever and Rachel insisted she sleep in. It had rained through the night and the temperature dropped to freezing. Channel Four news announced a two-hour school delay and the James' breakfast table became a festive site for light banter and a tasty breakfast of French toast with crisp bacon and soft scrambled eggs.

"Hey, Mom," Jason spoke around a mouthful of syrupy toast. "When you gonna let me shoot my BB gun?"

Rachel cut him a comical grimace, sending him into spasms of laughter. He loved to tease her about wanting a BB gun to shoot squirrels, knowing what an animal lover she was. In fact, all four of them were fervent ASPCA supporters.

As though led by divination, Gizmo, their rescued Heinz 57 mutt, appeared at the table side, black eyes a'begging for scraps he knew appeared at this time of the meal. Under the table, Jason discreetly dropped two slabs of bacon onto the floor.

"I saw that," Rachel said, back turned as she put dishes into the sink full of hot, soapy water.

"No, you couldn't see that," Jason argued then realized he'd been caught by virtue of confession. "I still want to go shoot my BB gun at those pesky squirrels across the road."

"Keep that up and I'll buy one just to shoot you in the hiney." That got more hoots from him. Peter had watched their dark-haired, pencil-thin boy, whose strong features—so like Peter's—showed promise of heartbreaker beauty. The mahogany hair was like his own while Rachel's genes were evident in Amber's sun-streaked dark blond waves. Both offspring had his green eyes.

Peter glanced at his watch. "It's time to get a move on. You've got that math test after lunch, don't you, Jason?"

"Aarrgh. I'm trying not to think about it." He slid into his jacket and grabbed his books.

"Brush your teeth first," Rachel called. "That sugary syrup breeds cavities." He already sported a mouthful of metal braces, which he hated, but when Rachel and Peter reminded him how beneficial to his appearance they were, he always relented.

Fact was, Jason was agreeable on most home fronts. The only way to paint him rebellious was by teasing, something he loved. He and Peter would bat roast-y comments back and forth until Rachel would glower at them, then erupt into helpless laughter. They were careful not to cross the line of disrespect.

The "roasts" were always so ridiculous they were funny. "You're the smartest (dumbest, ugliest, most handsome) son I've got," Peter would say.

"I'm the *only* son you've got, Dad," was Jason's dry reply.

That morning, as Jason detoured by the bathroom to brush his teeth, Rachel asked Peter, "Did you get those tires rotated yet?"

He snapped his fingers. "I forgot." He shook his head. "I'll do it right away. Leon said the last time they rotated them, the guy put the wrong tires on the front for my front-wheel drive."

"I know," Rachel snapped. An unusual thing for her. "You need to listen to Leon. Despite all his junk, he has a lot of wisdom to pass on."

"I just got busy with those rental repairs and forgot," he murmured, justifiably chastised while sliding his arms into a heavy jacket made for cold mornings like this.

"Maybe you ought to take the truck," Rachel, still worried, called as they sprinted to the driveway. Gizmo came yapping behind them, a streak of gold propelled by a wagging tail. Jason turned and called him. "C'mon, boy!"

Peter hesitated. Then decided on the car. "The truck's heater isn't working," he yelled, and they climbed inside, flipping on the heat full blast.

"Thanks, Dad," Jason gave him a thumbs up and gathered Gizmo in the car to settle at his side.

"For what?"

"For taking the car. I'm not into freezing, y'know?"

Peter chuckled. "Me neither."

They sang along with an oldie's radio station that Peter liked. When the Platters' "Twilight Time" played, Jason dropped out, obviously lyric-clueless.

Peter paused his sing-a-long. "That's our song, Mama's and mine."

"Shut up." Jason's lips curved up from ear to ear. But Peter could tell he was warmed by his old dad's revelation. Awed, in fact. He listened to the lyrics. "Man, songs like that—" Jason's skinny, broad shoulders shrugged.

"They don't write many like that these days." Peter resumed singing along.

"Right." Jason flipped to his test notes and studied them, pushing Gizmo's nose aside as he competed with the pencil and begged for petting. Finally bored, Gizmo moved to the back seat, turned a circle, then sprawled flat on his tummy.

Peter would never comprehend how it happened.

Till this day, it still wouldn't fit inside his brain.

He rounded the curve and his tires hit a patch of black ice. The car hydroplaned, fish-tailing as Peter fought frantically to gain control, using everything he'd ever learned to correct.

The pickup truck hit on the passenger side. The last thing Peter remembered was the crash of impact.

And then blackness.

He'd survived.

Gizmo had survived.

Jason had not.

Today, Peter blinked back the memory, not wanting to camp out there. His head threatened to go into whirl mode. He already had too much on his plate. Lately, stress made his mind go crazy and shut down. So he focused on relaxing and pushing back dark memories, struggling toward neutral.

At times, he wasn't able to do that. Those were the worst.

He blinked and looked around at the sunny garden oasis, whose beauty was dulled for him. He arose and started to backtrack to the OR waiting area.

Peter stepped inside and looked around. Where—

Nothing looked familiar. Panic rushed in.

His head began to twirl in earnest as he turned down first one hall, then another. He felt his breath coming in spurts and his heart pounding in his ears as his footsteps escalated.

Every hall looked the same!

Calm down. He could hear Rachel's soft voice telling him to slow down, take his time and all would fall into place.

"*Slow down,*" he muttered, stopped at a window, and peered out upon sun-drenched earth and moving humanity, taking deep breaths. He hated these moments of confusion. Pressure was the panic catalyst.

He back tracked until he saw the exit door and through it, the lovely garden sanctuary. He turned and saw the elevator doors at the end of the hall. Then he remembered. He breathed a sigh of relief, pushed the fourth-floor button and closed his eyes as the doors slid shut.

Thank you, God.

Leon Brown, Gabby's husband, met Peter at the OR waiting area. "Hey, buddy," he slapped Peter's shoulder and propelled him toward the cafeteria. "I need some java 'bout now. This sittin' gets my bones to achin' and my eyelids to droopin'." Then he whispered loudly, "Not to mention my poor numb hind-end."

Tall and still jock-featured, Leon's youthful hardiness was blunted by age and a few minor Korean War mishaps. But, thank God, no metal inside him, he always added in his thankful way.

Peter thought how his brother-in-law was—all things involved—lucky to have survived the war and near death skirmishes.

"I pray Rachel will be okay," Peter murmured aloud.

Leon efficiently poured two cups of high-test java. "J.C. left for a little while," he told Peter. "He'll be back later. But Drusilla's still here."

"Black," he said and handed Peter's to him, then carried his own as they retraced their steps to the OR waiting area, which now was even more packed. Drusilla sat beside Gabby, both clutching cups of tepid coffee. They looked haggard with worry. Peter's heart skipped a beat and he rushed ahead, finding and dragging an empty chair from another grouping to join them.

He tried to interpret Gabby's unreadable stoicism. "Have you heard anything?" he asked as he felt Leon's pilfered chair join his.

"Nothing." Gabby looked so—drawn. Peter was about to despair when a white coat appeared in the doorway.

"James family?" he inquired.

"Here." As one, they all stood and moved to get the news.

The doctor looked exhausted but upbeat. "She came through the surgery fine. Her ankle was repaired with eight screws and a steel plate. The other fracture, just below the knee, will heal with the aid of a cast and brace."

"How long?" Gabby asked.

"Three to six months, depends on how fast she heals. The neck brace will have to be worn for at least four months. All the time. She must not remove it for anything unless she switches to the other waterproof one while shampooing and bathing."

Gabby rose to her full height. "Sounds like she's gonna need a lot of care." She looked at Peter. "And I'm in it with you for the long haul, Peter."

"Me, too," Drusilla chimed in, reaching to squeeze Peter's arm.

Peter could have dropped to his knees for those vows of support. Tears rushed to his eyes.

And Leon's muscular arm lying across his shoulders and the strong fingers gripping his arm bolstered Peter in a way words could not.

Thank you, God. You heard me . . . and you allowed Rachel to stay with me. I'll never again deny you.

I will be forever grateful.

Because without her, I don't know how I'd face life.

\\//

Rachel's mind grasped at post-surgery hours in snatches. Two green-clad medics plastering a wet cast on her leg—not a comfortable experience—overhearing a couple of the nurses complaining about the mess made by the in-charge plaster-guy. "But he's good," she tacked on.

Gabby and Drusilla taking turns at her bedside. Pain. And Peter. Poor Peter, looking both grateful beyond words and, at times, confused.

Rachel tried to reach out to him as she usually did. But found that she could not.

Primitive instinct had switched her into unpolluted survival mode.

Another moment in time . . . a lovely big black Labradoodle named Francesca came to visit. Rachel glimpsed the curly therapy dog and trainer paused at her door. From her bed, as hurting and needy as any creature on God's earth, she reached out a limp hand to the oddly beguiling canine.

And in one swift movement, Francesca was on the bed snuggled to Rachel's length, as soothing and affectionately as Rachel had ever experienced. Francesca smelled nice and her soft curly head nestled for long moments against Rachel's face and shoulder. Rachel's fingers twined in the silkiness of her fur, and when Francesca lifted her head to lie quietly for extra unhurried moments, there was about her a nobility that Rachel had never before seen or felt in an animal. Something magical happened in those heartbeats, something soothing and warm and healing.

And when the time was right, Francesca left the bed as quietly as she'd arrived.

Her comfort lingered as Rachel drifted into slumber.

\\//

A high school friend from long ago appeared at Rachel's bedside, grinning from ear to ear. "Hi, Rachel, remember me?"

"Connie Northern," Rachel croaked, morphine-groggy. She'd heard that Connie was over the respiratory team at Greenville Memorial.

"Yup. I brought my posse over to take care of you. I've always told them that if I were to ever have injuries like yours, to bring me here and then to Roger C. Peace for rehab, because here they'll get you on your feet!"

That encouragement cut through the haze. Connie gave her hand a gentle squeeze.

Talk of Rachel's published novels always popped up. This time was no exception. Ruby, one of Connie's colleagues got the email link to access Rachel's titles and promised to drop by and see her as she settled into rehab.

Another battle raged as Rachel was transferred to the Roger C. Peace Rehabilitation Center. Food made her nauseous. Just the smell roiled her stomach. Violently. She fought to swallow nourishment but could only manage a few bites before sickness overtook her.

Mortality hovered more brazenly. At times Rachel felt she was nearing the end. But Peter remained nearby, holding her hand and murmuring encouragement.

"I'll order you something for the sickness," said the attending resident physician.

Ready or not, she was beginning twice-daily rehab sessions, during which she would nod off in the middle of her exercises. Pain debilitated her. Shaun, her wonderful, sympathetic therapist, told her that she was not able to complete her first day. *No joke.*

Thank you very much.

He wheeled her back to her room and helped her get herself out of the wheelchair and onto the bed. Not as simple as it sounded. First rule in a non-weight-bearing patient like Rachel was to wear shoes or hospital socks that grip the floor. Skid-proof ones. Next, lock the chair in a position close enough to the bedside, and then, using the good foot for weight bearing, hoist herself onto the bedside by pivoting on that foot. To get out of bed, she reversed the order of the procedure.

One thing was for sure.

"I'm going to get out of this bed," she told Peter and Gabby during those first tries, her teeth gritted in determination. "No way am I going to let this thing whip me."

"My sis is a real trooper," Gabby told everybody within earshot, echoed by Peter, Drusilla, J.C., Leon, and Gabby. Her cheerleaders.

Fact was, her fourth-floor room was somewhat of a gathering place for staff members whom she'd loved on sight. "You're my angels," she told each of them, bringing smiles to their faces and a spring to their steps. Their kindness overwhelmed her and made her even more appreciative.

"I feel so blessed," Rachel repeatedly reminded them all. Though she spoke from logic, not emotion. How close she'd come to death. *Maybe the trauma had killed part of her.* The thought flitted across her cerebral screen then dissolved.

In private moments, Peter sat at her bedside, holding her hand, eyes moist. "I'm so glad God left you here with me, honey. I didn't think you—"

"Shh," she would shush him. "Don't talk about it."

Rachel didn't want to go back there and visit that place and time. So Peter would comply until someone else came to visit and he would forget and she would have to remind him again.

On one level, had it not been for the pain, she'd have sworn she was already dead. She felt no emotion as she went through the motions of smiling and talking, but within minutes, fatigue would overtake her and she would turn her face to the wall.

Sometimes she wondered, *God, where are you? Why can't I feel you?*

Yet—on some level—she knew He was not far away.

\\//

Peter and Gabby alternated nights to sleep over and bed down on the lumpy cot near Rachel's bed. Gabby had to make Peter go home and allow her to relieve him. Drusilla offered to stay, but soon realized the lottery draw only had two ticket holders.

So she showed up during the free daylight hours bearing unique little treasures like new soft, stretchy panties that easily pulled up over Rachel's leg hardware. Or fragrant lotions teamed with a full-body massage.

Rachel was grateful for all the attention, but especially prized the constant nightly vigil because those hours were the trickiest. They required stealth and slyness to meet their demands.

"Peter's appointment with the neurologist is this Wednesday," Gabby again reminded Rachel the first week of her rehab stay. She lounged on the uneven fold-out chair-bed, dressed in PJs after Peter had reluctantly gone home for the night.

"You know he does not want to go." Rachel cut her eyes at Gabby, adjusting her neck brace and shifting her torso so she could better see. Her right leg twinged, then pulsed. "I'll insist that he go."

"Yeah," Gabby agreed. "I'll get Leon to talk to him—"

"No. I'll talk to him. Ganging up on Peter is the worst tactic possible. He'd dig in like a hedgehog for winter."

"Yeah. You're right." Gabby yawned, a wide one. The nurse entered with the med tray and administered pills, and soon Rachel felt the dip that preceded drowsiness. Her mind—what was left of it, she liked to joke—began to scatter into a spin.

Soon, the dizziness pulled her under.

\|/

Gabby arose early, and after assisting Rachel with the bed pan, left to go home and check on Leon. "I'll be back later this afternoon," she said and kissed her cheek.

The early morning occupational therapist, Debbie, helped Rachel get her sponge bath. Truth was, she just set the pan of warm water, washcloth, towel, and special antiseptic liquid soap close enough for Rachel to reach it. It took every bit of fortitude and craftiness to complete the task. Debbie would only help when Rachel asked her to wash her back.

And Rachel's stubbornness set in. Only through sheer will power and a sense of dignity did she reach her body parts for cleansing. By then, exhausted and thrumming with pain, Rachel was positive that she could not haul herself out of bed, much less do her little therapy exercises. By little, she meant that at first they didn't seem to mean much, but later she learned that they made all the difference in recovering the use of one's body.

Then came breakfast, one Rachel ordered nightly and one based on what her churning stomach dictated. This morning breakfast consisted of soft scrambled eggs, sausage, and a few grapes. The taste and texture of sausage made her retch before she spit it into a napkin. She managed to eat the small cluster of red seedless grapes and nibble the soft eggs.

The sustenance revived her somewhat and when the occupational therapist, Debbie, returned for her, she stood by closely while Rachel locked the wheelchair, struggled to angle her body—right leg encased in cast and heavy metal brace—pivot on her left foot (now wearing a black Adidas shoe with grip soles), and lower herself into the chair. She still wore the slouchy hospital gown with housecoat over it.

She looked like crap. And aberrantly, she didn't care doodle-y.

By now, her makeup was long gone and her faithful cousin, Drusilla, had fashioned her shoulder length hair up in a high ponytail to accommodate the neck brace, which, crazily, made her think of a Ninja Turtle in war armor. So from then on, she referred to it accordingly. The only concession Rachel made to cosmetics was a little eye pencil, blush, and lipstick so that she didn't blend in with her bedding.

Sheer habit.

Debbie did her best to keep Rachel going in the therapy session, but mid-exercise Rachel continually nodded off, dropping the weights or freezing mid-movement and awaking to see Debbie staring apprehensively at her. "I'm sorry," Rachel muttered several times. Debbie's look turned to something like pity and Rachel began to worry.

Is something wrong with my brain?

Narcolepsy?

Strangely, it was like one part of Rachel viewed the panorama from a distance, completely detached while the other replayed the atomic explosion 3-D vision—in living color and sound—over and over. Could something so catastrophic leave her brain unchallenged? Was it possible? Alarm jangled . . . then fizzled.

The loopiness really freaked her out.

"I can't stay awake," Rachel croaked to her orthopedic surgeon the second morning of their ungodly six a.m. rounds.

"Aha," he shook his head. "You need the pain meds but they're making you sick. It's the Phenergan making you drowsy. I ordered it for the nausea. I'll change it to a new drug that's being used for cancer patients on chemo. It's been pretty effective."

"What is it?"

"Zophran."

"Go for it." Rachel felt that without it, she would die anyway. What was nobler, dying from debilitating nausea or a drug reaction? Flip a coin. Hey, mortality was losing its edge. In her fuzzy estimation, survival was highly over-rated.

For once, her writer's inquisitiveness took a back seat. She gulped down the pill that morning, along with the pain meds. Oh, and the antacids for indigestion, and stool softeners to allay constipation, a by-product of pain meds. *Ah glory*, dignity had already jumped ship back in the ER.

Magically, the nausea let up. Her stomach still balked at the sight and smell of food but the grapes she'd ordered and soft scrambled eggs slid down a bit easier than before. The night before, on her menu form she'd ordered a baked potato for lunch.

Now, she stayed awake for both occupational therapy (learning to get about with little to no assistance) and then physical therapy (overall strength and range training) with Shaun. At times, Peter sat through the exercises with her, chatting with Shaun as Rachel did repeat sets.

"Be sure to always have those grip shoes or socks on during any transition from chair to bed and back." Shaun reminded in his laid-back, sensitive way. "You also need to get some regular clothes to wear in therapy, Rachel," he said with delicate care.

Why? was Rachel's first thought. She had, overnight, deserted her fashionista image, as well as modesty. The last thing on her mind was how she looked. Just getting through the day was her tunnel-vision goal.

In her vulnerable, primitive state, Shaun became her mentor. She could trust him because intuitively, she knew he really cared about his patients. It was in his gentle blue eyes and voice and the way, when she nearly fainted from weakness and pain one day, he wheeled her to her bed and told her to take a nap. And when she strained her shoulder at the parallel bar, he brought an ice pack and applied it, again taking her to her room and making sure she was comfortable before leaving.

He would check on her, too, as she lay exhausted and spent. One day, after she received the daily Enoxaparin stomach injection—to prevent blood clotting—she saw spots and nearly passed out. Shaun called the nurse in to check for a drop in Rachel's blood pressure, a rare side effect. Under close observation, she slowly came out of the crisis.

At the same time, Shaun consistently guided her through her therapy, slowly building her strength and endurance until she began to feel the difference when using her arms to compensate for her leg injuries.

He also fed her hope.

Rachel grew more and more thankful as she watched severely brain-injured patients struggling to achieve a fraction of what came easily for her. Shaun noticed.

"I work to offer them hope," he told Rachel as she lifted five-pound weights in each hand. "They need hope, too."

She looked at him and admired his—what?

Nobility. That was it. He had an extra measure of goodness.

She smiled at him, feeling lifted. "Lord knows hope's essential to get out of this wheelchair."

He chuckled softly. "Oh, you're going to get out sooner than you think," he said with conviction.

Yup. Hope was essential. And Shaun knew how to stoke it.

\\/

Mark arose early that next Saturday, endorphins cutting loose all throughout his wiry body as he scarfed down a quick breakfast of fresh eggs, bacon, toast, and cold farm-fresh milk. He was happy that his family tree social studies paper had scored an A+.

"Did you know Mrs. Dillon read my paper to the class?" he asked his mom, trying not to overly preen.

"Really?" She looked immensely pleased with that little ditty. Her smile tickled Mark's insides. He did so want to make her happy and lift the tiredness from her wan features.

He grabbed another slice of bacon and munched it in two bites.

"Slow down," his mother laughingly cautioned. "What's the hurry?"

He gulped down the remainder of milk. "Gotta check the incubator eggs. 'Bout ready to hatch!"

"Ahh," she chuckled as she scraped and rinsed plates for the dishwasher. "Couldn't miss that, now, could we?"

"Where's Sam?" He referred to the farmhand who'd been with them as long as Mark could remember. His wife, Maybelle, did most of the cooking and household stuff while Sam did heavier farm chores alongside Dad. Mama used to do a lot of it, but since she got diabetes when Mark was little, she'd had to slow down. Most of the slowing down was since she'd started dialysis treatments. She reassured him it wasn't that serious, that it simply took care of what her lazy kidneys didn't do.

He wanted to believe her. After all, she'd never lied to him, had she?

"He and Maybelle are gathering eggs. I insisted she go because I can pack the dishwasher. I'm not totally incapable." Mark thought she was scraping the dishes mighty hard, like she was irritated at them. And then it hit him—what she hated was being sick. Her anger was at *it*.

A ping of unrest zapped him, but when he caught her eye, she smiled at him and winked. "Just call me Superwoman."

"Yeah." Mark grinned back at her and relaxed.

Mark knew that egg gathering in itself would take hours, since they harvested an average of four hundred dozen a week, which Dad sold to area grocery stores year round, delivering them in their own truck. During mild and warm harvest seasons, they sold produce to the grocery stores and also from their red farm stand with its open front and battleship-gray wooden floor. Snowy shelves bore produce, and on each end, freezers stocked everything from sausage to range-fed chicken to rabbit to beef and pork. Man, they had it all.

His bony chest expanded a bit on that thought as his long legs spanned the yard and driveway. He paused only to open the gate and enter the fenced-in compound of red barn buildings of varying sizes, where he ducked into the steel machine barn and headed for the egg room. There, dozens of eggs perched, already washed, sized, and tray-ed. One Formica counter displayed two incubators, one over which Ralph Emerson hovered.

One incubator had a gentle rocking motion, to emulate the mother's nudges and warmth. The second one was called the holding incubator, in which the eggs were placed a day or two before they hatched.

"Come look," he coaxed, needlessly, because Mark swooped in like a gnat to mellow fruit, mesmerized by the activity inside the receptacle. The big man had tears in his eyes. Mark respected this man, who was not ashamed to show reverence for God and anything remotely connected to the Almighty. Ralph Emerson displayed a 3-D panorama of manhood that appealed to the boy on every level.

"It never ceases to amaze me," he murmured huskily. "The miracle of life. How these little fellers can peck their way out of those shells at just the right time. I've watched birthing from all species but this"—he shrugged, snuffling back tears—"just affects me more. You know?"

"Yeah," Mark nodded. He did understand the awesomeness of creation. "Maybe it's because they have to work more to get here—tackling that hard shell." The damp little chicks represented just a speck of the vast animal kingdom here on Sugar Hills Farm. Stepfather and son stood there in companionable silence for long minutes watching the miracle unfold.

His dad sighed, draped an arm over Mark's shoulder, squeezed, and said, "I've got to go check on the new calf. Wanna come?"

"I'll be on in a minute," He was transfixed on the cracking shell and emergence of the tiny beak. "I want to watch this last one finish pecking out."

"Can't blame you." Ralph chuckled, patted the boy's back and strolled out the door, whistling.

\I/

An hour later in the farm kitchen, Ralph lingered with Mary at the bar for another cup of coffee. "The calf's doing well," he informed her. Then he laughed softly. "Mark couldn't drag himself from the incubator drama."

Mary smiled at him over the rim of her limited one cup of java. The shrill of her cell phone interrupted the intimate moment. It was her mother, who shared the news of Rachel James' near fatal fall down her stairs.

"That's terrible," Mary said. "Yes, Mom, we'll pray for her."

When she rang off, she sat quietly for long moments, trying to still the trembling of her hands without her husband detecting her unrest. "Well?" Ralph prompted, curiosity evident. "Who are we supposed to pray for?"

She looked at him, then took a deep breath and plunged in. "Rachel James had a bad fall down her stairs, one that nearly took her out. She's in the hospital and her recovery is going to be difficult and slow."

"That's too bad," Ralph replied.

Her teeth bit her bottom lip and she dropped her gaze. "She's the wife of—"

"I know who she is." Ralph's reply carried not a trace of guile, astonishing Mary once again with not only his discernment, but his forgiving nature and grace. "She's still in need of prayer."

She stared at him, perplexed. "But how did you—?"

He sighed and rubbed his big, calloused hand over his face. "I wasn't sure. Just guessing—but I did hit the nail on the head, didn't I? Simple deduction. You worked for Peter James just before you left Manilowe so suddenly. Like I said, just speculation. But your reaction to the phone call and the expression on your face when I presumed—"

"You are incredible," Mary said, shaking her head, uncertain whether to laugh or cry.

He shrugged and smiled that devilish little grin of his. "Hey! I can't help it if I'm clever."

Mary burst into laughter, joining his, and it was a moment she would never forget. Her world remained intact and she was so grateful for this man who loved and protected not only her but her son by another man. Few men had hearts that big.

Her mother knew, and probably Peter and Rachel's families knew, but none other of Mary's acquaintances knew of Peter James' paternity. It was difficult enough as it was, without others running interference in her decision-making concerning her son's life.

Despite her protests, Peter had sent sporadic, generous, unofficial child support through the years but had never publicly acknowledged his paternity. And Mary was okay with that. She would not have wanted to drive a wedge between Rachel and Peter. That was not who she was. She believed in the sanctity of marriage, in biblical terms. Her mama had raised her well.

But she'd had to lie to her son to spare his feelings. And now that web of lies was closing in.

"Well," Ralph reached to take her hand across the bar. "Let's pray for her now."

Mary closed her eyes as her husband offered up a prayer for mercy and healing on one Rachel James. Her emotions swirled like a cyclone as she felt the weight of guilt crush in upon her. How many lies had she told her son and others? She'd stopped counting long ago.

Please, Lord, she silently petitioned, *please forgive me.*

\I/

At times, Rachel felt split asunder. One part of her lay in shreds, a mortally wounded animal, and the other, honored and pampered by a host of angels. The hospital team's synchronization kept the flesh, blood, and spirit tethered together in those weeks.

It was a tenuous one, but a connection nonetheless.

At times, Rachel felt so dead inside, she hardly felt human.

But, she was alive.

She approached the touchy subject of Peter's appointment with Dr. Ringel, the neurologist.

Peter balked. But this time Rachel found it difficult to find fault. "I've got too much on me right now," he rationalized. He lay curled on the miserable cot before night meds, simply being with his wife. "I just don't think I could handle it right now." His shrug was limp and cheerless.

Rachel understood.

She couldn't handle a diagnosis now, either.

"It's okay, honey. I know."

\I/

Peter was at her side as much as he could manage. His real estate duties pulled at him and his work ethic remained intact. That's what made Peter who he was. Only now, frustration at being torn from Rachel's side rattled his shrinking box.

Tonight, he relieved Gabby, who reluctantly left her sister's side to allow Peter closer and more private access. He knew she would stay every night, but he hated going home to the house that rang so hollow without Rachel's banter and laughter.

Even Mitzi, their little six-year-old blond Chihuahua, was boarding at Drusilla's house during the crisis. Mitzi had been shuttled away immediately following Rachel's accident. Good thing, because Peter would no doubt forget to check on her regularly. And it wasn't good for her to be alone so much. Mitzi's round black eyes adored him regardless of how he looked or behaved and was the most compliant of her breed, affectionate to a fault and obedient within a limited scope of commands.

Her word-repertoire mainly centered around *go outside, tee-tee, go to your bed, bad girl,* and *treat.* Not the most trainable of canine breeds but oh, so loving.

Anyway, he missed her when he came in the front door and she wasn't there dancing in celebration of his arrival. After Jason's death, their rescued mutt, Gizmo, had lived on for several more years. At his passing, Peter had had enough sorrow for a while.

Then, six years ago, he'd seen Mitzi's beautiful little face on the TV rescue segment and his heart had melted. He and Sarah had called and rushed to adopt her. Remarkably, and against all laws of nature, the little creature was as acquiescent as she appeared on the screen.

Well, most of the time. Just don't let her out the front door because—unrestrained by fence or leash—she would take off up the street like a proverbial bat out of hell. Then Peter would have to search the neighborhood for her. Most of the time, she wasn't far away and usually beat Peter home, but he just couldn't, with a clear conscience, leave it to chance.

And don't let a stranger encroach upon her family's territory. She gave plenty of warning growls but didn't nip unless a stranger was fool enough to ignore said warning and put a hand on her.

The upside, quote Rachel, was, "We don't have to worry about somebody snatching her from the car while we do a quick purchase at the 7-Eleven."

Yeah. He missed Mitzi now when he walked through the house.

That gaping hole in the sheetrock wall—targeted by Rachel's precious head—had to go. He couldn't stand to look at it any longer. His friends, Leon and J.C., had promised to help him patch it. With Peter's experience in building and rental unit maintenance, making the hole disappear was a piece of cake.

Only—he needed his pals' steady presence to bolster him to face the evidence of death's near claim on his wife.

Besides, Rachel didn't need to see it when she got home. She still *shhhh'd* him when he brought up details of her fall. The horror of it lingered with her. He could see it in her countenance. Could feel it.

The reprieve from neurological tests relieved him beyond exhilaration. For a while longer he could postpone dealing with it.

The big IT.

Thank God for his strong denial-penchant.

Rachel cleared her throat and reached for her water glass, snatching Peter's mind back to the present.

"There's food left for you," Rachel said from the bed, her pale face confirming pain's pull. She ate like a bird since the accident, leaving the bulk of her meals for him. He retrieved the salad platter, carefully wrapped by Gabby, and examined the contents: iceberg and romaine lettuce, diced tomato, grated cheddar cheese, cucumber slices, and slabs of grilled chicken.

"Looks good," he said, smiling at her, eliciting one in return. She always seemed to brighten when he walked in the room. That made him want to kiss the clouds. "Thanks, honey. I've not eaten much today."

"What have you eaten?" Concern bled through her weak timbre.

He pulled off the Saran Wrap and poured generous dollops of bleu cheese dressing over the salad. "I don't remember eating anything."

"Did you eat any of your protein snack bars?"

He kept those in his service truck for energy pickups. "I don't remember." he replied when he drew a big blank.

She kept watching him. "You don't look like you've gone hungry. You probably ate some of them."

He chomped into a mouthful of the mixture. "Probably."

They were beginning to make peace with his instant recall's minor erasures. Peter was thankful for that. At first, Rachel had been impatient at times. Even angry. But never at him, she always reassured him. At IT.

She hated it. The James' family plague.

He couldn't blame her. So did he. And he felt guilty that she'd ended up with someone who might inherit such a bummer disease. These episodes shook him more than he was always willing to admit to her.

He finished off the salad. The overhead TV played scenes from Mayberry and Sheriff Andy. Peter felt content just being there with Rachel.

\١/

Rachel watched Barney Fife and Andy harmonizing with the Mayberry church choir and felt fairly unwound. That could change in a heartbeat. Her emotions scampered all over the chart, erratic and unpredictable. She found that light and humorous television didn't make her as jittery as other pastimes. Her head was too loopy to read. Or talk much. Though she was glad to see visitors and church friends, after twenty minutes or so, engaging with them left her exhausted.

Not just tired—debilitated.

"What's happening on the news?" asked Peter, plucking and eating leftover grapes.

"I can't watch it. I'm sorry—" Rachel couldn't bear the newscasts nor, for that matter, anything controversial, solemn, sad, or violent. Her emotions became mercury in a thermometer immersed in still water. Heat disturbed and raised the temperature, shooting emotions out the top, tossing her mind into a cyclone.

Suddenly, amid the contemplation, dizziness caused her insides to quiver and shatter, like a skyscraper's slow motion crumpling.

"Hey." Peter was on his feet and leaning over her in a heartbeat. "Don't apologize. You watch what you want. You hear me?" Tears appeared in his eyes. "Okay?"

"Okay." He kissed her and went back to stretch out on the lumpy cot and watch Barney Fife vie for the solo in Mayberry's church choir. Rachel's heart heard Peter and something in his words made her feel better on some obscure level. *But why*, she wondered, *do I feel so dead inside?*

"Was the salad good?" she asked, knowing he needed *something* from her, even if only a few trivial remarks. The man spent hours a day on the road, working alone except when Gary, his friend and handy man, worked with him on repairs and such. He was lonely.

"Dee-lish," he said, wiping his mouth with a napkin and topping it all off with a cup of coffee he'd stopped for on the way to the hospital. The hospital kind got to you after a while.

"Peter," Rachel gazed at him, "I hate to bother you but I need to make a trip to the bathroom. I'm under orders not to go unless someone is here to—"

"Don't apologize, Rachel. Your every wish is my command." Peter was on his feet, angling the wheelchair to bedside.

Rachel slowly maneuvered her legs over the side of the bed, locked the chair, gripped the arm, and pivoted on her good foot to hoist her body into the seat. She refused to let others do what she could do for herself. Of course, Peter rushed to wheel her places and she had to admit that it saved time and energy she needed to simply survive. And she felt distinctly that if she protested his attentiveness too strongly, it would shatter him.

It was an intricate balancing act done on auto pilot. She prayed it would come out okay.

"Good girl!" Peter kissed her forehead. "You are such a trooper. Everybody's talking about how determined you are, honey." He rolled her to the cramped bathroom, where she did the reverse order of transfer. The entire process exhausted her. Pain spiraled everything inside her downward, slithering through each tendon and nerve like molten lava.

Peter wheeled her back and helped her to bed, though she pushed his hand aside mostly, preferring to navigate the transfer herself. It was, she was convinced, the right thing to do.

She lay back in bed, trying to negotiate a comfortable position with her braced neck. He offered more pillows. She accepted one and finally found a tolerable arrangement.

"What time is it?" she croaked, slanting her gaze to the wall clock. She groaned. "Two more hours."

"Till pain meds?" he asked, gently touching her cheek. She closed her eyes and grunted assent. He leaned to kiss her on the lips. "I'm proud of you," he murmured.

She gave a near silent huff. "Why am I still here?" she asked in a whisper. "It would be easier to go on."

\I/

Her words stunned Peter. "No! Don't you ever feel that way, Rachel."

Her eyes remained closed—features drained, empty. Panic threatened to swallow him. "Honey. Look at me." His finger plucked her chin upward. "Y'hear?" Slowly, her eyes opened but seemed not to see him. They were so desolate it broke his heart anew. He had to do something to get her *living* again. "Hey! I'm gonna take you for a ride. You've been in this room too long."

"I don't want—"

"No arguments. It'll do you good. Trust me." He already had the wheelchair in place and grabbed her robe. "C'mon. Sit up." Listlessly, she complied and within moments she was gliding down the hall with Peter pushing the chair, whistling a happy tune.

\I/

Thirty long minutes later, Rachel transferred herself back onto the bed, pain screaming at her. It had been a challenge to endure the discomfort this long, but she had to admit that seeing something besides her minuscule room stirred her mind and lifted her spirits.

Not a lot, but right then, a little went a long way.

And Peter had said the magic words to her.

Trust me.

It boosted her morale even more to realize that she did. The protector role fit him more than ever. His love vibrated in every look, word, and gesture. And somehow, that went a long, long way in justifying the *why* of her survival.

Finally, the med tray appeared. Nurse Emily smiled and doled them out. "I want to buy one of your books. And I want you to sign it."

Rachel swallowed the blessed pain relievers and smiled indulgently at Peter's shameless boasting about his published author wife. According to him, she was Pat Conroy, Anne Rivers Siddons, and Jill Marie Landis all rolled into one—except better. Yet, his singing of her praises was so folksy and sincere that folks accepted it all as gospel.

Right then, Rachel had no quarrel with Peter's adulation. In fact, it bolstered her as the combination of immediate relief from Oxycontin and longer lasting Oxycodone kicked in to assuage the suffering for another twelve hours.

An hour later, as she floated off into pain-free slumber, she felt Peter push down the safety bed rail and whisper in her ear, "Do you mind if I lie down with you?"

"Huh uh," she mumbled, lying flat on her back, the only position possible with all the leg and neck hardware and pain limitations.

He crawled in, curled against her, and snuggled. And honestly?

It felt good.

That last thing she heard as she floated off was his whispered, "I'm sorry I ever hurt you."

Chapter Four

\\|/

"Happiness can be found in the darkest of times, if only one remembers to turn on the light."
—Albus Dumbledore

Peter felt like a heel.

He hated to let Rachel down but he couldn't help it.

Despite her protests, he left the hospital at dawn. Cold January air beat against his cheeks, driving back grogginess. Rachel's disappointment smote him, but he could only be confined so long before the restless drumming started inside. It had to do with something like a trickle of fight-or-flight adrenaline. These episodes popped up more lately.

Anxiety is what Rachel called it. And he agreed.

Rachel had even been a little irritated with him this morning for leaving her alone. Said she needed someone to help her get to the bathroom and begin her bath ritual. Or else, she had to wait for Debbie, her occupational therapist who didn't come in until around eight thirty. The hospital staff was always busy during these early hours. Thus, she had to wait, which made her edgy, she explained.

He wished he could control this antsy thing inside him but he couldn't.

He turned on the car's heat and pulled out of the parking lot. He dreaded facing the scene at home where the wretched hole in the wall looked like the Grand Canyon and dredged up the horror all over again each time he entered his once peaceful haven.

Would life ever be the same? Would Rachel be the same? Bottom line was, he'd take her any way he could get her.

Early morning traffic was sparse and the sun sparkled across frosty lawns and foliage along the way. This was the same route the ambulance took all those years ago, when Jason died.

Peter shook his head, willing the anxiety away. His thoughts skipped backward, zeroing in on that night following the accident that took his son's life. Peter had been patched up and sent home. The family dog, Gizmo, was a little wobbly but recovered quickly. That Peter's injuries were so piddly had humiliated him, despite his loved ones' relief that he'd survived.

Thank God Amber had not been in the car. Had they lost her as well, he would not have been able to face life again. But in the end, he had lost Amber, too. Overnight, she'd changed from a bubbly, outgoing teen that lived to laugh and play and love to a somber, withdrawn shadow of herself. After she'd run away, only a ghost of herself appeared sporadically to taunt him about his failures as a father and husband.

Much of it, he deserved—the husband part at least.

Following the accident, guilt ate him alive. But Gabby and Leon—the entire Gang—had consoled him and told him it wasn't his fault, that bad things sometimes happen to good people. He could not, they insisted, blame himself.

That evening following the accident, Peter had gone to the upstairs bedroom to lie down and lick his wounds, clawing at a hint of redemption. That's when he overheard Rachel's outcry downstairs. He'd gotten as far as the stair landing when he heard something that stopped him cold.

"Gabby," she sobbed, "I told him over and over to have those tires rotated. So did Leon!" Her weeping froze Peter's heart. "But everything else came first. The rentals, the maintenance . . ."

Gabby's soft, "Shhh now, honey. You're overwrought. Peter has a lot on him. He didn't intentionally neglect to—"

"Not intentionally!" Rachel cried. "But his procrastination cost us our son's life." Then the turbulent weeping revved up.

Stunned and icy with shock, Peter had staggered back to the bedroom, shut the door, and sunk down onto the bed.

His procrastination cost us our son's life.

The edict had hit especially hard because Rachel was one of the most tolerant, forgiving people he knew. He'd always said that if he were on trial for his life, he'd want twelve Rachels on the jury.

So, her words resonated with veracity. They left Peter with a murderer's guilt bearing upon his soul.

Today, all these years later, they still stung. And all that followed only added to his sense of remorse. To his culpability.

He pulled into the driveway of their two-story Mill Village dwelling, one he'd bought at a modest price and remodeled to Rachel's taste when they first married. It was the intimacy of the village that held her heart captive, she told Peter, plus the fact that her father, Hampton West, had pastored the Manilowe village church when she was growing up. It was there that they met when Peter bravely ventured in one Sunday morning with his buddy, J.C. Johnson.

J.C. was dating Rachel's first cousin, Drusilla West, and since Drusilla was a good church-going girl like Rachel, J.C. knew that if he wanted to see her on Sundays, he had to brace up and become a church-goer, too.

Romance Psychology 101.

The two couples immediately hooked up for double dates. Peter smiled as he recalled how fast and how hard he fell for the preacher's pretty daughter. Her blue eyes, beneath thick, dark blond, sun-streaked hair, captured him. She came up to his chin and made him feel like Goliath when she gazed up into his eyes.

Today, Peter sat in the driveway, motor running, and closed his eyes remembering.

She sat at the piano that morning, sovereign in her loveliness and mastery of the keyboard. At sixteen, she'd already played in church two years. Before that, she'd accompanied during the church youth services. He would later discover that her singing voice was as exceptional as her playing.

Why hadn't he noticed her at Manilowe High? But he knew. He'd been so busy with his buddies that the quiet, unique splendor and charm of Rachel West had gone right over his dim-witted head. Her beauty emerged when she smiled at him that first time and her blue, blue eyes lit up just for him. He'd later told her many times that he'd simply not been that interested in girls at the time. He'd rather go carouse with J.C. and Leon, just looking for girls and doing the things guys do.

"We never found any girls," he was fond of revealing, then bursting into laughter at the absurdity of the truth. Sure, he'd dated other girls but none of them affected him anywhere near the wallop of Rachel.

Today, decades later, he opened his eyes and looked at their white house with its black shutters and rambling front porch. White rockers and cushioned wicker sofas beckoned even on wintry days like today—with memories of southern breezes and long intimate talks that sometimes lasted well into the evening. They'd talked about the children they would have when God thought the time was right . . .

His smile dissolved as the yearning resurrected, one so painful, so potent that it nearly drowned him. He pushed it back as a man fighting for breath, struggling against something so powerfully enthralling, a desire so great he felt he would die from it.

For something he could never have.

To have it would mean he would lose Rachel. That, he could not endure.

It was his own fault . . .

He felt the tears before he knew he wept and briskly brushed them away. He had to get on with life. Somehow, he must. He'd survived thirteen years, hadn't he? He could keep on putting one foot in front of the other, day by day, year by year. So he forced his mind back to when they'd moved into this house.

How in love they'd been. Their decision to wait until marriage had been difficult to hold to, but they had. He had to give

Rachel most of the credit for that. Her morals came straight from the Bible and years of sitting under her daddy's sermons.

Hamp. Fresh tears rushed to his eyes. Hamp had been his daddy, too. He'd seen them through the worst crisis of their marriage, his and Rachel's.

Lordy, how he missed that man and his wisdom.

Peter unlocked the front door and immediately missed Mitzi's tail-sweeping, whimpering welcome. He stepped inside the foyer, one he'd created while revamping both interior and exterior of the old double-storied structure. Everyone exclaimed over the transformation, especially Rachel, who declared it a masterpiece.

Of course, that pleased Peter. But today, his steps slowed and echoed as he ambled over hardwood floors through the den and into the kitchen. His eyes reluctantly found the spot on the wall at the foot of the stairs.

Peter was shocked to see that the hole was gone.

He hastened over and knelt down. The caulking was dry to the touch. So was the soft taupe paint.

Leon and J.C.

Peter's heart swelled with gratitude at his pals' generous gesture.

How good was the love of others in times like these.

And despite his bouts with heartache, he considered himself a blessed man.

Very blessed indeed.

\|/

Somewhere in time.

That's where Rachel found herself, but the song itself did not have its usual calming effect.

She listened to the jam box playing John Barry's arrangements of "Somewhere in Time," then "Out of Africa." Gabby had brought it with her today, along with several of Rachel's favorite easy listening CDs. Music usually lulled her, and though those particular compositions did not ruffle her fragile nerves, neither did they do their soothing magic. By now, she didn't expect total tranquility.

Flatlining did not equate serenity.

Trauma's reverberations were now a part of her.

In the beginning, she got through each day via pain meds. The rehabilitation activities were challenging and painful, especially when the walker came into play and she had to bear all her weight on her arms. Having fought fibromyalgia for years, she suffered aftershocks from both the parallel bars and later, the walker.

At the same time, something inside Rachel rose up and roared.

Something fierce: a force of will that bellowed, "I will not fail."

She spoke it aloud each day. "I will get up out of this wheelchair.

"I will walk unaided."

Shaun, her faithful therapist and now friend, said one day, "If you do all these exercises faithfully, when you get up on your feet, you'll take off."

She looked at his composed, assured features. And she believed him. It was as simple as that.

One day, as she sat before him doing her leg lifts, he revealed casually, "I've just been back to work for about six weeks."

Rachel blinked. "What happened?"

"Open heart surgery," he said as though it were nothing more than a trip to the dentist.

"*Shut up*. And here you are, not missing a lick with helping folks like me get their lives back on track."

He smiled and shrugged. Rachel noticed his face was smooth and unwrinkled. He couldn't be over fifty. So much, so young. And then she knew from whence came his compassion.

It came from that dark place her father had spoken of so often from the pulpit.

The valley. "It's in the valley that we learn of God's love and compassion. It's where we learn who we really are. And it's only through the valley that we develop that capacity for compassion."

Yep. That was Shaun's strength. It was in the way he always thought to bring her cold water and notice when she winced with pain and was beyond going. And the way he treated the most severely brain-damaged patients with respect and kindness, offering hope when there seemed to be little.

She smiled at him. "Thanks, Shaun," she said.

He angled her a curious look. "For what?"

"For caring. And for giving hope."

\|/

Peter faced down the dragons today, determined to slay them.

He took a break during Rachel's therapy session and ventured to the hospital cafeteria. He refused to kowtow to the blasted confusion. Why, a six-year-old could follow the simple route. Take the elevator down three floors, turn right—or was it left? His head began to do that crazy loopy thing and he closed his eyes tightly against it.

The doors swooshed open. Slowly, he stepped out. He looked left, a window. He let out his breath, relaxing. A right turn was the only way. Inside the busy food court, he purchased a strong cup of coffee and turned to re-track.

"Peter!" A big hand clamped him on the shoulder. It was someone from his church.

"Hi, there!" Peter grasped the man's hand in a firm handshake, knowing the face from church but the name danced vilely along the perimeter of his recall. "Who are you here to see?" Maybe that would give him a clue.

"Jeannie's here having an MRI. An outpatient. I'm batching for the day."

So Jeannie was his wife. Then a light came on. Jeannie was at the front desk in the church vestibule each Sunday. Her last name was Johnson. His name was, ironically, Johnny Johnson. An easy one.

Relieved—no, *elated* to solve the mystery, Peter blurted out, "You're kin to Horace Johnson, aren't you? We went to school together way back when."

Johnny looked blankly at Peter. Then he scowled. "No. I'm not kin to him. You've already asked me that. Twice, in fact."

Peter recoiled at the hint of irritation in the man's voice. He also recoiled at drawing a complete blank about having inquired previously about a family connection. He grappled for bravado. "Yeah. You're right. Sorry. Not getting any younger, you know." He winked and patted his acquaintance's shoulder. "Hope your wife's tests turn out okay." As calmly as possible, he managed to stroll away with a smidgeon of decorum intact.

Hurt roiled inside Peter. Why had Johnny been so—so acerbic about Peter's lapse? But at one time, Peter had to admit, he didn't know for sure that he wouldn't have reacted the same. In the next breath, he felt sure he would have been kinder. As it was, he felt flattened by a steam roller, depleted of dignity and self.

As he made his way back to Rachel's room, he experienced the infringement of a new fixation in his previously well-ordered life, one both dreaded and abhorred by every living human creature.

Its name was *stigma*.

\|/

Rachel faced another fear, one that persisted day by day, hour by hour.

Headaches and dizziness swamped her from the time of the accident.

She reminded herself each day that she was a miracle.

And she kept praying for another one—"*Lord, please let my brain be unchanged. You've given me the gift of writing. How would I cope without it? Don't get me wrong—I'm grateful to be alive.*" And she knew, on some level, that if her mind could no longer cooperate with words and language, she would somehow muddle through.

But she also trusted that the one who created her could certainly keep her intact—both mind and body. Each time she moved, even with the cantankerous cast and neck brace, she thanked God.

Yet, the kaleidoscopic sensations she experienced provoked anxiety.

In those first days, she refused to talk about the accident itself, resisted revisiting that time and place. She avoided thinking too deeply about it. The surrealism of it sent her head a'spinning. Not just a woozy thing—the Land of Oz's Dorothy-cyclone brand.

Peter dropped by during her physical therapy session that afternoon and laughed when Shaun said, "I hear rumors of a man crawling into bed with your wife." Peter got a real kick out of the teasing. Astonishingly, the hospital staff never reprimanded Peter.

"She's a real miracle," Peter launched into a discourse about the accident.

"Shhh," Rachel reminded him, not unkindly. Peter grinned and backed off the subject and Rachel felt a little bad that she was so anal about it.

"Is this normal—my avoiding talking about the accident?" she later asked Shaun while doing exercise repeats.

He tightened her leg brace, something she hated but didn't dare openly object to. She'd privately loosen it in her room to a tolerable degree. Her claustrophobia was doing a vile number on her via the leg and neck braces.

"Yes," Shaun replied, satisfied with the motion restriction of the brace. "Folks in traumatic accidents don't want to go back to that time. It's perfectly normal."

Rachel breathed a little easier. Maybe she wasn't too far off her rocker.

She'd always held her fears close. Now was no exception. When her head went through that wall, her emotions had scrambled like beaten eggs. She had her work cut out just getting through each hour of alternating cheer, apathy, dizziness, depression, feelings of helplessness, pain, and a myriad of other sensations of survival.

She reached out for something to latch onto and that something proved elusive, including God, on the level she'd always felt His presence.

"I feel so dead inside," she told Gabby one afternoon when she sun filtered through blinds and lay across her bed.

Gabby arose from the daytime easy chair and came over to hug her. "That's just the trauma aftershock," she assured her and poured some fresh water over ice for Rachel. "You'll get better. You'll see."

That's what reason told Rachel. Yet—the internal deadness was as tenacious as a dug-in wood tick.

Of course, the trauma was to blame, but that didn't lessen its frightening grip. Oh, how she wanted *to feel* again. Outwardly, she looked okay, talked rationally, and was a hit with the entire hospital staff, who loved to come by her room to chat and get her to sign her books for them.

Inside, nothingness screamed and howled.

Mortality's pull was dogged.

The hour-by-hour struggle overwhelmed her at times.

What did she have to live for? Really? Would she write again?

And then, that evening, as she floated into oblivion, she felt Peter slide into bed beside her and snuggle to her side.

And she reminded herself. She did have a reason to live.

Peter.

He needed her.

\\//

Memories haunted Peter.

The irony did not escape him as he struggled to remember small details of the past hour's happenings—and sometimes minutes. So, why couldn't he recall the short term as well as the long term?

Those weeks following Jason James' death, a heavy pall draped the James' residence. God only knew how much Peter had needed Rachel. But she was beside herself with grief, inconsolable. And her words the night after the accident had destroyed something inside Peter, a vital part of him that kept him leveled out—the heart part of him.

And what survived was set adrift on a sea of despair and aloneness.

When he later confronted Rachel about it, she'd begun to weep. "I didn't mean it, darling," she'd clung to him. "I was just so—so mindless with pain and didn't really know what I was saying at the time. Can't you understand that? It was grief . . . just—grief. I'm so sorry."

Peter tried to understand. He understood that grief and injustice had festered those sentiments deep inside Rachel. But they spewed from her mouth as truth that indelibly stamped itself across his soul and seared into his brain. And he numbly muddled on, a shadow of himself. Daily, he battled the guilt and the remorse that sawed his insides to grimy scum each time he thought of his beautiful son, pale with death, gone from him forever.

While Rachel spoke of seeing Jason again someday, Peter coldly rejected that possibility. God was no longer valid to him. Where was He on that icy road? While Rachel sought comfort from the Bible and church family, Peter withdrew, isolating himself and marinating in bitterness and self-loathing.

"Why do you no longer talk to me?" Rachel asked him again and again, confused, desperate to reach him.

Peter would shrug. "Nothing to talk about." And even as he slung redneck sarcasm at her, he recoiled at his callousness. But it seemed that once he set his face toward rancor he could not find his way back.

The tension built in the coming months until one day Rachel finally told Peter that she could no longer handle his anger.

Tearfully, she said, "I think it would be better if you moved out until you can decide to be a part of this marriage again."

The May day he packed his things and left was sunny as blazes and it seemed surreal when he stalked out, leaving Rachel silently crying and Amber stone-faced and pale, both standing in the doorway, watching him until his car disappeared. And he'd known that Rachel had hoped until the last moment that he would relent and the old Peter would return to her.

But she shouldn't have said those words.

His procrastination cost us our son's life.

Miserable months crept by and it was Christmas. He'd ignored Rachel's invitation to Gabby and Leon's house for the family celebration. Rather, he'd done something totally out of character—he'd gotten himself a bottle of Jack Daniels and returned to his office—a temporary place away from his usual residence office—to get plastered.

And to forget that this was the first Christmas without Jason.

His secretary, Mary Rivers, a pretty divorced Manilowe church member where they attended, was there finishing up some paperwork before going home for Christmas. When Peter offered her a drink, she'd expressed sympathy for his being alone on Christmas Eve and accepted. Unaccustomed to alcohol, they'd both ended up schnockered and on the office sofa, sympathizing with one another's sorry marriages.

The next day, Peter felt terrible. A hellish hangover was his first challenge. After that, guilt sat upon him like piggy-backed box cars. And heaped atop other offenses, it was too much. Seemed Mary had come to her senses as well. Before Peter could figure out what to do, she turned in her resignation and told him she was moving to another location a couple of hours away.

Left unsaid was *out of sight, with hopes of out of mind.*

Also left unspoken was that the feeling was mutual. Should she remain in town, even if no longer tethered together at work, they would be in church where the moral compass would implode in their presence. Mary's relocating was, to Peter, a godsend.

Relieved beyond belief to have the sordid thing behind him, Peter called Rachel and accepted the invitation to the family Christmas get together, despite the now amplified remorse he struggled with. Overriding that was the fact that he was certain he would soon expire from terminal loneliness. And when Rachel invited him over to her house afterward, he followed her home.

He apologized for all the grief he'd caused her and asked for forgiveness and mercy. He also asked Amber's forgiveness for his failures. Daughter Amber was silent, and though she allowed him to hug her, she was stiff and unyielding.

Rachel welcomed him back with open arms.

And Peter's world was turned right side up once more.

At least for a little while.

\|/

Life at Sugar Hills Farm remained tense.

"Gramma wants you to come visit her on weekends," Mary told Mark at the dinner table.

He cut his eyes at her, still not able to stifle the hurt he felt about family secrets. How he despised them! He could ignore them for a while but lately, the peaceful *denial* times were growing shorter and the anger more palpable.

"Why?"

"Why?" Mary frowned and lifted one shoulder. "She misses you. I would think you'd enjoy time away from the farm chores and seeing other young folks at church. It has to get lonely here for you. There's always somebody dropping by Gramma's house."

Mark took an aggressive slug of his milk. "I don't mind farm chores and I don't get lonely." He wiped his mouth with a napkin, knowing he was being purposely pigheaded, because he loved going to Gramma's house. But it seemed his parents were trying to get rid of him and something inside him screamed in protest, depositing him smack dab in the middle of a medieval moat that defied entry.

"No one's forcing you," Ralph inserted kindly. "It's entirely up to you, son."

Mark saw the sharp look his mother cut her husband and that only made him dig in deeper. He cut a bite of tender beef and chomped into it, though by now it was like chewing rawhide.

Why did he feel so unlovable? It *couldn't* be because his mother was trying to foist him off on *her* mother, could it? He bit his tongue to stem the brewing sarcasm. His father's sympathy would evaporate instantly should Mark insult his mother. He felt the vise closing in.

Mark stood and tossed his napkin on his plate. "I don't want to go. May I please be excused?" He knew that he'd better not desert his manners during this rebellion or he'd lose for sure.

"No, you may not," Mary objected.

"Yes, you may," Ralph overrode her with a firm nod of his snowy head.

Mark exited the dining room with as much dignity as he could, being as how he was feeling so—so *odious*. He'd learned that word recently when looking up a synonym to describe mean old Steve "Stinky" Dodger, his worst enemy at school. Stinky's nickname came from his love of baked beans and their effect on the gastric system. The attention did not deter Stinky's sense of self-importance a'tall. He gloried in his ill-gotten notoriety.

Stinky was the one who was always pestering Mark about who his real daddy was and how he'd died. His nosiness knew no bounds. Stinky's folks attended the same church as Mark's family and they remembered that Deacon Ralph Emerson had married the "widow" and had informally "adopted" Mark when he was born. The story had become a legendary testament to the man's epic decency.

Until recently, Stinky had stifled his curiosity.

This full-blown attack resulted from the A+ Mark had received on his family tree class assignment. Stinky's grades were pretty good and the fierce competitive streak in his wiring had awoken some dastardly *I wanna be number one* monsters.

In the end, Mark's mother had hedged—as usual—and suggested that Mark use his stepfather, Ralph's lineage, which, she concluded, was impressive.

But something in Mark had balked at the deception. He drew the line then and there to handle it in his own way. So, on his paper, he'd invented an imposing man with a distinguished military career. The fact of his dishonesty did not escape him. But, he reasoned, his mother had forced him into it.

His nemesis, Stinky, being Stinky, sensed Mark's raw nerves concerning his late father. His knowing dark eyes pierced Mark's armor mightily while he cunningly picked apart each point made in the paper the teacher had so eloquently read to the class. So Stinky went to the computer and tried to look it all up online—in spite of his obnoxiousness, he was a computer whiz—and he could not find anything to substantiate Mark's claims.

So when Stinky confronted him, Mark had tried to smooth over it by lying again, saying his dad had actually been a policeman who died in the line of duty. Of course, Stinky wanted all the details, when and where—the whole stupid nine yards. Mark revolted and refused to divulge one morsel more, stomping away in frustration and humiliation.

Since then, Stinky had been his worst nightmare. And to make matters worse, the fact that they attended the same church put him in even worse jeopardy should Stinky decide to spill the beans about Mark's deceitful ways.

Tonight, his gramma called and asked to speak to him. Mark pretended reluctance while inside he was elated to hear his gramma's sweet voice.

"Mark? I've missed you so much lately. I would really love to have you come and spend a weekend with me soon. The church is having a youth event in a few weeks and I'm baking a cake to sell to raise money for our orphanage in India. I'm also going to bake a cake especially for you. Know what kind?"

Mark gulped at how his heart responded to Gramma's love. "Strawberry?" His mouth was already watering.

She chuckled. "Now how did you guess that so quickly? Huh?"

He had to grin. "'Cause it's my favorite."

"So, is it a deal?"

What could he say? "Yeah, Gramma. It's a deal." Already, his heart was leaning that way.

"Love you, honey."

He grinned. "Me, too, Gramma. See you soon."

He clicked off his mother's phone and turned to return it to her. She was smiling and holding out her arms. He stiffened for long seconds as she angled her head beguilingly, her smile widening and easing the dark circles beneath her eyes.

Then he grinned like roadkill, took three long steps, and flung himself into her arms.

\1/

"Rachel?" Margie—pronounced like Magee only with an r—nudged Rachel awake in her hospital bed. She'd dozed off following her early afternoon physical therapy session with Shaun. Irritated, Rachel shifted her heavy leg cast and raised her bed half-mast. This was not a good day. She felt lousy and was so not in the mood to be around anybody or do anything.

Margie, an attractive brunette recreational therapist, remained undaunted as Rachel frowned at the news that she was scheduled for another four o'clock session.

"C'mon," Margie smiled and pushed Rachel's wheelchair to the bedside. "You'll enjoy this session."

Rachel knew better. The pain in her ankle and leg began rising again this time of day. It was about four on the scale, but that was enough to make her jittery and ill. The aching went all the way through bone and marrow.

She had, by now, limited herself to nighttime pain meds because having her head clear during therapy had risen to the top of her totem-goal.

It was either daytime pain or loopy head. Flip a coin.

As long as the throbbing was tolerable, she preferred it. And today, *tolerable* was not cooperating with her dogged MO. But reluctant to be stereotyped as a difficult patient, she grumpily complied.

Margie was cheerful beyond Rachel's forbearance today as she parked Rachel at the end of the Rec Room table. Not an easy placement since Rachel's Frankenstein-ish leg poked straight out, propped on pillows and thrumming like a rock concert's loud speaker.

Oh Lord, please let me die. She swiped her pale face with a damp wash cloth she'd brought along, just in case. Then she noticed that three more therapy patients she'd seen during her PT sessions were seated at the table.

One in particular drew her attention—Candy, lovely, slender young woman with warm, hazel eyes. When Margie asked them all to introduce themselves and their circumstances, Candy said she was twenty-nine and had suffered a stroke following a hysterectomy that left her left side weak and her speech slightly impeded.

Another patient, Jocelyn, a cute black girl, had also suffered a brain injury that left her silent and her movements awkward and unbalanced. Processing words came slowly. Rachel had seen her during sessions and felt badly for her because she seemed so out of it.

A fresh surge of thankfulness swept through Rachel. *Thanks, Lord, for sparing me that injury.*

Then there was Nadine, today accompanied by her boyfriend and mother. Tony, the spiked-haired, tattooed suitor joined in, ready to create a necklace for his love. So when Peter came wandering in, Rachel encouraged him to participate. He pulled up a chair beside her and settled in.

Margie presented several trays and bowls of endless, colorful beads, bangles, and bling-y little ornaments to be strung into bracelets, earrings, and necklaces. "Pick out what you want and create your own jewelry," she said, enthusiasm oozing from her.

When Rachel saw all the choices, an avalanche of despair nearly swept her away. Anything that hinted of challenge now undid her.

"I don't feel so good," she moaned. Peter took her hand and leaned to kiss her cheek.

Margie grinned, ignoring Rachel's angst. "Go ahead, Rachel. Pick out something pretty."

No sympathy there.

Sick as a puppy, she began to gather colors and textures from the different piles, not really caring. Peter joined in the treasure hunt, surprisingly adept and tasteful in his choices. Soon, Rachel found herself giving more detail to her preferences. When she gauged the number of ornaments she and Peter separated from the others, she threaded them in an arrangement she liked and sought Margie's counsel.

"Those look great," Margie proclaimed and in a few moments, her nimble fingers had the flexible, stretchy string ends clipped together and slipped on Rachel's wrist.

When finished, all the participants then modeled their jewelry for the others to admire, getting ridiculous chorused "oohs" and "aahs" along with good-natured laughter. Of course Nadine's boyfriend, Tony, got the most dramatic response as he blushed and presented the clunky creation to Nadine.

Peter, not to be outdone, informed the audience that he had helped fashion Rachel's bracelet, then stood and deeply bowed, to everybody's delight.

Rachel felt proud of herself as she bid farewell to the others. Everyone, by now, wanted one of her books. She promised that Peter would bring some more. She was delighted and amazed to see Jocelyn smiling and even more excited to see that she had chosen some lovely pieces for a necklace and strung them together.

"I would never have thought it," she told Peter over her shoulder on the ride back to her room.

"What, honey?"

She laughed. "I forgot my pain while creating this bracelet." She held up her wrist again, amazed. "This is special. I'm going to call it my healing bracelet."

\|/

Toward the end of the first week at Roger C. Peace, Peter wheeled Rachel to the elevator that whirred them down to the ground-level hospital cafeteria, where Gabby, Leon, Drusilla, and J.C. awaited them. He wanted this to be like a party for Rachel. Well, at least as much party as she could stand.

He knew she'd about gone feral in that tiny cubby hole of a room they'd put her in. The promised switch to a bigger, nicer room had never happened, but Rachel hadn't complained. She hadn't whined about anything.

Fact was, Rachel wasn't talking much now. But what she did say was upbeat and positive. Well, as upbeat as a hibernating woodchuck could manage. But Lord have mercy, he teared up at her courage.

Spotting the foursome waving them over to where they'd pulled two tables together to accommodate them, Peter aimed the chair in their direction.

"Hey, Rachel! C'mon, let's party!" J.C. motioned and helped navigate her to the head of the table where they'd granted the wheelchair wide birth. Then, each in turn gave her ever-so-gentle hand squeezes and air kisses.

"Party. Yeah, right," Rachel said. "Glad to see you guys. It gets boring here."

"You want me to fix you a plate, sis?" Gabby offered.

Rachel huffed her usual retort. "Heck no. That's the fun of dining out, isn't it? Checking out the choices?"

"Got that right," Leon said as he rushed toward the helm, but Peter's grip on the chair was ruthless.

He wheeled her around to each section, allowing her to select entrées of her choosing. Her fare was rotisserie chicken, candied apples, and a baked potato she'd squirreled away from lunch to bring with her. And though the pain in her leg was revving up, she ate well. The conversation was lively and entertaining.

"Why aren't you eating your squash casserole?" bossy Gabby challenged J.C.

"'Cause I don't like it," J.C. turned his nose up.

"Why'd you get it, then? Don't you know you're not supposed to waste food?" Gabby quipped a la Don Rickles.

"Listen how she's talking to me," sputtered J.C. at Gabby's comical sarcasm, their classic format. He crossed his arms and rolled his hound dog eyes heavenward. "Lord deliver me from evil cousins."

"I'm Drusilla's cousin," Gabby retorted. "Not yours. I'm not kin to you."

"Now just see how she treats me?" Features stricken, he peered at Peter, who burst into laughter. "She don't even recognize my family ties."

"Don't feel bad," Peter reined in his laughter and sobered. "She just *acts like* she likes me."

"Got that right," Gabby nodded, munching on French fries and chicken strips.

Usually Rachel enjoyed the banter. But after twenty minutes of it, her nerves were worn thin. The leg and head pain pounded in syncopation and she gazed at Peter.

"You need to go to your room," he said quietly.

"Uh huh."

Peter saw that exhaustion rendered her breath shallow. "Y'all can come up to the room and visit," she told them. Peter knew that lying down might revive her for a while. He also could divine that though tired, Rachel hated for them to leave.

On the way to the room, she asked Peter, "Did you bring more of my books with you? My night duty nurse wants a copy of *Promises Kept.*"

"They're in the car. I'll run out and get them when the family leaves."

Peter would run his legs off at her slightest hint of want.

He felt honored that she was left here for him.

\I/

Rachel transferred to bed and lay silently while the others kept up their banter about everyday happenings, which helped her feel a touch of normalcy. Only thing, the pain was taking over and pain-med time was forty-five minutes away. She forced herself to wait until ten o'clock so relief would last throughout the dark hours.

"Well, sir." Leon stood, stretching and yawning. "Now we've worn Rachel out, we should be going."

"Yeah, sweetie," Drusilla said. "I hope we didn't stay too long." She leaned to kiss Rachel's cheek. "Love you."

"Love you back," Rachel said, smiling. At least she hoped it was a smile. She was beyond tired.

"See you tomorrow, sis. Rest up." Discerning Gabby blew her a kiss and snatched up her stadium jacket, leaving swiftly.

"Hang in there, Rachel!" J.C. said. "Like a hair in a biscuit."

"You betcha." Rachel blew him a kiss.

Peter followed them to the door, then turned to tell Rachel, "I'm gonna follow them out and get those books you wanted from the truck."

Rachel watched them go with mixed feelings. With silence came blessed relief. But the dreaded sadness fell over her like black foam. She was alone. But—being alone was more peaceful. Wasn't it? Then why did she feel so wretched?

How she hated her emotions being jerked around.

She turned on the overhead TV, then fiddled with the unfamiliar remote, straining her pin-head patience and finally found the family channel that played *M*A*S*H* and *The Andy Griffith Show*. Mayberry she could watch. But *M*A*S*H* was playing and it didn't jive with her uneasy nerves at that precise moment.

Where was Peter?

He'd been gone long enough to be getting back—

Her cell phone loped into rhythm. She groped around on the bed for it until her fingers connected.

She flipped it open. "Hello."

"Rachel!" Peter's voice—frantic.

"Peter? Where are you?"

"I don't know." Panic laced his cry. "I finally found this door—I think it's the right one—but *it's locked.* I can't get in! You've got to help me!"

Her heart nearly broke. "Calm down, honey. I'll send somebody to let you in. It's always locked this time of night—for security. I'll get someone there right away. Okay?"

"Okay."

She pushed the emergency button on her bed and explained to the faceless voice her husband's situation and asked that the door be unlocked for him. Within five minutes Peter came rushing in, pale and trembling.

He shook his head back and forth. "I panicked," he said, disbelieving. "I just—panicked. My nerves are shot."

"C'mere." Rachel held out her hand to him. He came to her side and took it, the look in his sweet green eyes desolate. Rachel said to him, "Listen, sweetheart, you're going through a lot right now and you're bound to have these lapses. But soon, things will get better. You'll see." She smiled at him. "We'll get through this. Together."

He leaned over and she hugged him as close as she could manage with the odious neck brace and he lay wrapped across her bosom for long moments, heart to heart. She sensed when peace returned and he arose to search for food. He stretched out on the sofa bed and munched on some of her leftover grapes and peanut butter crackers, not really into the Mayberry scene.

Neither was she, but it focused her on something other than herself for moments at a time.

The nurse came by to administer pain meds and Rachel signed a copy of her novel, *Promises Kept*, and presented it to her.

"You're my angel," she reminded her, meaning it from her heart. Nurse Betty gave her an intense but careful hug of gratitude. After she left and Rachel felt welcome oblivion descending, she turned back the blanket and felt Peter slide in beside her.

He turned and wrapped himself around her.

It was good.

They would get through all this.

Together.

\1/

Where had her emotions gone to hibernate?

Through it all, Rachel had not shed a single tear since her accident. Despite the agony, vertigo, manic mood swings, and depression, underneath it all the soul part of her remained set apart, like a third person watching her situation from a secure, sterile distance. She knew that her mind struggled against returning to the traumatic fall. Denial became her friend and aided her survival.

At the same time, Rachel's determination to overcome was like a caged ravenous lion.

She kept up a running talk with herself. *I will not succumb to this . . . this will not do me in . . . I will walk again . . . I will write again . . . God is in this . . . this is happening for a purpose.*

She would trust God.

And even as she repeated this to herself, the spiritual part of her remained flatlined. There was not that familiar quickening of the Holy Spirit. So this was the dark valley her daddy used to talk about, one where one had to blindly trust God not only with the way *through* but the way *out.*

By faith, she would persist in saying, *this, too, shall pass.*

It had to.

Soon.

She must be there for Peter.

Chapter Five

\\\/

"However mean your life, meet it and live it."
—Henry David Thoreau

The Gang spent every minute they could at the hospital.

Tonight had been no exception.

"They've come a long way, haven't they?" J.C. asked over his shoulder. Leon and Gabby sat silently in the back seat of the sensible Honda Odyssey van. For the moment, all the junk talk was tucked away for later use when things got too somber.

"They have. Thank the good Lord." Drusilla yawned and ran her fingers through her short faded blonde curls, a habit rather than a necessity. It always sprang back in exactly the same order. At one time, she was so skinny her family nick-named her "Bony Maroney."

"Remember when old Dr. Bunton told me to give some blood and I'd start gaining weight?" she asked Gabby, then muttered, "Can't believe I was ever called 'Bony Maroney.'"

Gabby laughed. "I remember that he was right."

"Thanks a lot," Drusilla huffed. "That was just after Junior was born—and I donated blood. *Bingo.* I started fluffing up and by the time Anthony came along, I'd plumped up a good twenty pounds."

"On you, it looks great," chimed in ol' faithful J.C.

"Ha!" Leon snorted. "He's after something."

"How much that gonna cost me?" Drusilla whispered and winked at J.C. He winked back at her and they burst into laughter.

She didn't care that much about body image anyway. There were more important things in life than worrying about a few extra fat cells. Like being there for family. In this case, her cousin Rachel and Peter.

She, Gabby, and Rachel were more like sisters than first cousins. During childhood, they'd slept over at each other's homes nearly every weekend, attending Preacher Hamp's church on Sunday; the highlight of their week was when they occasionally sang trio numbers upon request. Yep. They shared the musical gene. But Rachel's was the phenomenal one.

"It's so sad." Drusilla said as they glimpsed the empty mill and warehouses. "Nothing left in Manilowe Mill Village but ghosts of the past. Except us, maybe, but we've changed so much we don't count."

"Yeah," Leon nodded. "NAFTA sold us out. All that machinery sent overseas." His huff was more bark than laugh. "And all the jobs as well."

"And the great exodus began. So many have moved away or died off." Gabby sighed. "I remember when this place bustled with life and . . ." Her voice trailed off as they all absorbed, once more, a sense of profound loss. Of melancholy. They all grew up here in Manilowe Mill Village. The mill hill had been, during their early years, a thriving textile metropolis of sorts. At least she was to her villagers.

Their collective loss was complete.

"Y'all come on in. I just bought some chocolate chip cookies from the bakery," Gabby said when J.C. neared the Brown's house, only two miles from the Johnson's dwelling.

"I don't think—"

"None of that!" Gabby cut off J.C.'s protest. "I've got some sugar-free goodies for you and Leon. So don't be a party-pooper, J.C.!" Leon and J.C. were both borderline diabetic and had to watch their sugar.

As predicted, the Johnsons accepted the invite.

"Rachel looks bad," Drusilla murmured.

"Yeah. She does." Gabby agreed. "But she's tough."

"That she is." Drusilla grew quiet as they pulled into the driveway of the remodeled mill house. This one, like theirs, was a one-story mill structure with added rooms, all a joint effort shared by Leon, J.C., and the "brain," Peter. Not unusual. The lifelong buddies did most everything together.

Even this.

\\\/

Gabby shivered from January's chill as she dashed across the large porch and unlocked the front door. The others caught up and they entered the toasty interior. "Thank God for a warm house," Leon called, throwing his arms wide. "I love you home!"

Nobody laughed because these were revered sentiments embedded in their close camaraderie.

Leon had been abandoned by his full-Cherokee Indian mother as a toddler and raised by a good father and his entire Mill Village clan. The Gang knew that a sense of belonging was vital to Leon, who remained—well into his sunset years—a striking blonde Adonis. He'd inherited his father's genetic fairness and his mother's proud features. His hair had gradually shifted from golden to platinum with little modifying of his firm facial angles and planes.

Gabby, Leon's brunette counterpart in her younger days now sported dark salt-and-pepper waves that needed only a comb and was still attractive with her deep-set blue eyes and perpetual smile that was mostly sassy but could turn compassionate in a heartbeat. She had fashioned their humble dwelling as welcoming and comfortable as her southern upbringing embossed. She prized Leon's homage. It validated and completed her.

Drusilla helped Gabby arrange the goodie trays while Leon and J.C. put on the coffeepot and soon they sprawled in the den, feet propped on the coffee table, sipping steaming java, munching cookies, and sharing their thoughts.

Their silence was relaxed and natural, spawned from a lifetime of intimate amity.

Gabby spoke first. "Rachel's had a rough time of it. All the way back. It doesn't seem fair—this disaster added to all the rest."

Leon took a deep breath, blew it out and scratched his head, a sign to Gabby that he didn't exactly disagree with the unspoken. But—

"So has Peter." When he saw Gabby's features tighten, he held up his palm. "Wait. I'm not saying that what Peter did wasn't wrong."

When Gabby composed her features, he continued. "But you know and I know that Peter wouldn't ever have done what he did if Rachel hadn't practically accused him of murder and then later asked him to leave."

"That's not exactly true," Gabby insisted, feeling her sister-temperature rise. "She only stated the truth. Peter had neglected to have the tires rotated and it did, in effect—according to the State Patrol—cause the hydroplaning on the icy road."

"But imagine how hard Rachel's words hit—"

"Well, he got even by treating her like a stranger for years. She finally had enough and asked him to leave until he wanted to be part of the marriage again."

All during the discourse, Gabby noted that J.C. and Drusilla had grown more fidgety, their gazes ping-ponging between Gabby and Leon.

Gabby waved a hand. "Stop." She closed her eyes for a moment, reined in her impatience, then looked at Leon. "This is ridiculous. We're arguing over something that happened years ago. They seem to have put it to rest. Now let's leave it there."

He relaxed and smiled at her. "Yeah. You're right." Then he shot his guests a chagrined glance. "Sorry, folks."

J.C. and Drusilla waved it off.

Gabby loved the way Leon smiled. His blue-gray eyes twinkled while his wide, generous mouth curled up at the corners as though reaching for his ears. She also loved the way J.C. grinned, like now, making them relax. Reservation found no place in him. His hair had long ago disappeared, save a white wispy horse shoe over which he usually wore his U.S. Army ball cap. When J.C. grinned, his eyes disappeared into half-moons and his lips were as wide as the ocean it seemed. Not to be outdone, Leon proudly donned his U.S. Marine cap over his full, wavy white mane.

"Peter and Rachel make a handsome couple, don't they?" Drusilla remarked, rather wistfully. "He's still as trim as ever and has hair to kill for." The change of subject was timely and appreciated.

That's where J.C. usually jumped in with some witty repartee, but tonight they all nodded in complete agreement. Of one mind.

"He was the only civilian amongst us who opted for a college degree." Gabby boasted without a smidgeon of shame.

"Yup," Leon agreed. "That's 'cause he tumbled so hard for Rachel. That set a different path before them."

J.C. added, "I remember when he was headed for the Air Force. Couldn't wait, doncha know?" He grinned.

Leon smiled at Gabby. "That was before he set eyes on that sister of yours, sweetheart. This family grows beautiful women. Great genes!"

Tonight, Leon's love spilled from that smile and wrapped Gabby with a warm coating of peace. Until she remembered her niece, one of the "beautiful women" the family no longer mentioned.

Amber.

She was both a blessing and, in recent years, a curse.

Family did not abandon family. They just didn't. Gabby's heart grieved the loss.

\1/

Rachel's aloneness spiked as time passed.

So she was glad when Ruth, a member of the hospital system's respiratory team, popped her head into Rachel's room during her breakfast time. "How's it going, Rachel?" she asked with a big smile.

"Ruth! Come in." Oh how good it was to have a visitor. Nobody, but nobody came much anymore because they feared she would be in therapy. And they were right. She usually was, what with occupational therapy after breakfast, physical therapy after lunch, and now, on top of those, she had speech therapy, which troubled her to no end because she had no speech problems. At least she didn't think she did. Her gabbiness had taken a powder at the foot of those stairs.

The old terror ratcheted up. Did the staff suspect something sinister was going on in her brain? In such moments of doubt, her self-esteem plummeted lower than a snake's belly and she felt herself stagger three steps backward—er, make that three wheel turns backward. Sometimes she wondered if her self-esteem still existed. Fear knocked her flatter'n she sprawled on that cranked down bed.

In a blink, the angst would leave. Two steps forward. "Jerked around" became the understatement of the millennium.

And right now, a living, breathing, intelligent entity positioned herself at Rachel's bedside, treating her as if she was normal. She felt uncommonly grateful as Ruth, a colleague of her old school friend, Connie, handed her a hardback copy of Jan Karon's *Recipes from the Mitford Series*, a favorite setting of Rachel's. She'd read all of Karon's Mitford series books and the characters had wormed their way into her heart and refused to leave. She'd not read this particular book.

"Here's something for you to read while you're here," Ruth said. "I don't have time to stay. Work awaits, but I wanted to drop this by to help you pass the time."

They chatted for a few more minutes before Ruth rushed off to work. Then Rachel began to thumb through the pages. The pictures and short stories drew her in, engaging her and filling her with something close to enjoyment. When Gabby came that evening, she showed her some of the colorful photos and recipes and the two of them started plotting which vittles they would cook up when Rachel got home. The leisure pastime laid fertile soil into which seeds of hope for the future began to incubate.

Trauma's ups and downs plagued her incessantly. From one moment to the next, Rachel could not forecast the course of her emotions. So the near pleasant intervals of Mitford diversion, however sporadic, heartened her.

It made her feel human.

\i/

One day, she looked at Peter across the hospital room and said, "I feel like Meryl Streep, you know, in that movie *Death Becomes Her.*"

He nodded, remembering. "That movie's a hoot." He laughed, thankful to be able to recall the image.

"Except when it's you who doesn't seem to have a pulse. You go through motions but you're dead. That's me."

"I'm sorry, honey, for laughing." He was instantly at her side, leaning over and nuzzling her cheek, gently kissing her. "You're going to get better, sweetheart. I promise, you will."

How supportive he was and, at times, Rachel felt she would have drowned had it not been for his strength and conviction tugging her from the rapids raging about her.

Oh, she prayed and she trusted that God heard her but she'd not—since the accident—had that warm downy connection. She took courage from her daddy's long ago counsel, that the Creator would use all things for good to those who love Him.

Even this? She could only hope.

\i/

The nights were the worst.

So far, Rachel had not been able to sleep on her side in her normal fetal position. But the pain meds had remedied that to an extent, plunging her into deep sleep that overrode the pain.

But how she hated the wooziness that rode shotgun to it and, by the fifth day, she realized that the pain was not as severe as it had initially been. Could she do without meds? Lucidity dangled before her, making her mouth water.

"Do I have to take the pain meds?" she asked her orthopedic surgeon on his irreverently early a.m. visit.

He lifted his shoulders and shook his head. "Not if you don't need it."

Bingo. "I think I can do without it now."

"Your choice. But if you find that you need it, you need only ask. Okay?" He patted her arm, then frowned at her leg brace that she'd always loosened at night.

"Who loosened this?" he asked, already re-setting it to unfeasible degrees of pressure.

"I did when I started to go to sleep. Otherwise, I can't adjust my leg and get comfortable."

He gave her a friendly yet firm response. "You don't want your leg to heal crookedly, do you?"

You should have to sleep with this on your leg. The hateful thought followed him as he left, trailed by an intern he'd brought along to observe.

Crooked leg. It resonated like a childhood bully's taunt.

Something to think about, huh?

Another dark distraction.

That night, alone because both Gabby and Peter felt under the weather, she did the cold-turkey with her pain meds.

When she finally sank into slumber, she dreamed. In it she wrestled the heavy metal monster brace, struggling to pull it off her leg. Claustrophobia panicked her.

"Aaiigh!" She awoke with a strangle hold on her leg, pointing the metal-bound appendage toward the ceiling. Her heart doing a tap dance, she slowly lowered it to rest on the extra nest of pillows that eased some of the choking around the ankle surgery site.

Something had to give.

And it was not going to be the brace.

She prayed, not feeling anything fuzzy or warm but simply operating on trust. "Lord, you know I need help in making friends with this leg brace. Please help me to find a place of healing that will be tolerable."

In that moment, Rachel felt a surge of strength to tackle a new venture—to roll onto her side, maneuver and prop her heavy-casted leg onto extra pillows, and finally bend her knees into the semblance of a fetal position. Aaahhh. *She did it.*

It was a pivotal moment in her healing.

She'd been able to make peace with the brace. And sleep without drugs.

\1/

Peter was having a lousy day.

"I can't focus on anything," he groaned upon arriving at the hospital a couple of mornings later. "I don't feel like working. I can't go on much longer like this."

Desperation reigned.

Again.

It was usually contagious. But there seemed no room inside Rachel now to accommodate the mental harassment. She wanted to fix it for him but it seemed that simply surviving was as far as she could stretch herself these days. So she did the only thing she knew to quiet the pandemonium attacking him. She held out her arms to him and he came into them and melted against her, snuggled across her bosom.

"Ah, honey," he breathed. "I'm so glad God spared you and allowed you to stay with me."

Rachel resisted shushing him for dredging up IT. She knew instinctively that he needed to vent, both the good and bad. "Me, too."

\1/

Rachel tried to flow. She really did.

Meeting life head on was the only way she'd ever known.

And now? Head on caused total meltdown.

Gabby came in at lunch time, carrying her own Hardee's fare and an extra Swiss Mushroom Burger for Peter, who'd not worked for a couple of days. But Rachel knew that if he missed some time, the sky wouldn't fall in. Their rental properties didn't require constant attention but, because of the number of properties in their ownership, the need for repairs stacked quickly. Late rent payments were another plague for bleeding-hearted Peter. Peter depended on his right arm man, Gary, to keep much of it going in his absence.

For extra income, Peter operated his own small pest control service, which Rachel's hospitalization had practically shut down. But that, too, could wait.

Gabby didn't tuck into her food as usual and Rachel sensed something amiss.

"What's wrong?"

"Hmm, I got a call from Amber today." Usually stoical Gabby looked uncertain. "I'm sorry. Maybe I shouldn't share this with you."

"Why not?" Peter came to full alert, laying aside his half-eaten burger.

Rachel said nothing. Couldn't. Amber's name alone brought darkness and right now Rachel was already digging her way out of a sunless dungeon.

"I'll give you the bad news first. She's in the hospital. The good news is that it's nothing serious. She had an appendectomy and is doing fine."

Thank God. Rachel closed her eyes.

"Why didn't she call us?" a tense Peter demanded.

Gabby laid her sandwich aside and presented both palms. "Look. I couldn't decide whether to share that with you or not but if it were my child, I would want to at least know." She shrugged tersely. "So, good or bad, I told you."

Even in her altered mental alertness, Rachel could feel Peter's anger. "Did she say why she neglected to personally let us know?" he asked sharply. His anger lashed at the thin thread tethering Rachel to sanity. She tried to shut out the discussion, vibrating with unrest.

Gabby sighed deeply. "Seems she had an emergency episode and had to be taken by ambulance from her work and only just today was able to call."

"She was able to call you," Peter snapped. "But not her parents?"

"Actually, she got a nurse to find my number in her cell phone and punch it in. She's still sort of—out of it."

"If I were a betting man, I would wager she didn't mention our names," Peter snarled, blasting a tsunami of fury throughout the small room.

Looking extremely uncomfortable, Gabby remained silent, confirming his suspicions.

"S'okay, Gabby," Peter declared. "I don't really give a rip." For emphasis, he resumed eating his food with gusto.

It slammed into Rachel like a freight train. "Peter, please—I can't take this right now," Rachel closed her eyes, dizziness drowning her. "Please don't discuss this. I can't—"

Peter and Gabby both dashed to her bedside. "We're so sorry, honey," Peter crooned, taking her hand and kissing her cheek.

"I should've kept my stupid trap shut," Gabby muttered. "I'm sorry, sis. You don't need anything contentious around you right now."

Faintness swamped Rachel and she whispered, "Lord, help me."

Amber sick . . . alone.

How much can a person take and survive?

\1/

The days following Jason's death later blurred in Rachel's memory. Much of it lay buried in darkness, rejecting access to light. In a way, it proved merciful. But when, out of her grief delirium, she'd foolishly spotlighted Peter's lapse in auto maintenance, she'd managed a brilliant kamikaze. Technically, she was right. Peter had procrastinated in servicing the tires.

The consequences of the procrastination were tragic. At the same time, her self-righteous rant inflicted lasting wounds upon Peter.

She didn't count on the aftershocks. The adultery was bad enough. His leaving the nest was even worse. That period of time following the ill-spoken words would forever haunt her. She had swallowed her pride when Peter later showed remorse and asked for forgiveness.

During the separation, she'd had time to remember all the ways Peter was a good husband. And how his fathering excelled, whether helping with algebra homework or shooting hoops in the driveway, chauffeuring the kids to piano lessons and soccer games, or even dressing up as Santa for Christmas school festivities, though J.C. and Leon had given him ample ribbing the one and only time he'd braved the Yuletide performance.

"Dang if you ain't the worst Santy I've ever seen," declared J.C.

That was one time Gabby kept her loose tongue still. It was too humiliating for her brother-in-law. But no such sympathy churned out from the Manilowe Mill Hill males.

Leon joined in. "My grandpa's coon dog coulda done a better job of *hohoho*-ing than you, Peter." He ignored Gabby's sharp elbow digging into his ribs. His was such that his wicked humor could not pass up such a rare, barefaced opportunity.

Rachel had studied Peter's angst with combined unease and pity.

It was true. He'd been convincingly pillow-plumped and stuffed into the red suit. And the white beard hugged his craggy features while Rachel's rouge lent the cheeks an elfin blush. Beyond that, the performance stank to the Manilowe Mill rafters.

Peter didn't have a thimbleful of drama in his DNA. Smart? Yes. Thespian talents? "No way, José!" was Jason's laughing critique.

Amber declared it a brilliant coup d'état of her genius father. One in which he'd created a hilarious parody of Santa Claus, much funnier, in her estimation than the stupid "Ho-ho-ho" patronizing image you usually get.

Everyone tried to downplay the disaster but Peter himself was his own scathing critic. "Don't ever ask me to do that again," he growled as he snatched off the hat and beard backstage.

J.C. deadpanned, "Don't worry, buddy. We won't."

Jason was the first of them to sputter with mirth, after which the entire Manilowe Mill Hill Gang hollered with laughter. Soon, Peter joined in.

They'd survived a failure of one of their own.

Together.

But Peter was always there for them all. He was, according to Amber in her pre-mutiny days, *a rock*. "I love you, Mom. You're the music and poetry in my life. But Dad's the earth beneath my feet, y'know?" And Rachel did know because her own father had been that to her.

That's why Amber's flight three years after her brother's death proved so bitter.

\|/

Rachel hated to do it.

But she had no choice.

"Can I lie down with you?" Peter hovered over Rachel's hospital bed when she turned over to position her body for maximum comfort, which only lasted for about two hours before pain drove her to struggle to roll to the other side. The process involved packing pillows behind her and in front to support and offset the leg brace's weight. In essence, she stacked her legs like logs, with a pillow between them.

It worked only if this pillow-fortress buttressed her.

"No, darling," she said sadly.

"I can't?"

"I'm sorry, honey, but cuddling is impossible now. Without pain meds, I have to be creative to get to sleep." Cunning was a better word for sneaking up on slumber. She was beginning to really catch on to the idea of mind over matter. It began with befriending the leg brace and now, she simply ordered her mind to think it was a natural thing to close her eyes and glide into slumber.

One device she used was to recall swinging on the old tree swing her daddy had strung up for her in her early childhood. Now, pushing a cerebral-video button, she replayed soaring like a seagull beneath a glorious blue, sun-filled sky. It required focus but she got pretty good at experiencing that gliding, mindless sensation that slid her into oblivion.

Sure, she woke up several times each night to turn over and pack herself into a pillow fortress like a sardine in a can, but she prided herself that mind-over-matter did the trick and that incremental sleep was beneficial.

But it could not be executed with Peter in bed with her. Not now.

"That's okay," he said like a little boy refused cookies. He leaned over and kissed her on the lips, then gazed longingly into her eyes. "I love you so much it hurts."

"Me, too," she murmured, drained enough to already feel a sense of swirling downward. That was encouraging. She was making progress with sleep. And the loopiness in her head had receded in recent days. Not that she was the sharpest tack in Peter's toolbox but there was a difference in drug giddiness and trauma aftershock.

Last thing she saw as she floated off was Peter lying on that impossible cot, keeping vigil over her.

\\//

Rachel would later recall the odd blessing of the trauma-cocoon.

It prevented her from obsessing about anything because nothing lingered long in her mind before scattering. Merciful was the reprieve from grief, however short-lived, over her son's death.

Those months following Jason's death were the worst of Rachel's life. Because not only had she lost a son but she'd also lost her husband. Oh, he was there in body, but it seemed his insides had been eviscerated. Her words had killed the elemental in Peter.

She'd tried to make it up to him but nothing she did brought him out of the inner sanctum he'd created from thin air and fortitude. He was like a resolute automaton, focused and polite—but so distanced she felt abandoned on the sinking Titanic.

Amber? She was another story. Seemed she, too, had gone off somewhere inside herself. Rachel tried, oh, how she tried to get her sweet girl to talk to her, but at times she saw flashes of something like resentment behind those lovely eyes.

Between Peter's coldness and Amber's detachment, Rachel felt sometimes that she would lose her mind. But the Maker pitched Rachel a lifeline. Writing. One that Rachel had never before recognized as a gift.

"That's His special gift to you," her father insisted, smiling his daddy smile at her, big hand patting her as she buried her face in his strong shoulder and wept. "Use it, honey. This will pass and writing will help get you through it, like my preaching helps me through trials."

"I don't know what to do, Dad," she sobbed. "Peter's just not the same. Sometimes I think he h-hates me."

The hand gently rubbed her back. "Aww, Peter doesn't hate you. He's going through grief, too, honey. Men sometimes have a tougher time of expressing themselves. Just be patient. He'll come around."

But Rachel could see the concern in her father's eyes. Later, he brought the two of them together for a conference time. Peter revered her father and Rachel knew that if anyone could reach him, Hamp could. He'd retired from the pulpit but the pulpit had not left him.

They sat stiffly in the living room of Hamp's small cottage, one bought when Manilowe Mill had sold their housing at nominal prices. The Wests wanted to retire near their family. Peter, J.C., and Leon had gutted the structure and turned it into what Rachel's mother, Lib, called a dollhouse dream. Her mother got to enjoy it for five years before cancer struck. Losing her had left a huge hole in Rachel's heart.

Hamp was still a striking man who Rachel fancied resembled one of her favorite actors, Efrem Zimbalist Jr., with his full head of salt-and-pepper hair, classic features, well-modulated voice, and polished manners. Besides that, he was the godliest man she'd ever known.

You get to know someone inside out when you live with them. Rachel's relationship with her daddy was tighter'n Velcro, her mama always said. While Gabby practiced shooting hoops in the backyard, Rachel sat quietly in her daddy's office studying and writing poems, just to be near him. When Gabby joined the girls' basketball teams and played soccer, Rachel took piano and voice lessons, spending hours practicing and doing private concerts for her father, who was always an adoring audience.

Later, she was his right hand during church services, sitting at the piano. He only had to blink and crook a finger and she knew exactly when to go to the piano bench and begin to play softly for the invitational. Soul mates, they were.

Rachel loved her mother dearly and spent much time in the kitchen with her. But Rachel knew her mom understood her youngest daughter's creative spirit and delighted in the tight father/daughter bond. She loved to comment on how Rachel would read her dad's sermon notes and offer suggestions, which he took to heart.

So when Hamp cleared his throat that day and began to counsel Peter and Rachel on a whole new level, Rachel's heart flung as wide open as the Grand Canyon. "I'm here, not as a father, but as a friend to both of you. You've had a marvelous marriage all through the years and for that, as a father and friend,

I feel extremely blessed." Warmth spilled from soft brown eyes that moistened for a long moment.

He cleared his throat again and swallowed soundly. "I want for you two, more than anything, happiness and peace. Along with that I covet joy in your union. I know that Jason's passing has weighed heavily upon your hearts, as it has upon mine. And he will always be here with us in spirit. That is as it should be."

Rachel felt Peter begin to tense beside her and nervously cross one leg over the other. Her heart plunged and her father, the perceptive one, must have noticed.

"I'm not going to spout biblical platitudes to you. You both know the Word and know what you have to do for spiritual harmony. What I want to offer to you is hope that this, too, shall pass. Lib and I have had our valleys, too. Some you may know about, Rachel, but others you don't. You do know that being in a pastor's family is not always smooth sailing. The flocks are human and the flaws limitless. The pastor's family is humanly flawed, too. As such we are predisposed to disappoint one another along the way."

He leaned forward. "That doesn't mean we don't love each other. That doesn't mean we should give up on each other."

Rachel slid her hand to touch Peter's, where his fingers lay between them on the sofa. He did not reach for it, as her heart yearned for. Rather, he withdrew and clasped his hands tersely on his lap. Rachel sighed defeat and only hoped that later, when Peter was alone, these words of wisdom would penetrate and germinate in fruitful soil.

"I want to leave you with this: to me, marriage is like the relationship between the hand and the eye. If the hand hurts, the eye cries and the hand wipes away the tears."

He stood and hugged them both. Eyes moist, he said, "That perception worked for Lib and me for nearly five decades. It can work for you, too."

Chapter Six

\\\/

*"You start with a darkness to move through but sometimes the
darkness moves through you."*
—Dean Young

Peter wished a thousand times over that he had heeded Hamp's
counsel that day.

But he'd stubbornly trudged on through the trenches he'd
created, tunnel-focused on how he'd been accused of killing his
son. He could not get past that. Rachel had tried in a thousand
and one ways to retract her words and meaning.

But Peter's heart had crystallized with the hopeless rage of
injustice. Beneath it all simmered a certainty that it was true.

During that time of self-absorption, he'd completely forgotten Amber, who'd retreated like a Cistercian nun over the past
three years. And then, during her first post-high school graduation year, his brilliant, beautiful daughter had cut loose like a
hellion on a punish-parents mission.

Today, as he drove to the hospital, he wondered "For what?"

At first, he and Rachel were slack-jawed with shock over the
alteration. That's because they'd not accounted for thin walls
during their history of home-front war.

For once, he wished his recall of those days was not so vivid.

He wished that when he'd confessed to Rachel of his one
night peccadillo, Amber had not overheard from the stairwell.
He and Rachel had worked it out. Somewhat. But neither had a
later clash gone unobserved by his poor daughter.

It was a collision that re-defined his life.

That one bombshell secret Peter had shared with Rachel had been the final proverbial straw for the sensitive teen. Overhearing her father confess that his "mistake," sweet, church-going secretary, Mary, had given birth to a son nine months after that fateful transgression had pushed Amber over the cliff.

Peter later learned that she'd heard it all—her mother's anguished cry, *"How much more can I bear, Peter? This loss of us is like a death knell. But this—"*

And Peter's impassioned, "Please, honey—I'll make it up—"

"I'm not your honey. Not any longer. And I cannot—" she broke off in wild weeping. "I cannot accept into my life a child spawned through betrayal."

"But the boy can't help it," was Peter's heartfelt cry.

"Neither can I!" Rachel screamed. "Don't you get it? Neither can I! Don't ask that of me."

"Please, darling. Calm down. You're right. You don't deserve this."

More sobs. "If you love me at all, Peter, don't ask me to accept this. I'll die if you do."

"Shhh. You're my life, Rachel. I can't live without you."

Amber had heard and spied it all from the stairwell of their home, hidden behind the blind stair wall.

Peter cringed today, imagining how the horrendous disclosures had invaded her, and lay there while she silently gestated their putridness.

The revelation of her savoir-faire happened two years later. The confrontation imploded on a Christmas after the family clan had gathered at their two-story home. Little brother, Jason had been dead three years and Rachel had seemed, to Peter, to come to terms with the loss.

Dear Lord, Peter would later think, *I've destroyed so much of my sweet family, I don't deserve to live.*

Everyone had departed, leaving the three of them alone in their cozy holiday-scented den to sip warm, spicy apple cider. The live fir tree that year smelled heavenly and was elaborately decorated with colorful ribbons, silken floral sprigs, and sparkly glass ornaments, a positive testimony of Rachel's efforts to over-come not only Jason's death but also Peter's subtle coldness.

Yes, he was a class A jerk, Amber was quick to tell him. And once she began, Amber let it all spew forth. "You've treated Mom like crap since Jason died." She went on to sharpen her observances in colorful language—formerly foreign to their daughter—and when he tried to shush her, she grew more irate. "Oh, I'll shut up all right. I've grown used to being treated like the light fixtures in this godforsaken shell of a home."

Green eyes glared at him, piercing his father's heart.

"Well, I'm tired of being the good girl lost behind the ghost of Jason. And lo and behold—now there's another ghost that Dad grieves for." Her sarcasm ended on a sob and she flung wide her arms. "I can't compete with both. I'm outta here. I won't ever bother you again. You can take that to the bank."

She rose to her full 5'4" height and pivoted on her heel to stalk from the room, her long, thick, wheat-colored, sun-streaked ponytail swishing. Rachel sprang up and rushed to capture her, forcing her to look at her. "Honey, you can't leave me." Then, the usually stoic, gentle mother burst into tears.

Amber smiled so sadly that Peter had to steel himself not to rush to rescue her from the terrible cynicism.

"I love you, Mama. I really do. And you've done the best you could under the circumstances Dad's tossed you. But this place—" She swept her hand around, "It's no longer a home. It's a war zone. I kept waiting, praying that Dad would stop being so mean and you would start really seeing that I need you, too. But you've had your hands full just surviving him. I've got to get away to find out who I am and why I feel so empty. Don't try to find me. I'm of age and can go where I choose."

"Please," Rachel whimpered, desperate. "First Jason, now you—"

Amber slowly shook her head and pulled away. "See?" Her voice was dead. "Even now, I'm seen in Jason's shadow. It's not about me. It's about you. Trouble is—it should have been me that day instead of him." She rolled watery eyes. "I wasn't even that sick. Know that, Mama? I could've gone to school and sat where Jason sat. But, no, I wanted to sleep in and have another free day. " With another snuffle and smile that didn't reach her eyes, she added, "It should've been me." She strode away leaving them devastated.

Peter had never felt so emptied as then.

Knocks on her locked door had gone unanswered.

Peter and Rachel spent a sleepless night, hoping against hope that Amber would change her mind, finally dozing restlessly at dawn.

When they awoke again, she'd disappeared in the used Honda Civic they'd passed on to her as a graduation gift. They'd rushed upstairs and her closet stood empty. They'd given their children what they could afford and Peter felt that he'd done a fair job of balancing "needs" and "wants" within his family. And Amber had always seemed grateful for his efforts.

Until then.

His head swam with the enormity of loss and poor Rachel was beyond consolation.

True to her word, through the years Amber kept her distance. On rare occasions she would call her mother to wish her a curt Happy Mother's Day or Merry Christmas. But as soon as Rachel would begin to pry, the connection would abruptly go dead. It was as though she'd wiped Peter from her life and mind as succinctly as bleach to a stain.

Peter blinked back the bad memories and hoped again that Amber's strong will would protect her from harm. He'd always said that if Amber were tossed from a plane in the jungle, she'd make friends with the wild beasts who would somehow help her find her way home. On one level, he still believed she would eventually return.

But this other Amber, the one who'd abandoned them in their time of need, caused something inside Peter to snap. It was a black blot on his fathering to have his daughter turn on the ones who'd given her life.

A new anger sprang up in him, simmering alongside the deprivation of an ill-gotten son who needed a father—it all boiled and bubbled in a red-hot cauldron labeled remorse.

Another burr was that he could not, at this stage, separate the selfish Amber from his egocentric alcoholic father, who'd died drunk, one he was loathe to even discuss.

Once the disappointment in Amber took hold, Peter's reasoning took leave.

"But she's still your daughter," Rachel appealed to Peter's former noble side when she needed to share concerns about their daughter. But somewhere along the slippery trail, Peter's nobility had fizzled.

"I didn't say I don't love her," he insisted. "But I can't stand to think that our daughter wouldn't spit on us if we were on fire—what would your father say?"

"Don't bring Daddy into this. He's fortunate to have already gone on, away from all this. But one thing I do know, he'd not give up on Amber. He'd still see something redeemable in her."

"I doubt that. Your dad didn't believe in her abandoning—"

"You didn't hear me. *He would not give up on her.* When did you get so judgmental, Peter?"

Now *that* really ticked him off, when she said that. Because unspoken were the words "Who are you to judge anybody?" And the truth of it was now an open, festering sore between them.

How dare she throw up all the past in his face? And be so sneaky with it? Like she'd not actually said it but it was doggone well implied.

"Where is mercy?" she asked him, her soulful blue eyes incredibly sad.

"The same place Amber hid away hers," he snapped. "I had to live in the shadow of another abandonment during my youth—one that sprang from my father's alcohol addiction. I can't go through another hell in my twilight years."

He knew that Rachel didn't understand because she'd always had a peaceful, loving home that fostered in her that reservoir of mercy and forgiveness.

So his icy treatment of Rachel had persisted in those years following Jason's death.

It was a battle neither of them could win, the one that had driven Amber away.

But at that precise time, Peter could not, for the life of him, forgive Rachel for denying him access to his son.

He climbed from his truck and headed for the hospital entrance. And he realized that through the years, although he and Rachel had slowly and laboriously mended that schism, the torment of separation from his son had not lessened.

He took a deep breath and blew out a wintry mist as he opened the glass entrance door, feeling the warmth inside welcome him. So it remained his punishment. One he would have to live with. Because he was the one who'd defiled his marriage vows. Not Rachel.

He would not put her through any more pain.

Especially not now, when he'd come so close to losing her.

\I/

Cabin fever struck Rachel.

Gabby had left mid-afternoon, when Peter arrived at the hospital.

The bright sun beckoned. "I need to get out of this cubby-hole room," she told Peter.

"Hey! Your wish is my command, darling." He proceeded to bundle her in her coat and put a shoe on her un-casted foot. On the casted one, he tugged a cut-off huge woolen sock that Gabby had fashioned from a pair of Leon's winter wear. It protected the toes from nipping temperatures.

Within minutes Rachel saw the nurse's station whir past, their faces all aglow at seeing her getting out. They unlocked the door passage for them and Peter navigated down to ground

level and then through the downstairs exit to the beautiful garden oasis.

Never had the outdoors looked or felt so marvelous to
Rachel. Fresh, brisk January air kissed her skin as the sun
warmed her. Peter carefully placed her chair where she could
see the activities of other strollers and traffic passing at a distant
point. Holly foliage and crimson berries rioted beneath golden
sunlight.

Another family wheeled their injured matriarch to a nearby
round table. Progress put them all in a celebratory mood and
they introduced themselves all around. Rachel and the mother
shared the history of their injuries, and soon the stimulus began
to tire Rachel. She politely excused herself, unlocked her chair
brakes, whipped around, and wheeled away.

"Where you going?" Ever vigilant, Peter watched her man-
ually distance the wheelchair toward a lovely, multi-columned
walkway shelter. Navigating the chair was simple because PT
had strengthened Rachel's arms and upper body. Peter joined
her and offered to push.

"Thanks, honey, but I need the exercise." So he watched as
she moved about on her own until she tired and beckoned to
him. "Have at it."

Pain and exhaustion soon became obvious. Peter veered his
cargo back to the elevator and up the halls.

In the room, supper arrived and Peter solicitously arranged
the fare on the hospital food trolley, actually an over-bed trolley, after which Rachel split the entrées with him, knowing he
looked forward to this little meal-sharing time together.

One entrée was a reheated baked potato left from lunch.
She'd ordered another one for supper for Peter, who was pickier
about his food being hot and fresh. Gabby, Drusilla, and the
hospital staff kept her supplied with extra plates and forks, so
by now she and Peter had the drill down.

Tonight, the large baked chicken breast, divided, provided
well for the meat entrée. She'd ordered sliced peaches, which
she presented to Peter, who loved them. Her appetite was

nonexistent and she could have skipped food at any time had it not been for the weakness that invaded her when she fasted past mealtime. Her body balked at food and caved in without it. So she nibbled like a mouse and collected leftovers for Peter like a pirate. The game was but one that kept her mind busy and diverted from dark places.

The beautiful nurse named Betty came in later to check Rachel's vitals. Rachel had gleaned from brief chats that Betty's husband had died over a decade ago, leaving four children for young Betty to raise alone.

"The weather's supposed to get icy later tonight," she informed Rachel as she left.

"How icy?" Peter asked, sitting up on the daybed, brow creased in worry.

"Supposed to snow," Betty said, smiling. "See you later tonight, Rachel. I've got the night shift."

"Great," Rachel said, smiling. Some staffers, like Betty, had this mystical winsome-presence that lifted one's spirit. Same as Shaun, her physical therapist. Their quiet assurance and innate goodness had healing powers.

Peter grew quiet for long moments. Then, "Would you mind if I go sleep at home tonight? If it's gonna snow I don't need to get stuck here. I've got a repair to do at number nineteen, Sycamore Drive. A busted pipe. Can't go unheeded."

"You go on. I'll be okay." Mentally hoofing it, Rachel surmised a night of solitude might be fine. At least that's how she felt at that precise moment. Her sleep-increments now stretched longer as her strength inched upward. She gauged this by her stamina-therapy index.

"I'll go out and check the weather. Can't believe such a nice day could turn that quickly." Peter slid into his all-weather lined jacket.

Moments later, he returned, his brow creased. "The temperature's dropping. I can feel and smell ice in the air. I think I'll go on home. I wouldn't if it wasn't for—"

"You don't have to apologize, honey," Rachel reached out her hand and he clasped it. She could feel January's icy sting clinging to his fingers. "I'll be fine. Nurse Betty's on duty. She'll take care of me."

"Not like me, though." He gazed longingly into her eyes.

"No. You got that right. But I'm okay alone." Peter kissed her and left.

No sooner had his image faded from the doorway than the old melancholy dropped over her like thick gray foam. Her phone jangled and she snatched it from beneath her pillow.

"Hello?"

"Did you hear about the snow?" Gabby asked, little girl anticipation ringing in her voice.

"Uh huh. Peter just left. Didn't want to get snowed in because he had critical repairs at one of the rentals. You excited, huh?"

"What do you think? Snow ice cream, here comes Gabby!" She laughed. Then abruptly fell silent. "Say . . . do you need me there? I mean, I can—"

Hearing Gabby's voice had lifted her somewhat. "No. No, that's not necessary, sis. I'll be okay." And it was a relief to know that at that moment, it *was* okay. Only later did the helplessness swamp her again when she needed a bathroom break and couldn't get anyone to her room to oversee the transfer. She was still under restriction.

That was the worst part of her current regimen. The vulnerability. It heaped emotions on Rachel she could not define.

Humility reigned.

Something else had shifted. Her attachment to Peter had stretched to an uncharted scope. The only thing was, love had morphed into something she could no longer adequately pigeonhole. The intense chemistry of youth seemed to be in hiding since the trauma.

Of course, this was the winter of life, wasn't it? Getting older figured in but . . .

The trauma made it more factual.

Later that evening, Nurse Betty came by to check her vitals. Rachel, again plunged into aloneness, pulled her into conversation. "How did you raise four children all by yourself?"

Betty, a lovely middle-aged brunette, smiled and relaxed against the over-bed trolley. "I've been blessed to have my RN license. I've worked here for thirty years."

"Wow. I'm impressed. Tell me about your husband." The writer in Rachel lay enthralled as for the next twenty minutes, Betty shared the wonders of once-in-a-lifetime love and the agony of loss. The time spent there was costly for a night duty RN and soon, she was forced to proceed with her rounds.

"Thanks, Betty. You're one of my angels, you know?"

She smiled again, blushing. "Thanks." She leaned in close. "If I see snowflakes tonight, I'll come get you. I'll take you to a window to watch."

Rachel could only reach for her hand and whisper. "Thank you."

Snow in the south rates a ticker tape parade, a phenomenon for which Rachel ordinarily would have broken into a Piney Mountain clog. Tonight, she hadn't the strength or will to feel elated. She hoped it wouldn't snow. But if it did, Betty would see that Rachel wouldn't miss it.

Exhaustion overtook her, sliding her into deep slumber.

\|/

Peter's face swooped in while he kissed her awake.

Rachel's morning nap ended on that note. Sunlight spilled over the hospital room. Peter had raised the blinds to brighten things up.

"I'm glad it didn't snow," he said. "Gary and I got the busted pipe fixed last night. Thank goodness the freeze didn't knock out any more of the rentals' water pipes."

"That's good," she whispered. She'd already been awakened by the predictable ghastly pre-dawn doctor's visit, as well as having finished her morning bath and hair routine, such as it was. The Ninja armor-looking neck-brace style took all of three minutes to tether the top knot ponytail.

One glimpse of her reflection anywhere continued to remind her of a turtle's head barely poking out of a medieval armor shell. Heavens to murgatroyd. She had to find humor somewhere in all this experience.

Her half-eaten breakfast lay forlornly on the trolley.

The process exhausted her. But it kept her busy and she didn't have time to think of the pain and desolate, erratic mood swings. Peter scarfed down her leftover bacon and egg remnants, and then finished off her strawberries. He'd brought his Hardee's coffee with him and sipped contentedly, watching her from the saggy day seat.

The TV droned in the background, tuned into Mayberry, an easy-on-the-brain pastime. But still, she snapped it off, needing silence—at least for that moment. That could change in a heartbeat when she needed stimuli to remind her that she still had a faint pulse and to tether her to wakefulness.

"How you feeling?" he asked. "I figured you'd be in therapy."

"It's Saturday. No therapy."

Surprise flashed over his face. "Oh. I thought it was Thursday."

A staffer came by and picked up the now empty tray, greeting the two warmly.

"How're you feeling, Peter?" Rachel asked, seeing that familiar shadow of desperation engulf his features. He hated when he mixed up days. So she tried to ignore it as much as possible but sometimes, like now, it was necessary to spell out why today was Saturday and therapy-free. It was a thin line between patronizing and clarifying. And Peter knew the difference. Oh, yes, he knew the difference.

He shrugged. "Same ol' same ol'. I really had a bad day yesterday. Couldn't think my way out of a paper bag. I'm serious." He sighed deeply. "Couldn't find the right exit out of the hospital parking area. I've been in and out enough that I should—" His shrug was limp and his features bleak.

He'd only recently begun opening up about the lapses. She felt herself a privileged recipient of his rare and difficult trust.

"Honey, you're going through a lot right now. It's just natural that you have these blips."

She could see him begin to relax. "Yeah, you're right. Everybody my age begins to have them. I do good for my age, actually, don't you think?"

"You do wonderfully." Positive feedback kept him going. As soon as she got discharged, she'd see that he kept his appointment with the neurologist. He needed a diagnosis—though he did not want it. He needed treatment. Time was swiftly passing and she didn't want this to go too far before. . .

"Just look at all I handle—all these properties and repairs, plus pest control and finances. . ." Denial was alive and well.

But sometimes it was essential for one to survive.

He gazed at her then, eyes moist. "And now, this. Don't know what I'd have done had you not made it."

"But I did." Unrest swept through her but she didn't have the heart to shush him, to stop him from ushering her back there to the nightmare.

"I thank God every minute of the day for that." He came over to the bed, wedged onto the side and leaned in to snuggle her cheek. "I love you . . . so . . . much . . ." She welcomed his coddling and responded as affectionately as the blasted neck brace allowed, which was not much. Plus the pain of adjusting her upper body deterred much expression.

But Peter did not demand anything from her. Not a solitary thing. And that was a precious gift in itself because she had nothing to give. Surviving sapped every morsel from her. Somehow, he understood. He got it. It was enough that he could be with her. She got that.

She sensed his restlessness before he slid away and paced across the floor and back. He stopped and looked at her, hands on still firm hips. "I'm afraid." He looked ready to panic. The change in him cut her breath short.

"Of what?"

But she knew.

"I don't want to go down the road my mama and three siblings did. I don't want to have somebody wipe my butt and change my diapers. I'd rather die. Before I go into a nursing home and not recognize you, I'll blow my brains out." His eyes told her it was no empty threat.

"Please, Peter," she whispered, reaching out a hand to comfort him, suddenly overcome with faintness. Her head began that hateful spin that separated her from clarity.

Peter rushed to her, looming near her face, taking her hands in his. "I'm sorry, darling. I shouldn't dump on you now. I promise I won't do that again. I'm okay. I'll do fine. You just get better. That's all that should concern you. Just get better."

She whispered, "S'okay. You need to vent." The room swirled relentlessly for long moments as he held her hands in his as though she were drowning and he was her anchor.

As the spinning slowed and ebbed, he watched her closely, features overcome with concern.

Alertness slowly returned and as he read it, she felt the comeback of Peter, the nurturer, her protector. The Rock, as her pastor father, Hamp, had addressed his son-in-law—giving credence to his biblical name.

How Rachel admired his courage, his propensity for being able to rebound when the terrible reality kept scuba diving into his mind. He'd never looked as noble as just then.

"You're my hero," Rachel whispered, smiling weakly to reassure him, feeling the heaviness inside her compound. "We'll get through all this and get you some help."

He drew a deep breath and expelled it tensely. "I think I'll be okay. There's just so much going on—"

Just look at us, she thought, *enough black-and-blue freight between the two of us to keep the hospital busy for decades.*

She would have laughed had she not been so ill because she, too, was in a predicament that lent itself to fear and doubt and desperation. Not the same as Peter's for certain, but one that taxed her endurance and all but annihilated confidence and optimism.

One that left her shrunken. Struggling.

Vulnerable.

At least for now.

So much going on. "You're right," she agreed, sensing that was as much as he could juggle for the moment. And she wondered, if she were in his shoes, could she be as brave? She did not think so.

His sea mist gaze darkened. "I'm so sorry I ever hurt you, Rachel." The words were guttural. Hoarse with emotion.

"Shh," she whispered. "When?"

Tears suddenly shimmered in his eyes and he gulped back a sob. "Thank you," he husked.

"You're welcome. C'mere."

She embraced him and he melted against her bosom. And in that heartbeat, she recognized the truth. In that one word, she'd rendered Peter's roster of offenses null and void. The release gave her a sense of freedom so sweet that she seemed to float for long moments toward light. Not euphoric, just—serene. She smiled, fingers gently caressing his cheek, threading his silky hair, and murmured, "Our love will get us through. Nothing can defeat us while we're together. You'll see, darling."

Something stirred from the embers of trauma's fender-bender, from the deadness claiming her. A fresh empathy for Peter sprang forth.

And from the depths of mortality's pit, her love for him burgeoned to unparalleled magnitude. And in that moment in time, she didn't know where he ended and she began.

\|/

Early memories caught up with Rachel during those endless twilight hospital hours.

They played—not like entertainment or pleasure-getting videos, but more as documentaries. Or like old dramatic movies she'd seen over and over until her emotions became flattened.

Yet—they maintained their Technicolor appeal.

From the get-go of their relationship, Peter's appeal was his sense of adventure and humor. She loved his sea mist-green eyes' gleam when he saw new horizons to explore. She'd fly along in his wake tasting new discoveries that had eluded her sheltered life. Not bad things, but decidedly ones that veered from her church-lady upbringing.

They had, in those college, pre-children years, explored campus disco scenes, laughing at Peter's two left feet but diligently finding a common meeting of footwork to employ pleasure. And rebel Gabby had been right—dancing was so much fun!

She and Peter had agreed that alcohol was out. Why would they need it? Amusement for them flowed easily and needed no chemical enhancement. And though not judgmental of others, they both respected and followed her father's teetotaler example. Rachel was in awe of Peter's love and respect for her father.

After the children came, days became even more boisterous and spontaneous. Peter loved little Amber and did daddy things with her from the beginning, attending her piano recitals and helping her with science projects. With Jason, he really cut loose with guy things like fishing and golfing and ballgames.

Tender-hearted Jason's love of animals had turned Peter on to the appeal of God's creatures. At one time, the two of them had built an atrium for rescued birds. Many a homeless pet had they cleaned up and delivered to the Humane Society Shelter for adoption.

Another time, they'd heard about old retired U.S. Mail Trucks being sold. They decided they wanted to refurbish one for an ice cream truck, a way Jason could make extra cash in the summer. It had worked out because Peter had driven in the evenings, after his own day's work, while Jason, and sometimes

Amber, served ice cream out of Peter's engineered and fashioned side window of the big cab.

Peter's ideas were often radical. At one time, his daring would have ruffled Rachel's peaceful world. The James' name emblazoned on an ice cream truck would have sent Rachel into hiding. Before Peter, unlike her sister Gabby, she'd not liked making statements. She'd liked to fit in, not stand out.

"Life's too short not to have fun, Rachel," was Peter's favorite adage.

And through the years, it began to take hold with Rachel. His individuality was refreshing and its magic pulled her along until she, too, appreciated that her husband didn't want to be just like everyone else.

She thrilled to his strength and confidence.

Peter's brilliant handling of finances dazzled Rachel because she was no more adept at numbers than a blonde Barbie Doll.

Their marriage had been a dream.

Today, she blinked her eyes against sunshine spilling over her hospital bed as he snored softly, curled up on the lumpy cot.

"He's dependable and honest," her father had been fond of saying. "An absolute workhorse. You couldn't have done better. You and Gabby both blessed me with fine sons your mother and I never had."

Peter's fearlessness thrilled Rachel.

And now, a dragon had appeared on his horizon.

And for the very first time, she saw a fearful Peter.

\\|/

Peter wasn't the only frightened one.

Rachel's hospital therapy sessions now included two more therapists. Millie, the speech therapist, struck fear in Rachel's erratic heart. The lovely brunette was warm and personable and soon put Rachel at ease—until she mentioned the tests.

"What tests?" Rachel's heart tripped into staccato.

"Oh, I'll just read short paragraphs and then I'll ask questions about what I've just read."

Rachel felt terror's icy grip but she forced a smile. She'd gotten through much of life's messiness by smiling her way through. *Fiddlesticks.* She couldn't even read without her nerves jangling, so how on earth could she retain something she heard read?

Time to pray. *Help!*

Millie began to read and Rachel willed herself to calmness, even as her insides clamored. She listened as carefully as one can while careening up, down, and sideways on a roller coaster.

When Millie asked her the first question, Rachel surprised herself by recalling the details. The next ones were also subjective enough that she could piece together logical responses.

When the session ended, Rachel hoped Millie would say, "You're okay, Rachel. You don't have to come back."

But Millie did not. More tests lingered in the wings, she informed Rachel, leaving her more ill at ease than ever.

Then Shaun did a flip-flop on her PT session the next day. He turned her over to a young brunette therapist named Patricia and watched carefully as she paced Rachel through her PT exercises.

Rachel's mind flew into a tailspin of imaginings. *Does Shaun know something I don't? Has Millie decided that I've sustained a brain injury? What will the scheduled session with Dr. Mills, the psychologist, turn up?*

Am I becoming paranoid?

Without a doubt.

Oh how Rachel could relate to Peter's fears.

That night, as he kissed her good night, she whispered with new-fangled fervency and a ratcheted-up respect for Peter's ongoing warfare, "Whatever happens, darling, we'll get through it all together."

Peter smiled. "Got that right, honey." His eyes moistened. "Together."

Rain.

Even during Rachel's best of times, rain equated bleakness.

But despite the monsoon-like day, the session with Dr. Mills went smoothly, being more a get-acquainted session of questions/answers and delving into her philosophical depths. Rachel felt relief that her intellect experienced no strain.

Still . . . no one gave a verdict on her brain-health. The silence roared. The only response to her apprehension was, "This is standard procedure with patients who have injuries like yours."

"I couldn't bear not being able to write again." She gazed at Peter from her wheelchair where she tried to sit as long as strength allowed, whose increments were squat. He slouched on the daybed. "I've just got to trust God on this one."

"Absolutely," he agreed, sitting forward, intent. "You're going to be all right, Rachel. The Lord's already given us a miracle by you just being alive. Plus, you're moving and talking and—well, you're as lucid as anybody I've ever come across. Bar none"

"Thanks," she whispered, comforted beyond words at his matter-of-fact assurance.

Peter stood. "I think I'll go get those books from the truck that you wanted."

She'd asked him to bring yet more copies of her novels for staffers who cared for her and sometimes snatched a moment simply to drop by and chat. How priceless those gestures. She could never actually repay them for their acts of kindness, like taking her clothing to the floor laundry at night, washing, drying, and folding them for her or assisting her to the bathroom or getting her ice water when other staff members were occupied elsewhere.

Small acts? Hah!

Mammoth acts when one is lying at the bottom of the helpless heap.

So gifting them with books was the least she could do, especially when they almost fought over the copies.

Her window view today of the outdoors was beyond dreary. "I've got terminal cabin fever," she told Peter. "Would you mind getting me out of here for a few minutes?"

Peter laughed as he began navigating her from the tiny chamber called "room."

"Darlin', you only have to grunt and your wish is my command." His hoarse declaration vibrated with emotion. It stroked something deep inside the deadness that weighted Rachel down like cement.

And for just a few heartbeats, she felt something flutter and strive to flounder upward, but it didn't ignite.

That's okay, she told herself, *I'm healing. By faith, I'm healing.*

"You'll get better, baby," Peter spoke as if reading her mind.

Yes, it did help for him to say it aloud. And often. It fueled something inside her that resonated just a bit, like the flutter of a tadpole that flatlined away in the next heartbeat or that first quiver of life inside the womb.

Peter wheeled her to a lovely ground-floor waiting area and parked her chair next to the exit glass doors, clear of the walkway. She watched through glass panels as he went about the task of sorting and unloading the books. Restless, she wheeled over to the coffee table and spotted a Bible.

Up until now, reading had rattled Rachel's nerves. But without hesitation she picked it up and as she did so, the pages fell open to Psalm 91. Rachel felt compelled to read and as her eyes scanned the words, something stirred inside her, something profound.

Emotions welled, ones she'd not felt since the accident. The words immediately sprang to life . . . *"He that dwelleth in the secret place of the most High shall abide under the shadow of the Almighty . . . He is my refuge and my fortress: my God; in Him will I trust."*

Heart racing, she read on past all God's promises of protection to those who trust in Him and Rachel's quickening grew.

And then the words in verses 10–12 plunged into her, head first. "*There shall no evil befall thee, neither shall any plague come nigh thy dwelling. (11) <u>For He shall give his angels charge over thee, to keep thee in all thy ways. (12)They shall bear thee up in their hands, lest thou dash thy foot against a stone.</u>*"

That text leaped from the page and Rachel felt the message of them pierce straight to her heart and mind and she began to weep uncontrollably.

Now she knew.

Angels had borne her up on that horrific downward spiral. How many times had she heard Peter share with others that she had landed in the only spot that could have spared her life and limb? If she had veered three inches in either direction, her head would have hit a solid beam, causing at best, paralysis, at worst, death.

At the same time this revelation seized into Rachel, a woman with a leashed beautiful Yellow Lab/golden retriever mix, paused at the reception desk, just feet away. Rachel reached out to her pet.

"Is he a comfort dog?" Rachel asked. The lady looked at her, taking in her teary condition and compassion spilled from her as she brought him over. "Yes, his name is Lionel and you can pet him."

Rachel leaned down to hug him. He nuzzled her and began to lick the tears from her cheeks and—as with Francesca, the black comfort dog—she felt a startling connection of Holy Spirit love from God's creature.

Again, it struck Rachel.

I . . . am . . . a . . . miracle.

Part Two

\|/

*"Out of the mist your voice is calling.
'Tis Twilight Time"*

Chapter Seven

\\I/

> *"You only know yourself because of your memories."*
> —*Andrea Gillies*

Memories are both blessings and curses. It's all relative.

Sometime during those twilight hours of hospital captivity, Rachel caught ephemeral recall flashes of Peter's anger toward her slowly morphing into devotion. It coincided with his short-term memory bleeps. She wasn't certain exactly what precipitated the change—save prayer—but she welcomed it with outstretched arms.

In fact, the transformation was so profound that, at first, it threw her off-kilter. His growing attachment to her was so far from the old do-his-own-thing Peter that she didn't know how to feel or react. Faced with constant attention, her own need for solitude—a writer's oxygen—felt stifled.

Smothery.

But that ensnared-reaction lasted only momentarily.

A slight attitude adjustment fixed that. On some level, she knew that Peter's dependence on her was growing and that accounted—to some degree—for his new vision of her. She also found that it was okay.

She opted to flow with it and count the new Peter and lifestyle all joy.

Rachel welcomed the lingering looks and embraces and words of affection, returning them in kind—singing the words of their song . . . *Deep in the dark your kiss will thrill me like days of old, lighting the spark of love that fills me with dreams untold.*

She considered it a return to their young courtship and early marriage years and relished each moment now, just like in their song . . . *I fell in love again, as I did then.*

\\\/

How could he have been so stupid?

Mark loped up the long paved driveway from the bus stop, for once oblivious to the sentinel of perfectly spaced crepe myrtle trees zooming past on each side. His breath came in gasps by the time his feet hit the front porch of the stately farmhouse.

"Mama?" he called upon entering the front door, hating the trembling in his changing voice. It already sounded like a rusty, uncertain woodwind instrument and panic amplified it.

"In here," she responded, coming from the kitchen wiping her hands with her apron. "What's wrong, honey?" She came to him and captured his sweaty face between both hands, her brow wrinkled. "You're pale as a ghost."

Maybelle, the housekeeper, appeared in the kitchen doorway. "You okay?" she asked, looking mighty worried.

"Yeah. I'm okay, Maybelle." Then he grabbed his mother's hand and tugged her toward the stairs, slowing his pace to hers. "C'mon. I've gotta talk to you."

Visibly alarmed, his mother followed without question. In his room, he shut the door and sat down beside her on his bed. "Mama—I did something bad and I've been caught. I'm sorry. I shouldn't have done it. I hope you won't be mad at me. It was wrong and—"

"Slow down, Mark." She patted his cheek and shook her head. "You're a good boy so I know it couldn't have been as bad as you seem to think." Mark saw her lick her lips nervously and his heart skipped a beat. How he hated to worry her. But he had to tell her.

He took a deep wobbly breath and blew it out. "Remember the class project—you know, the family tree subject? I asked you how my real father died and all? Well, I had to put something on my paper so—" He gulped back tears. "So I made it all up. I lied."

He saw his mother's face go slack with something he was loathe to see. Grief. How he hated to cause that. He took another deep breath and looked away, unable to meet her eyes.

"And Steve—you know, Stinky Dodger? Well, he got online and tried to find something and of course, he couldn't find anything to back up what the teacher read to the class. So he told the teacher and everybody else who'd listen."

He cut his eyes to gauge Mama's reaction. She was silent as a gnat. And her already wan features appeared white as alabaster. Her gaze met his and the desolation he saw—the absence of her behind the hazel irises—caused his heart to plunge even lower.

"Mama? I'm sorry to dump this on you," he murmured in one long squeaky breath. "I'm so sorry." His voice broke.

Suddenly, she blinked and returned behind her eyes. Her arms reached out to gather him close. "You have nothing to apologize for, honey. Let it go. It's not your fault."

He swiped at his wet cheek, hating his weakness. "But the teacher had to lower my grade because of—" He snuffled loudly. "Because I wasn't honest." Then he broke down completely. "I—I never lied before, Mama. And—and I won't ever lie again."

"Ahh, sweetie," she kissed his damp cheek. "I'll talk to your teacher and explain that I put you in that position. It's not your fault."

Mark pulled away and sat up straighter, wiping his nose on his jacket sleeve. "Mama, nobody can make you lie. That's your own choice. You know? And I take full responsibility. Dad's taught me to always face up and take it on the chin when I make mistakes. So, that's what I'm doing." He squared his shoulders and felt a burden lift.

"He says to always do the right thing and everything will work out." He turned to look at her and smiled, feeling much better. "Just don't you worry about it, okay?" He hugged her again, kissed the top of her head, and sprang to his feet.

"Love you, Mama!" he called on his way out, descending the stairs two steps at a time. He gave a startled Maybelle a big hug and twirl in the kitchen and by the time he reached Elsie, the Jersey cow's fence to nuzzle her velvety calf, Honey, he was whistling.

\\//

"Poor kid," Ralph murmured an hour later, sipping steaming coffee in the kitchen. Maybelle had already gone, leaving supper in the warm oven to be eaten later. Today, the tantalizing aroma of pulled pork barbecue went unnoticed as Mary shared Mark's school calamity with Ralph.

She spared no details, from Mark's lies being discovered, to his humiliation and finally, to his owning his mistakes. She saw pride dawn in her husband's eyes.

"He's a good boy," Ralph's emphatic nod brooked no arguments. "Good ethics springing forth." A smile played over his lips.

"Funny—he takes after you."

Ralph's smile faded. "We've got to tell him, Mary. It's not right letting him go on not knowing. Lord knows I love him as my own but it's just not right—"

Mary raised her palm and closed her eyes. "I know. I know." They'd had this conversation many times over the years and she'd never felt the time was right. And now, she wondered, was it too late? "I don't know how he'll take it, Ralph. I couldn't stand to—have him turn away from us."

He gazed at her with kind eyes. But Mary saw determination in them today. It sent her heart a skittering. "Let's pray about—"

"We already have, honey. And I know in my heart it's the right thing to do. Mark's thirteen, a young man. We should've told him years ago, let him get used to it and then it wouldn't be such a shock."

Tears pooled in Mary's eyes. "He's always believed his real daddy's dead. I let him. That's the terrible thing. But what could I do when Peter refused to openly acknowledge him as his son? I didn't want him to feel—rejected."

She froze at the sudden stiffening and shocked expression on Ralph's face, his gaze riveted to the door behind her. The hairs on her neck stood up. And she knew.

She swiveled about and sure enough, Mark glared at her from the den doorway, pale as chalk.

"Mark!" she croaked. "How long have you been there?"

He blinked, then scowled. "Long enough! What I want to know is, *why?*"

With that, he pivoted and raced from the house. Ralph, poor Ralph, ran behind him calling, "Son? Come back, please!"

From the front lawn, Mark stopped, turned, and eyes ablaze yelled, "Last I heard, I wasn't your son, *Ralph.*"

And then he disappeared across the pastureland into the forest.

\\\\/

The world looked upside down.

Mark loped in no particular direction with brisk Carolina air biting at his nose and ears but he didn't resist it. Fact was, he welcomed the pain. His resolve to escape could not outrun the sorrow that flooded him. Sobs, sudden, like a violent cloud burst rode out encased in vapor upon icy air.

He kept sprinting away until he no longer heard Ralph's desperate yells for him to come back. Only then did he pause to look up into the clear sky and fling wide his arms.

"Why?" he sobbed. Why had no one told him his father was alive?

Which brought on another fresh burst of grief. Why hadn't his real father wanted him? Mama had said that she'd kept it secret because she didn't want Mark to feel rejected. That thought brought an icy realization that stunned him and stemmed his tears.

Rejected?

For the first time in his life, he now knew how that felt. Footsteps slowing and heavy by now, he unfastened the gate of the black four-board wooden fence that enclosed the assorted cheerful red buildings that to Mark had always represented HOME.

In that moment, Mark no longer knew what *home* meant.

Tears blurred the large Event Barn and as his shoes hit the concrete porch floor, he nearly bumped into one of the white swings suspended from the overhead ceiling. He collapsed into it and gave vent to the cyclone of emotions pummeling him.

He didn't see the big man he'd always called Dad hovering in the distance, wiping his eyes and praying.

\\/

No pain, no gain.

How many times she'd heard that. Now she lived it.

If the parallel bars were painful to execute, the walker was torture.

"Look how far you've come, Rachel," ever-optimistic Shaun encouraged her. She looked back to where she'd started and was amazed that she'd moved nearly the length of the hospital corridor. Every little one-foot-hop/step had been excruciating but her determination diverted her mind from the nasty pain to latch onto triumph.

Yup, there was merit to gain's prerequisite of pain.

And yes, she was pleased. But fatigue and throbbing pain vied for preeminence. "My arms are about to drop off," she muttered as she felt Shaun move the wheelchair to touch the back of her knees. She sat. "And I'm beyond pooped."

Shaun chuckled. "You've made great strides," he said in his laid-back way that comforted and made her feel she'd finished the Boston Marathon. "We'll call it a day."

Ahh, how she loved those words.

On the way back to her cubby-hole room, Rachel could no longer resist asking, "Shaun, why did you watch me the other day when Patricia, the new therapist, worked with me? Do you think I'm doing okay or—what? I'm a little worried about having to be studied by a speech therapist and a psychologist." She shrugged self-consciously, feeling naked about exposing her inmost fears.

Shaun looked surprised. "Actually, I was watching Patricia's way of handling therapy. We're thinking of hiring her on." He grinned. "I gave her the best patient I had. You."

Rachel smiled and felt herself relaxing. "How did she measure up with you? I thought she was great."

"She was. But I'm keeping my best patient-specimen for my own glory. As for the speech and psychological therapy sessions—they're—"

"Standard procedure for patients with injuries like mine," Rachel duet-ed with him and they both laughed, though Rachel's was still a bit uneasy.

He may have called it a day but by four o'clock recreational therapist Margie had other ideas. By now, Rachel had pigeon-holed Margie's itinerary as pleasurable rather than struggle. So she participated in a word game that was just challenging enough to haul up the competitive-strain in everyone who breathes.

Yet—camaraderie prevailed. Personalities had emerged. So had caring. Rachel's books dispersed like startled ants at a picnic.

Her mood, when Peter wheeled her back to her room, was light and calm.

It was nearly suppertime. Slowly, she had begun to anticipate meal time. Not because of appetite but because it was a respite from pain and aloneness. It was an occasion. At least with Peter and her. It strung together spurts of *I'm living* to bolster and make endurable the *I'm dead* moments. Tonight, The Gang would come together in the lower level cafeteria, making it special.

"They're meeting us there," Peter informed her as he navigated her down the hall. Since the end of her first week, her daily attire consisted of classic plain black yoga pants and a fitted pullover, practical and comfortable with its soft, stretchy material. Shoppers Gabby and Drusilla happened upon some soft black sneakers on sale, of which Rachel wore only one over her grip sock. Her mummified right leg propped half-mast on the chair's leg rest.

The Gang was in exceptional form tonight. Rachel suspected it was because she was looking less deceased. Her out-of-bed increments were slightly lengthened and her leg's thrumming was slowly becoming more bearable. Two weeks without pain meds. She'd gained ground.

She could think pretty straight.

At least she thought so. She had not truly engaged in conversation outside the crazy Gang jousting. And that was not a true test. Actually, even amongst them, she was mostly silent, simply listening. She shoved that disturbing observance away.

Rachel nibbled at her hamburger patty and baked potato—still her most tolerable filler—listening to junk talk, relieved for this reprieve from untainted survival mode.

"Hey!" Leon grabbed the floor. "Did you know J.C. was a boxer in high school, Peter?" In their teen years, J.C.'s dad had taken a job at a nearby mill and moved his family from Manilowe. For the next year, J.C. and his two friends had been separated.

"Naw!" Peter, of course, knew. This was one of the favorite junk topics.

"J.C. can box good," Leon proclaimed.

Gabby *harrumphed.* "He can lay on the floor good."

J.C. put on his angel face and folded his hands across his midriff, eyes focused on the faraway. "If you lay on the floor you don't get hit."

"*Wimp,*" Gabby retorted.

Rachel broke in. "Gabby, did you make sure Peter took his coconut oil this week?"

"I called to remind him. Did you take your oil this morning, Peter?"

Peter grew quiet. Then, "I don't remember."

Leon said, "Whaddaya mean—"

Gabby elbowed him sharply in the rib.

"I might have," Peter said uncertainly. Then shrugged tersely. "I can't remember."

Gabby snorted gently. "I'll have to come by and shove it down your throat every morning. Would you like that?"

Peter laughed. "Come on and make my day."

Rachel appreciated her sister making light of Peter's bleeps.

"Ya think coconut oil will help J.C." Leon asked, grinning.

Drusilla jumped in. "I'm already slipping it in his morning coffee,"

"*What*?" J.C. raised his eyebrows. "I thought that coffee tasted funny. Felt funny in my mouth, too."

"Ah," Drusilla waved a hand at him. "You smack your lips on it."

He smiled his Franciscan monk smile. "Yeah. It does taste kinda good. But what does it do for me?"

Drusilla and Gabby had both read the book and seen the viral video so Drusilla began extolling the coconut oil benefits beyond the liver converting the oil into ketones and nourishing the brain. "It also helps depression, cholesterol, diabetes, and lots of other health issues."

J.C. folded his hands over his chest and smiled. "Well, I'll take a gallon a day of that stuff if it's that good for me."

Months earlier, when Rachel noticed Peter's lapses growing more frequent, she began an online research on dementia and Alzheimer's sites. One report in particular drew her attention.

Dr. Mary Newport, whose husband, Steve, age sixty-one, had progressed to advanced Alzheimer's, wrote a book, *ALZHEIMER'S DISEASE, What If There Was a Cure? The Study of Ketones*. The lady doctor had, years earlier, begun to research the disease and discovered a high-energy fuel that nourishes the brain.

"What are ketones?" asked Leon, whose pizza cheese strung hot and long from food to mouth.

Rachel, the more knowledgeable Gang member, responded "Ketones are tiny molecules of organic fuel that have been around since the beginning of life on planet earth and have ensured our survival as a species. These are molecules of hope for people suffering from Alzheimer's and other degenerative brain diseases." She surprised herself with the vivid recall and she felt a kick of hope that her intellect just may be intact.

They all listened carefully, even Peter, though it was a given that none of them openly attributed the affliction to Peter. For that Rachel loved them even more. They danced all around it but even torture wouldn't drag a hint of it from them. After all, there was not yet a diagnosis a'tall.

One redeeming quality The Gang possessed: they thought good thoughts.

Rachel alone carried the 24/7 evidence of probability, of the acknowledgement of his family genetics pointing to it—of having watched Peter's three siblings and his mother succumbing to the disease.

At the same time, the luxury of not knowing for certain remained hers.

She felt a mixture of hope and desperation, like the donkey following the unreachable carrot. Hope prompted her to keep going. "A drinkable form of ketones can already be made in the National Institute of Health lab—I think that's the correct name—of Richard Veech, MD, PhD, a world-renowned researcher who's been working with ketones for decades." She took a deep breath and shook her head, dizzy from the concentration.

"But" Rachel's most despised word in her Alzheimer's study.

"*But* it will take lots of money and years of clinical trials—even after the money comes through—to be available to the millions who need this."

Rachel felt the heaviness of grief and her voice grew weaker than usual. "Competition is fierce for research dollars, and the money to mass-produce this ketone compound has not come through yet."

Gabby snorted. "As often happens, politics get in the way of true progress." She paused to take a long drink of iced tea. "Dr. Newport's book would help raise awareness to the critical nature of this issue and perhaps prod the powers-that-be to take a closer look at the need for research funds and also cause an explosion of research." She winked at Rachel and nodded for emphasis.

For Rachel, that could not happen soon enough.

In the meantime, she wanted Peter to daily, *religiously* ingest the pure form of coconut oil in his oatmeal and other entrées. It couldn't hurt and according to Dr. Newport, could help. Actually, just before she'd entered the hospital, he'd taken to putting it into his morning coffee and drinking it. Yet, sometimes he ate it right off the spoon.

She'd tried it and found it to have a pleasant texture and coconut flavor, that is, for folks who love coconut. It was quite palatable when stirred directly into ice cream, too.

"It's good on a baked sweet potato," she offered. "It even works on a regular potato."

Drusilla said, "Wonderful! I use it in my cooked veggies. Not bad."

Gabby added, "Dr. Newton also prescribed daily doses of MCT oil for her husband, Steve. I remind Peter to take that, too, don't I, Peter?" She challenged him good-naturedly, because in Rachel's absence, the confrontations fell to her dear sister.

Peter ignored her.

"What's the difference?" Leon asked, finishing off his pizza.

Rachel forced herself to focus. Her strength was ebbing fast. "MCT is derived from coconut or palm kernel oil. MCT translated is medium chain triglycerides or medium chain fatty acids. I studied the facts, which are: these MCTs also are metabolized in the liver as ketones. And in my sophomoric interpretation, it boosted the ketone benefits for Dr. Newton's husband, Steve."

"*Woo hoo!*" hooted Leon. "Listen to Ms. High IQ, spoutin' them big words!"

"She's a writer," Peter enunciated pompously, nose in air. "And don't you forget it."

Rachel smiled at his proud boast and continued. "Dr. Newton's husband Steve was really in bad shape when she began him on the MCT and coconut oil regimen. His personality was flat and he'd stopped reading, had become a virtual recluse, hardly able to match socks or even put them on. And on his initial testing, the doctor requested he draw a simple clock.

"His version didn't even resemble a clock face with numbers and hands. But after he dove into the regimen, Steve's condition did a dramatic turnaround. The video I have shows that he eventually drew quite a good picture of a clock and regained much of his personality and vitality."

"Hey," J.C. said. "I can draw a pretty good clock, too."

"Hah!" Gabby sniffed.

Everyone burst into laughter.

What, Rachel wondered, would she and Peter do without them and their rose-colored glasses?

But her long discourse had taken its toll on her. She felt like bruised cement when she tried to move. Had it not been for the neck brace, her head would have lolled in every direction.

"Peter, take me to my bed before I slither out of this chair and have to be scraped up off the floor." Rachel would have sworn a ping-pong ball had flown into her ear and was bouncing around.

J.C. leaned in close. "Sweet girl, ain't no way that steel brace gonna let you melt anywhere, doncha know?" Then to the others, "Let's move 'er out and head 'er up!"

Leon brought Rachel a laptop to the hospital. How she missed the social media connection, a huge hunk of a writer's life.

Brilliant as he was, Peter was not tech savvy. Not one bit. So Leon and Gabby hooked up the computer and got Rachel online. She tried, lying propped in bed, neck brace blocking any angle for adequate view of the screen, to compose a warm, folksy message.

Peter was doing some of his pest control routes today and would arrive later. She hoped that, amid all the chaos, his mind would tether properly to directions and such. He'd so far had little to no difficulty in his travel navigation. She prayed that would hold during these trying days.

Thirty exhausting minutes later, she'd managed to blindly fumble with the laptop keys and compose a short email paragraph to her special friends and readership, letting them know she missed them and that she was healing.

To her, the completed task would represent a landmark much like the Declaration of Independence bell-toll.

The effort left her shattered and ready to crash the laptop through the blasted window.

She closed her eyes, ready for everybody to leave. Sensing it, J.C., Drusilla, Leon, and Gabby quietly left for a cafeteria coffee break. Good. She wanted to be alone.

She closed her eyes and basked in the silence.

For all of five minutes.

Until her head began its wild harebrained descent into despair. She struggled to overpower the sinking spiral with prayer. Her prayers dissipated midsentence. *Is my mind okay?* The relentless panic rose up like a fire-breathing Loch Ness-er. *Was her laptop fiasco a presage of things to come?*

Peter appeared at her bedside and she felt his big, warm hands wrap around her icy ones and gently massage warmth into them. "You okay, honey?" he asked softly.

"Not really," she murmured, breath shallow. "So down."

He leaned to brush his lips across hers. "You're a real trooper, Rachel," he whispered. "You're hanging in there beautifully. You're so brave and I'm so proud of you."

"Don't . . . feel . . . so brave," she whispered, feeling like a beached sea creature gasping for oxygen. "Wish—"

He leaned in closer. "Wish what, darling?"

"Nothing." She couldn't tell him. It would discourage him when he was giving everything.

Truth was, in that moment, the struggle was too much. She wished she'd died.

\\//

Rachel may have been out of circulation.

But she was far from forgotten.

From the get-go, Gabby daily posted Rachel updates on Facebook and in emails so her social media friends were savvy to Rachel's trauma.

Gabby's tech expertise impressed Rachel and enthralled Peter. The photos she'd taken in the ER, therapy, hospital room, and even ones with Francesca, the comfort dog, had been splashed over the Internet, keeping those who cared connected.

Members at Manilowe Community Worship Center, The Gang's church, trickled in. Rachel was disappointed that more did not visit, but at the same time, she didn't know how her emotions would hold up to a steady flow of well-wishers. The near two thousand member congregation had several associate ministers who dropped by for brief intervals of prayer and encouragement.

That worked well. She loved when friends called. The outside contact was refreshing but she quickly discovered that any conversational engagements past five minutes shriveled her into a flaming heap of exhaustion.

On Saturday, Tammy, one of her favorite people, stuck her blond perky head around the corner of Rachel's weird off-set-space cubicle. "*Yoo hoo!*" she said softly.

Unable to turn her head, Rachel said, "Come on in. I can't see you."

When she saw Tammy, her eyes grew moist. "Hey, darlin'. Come give me a hug. I need a hug." She held out her arms and she and her friend embraced warmly, if a bit awkwardly.

Hugs were so life affirming these days.

Rachel would forever view physical affection differently.

Tammy stepped back, all sympathy. "I didn't hurt your neck, did I?" Her soft brown eyes were all concern.

Rachel huffed. "If that fall didn't kill me, honey, neither will a hug."

Tammy's eyes grew moist as she held Rachel's hand. "I'm so glad you survived. Don't know what we'd do without you at Eli's Place, doncha know? Everybody there's asking about you every day. Your table is being kept open out of respect for you."

"*Shut up*," Rachel said softly. "Girl, you keep that up, I'll start blubbering and you will have . . . a . . . mess . . . on your hands. At first I couldn't cry. Now—" She held her palms up, "I cry at most anything."

At that, she burst into silent tears and Tammy carefully hugged her again. "Now, now. You just go ahead and cry. Sometimes it's a good thing."

Just as quickly, Rachel's waterworks dried up and Tammy took a seat on the lumpy daybed.

Tammy waitressed at Eli's Place, a wonderful buffet style eatery, where The Gang hung out most days to toughen up and harass each other, love, and eat together. Tammy was theirs. She belonged to J.C., Drusilla, Leon, Gabby, Peter, and Rachel. And they belonged to her. Like family.

Through the years, they'd borne each other through a collage of experiences both glorious and tragic. Like Tammy's divorce. Gabby's hip replacement, Drusilla's breast cancer. Leon's struggle with Meniere's disease of the inner ear, J.C.'s battle with skin cancer, Peter's memory lapses, and now, Rachel's trauma.

Tammy had been there about five minutes when the rest of The Gang spilled through the door. A big to-do over Tammy's presence ensued.

They were at their shining best celebrating each other in their own unique nonsensical way. "Tammy," Leon gave her a big bear hug. "You're a sight for sore eyes, honey. Thought we'd give you a rest from J.C. for a while."

Drusilla took his place and said. "We miss seeing you every day, sweetie. But duty calls."

"Duty?" Rachel croaked, making every effort to slide into her role. "Now I'm a duty, J.C., did you hear that?"

"Yeah," His face morphed into Mona Lisa melancholy, "That's how they do you when you're down." Then he grinned, gave Tammy a hug, and took off his Army cap and pretended to wet his finger and meticulously smooth down nonexistent hair wisps atop his bald head. "Now, you can do your thing," he told Tammy.

She kissed the top of his head, a ritual that deposited her lipsticked imprint. J.C. replaced his Army cap with a sweetly smug look on his face.

Tammy held out her palm. "That calls for at least a five dollar tip."

This always drew guffaws and good-natured ribbing.

They perched on every inch of available space, including both sides and foot of Rachel's bed and in her wheelchair. About that time, Nurse Betty came in to do her vitals check and they enjoyed complimenting her beauty and proficiency, drawing pretty blushes.

"By the way," she told Rachel as she finished checking her blood pressure, "I'm loving your book."

"Which one?" asked Peter, the unflappable PR man.

"*Rainbow*—um . . ."

"*Once Upon a Rainbow*," Peter supplied with finesse. "So you're enjoying it?"

"Very much so. I can't wait to order her others."

"Thanks, Betty." Rachel smiled, pleased to have gained a new reader. The professional's exit left a trail of some clean, powdery fragrance in her wake.

J.C. related how Peter loved to play with their frisky Yellow Lab, Porsha. "That girl will keep fetching that stick to you till the cows come home," he declared.

That caught Rachel's ear. "And Peter loves to play fetch with her till the sun goes down," she murmured, feeling a trickle of affection for the animal lover, Peter.

"Huh! That shows how dumb he is," J.C. said, looking angelic.

Peter laughed, then countered with his nose in the air. "That shows that Porsha recognizes nobility when she sees it."

That really tickled everybody's funny bones, including Rachel's. She loved Peter's wit.

The usual bantering went on around Rachel and for a while she experienced it as one looking in from the outside. Then exhaustion swooped in. She could hardly hold her eyes open or lift her hand when they all tuned in and began to quietly slip out.

Finally, only Peter remained. By now, she didn't need an overnight sitter. She could ring for a staffer to help her to the bathroom at bedtime or to fetch the TV remote that had fallen to the floor or a dozen other mishaps that a normal situation defies.

Actually, only thing that had changed was her tenacity. Assertiveness slowly moved to the top of the totem pole.

A couple of times, desperate when help did not promptly appear, Rachel had transferred herself to her wheelchair alone. Not good if she got caught because she was still on restriction. She'd made it fine to the bathroom, transferred to the toilet seat, then back to the chair and on to bed. An exhausting task, but by George, she'd done it.

A small seed of confidence took root.

She felt that if need be, she could function without help.

But Peter wanted to stay.

"I want to be near you," he whispered as he later slipped in beside her, spooned against her in odd fashion. And she knew that he would soon slide from the bed and retire to the let-out detestable cot.

But for the moment, he was content.

For the moment, so was she.

\\/

This, too, shall pass.

Though it crept by like a sluggard on Valium, time crawled on, validating the old cliché.

The last week arrived. According to her PT's agenda, Rachel should be wrapping up her three-week hospital stay. Her concern over the psychological evaluation remained on alert until the very last day of the sessions, during which the psychologist and speech therapist both informed Rachel that not only was she A-OK but they'd each enjoyed their time with her and really hated to see her leave.

"Do you have the ramp in place at home," PT Shaun asked Peter again. He'd been reminding him for days now about the critical nature of having a stable ramp in place on which to transport Rachel's custom measured wheelchair up the porch steps and into the house from one level to the next. He'd insisted on the smaller measurements to fit Rachel's near-petite frame.

Too, the Manilowe Mill Village house had some narrow doors to span.

Peter looked uncertain but quickly recovered. "Uh, not yet. But it will be ready when Rachel leaves."

Shaun went through all the equipment she would need to function at home. Peter seemed confident enough, so Shaun took Rachel through her newer tests of using the walker to one-foot-hop onto a short curb. She passed with flying colors.

The backward hop was more difficult. She accomplished it.

Barely. And she vowed to avoid it at all costs.

Her worst nightmare now was of falling again.

\\|/

This was the day!

Rachel awoke feeling something akin to anticipation.

She was going home.

Gabby arrived at Roger C. Peace right after Peter did. She was there to help pack up all the paraphernalia collected in three weeks of pack-rat living.

All morning long, medical staff members dropped by to say warm good-byes. Rachel sat in the middle of her bed—dressed in her black yoga ensemble—fortressed by a hodgepodge of "stuff" stacked like lumber all around her, ranging from extra yoga attire to spare bathing supplies and neck braces for different purposes.

They'd even provided her with extra-large plastic bags with which to wrap her mammoth braced and casted leg, to waterproof it for bath time. "We got the shower thing-y hooked up for her to use in the tub," Gabby told Drusilla, who'd just walked in to help out.

"Tub?" Rachel was curious as to how she would accomplish that.

"You don't actually sit in the tub but use a seat that sits across the tub and you sit in it and use the shower thingamajig to—well, shower."

"Where does all this come from?"

"Don't worry, honey," Drusilla soothed. "We got you all fixed up. This friend from church—" She halted and cast Gabby a startled glance. Gabby shook her head and kept on packing things.

"Anyway, the woman's husband had been an invalid for a long spell before he passed away. When she heard about your need, she insisted we move it for you to use."

"Well, that's sure nice of her," Rachel said. "Who was—"

"You don't know her," Gabby rushed in and began clearing off the over-bed tray.

"I know lots of folks at church," Rachel said. Though there were many she didn't know because the church had two services and some members never connected.

The two women glanced at each other. "She's fairly new," Drusilla said.

Gabby rolled her eyes and turned away.

Rachel felt something in the air, a subtle tension. But these days, that was par for the course. "Oh. Well, anyway, it sure is sweet of her to do that."

Peter strolled in. "The car's ready. We can load the trolley and then the car."

This continued until only Rachel remained on the bed and, for the first time in weeks, she could see the floor and walls with no problem. Drusilla collected Rachel's handbag and Gabby her blanket, to cover her foot protruding from the ghastly cast/brace. She shifted herself to the edge of the bed and transferred to the wheelchair, the new, smaller one customized for her. She liked the feel of it—the fit was cozy.

Outside at the nurses' station, about a dozen staffers gathered to bid her farewell.

Margie, her recreational therapist, swooped in to air kiss and hug her. "Stay in touch," she said. "We'll connect on Facebook, okay?"

Rachel grinned and lifted her wrist to show the beaded bracelets she'd done in therapy. "My healing bracelets," she said and then pointed to her matching earrings, whose sea mist green matched her crazy Ninja neck-brace trim. "I'll think of you when I wear them."

In turn, each of her angels embraced her and wished her well, promising to stay up on all her upcoming book publications and such. She was even asked to sign a few more books.

"Did you get the ramp in place, Peter?" Rachel asked after the last good-bye.

"Uh, no. But we'll manage."

Rachel felt a frisson of alarm. Then, just as quickly, she released it. She had to trust Peter to get her into the house.

As Gabby strolled along beside Peter, pushing the wheel-chair down the long corridor, she said, "Wouldn't you know I wouldn't have my camera-phone with me to photograph that great good-bye scene?"

"Where was it?" Drusilla shifted the flowers she carried to her other arm as they strode out the exit.

"In the car with my purse." Gabby shrugged. "Oh well. Facebook will just have to miss it. Let's get our girl aboard."

Rachel did the transfer from chair to front passenger seat in a jiffy, thanks to Shaun's relentless drilling those last days. Gabby's car, a 2005 Nissan Altima had the lowest sitting body in the group, one with which the transfer worked. Peter's pickup was too high and their second car's floor space was too short to accommodate her long leg brace.

The drive home felt surreal to Rachel. Passing scenery looked foreign; even as they entered Manilowe Mill Village, landmarks seemed otherworldly. Her house could have been designed by space aliens.

Where was that warm fuzzy feeling of home?

Warm fuzzy feeling?

Immediately, Rachel knew that warm fuzzy feelings were currently in short supply. Nonexistent, in fact.

Recovery was now at the top of the bucket list.

And how, oh, how was she going to span those three steps from mother earth to porch?

Like the tragic tire rotation Peter disregarded years ago, the missing ramp issue rose up like Mt. Kilimanjaro. She tried to ignore the letdown. No worry. Her mind refused to entertain any contemplation for more than a few seconds before spitting it out.

"Don't worry," Peter leaned down to speak through her car window. He smiled encouragingly. "Jesse's on his way."

Chapter Eight

"Affliction is a good man's shining time."
—*Edward Young*

He wasn't Jesse James, but he came riding in just as dramatically.

Only it was in a big red fire truck.

Sure enough, Manilowe Fire Department's big red fire truck rumbled to a halt at the end of the James' driveway, followed by several more vehicles. Fire Chief Jesse West's volunteer firemen spilled from various autos to rush to the aid of the disabled damsel, one of their very own villagers.

Peter opened the Nissan's door and Rachel swiveled to transfer to the wheelchair when a zealous young volunteer swooped in, slid his arms under hers and—grasping her to his strong chest—began to tug.

"No, no," she said kindly, "I can get in the chair myself and then it can be lifted to the porch."

Nonplussed, he backed off and Rachel deftly transferred and locked the wheels down.

With few words, four strong firemen hefted the entire package from pavement to front porch amid a chorus of relieved and triumphant murmurs.

"Thank you," Rachel called out, uncommonly appreciative to finally have successfully spanned the impasse to home.

She wheeled herself across the shiny gray concrete porch, her peripheral vision vaguely taking in the white-cushioned black wicker furniture that usually welcomed her to a peaceful passage of time.

Emotions flatter'n a busted balloon, she allowed Peter to help hoist her chair over the raised entrance threshold. Inside, the atmosphere beggared description. Key furniture pieces had disappeared to storage to allow her ambulatory space. Hence, the bareness approached the Spartan.

But it's home. The thought flitted—then fizzled, leaving only a trace of homecoming effect.

Clairvoyant Gabby asked cheerfully, "How does it feel to finally be home?" Her ebullience over Rachel's progression splashed over. "By George, we worked all week to get everything squared away so you could wheel that contraption around like ol' Danica Patrick!"

Rachel looked at her. "Who's Danica Patrick?"

Gabby stared at her, taken aback. "Why, she was the first woman ever to lead in the Indianapolis 500 race. Patrick also won the time trials at the Daytona 500, becoming the first woman to win the pole position at the famous NASCAR event, and went on to place eighth in the race!"

Unimpressed, Rachel wheeled to the kitchen, meeting resistance from yet another threshold hump. She had to heave three vicious thrusts to the wheels to gain a limp victory of entrance to the home's hub.

"That'll have to be removed, for now," vigilant Peter told J.C., who hovered with Leon on the sidelines, attentive to each of Rachel's wishes.

"No sooner said than done," Leon was already striding to the tool box.

Rachel's wheelchair rolled to a stop at the stair bottom. She gulped in a deep breath, then creased her brow. "Where's the hole in the wall?"

Peter took her hand and squatted to gaze into her eyes. "Leon and J.C. fixed it, honey. And I'm so grateful. We didn't want any reminders for you to see."

Rachel blinked back sudden tears. "Thanks, guys," she called out to J.C. and Leon, who now worked like two beavers taking up all door thresholds throughout the dwelling.

"You're welcome," J.C. replied.

"I owe you two big time," Peter called out, arising and heading their way.

"You got that right!" Leon yelled. A smile vaguely grazed Rachel's lips. Leave it to them to provide flippancy.

"We moved out the large dining room table and used my spare smaller round table in here." Drusilla pointed to the dining area. "This way, you can get in here easily and have room to spare."

The little bathroom loomed. THE challenge. Rachel wheeled to the tiny chamber and just barely cleared the door. *But jumping jellyfish, she was in.*

"Hallelujah! Shaun did his work *good!*" Gabby crowed. Therapist Shaun had been nigh on neurotic about Peter measuring the doorways at home, to exact dimensions. His orchestration of Rachel's ambulatory scheme proved near genius.

Her office. Rachel hastened to wheel to her favorite ground-floor room. At its door, she came to an abrupt halt. Seemed much of the relocated "stuff" had ended up there, stacked in the middle of the floor, a virtual blockade.

Suddenly exhausted, she pivoted the chair in another direction.

Another monumental change faced her: her bedroom was now downstairs. They'd moved and swapped it all out to accommodate her needs. The task had been colossal for The Gang but *by cracky*, they'd done it!

But . . .

From her crunched down height, the chamber was distorted. *Bizarre.*

She wouldn't tell The Gang for the world. They'd worked so hard to make things simple for her and to ease her back into normalcy.

But her homecoming was anything but normal.

For one thing, changing locations did not alter suffering. Physically, home only intensified the awareness of traumatic injuries. She'd acclimated—to an extent—in the hospital. After all, there, pain existed on a wholesale scale, varying in severity up or down, from case to case.

At home, Rachel's psyche sought pre-trauma peace and relief. It was not there. Her mind grieved the crush.

Rachel closed her bedroom doors—difficult to do from her chair, taking several attempts—and sought the quiet and consolation of her bed. Even that had changed. One of her "Pineapple" poster bed mattresses had been removed, lowering the surface to her level. That way, she could transfer from chair to bed with no assistance.

She shifted herself onto the bed and sat there for long moments, gazing about for familiarity, her weighty casted leg dangling, pulsing. Her angled view of the dresser and entertainment center and wall decor was warped.

So many alterations. Nothing looked right. Nothing *felt* right. The darkness of twilight was closing in on her, *when purple-colored curtains marked the end of day.* The words and melody played dissonantly along her psyche-music track.

As of yet, music had not found its way back into her soul— it did not fill that space in her head devoted to wonder.

Nothing did.

"Rachel?" Peter called from the next room and she knew he sought her. Needed her.

The knob turned and his face poked around the door. When his gaze zeroed in on her sitting there, he softly closed the door and came to sit beside her, wrapping his arm around her.

"You okay, honey?" Concern marked his features.

"I'm okay," Rachel murmured, abruptly lifted by his sweet rumbling voice.

It drove back the mist.

At least for the moment.

At the same time, the James' pet's homecoming proved as bizarre as Rachel's.

The little Chihuahua trailed Rachel to the bathroom, where Rachel transferred to sit on the closed commode during the first week into her new agenda.

"Mitzi's got her job cut out avoiding my chair wheels," Rachel leaned to ruffle the small blonde Chihuahua's medium length fur. Mitzi propped front paws on Rachel's good leg while obsidian eyes gazed up into her mistress's face with rampant adoration and just a smidgeon of confusion.

"How's my little thang-y doing? Huh?"

The tail thumped happily from side to side before she hopped down and trotted to the back door to be let out for her morning romp and relief. Rachel heard Peter open and close the door.

"Did you take your coconut oil yet?" Rachel called from her undignified perch.

A long silence. "I'm not sure." Peter moved around in the kitchen, scrambling eggs for their breakfast and taking fresh fruit from the fridge to serve.

"Well, you can take more if you're not sure. It certainly won't hurt you."

Then a decisive, "I did. I put it in my coffee."

Rachel had remained on her hospital schedule of arising early and trekking to the bathroom. Mainly because her body ached so badly that lying over seven hours in bed proved impossible. This sunny morning, she brushed her teeth while sitting on the closed commode, her casted leg propped in the wheelchair's seat, using the hospital's standard, weird little half-moon plastic bowl as a mouth rinse catcher and when washed, as storage for toothbrush and paste. She left it on the sink where she could reach it.

Organizing necessary paraphernalia within reach required much of all three female Gang members' ingenuity. Mostly it was Gabby's and Drusilla's cunning and skill that rescued Rachel from absolute powerlessness.

And in moments of aloneness, which came rarely but did happen, bananas, peanut butter, and snack items sat within Rachel's reach along the counter.

Drusilla did the shopping for phenomenal paraphernalia like the Grabber—a long handled do-jiggy used to get to and grasp hold of anything out of Rachel's immediate reach. When settled in bed, Rachel used it to grab hold of clothing now stacked on a chest at the foot of, and level with her bed. Drusilla and Gabby had early on folded and organized them into yoga pants, shirts, and underclothes.

The arrangement would not have made *House Beautiful* magazine but sweet granny, it made life bearable for Rachel. Unlike Rachel of old, she let go of her idealized standard of order and got on with the business of overcoming her restrictions.

Limitations which, at that precise time in her life, were mind-blowing.

One situation at a time became her misty mantra.

Daily, Rachel endeavored to use her chair for mobility as much as possible, refraining from calling Peter or Gabby unless she was battered beyond going on.

Past that, the Grabber aided in her independence quest by retrieving the dozens of whatevers evading her every hour, such as the TV remote, cell phone, glasses, book, etc.

She'd also managed to sponge bathe—perched on commode—by having Peter fill the larger hospital plastic basin with warm water and placing it within reach. Not ideal, but it beat the hospital ritual of lying in bed doing the same cleansing.

Gabby and Drusilla promised that any day now, they would officiate a genuine shower via the across-tub seat.

Peter hovered and helped in every way possible as she began carving out a schedule of sorts. "Gabby will be here by nine," Peter said as he placed silverware beside their plates of soft scrambled eggs. A cup bearing berries appeared while coffee perked.

"Those are pretty," Rachel said. The mixed colors and fragrance of blackberries, blueberries, strawberries, raspberries, and red seedless grapes gave her spirit a peculiar little pick up. Eaten along with the eggs, the result was tasty.

"Gabby picked them out," Peter admitted modestly. "She's a great gal."

"Yes, she is." It did her sluggish heart good to hear Peter extol the virtues of her big sis. She'd always told Peter that when he praised and did good deeds for Gabby, he was doing them for her as well. Actually, she was blessed with the entire Gang, each of whom would—she was certain—take a bullet for her.

And vice versa.

"*Yoo hoo!*" Gabby trilled from the front foyer as she traipsed her way to the kitchen, clad in sneakers and sweats, armed for work. "I'm a little early. Thought you might need me to fix breakfast for you." She halted at the threshold, then scowled. "You already ate."

"I went ahead and fed her," Peter said, taking the dishes to the sink of hot sudsy water to swish and rinse them clean.

"Don't look so disappointed, sis," Rachel said. "You'll have plenty to do before the day's over. Trust me." Her attempt at humor mingled with perplexity. Limitations loomed like King Kong on the warpath. Her drive was in hiding while that machine inside her battered skull kept sporadically churning her emotions and hissing to her brain, "Do something."

Do something.

What? How? With no strength and slight mobility, she could do squat. Desolation flooded her anew.

"You okay?" Peter asked as he passed her chair, still parked beside the tiny maple table. He gazed down into her face, searching. "Can I do anything for you? You know I'll do anything within my power to help you."

She sighed. No way could she load him down. "I know, honey. I'll be okay. Gabby's here with me. You go on and work your pest control routes."

He peered at her a few more lingering moments before, satisfied she was all right, he leaned to kiss her. "Call me if you need me." Then he was off.

Rachel tried to sit and chat with Gabby as she puttered around the house, picking up and dusting and doing the dozen and one things a woman does when she's supposed to be busy. But the chat inside her had gone off somewhere far away. Within thirty minutes, Rachel's leg throbbed so badly she returned to her bed, where she propped herself upright against a husband cushion padded with extra pillows.

With both hands, she lifted and positioned her hardware-burdened leg to ease the pressure. Then she undid and refastened her neck brace, loosening it a bit to accommodate her body's slightly tilted back sprawl.

Rachel decided to watch television since reading was not yet an option. Where was the remote? She grasped the Grabber and cut her eyes as far as possible in every direction without moving her neck. She didn't see it. *Oh, smaggle!*

"Gabby?" No answer.

Louder. "Gabby?" A rustle of footsteps coming.

"What you need, sweetie?"

"The remote, please? I'm sorry to bother—"

"Hush your mouth this instant. That's why I'm here." Within moments Gabby handed her the magical connection to entertainment's galaxy. Rachel clicked on the high-definition screen and began surfing channels. Within itself, exposure to normalcy proved harrowing to her nerves. So she turned it off for a few minutes to level out—but that weird restlessness regrouped in her and she flipped the switch again searching in earnest for something distracting.

News? Too stressful.

Talk shows? Voices clattered about inside her skull.

Adventure? Top-of-Richter-scale nerve-rattling.

ID, formerly her favorite true crime channel? Inflammatory at best.

Finally, she found an Inspirational channel that played only spiritual and family shows. Those proved to be more emotionally palatable, though heavy preaching battered her into a heap. Joyce Meyer's upbeat-ness was more tolerable.

She quickly began to flow with a *Little House on the Prairie* episode. Then another—it was a double feature that day. Peter called twice during the morning to check on her. He kept the calls short and sweet.

Thank you.

Soon, lunch time emerged.

Progress. She had made it through two hours without an emotional meltdown.

Thanks be to the Almighty.

Gabby planned a full dinner for The Gang. "You'll enjoy seeing everybody," Gabby assured her. The prospect did appeal to her neediness.

Oh my, was she needy. And now, it was okay but only if she was going full throttle on her own.

Peter joined them for lunch, warming Rachel with his presence. Her appetite still drooped but at home she could at least be finicky and get something her taster called for. Today, it was Burger King Whoppers. Peter had grabbed them on his way home. Not the healthiest choice but it did arouse her taste buds a bit. She ate half of one and wrapped the other half for Peter's nighttime snack. Old habits do indeed die hard.

Gabby finished her burger and sat back, arms crossed. "I've got to call and make your appointment with the neurologist, Peter. The sooner you see him, the sooner you can get on medication."

Peter laid down his half-eaten sandwich and sat there like a knot in their pine floor, staring at the far wall as though it had somehow affronted him. Rachel saw stubbornness raise its horns and spoke. "She's right, honey. You need to get it over with. Hey! It may not be serious after all."

"That's right, Peter," clueless Gabby took a drink of her iced tea. "Want me to take care of it?"

Rachel knew. Her sister was being too in-his-face, crossing the line.

Peter's head already moved from side to side. "We'll take care of it."

Gabby nodded acquiescence. For the moment. Rachel knew her big sis wouldn't let up, as she shouldn't, but she'd have to soft-pedal to get Peter's cooperation. A rogue wave of fatigue slapped her as she realized that she alone, Rachel, was the key to Peter's compliance.

While Gabby tidied up the kitchen, Peter trailed Rachel as she wheeled herself to the bedroom. There, he sank into the little glider facing her. She was determined to be self-sufficient and navigated the chair close to the bedside, aligning it for transfer when exhaustion and/or pain dictated.

Peter watched her maneuver, admiration spilling from his gaze. "I'm so proud of you, Rachel."

She locked her chair and looked at him. "Thanks," she murmured, tired beyond words as she adjusted the leg rests, adding two extra pillows to raise and cushion the throbbing limb a bit more.

"I've got to sit up more to build up endurance, even if I have to do it in short increments."

Peter's head moved side to side in amazement. "You're a real trooper." The statement breathed reverence, making Rachel feel—undeserving.

"Not really," she sighed. "You do what you gotta do. You know?"

"No. Your attitude goes beyond that." He spoke with such conviction that something inside Rachel reacted, a barely registered tickle of contentment. A rustle of fulfillment.

Her gaze met his in a soul connection.

"Gabby's right, you know," Rachel said gently.

"I know." Peter's smile evolved into solemnity. "I just hate to think about it. I want you to go with me when I go."

"Of course. There's no reason I can't go if the ramp is in place. Have you checked on one?"

He looked sheepish and cleared his throat.

"We're checking on it," Gabby spoke from the doorway. "Actually, J.C. and Leon have a lead on one and should know something by tonight." With that, she turned and went back to work.

Peter's relief was evident and Rachel stared at him. He didn't meet her gaze but fastened it on to the television screen as Grandpa Walton gave one of his fiery supper table blessings. Then she mentally let it go. She wouldn't embarrass him more over the lapse. He was feeling the stress, too, and that intensified his symptoms.

Within minutes she was forced back to bed, nursing the aching appendage made for walking. Changing positions did relieve the leg enough to pass time and redirect her thoughts, misty though they were.

Peter decided to take the rest of the day off and stay with her. She didn't object. Was, in fact, comforted by it.

Gabby stuck her head in the bedroom door. "I think I'll go on home since Peter's here. I'll see you tonight. Don't forget The Gang's coming!"

"Thanks, Gabby," Peter arose and hugged her. "For everything."

Gabby leaned in to kiss Rachel and then left. "Thank you, Gabby," Rachel called after her. Gabby gave a breezy wave over her shoulder, never looking back.

Peter carefully stretched out beside her and reached for her hand. They snuggled a bit, now a little less encumbered by lack of bed space. It felt heavenly despite her trussed-up leg and neck and her limited range of vision and motion.

He spent the afternoon with her, simply being there, enjoying episodes of *Little House*, *The Waltons*, and *Dr. Quinn, Medicine Woman*, and at times napping. The words of their song echoed in her heart as she drew strength from him . . . *lighting the spark of love that fills me with dreams untold . . .*

Dreams untold. What were they? She didn't yet know. But the Creator had left her here for a reason. And in her heart of hearts she knew: Peter was the essence of that reason.

\\/

The Gang was in extraordinary form.

That evening as they positioned Rachel's chair at the small table, which—with both drop leafs raised—barely accommodated them.

"Cozy," Rachel murmured, smiling. Even smiling could be difficult and tiring, her brain reminded her each time she did it.

"Like sardines," J.C. said grinning, then added angelically. "But I love sardines."

"Huh." Gabby placed the last entrée on the countertop to join all the others of Rachel's favorites. "You love anything edible."

"Huh uh," he sobered. "I don't like your collards." He said it so kindly one would have thought it a compliment.

Leon spoke up. "I love Gabby's collards."

J.C. assumed his Father Tim hands-folded stance. "You know you better say that. Else you'll not sleep in your bed tonight."

"I'm hungry," Rachel injected, a bit sharply. It wasn't that she was starving but since her surgery, she'd found that hunger had evolved into a jittery thing of desperation and pure survival.

"Okay, sweetheart," Peter reached to gently squeeze her clenched hand.

"Of course you are, honey," Gabby crooned and then snapped, "Shut up, y'all! And let's get this girl fed." She grabbed Rachel's plate and commenced to spoon up generous portions of pork tenderloin with fresh herbs, roasted garlic mashed potatoes, tenderloin gravy, roasted butternut squash with rosemary and olive oil, and grilled brussels sprouts.

Drusilla had concocted a balsamic, olive oil, Dijon mustard, and fresh herb salad dressing drizzled over a green salad made crunchy and tangy with walnuts and fresh cranberries.

The others crowded around to help themselves and squeezed in around the round table.

"Peter, would you say grace?" Gabby seated herself last.

Peter complied and added at the end, "And thank you, Lord, for Rachel's homecoming. We're so thankful for—" His voice choked off as he dissolved into tears, squeezing Rachel's hand.

Rachel's emotions were in frozen mode at that precise moment. Like they were Novocained.

A chorus of sniffles and "Amens" ensued.

Rachel's first taste of the gourmet loin was divine. Tastelessness had become so routine that this reemergence flooded her with endorphins. *How incredible*, she thought at the pleasant invasion.

Leon finished first and leaned back in his chair, ready for banter. "J.C., by the time my Marine battalion got to Korea, you'd already killed half our leaders at the officer's dining club with your cooking."

A favorite joke topic. Rachel only half listened to the oft told tale.

"Oh no," J.C. gave a benevolent smile. "I helped win the war by feeding 'em good."

Leon guffawed. "We won because they sent you home early."

Drusilla asked, "Rachel, you need anything else?"

"No, thank you. I've not eaten this much in weeks and I'm about to explode." Her plate was nearly empty. Amazing.

"What day is it?" Peter whispered to her.

She stared at him in amazement and whispered back. "You're asking *me*?"

Then the two of them chortled aloud.

"What?" Gabby and the others swiveled to look at them, puzzled.

"Let us in on it," Leon demanded, already grinning.

But the two of them just continued possum grinning, and Rachel hugged it to her bosom, the shared recall-limitation.

"Oh, well," Gabby quipped, standing to get another helping of pecan pie. "Be that way. We don't care, do we, guys?"

"I do," J.C. folded his hands across his bosom and rolled his eyes heavenward. "They hurt my feelings."

Another round of laughter unleashed more fun vignettes to bat about.

Without warning, Rachel felt the life begin to drain from her, like a plug had been pulled. Within moments she began to slump and reached for Peter's hand. "What's the matter, honey?" He sprang to his feet, sensing her dilemma. He flipped her wheel lock off and said to the others, "She needs to be in bed."

Apologies rumbled forth in an avalanche.

Then, the room grew very quiet as he wheeled her away and assisted her into bed. "Can I do anything else for you?"

Melting into the mattress, Rachel whispered, "No . . . thanks."

He leaned to kiss her gently on the lips. "I love you, darling."

"Me . . . too. Go back to . . . Gang. They're so sweet."

"You sure?" He hovered until she gave him a weak smile. "Okay. But I'll be checking on you."

Rachel heard the soft click of her door closing and she swirled downward into a misty gloam. Nothingness swathed her.

A little while later she heard car doors closing and then motors fading.

A soft body slid in beside hers, wrapping her in warmth and the voice she loved so much soothed her . . . "I'm here, darling. Just rest and things will get better. I'll take care of you. Always."

Safe. Peter's here.

Heavenly shades pulled her into slumber.

\\\/

"Come and see!" Peter stood proudly in the bedroom doorway the next afternoon.

He hastened to align Rachel's chair alongside the bed for her transfer. Patient as a saint, he adjusted her leg rests and added pillows to elevate her injured leg.

"What?" Her curiosity peaked. She'd heard J.C. and Leon's voices outside and some bee-like activity around the front porch but remained clueless. Gabby put away her dust cloth and trailed Rachel's path to the porch.

"Oh. My. Goodness," Rachel put her hands to her cheeks and nearly burst into those unpredictable tears. "A ramp! *Alleluia Chorus!* Now I'm not trapped here." Then tears did release and trickled down her cheeks.

"Yup," Leon said, visibly moved. "We just couldn't stand seeing you caged up any longer."

"Where did you—"

"A secret angel. Uh . . . asked to be anonymous." Gabby hastened to her and readjusted the scarf unnecessarily.

Rachel peered at her. "But I just want to thank—"

Gabby peered down at her, annoyance barely below the surface. "Some angels don't want to let their right hand know what their left hand is doing, doncha know?" With that she turned to the guys. "Let's get her out of the cold."

"Yeah." J.C. dusted his hands on his old coveralls. "Eli's having a fit to get you back over there. Everybody's missing you, doncha know?"

Then Rachel saw Drusilla standing nearby, next to the ramp, and held out her arms, tears still flowing. "Y'all didn't say a word," she accused.

Drusilla wiped her eyes and swooped in to hug Rachel. "Don't let me hurt you, now, hon," she said, gently, squeezing her then untangling their arms. "We just thought you deserved a little ol' surprise about now."

Rachel snatched a tissue from Gabby and blew her nose. "Oh . . . I can't believe it."

She hadn't realized until that moment how trapped she'd felt. How—ensnared. The hurdles had been impossible to conquer. But now—that strong metal ramp represented the world's gateway opening up to her.

She grinned at them all as they stood around, watching her like chicken hawks ready to swoop. "Y'all don't know," she looked at each in turn, love splashing through her very pores. "Y'all just don't know."

Then she laughed out loud. "Tell Eli to get my table ready."

\|/

Mary watched her deacon husband greet church folks.

Ralph shook hands and smiled that big ol' smile of his that melted everyone's heart. Except Mark's.

Mark.

Ever since Mark had overheard their conversation about his biological father not being dead, as his mother had always contended, things between the boy and his family had gone south.

Mark's cold demeanor took the spring out of the big man's step and twisted a knife in her mother's heart. But she understood. She had betrayed him with her stubborn silence, thinking she had been protecting him.

A movement caught her eye. Pastor Pate approached Ralph.

"Ralph, may I speak to you after service, please?" he addressed him quietly and Ralph nodded.

Mary was within inches of them and overheard. The somber tone of the request smote her, left her uneasy.

In the church auditorium, he slid in next to Mary, who was barely able to sit through the entire service. Months ago she'd begun to forego the Sunday school classes, opting to drive alone to join her family for the preaching hour. Her strength these days played hide-and-seek, mostly hide. Even the worship hour stretch got to her. She noticed Ralph grimacing and lightly rubbing his chest. "What's wrong?" she asked her usually robust husband, realizing that he, too, was troubled by the pastor's summons.

The grimace dissolved to be replaced by a reassuring smile. "Just a little acid reflux," he whispered. "Did you see Mark?"

Mary glanced around and spotted her son sitting alone in the back of the auditorium, away from his former church pals.

He didn't look her way but sat rigid, eyes glued to the front wall, features empty as a gourd.

"He's sitting in the back," she relayed to Ralph.

"Alone?"

"Yes." That shook her even more, that Ralph noticed the isolation. "It's probably his choice," she whispered, more to convince herself than him. Mark had been so withdrawn lately, since the school upheaval, despite the fact that Mary had talked with Mark's teacher and explained Mark's dilemma, one Mary had caused. The teacher had been extremely sympathetic and understanding.

But, as Mark later told her quite stoically, the damage had been done. Since that day, her son had moved about like an old automaton who'd seen better days, who operated on empty diplomacy and dead emotions.

Ralph had chosen to give him a wide berth to level out. "He's frustrated," he told Mary. "I would be, too. I won't push him right now. He deserves this pity party, honey, and you know it."

How she loved that big hunk of farmer. She sighed and realized she'd missed most of the sermon while wool gathering. She felt Ralph's supportive hand at her elbow as she struggled to her feet to join the congregation now standing for the benediction.

"Excuse me," Ralph murmured as the members filed out through the vestibule where the pastor greeted each cordially, regal yet home-sy in his black clerical robe. Mary made her way to her sporty little red Mazda and saw Mark sitting in the passenger seat, looking unseeing out the side window, ignoring her as she climbed in. She was certain the drive there with Ralph had been as dismal.

Grief seized her. She turned the ignition and the vehicle purred to life. "Hi," she ventured, only to receive a grunt in response.

She remembered Ralph's counsel to give him space, so the drive home was silent. As soon as she cut the engine, Mark was out of the car in a flash. She caught sight of his hind parts disappearing into the meadow. It took all she had to not call him back.

Maybelle had left food warming in the oven as usual. Mary thanked God for the woman's thoughtfulness as the aroma enveloped and welcomed her. If only—

She pulled herself up and slipped out of her Sunday shoes, retrieving them and slowly making her way to the bedroom. She slid into comfortable jeans and pullover and crawled onto the bed to rest for just a few minutes.

Next thing she knew, Ralph sat down on the bed beside her. She woke with a start. "I'm sorry," she mumbled. "I was so tired—" His expression halted her flow of words. "What's wrong, honey?" she asked, struggling to a sitting position while plumping pillows behind her. She narrowed her gaze on him. "What did Pastor want?"

He was pale. But he gave her a lopsided smile. "Aww. You know. Gossip starts all kind of rumors."

He heart skittered. "About Mark?"

He hesitated and then nodded, going solemn. "Seems his classmate, the Dodger boy, has been busy stirring up trouble. His dad's offended, demanding I resign as deacon. Says if a man can't control his own household, he's not fit to rule in church."

"Look at who's talking." Mary bit her lip to stop the angry tirade that gripped her. "He's not doing so good ruling that son of his. And rumor's had it that he and that woman at his plant were—"

"Whoa," Ralph cautioned. "We can't fall into the same rumor-mill trap, sweetheart. Though he didn't ask for it, I told the pastor that my resignation will be forthcoming. He wants me to wait, thinking Dodger may cool down and hush his foolishness. He's not usually a bad guy—he just believes his son. But Mark is more important to me than a title." He patted her arm and smiled. "So I'm going to turn in my resignation this week. No big deal."

Tears burned behind Mary's eyes. "Oh, Ralph." She reached and slid her arms around his big neck. "You are such a big deal." Tears splashed over and she tightened the embrace. "Such a big deal."

\|/

Mark stood unmoving on the staircase. He'd stopped there after having rushed into the side door to try to escape to his room. He just missed the opportunity when Ralph came in the back door and beat him up the stairs.

When he heard the emotional tone of his parents' conversation, he grew curious and crept closer to listen. Now, he sneaked back down to the lower level and exited by a side door to the sun porch, a seldom used retreat. He slid into the plush lounge chair and rested his head against the floral cushion.

Despite his resentment toward his stepfather, he knew how Ralph felt. Mark's church friends had already scattered in uncertain censor of his rumored dishonesty. Some had tried to approach him for what—he was certain—was his denial of the charges. But he could not deny the truth, so he'd set himself apart. And now, his dad was being ostracized as well.

Not fair. It wasn't Ralph's fault. He'd been nothing but good and still he was being maligned, along with his son.

His son. Mark's eyes popped open. Yeah, Ralph was his dad as surely as any man could be. A little of the ice around his heart began to crack and melt. But in the next breath, Mark stumbled upon the reality of the lie he'd been fed since birth: that his birth father was dead.

At any time, Ralph could have set it straight. And he had not.

Anger oozed and froze back into place as swiftly as it had leaked. Mark arose and slipped quietly out into the cold, sunny day where farm creatures sang in symphony to him a song of belonging.

Besides Gramma, they were his only family now.

\⁄/

"Will you fetch my pill bottle, Gabby? The Meloxicam?"

Gabby quickly brought it to the table, where Rachel popped one in her mouth and washed it down with tea. She felt a spurt of hope that it would provide a measure of pain relief.

"There. The doctor said I needed anti-inflammatory meds now so he okayed my old standby, easy-on-the-stomach Meloxicam."

Gabby had taken Rachel to her two week orthopedic surgery checkup that morning.

Gabby agreed. "It should help you sleep better, too."

Rachel still ached terribly at the injury sites and hoped this would reduce the inflammation.

Within moments, her head felt like a sledge hammer smacked it and began to spin. The impact was so severe she fought panic. A concerned Peter hastened her to bed. But the bed spun and agitated like an old fifties washer, rattling her entire body.

"Peter, I feel like a tall building crumbling to the ground but it never lands. Just keeps on and on . . ."

He perched on the edge of the bed, gripping her hand, watching her closely. "What do you think caused it?"

"The Meloxicam. Don't know why. I've taken it for at least a year and never had a reaction. But my body's changed since the fall and surgery." She pressed her hand to her forehead and closed her eyes. "*Whywhywhy?*"

"Can I do anything to help?" Peter peered into her eyes, his face blurred in her sight, she was so alarmed she could feel it in her bones. Well, that was, if she'd been able to feel her bones at that precise time. As it was, the cage rattling was not letting up.

"I'll be okay," she lied. She just wanted to be alone for a few minutes to try to level out. Twilight was closing in on her—the horrible deepening of shadows that left all dark and hopeless.

Rachel carried a secret—one too shameful to reveal because of her moral upbringing.

Suicide beckoned.

Thoughts of suicide stalked her in her most vulnerable moments. Like now.

Life had become such a minute-by-minute struggle. She was so tired. She couldn't even take a tiny pill to relieve the pain that sporadically tormented her.

Then, like a candle lighting up the darkness, she was reminded that the hurting was no longer constant. That it did let up for short increments of time.

That was progress. Wasn't it? Yes, it was.

She prayed. And though it was as mechanical as pulling a slot machine handle, she did it.

That was the right thing to do. And when she did the right thing—her daddy always said—it would all work out to the good.

She would trust. Yes, she would.

The purple curtains closed on that thought.

\|/

Initially, the nights were difficult.

Oh, she could fall asleep. She'd learned that by telling herself she was resting, it would actually help her to slide into slumber. Too, her body seemed to be on automatic, taking care of itself after being overtaxed by trauma. At least that's what she kept telling herself, and it seemed to be working.

The only thing, after three to four hours, her body would begin to ache and scream "turn over." Then her bladder would command relief. She hated to disturb Peter, who fought fatigue much of the time in recent months.

Any time Rachel attempted to slide quietly from bed and wheel herself to the bathroom without disturbing him, Peter would immediately be behind her, swiftly pushing her to her destination. And while she transferred and relieved herself, then shifted back, he waited patiently, never emitting any signs of impatience or even tiredness. He was like a vigilant soldier guarding a national treasure.

Peter awoke each time Rachel shifted. "You okay?"

"I'm sorry I'm disturbing you but—" she said one night during that first week.

The room flooded with light. He was already on his feet. "Don't apologize. You need to go to the bathroom?"

Rachel swallowed back nausea. "Yes, I need to pee, but I'm too sick to get up."

"I'll get the bed pan." He was off before she could protest, which she knew was futile because she was indeed too sick to do the transfer twice without passing out.

Peter was back within moments, expertly helping her through the painful process of lifting her body enough to slide the pan beneath her. Had he not been exactly who he was and had she not known just how much he loved her, the act would have mortified her.

As it was, she felt like a liability.

Emptying her bladder was a blessing and she felt uncommonly grateful for Peter's gesture.

"Okay," she said when finished. He handed her a moist wipe from the box on her bedside table, slid the pan from beneath her, and disappeared to the bathroom where she heard him flushing and rinsing the utensil. Each sound was like a nail being hammered into her spirit, crushing her sense of self-reliance.

When he returned he asked, "You thirsty?"

"No." She reached out to take his hand and squeeze it. "Thank you, darling. Somehow, I'll pay you back for everything."

The room plunged into darkness. "Shhh," he said as he slid in beside her, nuzzled and kissed her cheek and when she slowly rolled back onto her side, balancing the heavy metal brace with a pillow tucked between her legs, he spooned against her. "You don't owe me anything. Just having you here with me is all the payment I need."

The assurance of those words sank into her, trickling through her in a peaceful way that nothing else had recently.

Out of the dark, his voice floated softly. "I don't deserve you."

Somewhere there in the fingers of night, a fragment of humor stirred and—with a touch of sass—she murmured his favorite retort. "Peter James, you got *everything you deserved.*"

He chuckled and wrapped his arm across her midriff. A long sigh. Then, "That's my girl."

\|/

"Your appointment is next week with Dr. Ringel. He's with Neurology Associates in Spartanburg."

Rachel continued eating her fruit at the breakfast table, hoping for the best, by way of his collaboration. Gabby had masterminded accessing an appointment, knowing Rachel wasn't up to the task. But Peter didn't have to know that. His reactions to intrusion could sometimes be persnickety at best. It was growing increasingly hairy to motivate him.

From the corner of her eye she saw wariness set in. "What's he gonna do?"

Rachel assumed a casual tone. "Oh, just do some memory tests, I assume."

He visibly stiffened. "My memory's probably as good as anybody else's at my age."

Good ol' merciful denial.

Rachel felt her gut gather into a knot. "Yes, it is. Like I said before, he'll probably not find anything seriously threatening. Most of the time, the things we fear most never come to pass."

Please, dear Lord.

She felt it. His relaxing. "Yeah. You're right." A long nervous sigh. "Might as well get it behind me."

She smiled at him and took his hand as Gabby, silent as a background fly on the wall, refilled his coffee cup.

The two sisters locked gazes over his head, relief palpable. Strike one.

\⌄/

Lunch at Eli's Place was postponed a couple more days until Rachel's appetite could better tolerate the food smells and sights. The first trip was eventful, with the entire Gang invading Rachel's dwelling and bustling about to see that she got properly transported in the unseasonably frigid weather.

Gabby gently stretched the knitted sock over her sister's casted foot. "So your toes won't get frostbite. " Actually the temperature was in the mid-thirties, mild for northern Yankees but icy for southern folks.

The first trip down the ramp was like a school house fire drill. Rachel was not in the least anxious about it, not with the view of the Keystone Cops' slapstick playing out before her. She had every confidence in The Gang's ability to deliver her safely into Eli's capable hands. Besides, Lizzie, the in-house physical therapist, who'd by now begun bi-weekly visits to the James' residence, had gone through the dos and don'ts with Peter and Gabby.

Today, the trip to Eli's Place deemed her liberation official.

Drusilla added a scarf to Rachel's warm coat, to cover her ear tops, where the neck brace ended.

After huffing like Japanese sumo wrestlers and hovering as the wheelchair spanned the descent, the guys held their breath while Peter locked the wheels and Rachel expertly stood on her good leg, pivoting and sliding onto Gabby's low-setting car's passenger seat.

"Good girl!" The Gang chorused, grinning broadly and shooting thumbs up all around as she acknowledged them with a thankful gaze.

J.C. and Drusilla followed in their car and the ride was pleasant for Rachel. Just the change of scenery was awesome. Not exactly exhilarating—more like overwhelming, emphasizing her tattered condition.

She let those impressions fizzle into the mist as they parked at Eli's and Peter wheeled Rachel up the curb ramp and into her second home, where she received a rousing welcome from Eli and all the other regular diners. It touched her, the sense of belonging and caring that showered over her.

The buffet looked colossal and—*overpowering.* But she found the atmosphere welcoming and the sights and aromas not unpleasant. "Want me to fix your plate?" Peter offered.

"*Heavenly hash*, no!" She surprised herself with her reaction's punch. "You know better than that. Picking out what I want is the fun part."

This drew *woo hoos* galore and lively banter while Peter allowed her to navigate her chair to choice selections where he spooned the entrées onto her plate. *Great teamwork*, she thought, warmed by it all.

Back at the table, a huge serving of Eli's zesty chicken salad—Rachel's favorite—magically appeared before her and when she began feasting, she found it all good.

"J.C.," Gabby peered at him. "What happened to your nose? It's all skinned up."

"Oh, I walked out of the shoe store a couple of days ago, looking down at my new shoes, and I tripped over a parking curb, doncha know? And I fell flat on my face."

"Oh my goodness!" Gabby grabbed her cheeks. "That's terrible."

Drusilla drew herself up and said, "When he came home all bloody and bruised, know what he told me happened?"

"No telling," Peter muttered between bites.

J.C.'s mouth curved in pious sweetness. "I told her this big ol' feller hit me and I beat him up so bad that they don't know whether he's gonna live or not. Had 'er goin' there for a few minutes."

Drusilla glared daggers at him. "I can't believe you lied to me like that. Stupid me."

Leon chortled. "Teaches you not to believe everything he says."

"You okay?" Peter asked Rachel, observing her growing silence. Her strength had begun to slowly leak out. The stimulation of engaging with the others sucked out even more. But she was so ravenous for normalcy that she pushed back the encroaching gray-ness.

"Yes, darling. I am." She couldn't eat all her food. So Eli brought a carry-out box for her leftover chicken salad. "For later," he said, winking at her and putting in her leftover baked sweet potato for good measure. "Gotta get you well and strong."

"Thanks, Eli," she said. "I've missed you."

He saluted her. "Me, too." She watched him move on to others' needs and thought about how some folks could be so giving. Every day now, she found herself more appreciative of kindness.

Peter nudged her, interrupting her musing. He grinned and asked her, "What day is it?"

She went solemn, trying to focus.

Then he winked. "Just testing you."

\\\//

Seemed to Rachel she lived on the edge.

She never knew when something would create instant cranial-pandemonium.

So she tried to flow as smoothly as a short-fused android could.

Some days, when Gabby finished laundry and tidying up, she carved out time to sit with Rachel in her bedroom. They would catch an old forties movie on the American Movie Classic channel or maybe turn on Sirius Music channels for soft background music while they chatted.

Rachel sat in her wheelchair today, leg rest elevated, as Gabby shuttled back in time to when their kids were all little and boisterous. Rachel mostly listened now, too sapped to engage, soaking up other times and memories, ones simpler and uplifting.

"Remember when we sang that trio for the Christmas musical at church, you, Drusilla and me?" Gabby rocked and mused. "What was that song? Oh, yeah, 'Birthday of the King,' and you reached for that high note on the chorus and ended up on a scream?" She burst into laughter.

"How could I ever forget? I don't know what happened that day—I just remembered what the voice teacher had said—that when you approach a note you find too high, to scream it on key. That note looked as high as the moon so I screamed it out. It just happened to be tone deaf."

"You didn't expect us to follow you, did you? You should've known that in music, we'd follow you off a cliff or up a scream." Gabby wiped tears from her eyes and burst into fresh laughter. "We ended up sounding like the Three Stooges in a drag concert."

When their laughter died down, Gabby grew pensive. "I remember our harmonizing when your kids were beginning to really connect with music. Remember how your Jason could sing such beautiful tenor with Amber's soprano?"

Rachel did. And it pricked her heart.

"My boys?" Gabby did a hand flip and shook her head. "Didn't get excited over anything unless it had a ball in it."

"Wonder who that came from?" Rachel gave a soft snort.

"Yeah. I never was able to steer my boys away from sports to the finer artsy stuff."

They sat quietly for long moments, marinating in memories. Then Gabby said softly, "Remember after Jason's accident, when I came over that next morning and we shared our—"

Wham!

Rachel felt the cerebral impact of a mallet blow and her head began spinning like a wind turbine. She grabbed her skull to still the swirling.

"What is it?" Gabby called out, rising out of her seat. "What's wrong?"

"Dizzy," Rachel moaned as the room reeled and tilted. "So—woozy."

"Ahhh, sis," Gabby was at her side, kneeling. "I'm so sorry to bring that up. I didn't think."

"You didn't know," Rachel whispered, taking deep breaths to slow down the swirling sensation. "I didn't know either . . ."

Gabby helped her to bed, where she half reclined, propped on her pillow stack. "I'll be okay," she murmured. "Just give me a minute. It's slowed down but not gone yet."

"I could kick myself," Gabby muttered as she left the room to check on the clothes in the dryer. "Stupid, stupid. *Stupid!*"

Peter soon arrived and a subdued Gabby departed for home. Rachel kept silent for the duration of the day and the loopiness finally subsided, leaving her strangely sapped.

That night, Jason reached into her dreams, alongside Amber. Rachel's cozy bed offered no defense from the sense of loss—not even in the midst of the Disney setting—as she watched the two of them, dressed as angels, singing on a Christmas parade float.

She approached them, overjoyed, and reached up to them. Unexpectedly, Amber leaped from the float and ran helter-skelter into the throng gathered there. Rachel chased her until she lost sight of her in the crowd. Desperate and weeping, she pivoted and looked back at the float, searching for Jason.

He was gone.

Oh, God . . . She's missed her chance to find him. To hold him once more. "Noooooooo . . ."

"No!" Rachel awoke with her mouth wide open, her face tear-streaked.

"What?" Peter bolted upright beside her and reached out to soothe her. "What's wrong?" he asked, his voice husked with panic and sleep.

Rachel inhaled a deep ragged breath and blew it out, blinking back spots and vivid images. "A nightmare," she whispered and struggled over on her other side to regroup for sleep.

Peter changed sides in order to spoon against her. "Get some rest, honey."

"Okay." But it was near dawn before slumber reclaimed her.

\\I/

Peter's bad days taxed Rachel's coping ability.

Of course, the accident had already destroyed most of it.

The Gang offered a continuity that helped her ford many of the daily rapids.

"We're gonna come and fetch you to church," J.C. insisted during Saturday lunch at Eli's Place. A chorus of assents followed.

Rachel glanced at Peter but he didn't seem to remember. *Good.* Earlier that morning, she'd awakened to find him already dressed in his Sunday suit. "Where you going?" she'd asked.

"To church." And then when she didn't respond, he'd asked uncertainly, "It is Sunday isn't it?"

"No, honey, it's Saturday."

Wordlessly, he had carefully hung up his clothes and redressed in his everyday jeans and pullover. More than anything, his silence had tugged at her heart.

Tammy, their cute blonde, pony-tailed waitress poured more coffee and tea, overhearing the church plans. "That's great, Rachel. I'm gonna be there. It sure was dead around here with you gone, I'll tell you that."

"I'm looking forward to it," Rachel said, lifted by the prospect.

"Church isn't the same without you, either," Tammy said and moved on to the next table in her efficient nonstop way.

Gabby spoke up. "That is, Peter, if you don't wear that ugly orange jacket you've got on." She referred to the neon jacket Peter bought primarily to wear for bike riding and had ended up wearing on chilly days because of its comfort.

Peter grinned at Gabby. "You talking about my favorite yellow coat?"

"No, dummy. That coat's as orange as a tangelo. You know I don't like orange! See?" She pointed to the large rhinestone rooster pinned to her blouse. She was a dyed-in-the-wool Carolina Gamecock fan, loving a chance to defile anything Clemson orange.

"Huh." Peter took a big bite of ice cream. "I'm color blind."

Gabby peered at him, disbelieving. *"Shut up."*

He looked at Rachel. "Tell her, Rachel."

"He *is* color blind." And he was. "Can't tell fire engine red from green." And that was a fact proven when he one day miss-labeled Amber's Chinese red pom-pom puddled in the car's passenger floor.

He'd pointed and asked Rachel "Where did that cabbage come from?"

She related the incident to The Gang. "So that's how I know for sure."

"Why didn't I know that before?" Gabby asked Rachel.

Rachel shrugged. "It never came up."

"No wonder you chose that." Gabby narrowed her eyes at Peter. "That's the butt-ugliest thing I've ever seen."

Peter grinned at her, delighting in every little morsel of their sparring match. "You just don't know real beauty when you see it."

"Huh!" Gabby ate a few bites, silently reloading. Rachel mused that Gabby and Peter mostly only sparred when hanging out at Eli's Place. She was glad. She wouldn't be able to stand it nonstop.

They all pulled out their tips and passed them down to where J.C. sat and he began adding up the bills.

Their waitress friend sidled up to him and trilled, "You need help with that, J.C.?"

"Naw, Tammy. I'm just a-counting it."

"He's just hanging on to that money! Give 'er the money, J.C.!" Gabby ordered.

"Goodbye, Lincoln and Jefferson," J.C. muttered, kissing the greens and handing them over to Tammy, who, in turn, leaned to kiss his cheek and thanked them all.

"You don't mind me kissing your ol' man, do you, Drusilla?" Tammy added, tucking the money into her apron pocket.

"Huh." Drusilla rolled her eyes. "You kiddin'? I guess he does deserve a little thrill every once in a while."

J.C. smiled benevolence at his wife and said. "I wouldn't touch that with a ten-foot pole."

Rachel decided she'd had enough for one day. "Let's go, Peter. I'm tired."

"Sure, honey." He dramatically slid into the neon orange work jacket, unlocked the chair wheels to align and push her to the exit. "Bye Gang."

"Bye. Be ready about nine in the morning." J.C. called.

"Okay!" Rachel was already feeling buoyed by the prospect of church.

\\/

Getting to church proceeded without incident.

When Peter rolled Rachel into the sanctuary, however, many eyes turned her way and jaws dropped at the sight of her pale face and her trussed, braced and casted body in the wheeled contraption.

Rachel surmised that their first glimpse of her must be pretty dreadful. The Gang had gotten used to her battered appearance and any improvement to them was monumental.

The guys parked her in the wheelchair section. Actually, Rachel liked the slightly elevated view, even though it was a bird's-eye observation compared to her normal front section seat. Today, she found the view unencumbered. Peter loved sitting up front because he said he didn't get distracted by people-watching.

People-watching. That was Peter. In fact, that was the whole Gang thing, finding humor in everything and everybody. Though they didn't use derogatory put-downs, thank goodness, only amongst themselves where it was blatantly utilized for laughs. No, theirs were mostly upbeat observances.

"You guys go on up front to your regular seats," she attempted to shoo them away.

"Huh uh," J.C. grunted and planted himself in a nearby seat. The rest of The Gang followed like dominoes dropping, leaving for Peter the chair adjoining Rachel's.

The hundred-plus member choir filed in and began their rousing call to praise and worship and Rachel's emotions began to clatter about and by the time Pastor Gladden delivered a brilliant, rich message of hope and deliverance, her emotions had roller coaster-ed all over the chart, alternating tears, ebullience, remorse, grief, repentance, and redemption.

Through it all, Peter held her hand and watched her as though she might implode into the atmosphere. In those moments, she knew—*felt*—his affinity and above all, his gratitude that she remained with him.

The validation wrapped her in a soft, consoling way.

At service's end, folks filed past her to the vestibule, and for the first time, she experienced what a chair-bound person feels. Her scrutiny of passers-by flashed in tiny increments because she couldn't move her head to follow the moving entities. Some looked everywhere but at her, walking briskly to more important affairs.

The forgotten one. Not a great rank but hopefully a temporary one.

She would never again view physically challenged folks the same.

Then, one by one, others began to stop and speak to her. Many did not know of the accident and expressed genuine regret that they'd not known. She received careful shoulder hugs, air kisses, and words of encouragement and hope.

From a distance, one adolescent boy caught her eye. He stood beside an older woman and something about him made her look again. And again. He reminded her of Jason. Unexpectedly, tears puddled and she tore her gaze loose.

Tammy, all spruced up in a chic suit and fashionable hairdo, rushed to greet The Gang. "I'm so glad to see you back, Rachel!" She carefully kissed Rachel's cheek. "See you tomorrow at Eli's!"

Eli's Place closed on Sundays to honor the Sabbath, a thing important to the proprietor. Because of his Christian faith, Eli and his family were forced to flee Egypt years earlier with only the clothes on their backs. His work ethic and faith had helped him work his way up in America to the realization of his dream: owning his own restaurant.

While Peter aligned her chair to the car for transfer, Rachel felt a little surge of triumph.

She'd ventured to church today! My oh my, that meant she was becoming not only human again, but the spiritual embers of Rachel had, during that time of reverence, flickered—albeit in brief spurts.

That had to mean something, didn't it?

Yes. The still small voice spoke. She didn't feel a thunderbolt of faith but she did decide to trust that voice. Yes, she took a deep, affirming breath. There was hope.

\I/

Mark looked around at the youth of Manilowe church and felt—peace.

At least he did in that moment.

He hung close to Gramma today at her church, one much larger than his own country house of worship. Visiting her was a welcome relief, much greater than he'd imagined possible. With her, he felt a belonging. A sense of place. One he'd not even realized he'd lost until he landed here with her this weekend.

The youth event last night was super, pulling him into contact with teens who knew nothing of his notoriety back home. He'd enjoyed a sense of camaraderie he'd not had in weeks.

In the past week, he'd had a run-in at school with Stinky Dodger. After overhearing him at lunch replaying his tale of Mark's lies, Mark had seen red and lit into him. He'd actually hit the boy in the mouth, leaving him with a busted lip. Stinky squealed like little Petunia, his pet pig, squeezing the drama for all it was worth.

None of the witnesses stuck up for Stinky either. They'd all treated Mark with respect since the incident. He'd been suspended for the rest of the week but his parents had not scolded him—a real surprise, considering all concerned. He knew his dad didn't approve of fighting but this time he'd said the kid had it coming. He'd had no business running his mouth all over creation and dragging Mark's name through mire.

His parents didn't even punish Mark by calling off his weekend trip to Gramma's house.

That touched Mark in some unprecedented way but he didn't want to analyze it too closely. The hurt of betrayal still lay heavily upon him.

Today, he basked in Gramma's presence and couldn't wait to get back to her house and eat a huge hunk of that fresh strawberry cake she'd baked just for him.

"It's your special cake, honey," she told him as she drove home, sliding him her little doting smile. "I don't get to see you often enough so this will be our very own private celebration of being together."

Mark felt tickled inside with a feather duster, anticipating the time together. He'd not enjoyed his family times lately. He'd gone through polite motions but he could tell they knew his heart wasn't in it.

Good.

He'd tried to disassociate himself from religion. He'd gone sour during this siege of his parents' duplicity. But something Pastor Gladden said today stuck inside him, like corn in old Tom Turkey's craw. He'd said that we all have sinned and come short of the glory of God. That there was none righteous. No, not one.

He got that. Mark knew he was the worst of sinners. Bar none.

It was the other scripture that really bugged him.

"Gramma, was what the pastor said about judging others really right on? I mean—does that mean when I judge somebody of something, that I do the same things?"

Gramma smiled and nodded. "Yup. That also applies to me and anybody else who accuses others of sinning. Romans 2 says 'You, therefore, have no excuse, you who pass judgment on someone else, for at whatever point you judge another, you are condemning yourself, because you who pass judgment do the same things.'"

Then she shook her head. "Plain as the nose on your face."

"Huh." Uneasiness crept through him.

She cut him a glance. "Not fun hearing that, is it? I don't especially like to hear it, either. But it teaches me to be kind when assessing others' actions. I mean—how can I even recognize wrongdoing in others unless it has at least crossed my mind to do the same things."

"You?" Mark peered at her, doubtful that this shining example of virtue could be tempted to do the big S.

The white head nodded. "Even me, sweetie. So, to forgive is high on my list of priorities. There may be a day that I'll need forgiveness for something stupid. Know what I mean?"

Mark fixed his gaze on the road ahead. "Yeah." *Boy, did he know!*

He had a lot to chew on.

He needed to talk with Gramma about wanting to know who his real father was. He also wanted to share his hurt at the man's rejection. He wanted to vent about his parents' betrayal. There was a lot to unload. But Gramma loved him, despite all his faults. She would not lead him on a wild goose chase.

Yup. He needed counsel.

After he ate his strawberry cake.

\|/

The Gang migrated to Rachel and Peter's house for lunch.

Today, they stopped at Burger King and stocked up on enough Whoppers and fries to feed a platoon. Gabby had hauled a gallon of sweet tea to Rachel's house that morning when they collected Rachel for church. It now sat chilled for iced glasses.

Gathered around the small table, they ate heartily, in silence for a while. Rachel knew they were now assimilating the praise, worship, and message of the day. Despite their sometimes boisterousness, they all were stone-cold serious when it came to their spiritual walk.

Gabby broke the silence. "I'm surprised so many folks didn't know about your accident, Rachel." She dipped her French fry in ketchup and chewed it thoughtfully. "Reckon it's because Manilowe Community Church has grown so big in membership in recent years? I mean, when you get up to two thousand members, you can't even get to know all the faces and names, much less keep up on what's happening in all their lives."

Drusilla nodded. "When Uncle Hamp pastored there, we thought five hundred was a large church. But when something bad happened to a member, everybody heard about it and rallied."

Rachel sighed and played with her half-eaten food. "Actually, I'd have been overwhelmed with lots of visitors and calls, anyway." But it did hurt a little that her ordeal was not newsworthy enough to spread. She mentally shrugged and let it go. Daddy had always said "get over yourself."

"You would have," Peter agreed. "Who did you say loaned the ramp?" he asked to The Gang at large.

"We didn't," Leon quickly replied, frowning, while the others exchanged quick blank looks then focused on their food.

Peter looked a bit puzzled. Then he shrugged. "I thought you did."

Rachel's curiosity was piqued again. "You said a secret angel loaned it?"

"That's right," Gabby said sharply, not looking at her. "Wasn't the message good today?" She abruptly changed the subject.

Rachel glanced around to find each of them studiously avoiding looking at her.

Why?

She pushed her plate away, more curious than ever.

Chapter Nine

\\ /

"The struggle you're in today is developing the strength you
need for tomorrow."
—*Robert Tew*

Peter's black moods were perilous due to his penchant for rage
and fickleness.

Now, more than ever before, Rachel dreaded them. Despite
his deep devotion to her, the black moods sporadically popped
up to jangle her hard-earned moments of peace. She sensed they
were part and parcel of the James bloodline's encroaching infir-
mity, which unnerved her even more. And these days, she had
few nerves left.

That morning, Peter found a water bill statement, still sealed,
buried in his desk paraphernalia. "I can't believe I missed this
bill!" he all but shouted. "They just called me, wanting to know
why the payment hasn't been sent. I hate that!"

Craaash!

Propped in bed, Rachel startled—she felt every axon in her
nervous system screech into emergency flight-or-fight. "What
was that?" she rasped, her nerves shattering like glass.

She peered at him, this stranger whose face blazed with
fury, eyes dark and sinister focused on her. He'd dashed his
bulky keys-cluster against the hardwood floor. Now, he pivoted
away and grabbed his head with both hands. "I feel like getting
my gun and blowing my brains out."

From the bed, Rachel gazed beseechingly at him. "Please don't talk like that, Peter." She tasted the fury in him, knowing he would not harm a hair on her head but at the same time, she knew that he was capable of harming himself.

He spun on his heel and peered at her, eyes a-glitter. "I'm so tired of it, Rachel. All I do is work, work, work." He paced back and forth. "I can't keep up with the bills anymore."

"Just calm down, honey. When I get better, we'll work it out." Her insides already knotted and her head forecast that dreaded spiral-threat.

He gave a dry, humorless laugh, one that struck fear in her heart. This was the Peter that drew murky memories from the past, of when he'd shut down his love and closed her out. She took a deep breath and closed her eyes, silently praying. She could not go back there.

Not now.

"Calm down?" He shook his head, disbelieving, staring unseeing out the window into a cold overcast day. Long moments passed in silence.

"I don't know how long I can hold it all together, Rachel. I don't know where the money goes. We should be living worry-free now but it's not happening. At my age, I should be completely retired. But I'm not."

Rachel's head ballooned to capacity. She sat up, swung her bulky hardware over the bedside and placed her good foot on the floor. She pivoted herself into the chair and wheeled from the bedroom.

Peter called out, "Where you going?"

"Anywhere," she replied. She'd reached her limit of doomsday for one sitting. This was a different Rachel than the one from the past. The Rachel of old would have hung in there to the death.

This Rachel had no choice but to remove herself from what was—to her bruised and fragile brain—pandemonium. The middle ground had vanished at the foot of those stairs. Now she had to sail above the rapids to survive.

She heard him come rushing as she stopped in the den and parked in front of a window to watch the squirrels outside scampering along the tree branches.

"Ahh, baby," he was on his haunches beside her, gathering her hands in his, frantic eyes level with her empty ones. "I'm so sorry. Sometimes I forget that you're not able to handle all this stuff."

Rachel looked away and watched a feral cat cross the road. Or was it feral? Her heart went out to it, knowing its vulnerability. Its aloneness pinched her heart.

"Please, sweetheart, will you forgive me?"

She looked at him, taking in his repentant features and his desperate hold on her hands. She nodded slightly, the only movement range in her neck. "It's okay," she whispered. Because on some level, she knew—he couldn't help it. No more than she could help her need to flee.

Peter smiled at her, his eyes remained somber. "Soon, we'll work it out. Together."

\i/

Peter's cuddling was growing more amorous. He couldn't help it. He really missed marital intimacy. Rachel still couldn't even snuggle, not really. The bulky neck and leg braces were like something worn by medieval warriors. All she lacked was the iron face mask.

He hated to think like that. But, holey moly, it had been weeks since the accident and there was still no light at the end of the abstinence tunnel. Today, he was finishing his pest control route when his cell phone jangled.

""Hello?"

A pause. "Peter James?" A strange voice. A woman.

"Yes?"

"I hate to bother you like this. I know lots is going on with your wife's accident and all."

"Who is this?"

Another long pause. "I'm Dorothy Rivers."

"Do I know you?"

"Not really. We do go to church together but don't ordinarily bump into each other, so you don't know me. You might recognize my face but not my name."

"Can I help you with something?" Peter asked politely. He was always getting calls for pest control service or inquiries about his rentals.

"Well. Maybe. You see—I'm the grandmother of your son."

Peter felt like a bus had rammed into him, knocking the breath from him. "W-what—?"

"I'm so sorry," she hastened on, kindly, "dumping it on you this way. I know it's a shock hearing from me out of the blue like this. But it's about my grandson, Mark. He's thirteen, just the age where he wants to know who his daddy is, you know? My heart just breaks for him. Is there any chance—"

"Just a minute. I need to pull over to the side of the road." Which was true. But mostly, he needed time to catch his breath and think. *Behave, brain—please.* He saw an I-85 rest area and pulled in, cutting off the engine.

"I'm so sorry, Mrs. Rivers. I wish I could feel free to—" He took a deep ragged breath and blew it out. "Fact is, left up to me, I'd have been in his life all along. I tried to pay child support but his mother would send the checks back, most of the time—uncashed."

A soft chuckle. "That's Mary. Too much pride, I tell her. It's not about money that I called. It's about Mark's emotional needs. Mary doesn't completely understand—well, maybe she does, but she knows your dilemma and—" A long pause. "But she loves that boy better'n anything on this earth."

Peter sat for long moments, trying to absorb the shock of confrontation. The trembling and trauma of it played with his mind. *Please, Lord, let me make sense of this. Help me to concentrate because this is important to me.* Then, in the next breath, a calmness and clarity stole over him.

"I'm glad he has that, at least. With all my heart, I'm thankful for that. Rachel was hurt so badly by the—indiscretion—and any mention of it devastates her. Right now, being in the shape she's in—well, to raise the issue at this time would send her off the deep end. I just know it would. I can't do that to her. I came so close to losing her."

"I know. And I'm so sorry," the sweet voice sounded sincere. "I've been praying for her and all . . . she's had a hard time through the years and I wouldn't want to add to her burdens. I just wanted to run it past you, about my grandson. He's—he's going through hard times trying to make sense of it all."

"Please—fill me in a bit. Is he okay? I mean, is he healthy and happy?" Oh, how he prayed daily for this.

She chuckled. "Yes. He's a fine boy. Smart, too. And he's been happy. Up until now. He feels betrayed by his mama and his stepfather because they let him believe you were dead. He just recently found out it wasn't true. Quite a shock for a young fellow, wouldn't you say? Now he needs to know more about his biological dad. But with your situation with Rachel—that's not going to happen any time soon, is it?"

Peter felt backed into a corner, confronted by a legion of guilt demons, all fangs and bloody claws, snarling and resolute to rip out his heart. "Oh my," he moaned, rubbing a hand over his face. "What a catch-22! I'm damned if I do and damned it I don't. Literally." His head began to reel and his hands to tremble.

"I—I don't know what to say," he groaned, his mind going more blank than it ever had before. Oh no!

"Look," the woman's voice gentled even more, "you don't have to deal with this now. You've got too, too much on your plate, Peter James. You just take care of Rachel, now, you hear? I'll handle things from this end for the time being. Okay?"

Peter struggled to comprehend what she was saying. The harder he tried, the more blanks he drew. Dear God in heaven—help me! What a time to bleep out.

"Peter? Are you all right?" The voice penetrated his fog.

He cleared his throat and managed to murmur. "I'm okay."

"Good. Take care and know that I'm praying for you and Rachel. If you need me, I'm as near as your phone. Good-bye."

Peter looked at the dead cell phone in his hand and slowly closed it.

What had just transpired? He realized it was important.

But for the life of him, he could not remember.

\I/

Peter seemed blanked out about this morning's appointment.

The emptiness behind his eyes was difficult for her to read. Most of the time, she kept quiet and it passed.

Gabby drove Peter and Rachel to Dr. Ringel's Spartanburg clinic. Peter had not been crazy about her sister going with them but, *tough toodie*. Rachel needed Gabby. It was no longer all about Peter.

Heavens to murgatroyd. Together, she and Peter had such an explosion of baggage to place under one roof. She had to not only survive all this but she had to *heal* in order to carry Peter during his dark times.

After Gabby parked her car, still the only vehicle into which Rachel's bionic-like leg fit, Peter unfolded the wheelchair and brought it around for Rachel's transfer. Inside, their wait stretched long, during which Peter went outdoors. Rachel watched him through the glass windows, pacing tensely outside on the sun-washed sidewalk, back and forth, his ear plugged to the cell phone.

Her heart went out to him. His duties never stopped. No doubt the caller was his helper, Gary, discussing rental repairs that continually popped up. Or worse still, a utility company employee, scolding him for a late payment.

Fiftyish Dr. Ringel was a pleasant, clean-cut man who immediately put them at ease by chatting about his own rental properties, having seen Peter's work information on his chart. Rachel could see Peter slowly relaxing as he shared his expertise with the doctor.

Then Dr. Ringel asked him, "What day is it?"

Peter's face grew tense. "Thursday," he said without hesitation.

Blaaaah! Wrong answer.

"What year is it?"

Peter, not one to cower, threw out, "1999."

Blaaaah!

"Who's the president?"

Peter hesitated and then decisively, "Clinton."

Blaaaah!

"Who's the vice president?"

Blaaaah!

Peter's confusion tormented his sea mist eyes.

Rachel could stand it no longer. "Peter," she said gently. "Take your time."

The doctor held up a cautioning hand. "Don't interfere. Let him answer. Who's the vice president?"

Peter, still bluffing it, said, "Ford."

Rachel's heart fell to her feet. Peter never seemed this befuddled. Why now? She knew that stress would badly affect his presence of mind. But this—

Her hopes, that the memory bleeps were somehow harmless and inconsequential, burst like an overblown balloon and smacked her in the face.

The doctor, bless him, did not address the bleeps. Instead he scheduled a series of tests for the following week. Peter said little on the way home but his features remained tense and closed. Gabby, for once, was silent as falling snow.

Not until Gabby dropped them off at home and left did Peter say, "He shouldn't have come at me like that. If he'd told me he was going to test me, I would've been prepared a little. When he started throwing all those questions at me like that— my mind just shut down."

Rachel held out her arms to him. He came to sit on the side of her bed where they embraced each other, resting against her pillow cushions. She stroked his temples and murmured soothing words.

"Honey, they haven't done the tests yet. Dr. Ringel said that there were a couple of things that could possibly be affecting your short-term memory, besides Alzheimer's. We'll just trust in the Lord and pray like crazy."

"Yeah," he muttered. "There's still not a diagnosis, is there?"

"Nope. So just relax and let's enjoy each moment."

He snuggled closer. "Sounds like a winner to me."

\\/

The next week brought with it a bustle of activity.

The Mind Streams Assessment testing drove Peter up the wall. "They left me in the room with a computer and told me to click on the images that were alike. Rachel, I told the lady that I was computer illiterate. Like 'read my lips' I. Do. Not. Know. How. To follow simple instructions. She just walked out and left me there to fend for myself."

He threw his arms wide as he paced across the bedroom and back. "I started out the test with my nerves in a wad!" He turned his tormented gaze on her. "And you know what that does to my mind."

"Ah, honey," she said, reaching out to him from her bed. "C'mere." He slid into her embrace and lay there with her until his panic began to subside.

"Remember this, Peter," she murmured. "These tests do not define you. It says on the NeuroTrax Disclaimer that this assessment does not render a neuropsychological diagnosis or any treatment recommendations. Dr. Ringel, consequently, has not given us a definite diagnosis of Alzheimer's. So, we can move in faith and take the medications known to help or slow down memory loss, trusting for a good outcome."

"You think so?"

"I know so. We won't let anyone or anything dictate that you won't come out of this intact. Who knows? A cure could be just over the horizon. We must think like this, Peter."

"Yeah. You're right. We'll do what the Bible says . . . 'think on good things.'"

"Y'know, this entire experience—both our voyages—has made me think more about my mortality and given me a more carpe diem approach to life."

"What's carpe d—?"

"Carpe diem means to seize the moment. You've already said that you live in the moment. That's not all bad. I now know what's important in life, Peter. Not money, though we need it to survive. Nor fame. If I become another Pat Conroy or Nora Roberts is not the important thing. It's the time I spent making cookies with Amber and going to Jason's ball games and singing with them when they were happy. It's the time I spend now with you, each moment . . . snuggling and kissing and—"

"And what?" he raised his head to gaze into her eyes with such hangdog longing that—incredibly—she burst into laughter.

Then he too dissolved into guffaws. "I'm pathetic, huh?"

"You are, you big ol' hunk, you. See? I'm just as big a goofball. But soon, we'll be able to put this insanity to rest."

"When?" he reached to move a stray hair wisp from her forehead.

"Soon as we get this iron cast off my leg."

"Carpe diem, huh?" His eyes drank her in.

"Yup. Carpe diem."

\!/

Healing.

She knew it was happening because she only had to look back to weeks before, right after the fall, and see how far she'd come.

But land sakes alive, it was so slow she sometimes doubted it was happening.

Rachel tried to explain to Gabby one day how topsy-turvy her psyche now operated. She talked as she worked the five-pound weight lifts with both her arms and good leg. Her injured limb received therapy but not yet with weights.

"It's like—my inner battery has been altered since the trauma. The positive- and negative-charge synchronization is so off-kilter that I can't even explain it. At times, I'm hyper with purpose and direction when at others, I'm in meltdown, lower and shiftier than a sidewinder's belly, going round and round in circles. There's little middle ground in this ol' girl. Not yet, anyway. I'm still grasping for trust."

Gabby rocked sedately in the small bedroom chair, thoughtful. "You'll find it, honey. Just hang in there, like you've been doing. By the way, I'm proud of you and the way you dig into the therapy exercises. Tomorrow, I'm going to see that you do a real shower bath."

"Can't wait," Rachel huffed while doing knee lifts while sitting on the bed's edge.

On the bed, propped up on pillows, Rachel flexed the upper thigh muscles in her bad leg and held them till the count of ten, then relaxed. It was not painful, surprisingly.

"Lizzie said I needed to keep building strength in every uninjured muscle," Rachel said between sets. As the PT had predicted, as she worked on every muscle in her body Rachel could feel strength slowly building as the days passed.

"Wish I could build up my emotional stamina so easily," she said, lifting the five-pound arm weights.

"It's coming, honey. You'll see. Soon, you'll be good as new."

The next morning, true to promise, Gabby, with Drusilla's help, wrapped Rachel's hard-wared and casted leg with a large plastic garbage bag, waterproofed thigh high with tape, and watched as Rachel pondered hoisting herself onto the heavy duty sliding transfer bench placed across the tub.

"Piece of cake," said a naked Rachel as she transferred from chair to bench, sliding herself with her conditioned arms to the center. With her hands she propped her heavy, shrouded right leg onto the side of the tub while sliding her good leg into the deliciously warm water of the filled tub. She couldn't yet submerge her entire body into it because of the threat of water to her injury sites and also, she was not yet able to lower herself so low and climb back up and out.

Once taken-for-granted goals now loomed like steep, jagged rock fortresses to conquer.

"One more thing," Gabby reminded her, holding up the waterproof neck brace. Rachel loosened the Velcro straps and swiftly exchanged old faithful for the waterproof one, while Gabby held her head to prop up her neck in the process. She noticed that the slightest tilt made her neck feel rubbery and useless, unable to support her head.

Gabby turned on the hosed showerhead adapter, testing the water with her inner wrist before passing it on to Rachel, who began hosing every inch of flesh she could reach.

"Aaahh, this is heavenly," she murmured, then grabbed the nylon scrubby and soused it with Bath & Body Works shower gel. She began scrubbing and nearly swooned from the scrumptious Sea Island Cotton fragrance.

While Drusilla washed then rinsed her back, Rachel cried out, "I feel almost human again!"

"Just tilt your head back a little," Gabby instructed and took the shower hose and began irrigating her hair.

"*Gina Lollobrigida,*" Rachel moaned. "Do that all day."

Drusilla handed Gabby a floral smelling shampoo and she lathered, getting down inside the top of the brace to reach Rachel's entire scalp and gently massage. She rinsed, then lathered once more. The final rinse convinced Rachel she was once more not only human, but squeaky clean.

A glorious feeling.

The reverse transfer this time was more involved because of her sopping wetness, but Rachel felt so revitalized in those moments, she didn't mind the extra effort it took to slide over to place her legs over the tub's rim, twisting sideways to face the wheelchair, her goal.

"Can I help?" Drusilla asked.

"I got it," Rachel insisted.

There, she turbaned her wet head and then toweled her good leg and body as dry as possible—while Gabby and Drusilla removed the plastic garbage bag from the casted leg—before transferring to the towel-draped chair for the ride to her room where her clean clothes lay ready and waiting.

Rachel had insisted from the get-go that she dress herself and do her makeup as usual each day. That also included working with the tangled hair and blow drying it until she could fashion a ponytail and then exchange the plastic waterproof neck brace with her softer, more colorful one.

Propped in bed, she looked into the mirror across the room and liked what she saw; a more alive Rachel than she'd seen in weeks.

Maybe she'd make it yet.

\\//

Angels began to pop up at the James residence.

Church friends, Rollie and Sheila called the third week following Rachel's homecoming. "We're going to bring a meal tonight. Will around six be okay?" Rollie asked in his deep, warm voice.

Rachel's heart lifted. "Ahh, Rollie." Gratitude stirred inside her, like rich, warm chocolate. "Six-ish would be great. This is so sweet of you and Sheila."

"Hey, we didn't even know you'd had an accident until we saw you at church in the wheelchair. We feel bad that we haven't already reached out to you and Peter."

"Well, I'm overwhelmed with your kindness. And I look forward to seeing you." The gesture lifted Rachel to new heights. By six, she was rested enough to be a little excited—well, as wound up as an android could be. But, *fiddlesticks*, she would take any affirmative emotion handed to her.

Her friends arrived, arms loaded with fragrant fare. Rachel sat on her bed and invited them to visit for a spell.

"No," Sheila replied. "We want you to eat while it's hot. We'll visit while you eat." The lovely blonde who sang church specials like an angel—who also could have been a model—transported entrées to the kitchen counter as Peter pulled up chairs for them and Rachel wheeled in and positioned her own seat at the table.

"Aren't you going to join us?" Peter asked as he poured tea over ice.

"We already ate before we came. You two go ahead and dig in." Rollie, a tall, clean-cut big-farmer guy was equipped with endless good cheer. In fact, together, the duo gave off such positive vibes that, as Rachel tucked into the feast of luscious rotisserie chicken, seasoned mixed veggies, braised potatoes, and a rich dessert, she felt absolutely coddled.

Conversation flowed comfortably and by the time their friends departed, both Rachel and Peter talked of how the bountiful love of friends was so healing and affirming.

The next week, Jim and Frieda called ahead and then dropped by. They, too, brought along a love gift of succulent baked Cornish hens and upbeat camaraderie, offering prayer for Rachel's recovery before departing.

Another evening Terry and Mary Lou visited and shared fantastic, still warm home-cooked cinnamon rolls. *Nom nom.* Rachel noticed that each time such affection abounded, her spirit would lift—at least momentarily—from the pit that seemed determined to own it.

Friends. *Such gifts.*

She especially liked those who didn't want their identity kept secret.

Then one day, Frieda called to check on Rachel. Up till now, Rachel had been able to talk for short periods on the phone. The conversation was pleasant. But Rachel suddenly felt her energy begin to dissipate. Her friend, a marvelous holistic doctor, was suggesting treatment options for her recovery when Rachel's head began to spin.

"Frieda," Rachel muttered. "I can't do this."

"What?"

"I can't go this deep in—discussing this."

A short silence. "Oh. Okay, Rachel. I'll let you go." Kindly and considerate—yet, Rachel was aware of disappointment. But she wasn't able to articulate beyond what she'd already expressed. She'd simply drained out.

Rachel rang off. She felt badly but wasn't able to grieve over the limitations she now bore. It was a big switch from the old Rachel, who would have spent sleepless nights flogging herself for such insensitivity. Now, her mindset was altered to survival mode. It was something over which she had no control. And she trusted that true friends would come to understand that. Gentle, patient, courteous Rachel now had limitations.

She had to live with it.

"It's okay," Peter soothed her when she shared it with him. "She'll understand. She loves you."

"Thanks honey. Did you take your pills today?"

"Mmm, I don't remember."

"Check and see if the little bowl is empty. If so, you took them. I dole them into the bowl each night and set them on the counter each morning. Gabby checks behind me. Go check." It was one of the things she *could* do.

Peter left then and within moments was back and climbed into bed beside her. "I took them."

"Great."

She felt him looking at her. With the neck brace, she couldn't turn her head to return the love gaze. "Why do I love you so?" His question was pensive. Reverent.

She smiled. "'Cause I'm so *good*," she drawled and was rewarded by a full belly laugh.

"That you are," he said, reaching to take her hand in his, still chuckling. "I'm still amazed that, in all the world, we found each other. How do you think that happened?"

Rachel struggled to focus in on it. "Because it was ordained."

"You think so?"

"Absolutely."

"I do, too." He rolled over and placed his arm across her. "We've always fit perfectly."

She smiled and enjoyed a moment of peace and contentment, things in short supply these days.

He held her hand as they lay together and fingers of night began to surrender the setting sun. Neither knew what tomorrow would bring. But right now, they were together in the sweet and same old way.

For tonight, that was enough.

\\/

In private moments, Peter felt the pinch of guilt.

It sat heavily upon him. So he tried to drown it with work and spending every possible moment with Rachel. Only thing, together, the two goals could prove to be counterproductive.

Today, he drove his pest control route, trying to cover all his accounts. Some months lately, he was leaving money out there. That hurt his finances. He found that some days, he just didn't feel like running the race. Even at that moment, his heart was urging him to turn toward home.

To Rachel.

He pulled his cell phone from his side holster and punched in her number.

"Hey, darlin'," she answered. She sounded weak. Not good.

"Just wanted to hear your voice. You okay?"

"Mmm, more tired than usual. Resting for a few minutes before trying it again. Gabby's cooking us some pinto beans for this evening. I'm going to try to sit at the table and do some cornbread to go with them. We'll see."

"I'm so proud of you." His eyes welled with tears.

She huffed a little laugh. "Thanks. Wait till later to praise me, though. I can hardly hold my eyes open right now."

"Want me to come home?" *Please say yes.*

"No need, honey. I'd love to have you here but you need to get your route done. You'll feel so good to accomplish that."

"Yeah." He knew she was right. And suddenly, he felt bolstered. Protective. Felt the provider in him rise up. How in *Sam Hill* did she do that? Balance him out?

"Cut up a Vidalia sweet onion to go with that and you'll have one happy guy on your hands, darlin'."

"I'm sure Gabby already has that on the order. Love you."

They rang off and instantly, he felt bereft.

Regardless of his ingenuity he could not be in two places at once. "No way, José," Jason would have said, laughing that uninhibited hoot of his. Then, thinking of Jason, his mind automatically ricocheted to Mark, the son to whom he was forbidden access.

Ah, the twilight hours of grief he experienced over that one.

He wondered sometimes if maybe folks should not be as happy as the two of them were way back then. Maybe they'd not suffered enough. But losing Jason was not fair. The beautiful boy hadn't had a chance to live life to the fullest. Cut down at thirteen when he could have lived to be a hundred.

Humpty Dumpty—all the king's horses and all the king's men couldn't put the pieces back together once they'd been shattered.

On top of that struggle, his finances harassed his mind. Before her accident, Rachel had begun to help keep track of monthly bills. Now, with her out of the equation, he trudged along a dark maze of elusive, *terrifying*, numbers and deadlines. For a man with perfect credit, delinquency was his ultimate horror.

Bottom line: he could not bother Rachel with any of it now, not with her stability so fragile. Occasionally, he slipped and complained and was forced to witness her plunge into a distress she did not ask for nor deserve. No, he would have to watch it.

But it was driving him nuts, trying to keep track of what bills he'd paid and what statements still floated around out there. And balancing the checkbook was literal hell on earth. He'd thought of asking Gabby to help but quickly nixed that idea. He cringed at the idea of exposing his vulnerability and inadequacies. Only Rachel loved him with the love that covers all; the unhampered kind.

On some level, he knew The Gang loved him like that, too. But—he wasn't yet ready to risk losing their esteem. He was aware that they overlooked his little short-term memory lapses and for that, he could kiss the ground they walked on.

He wheeled into the next residence, pulled out his back pack and sprayer, and commenced treating the dwelling's outside perimeter, wondering how long he could continue this activity, day in, day out?

Please, Lord, help me to stay strong and well.

Rachel needs me.

\I/

Gabby set the charming pink cake on the counter and turned to wash up the breakfast dishes.

"You bake it?" Rachel asked as she sipped coffee at the table.

Gabby turned, hands on hips. "What? You don't think I can bake a cake?"

Rachel laughed. "I know you can but it's not something you would usually do—that is, without having a monumental event to justify it." She watched Gabby, who had gotten inordinately busy, eyes averted.

Rachel felt a subtle tension about her sister. "Did you or did you not bake the cake?" she asked.

"No," Gabby snapped. "A lady from church sent it. She brought it last night to prayer service and wanted me to bring it to you." As of yet, Rachel's stamina did not stretch to church attendance beyond Sunday morning services.

Rachel frowned. "Why are you so uptight about this? Who was—"

Gabby whirled and faced her. "That's why I'm so uptight." She did an elaborate sweep of hand. "You just cannot let things go without analyzing and taking it apart, piece by piece and—"

"That's the writer in me," Rachel retorted, stung by the reprimand.

Seeing Rachel's hurt, Gabby immediately backpedaled. "Ah, honey. I'm sorry. Someone wanted to do something nice for you without you knowing who, that's all." She turned away and resumed her tidying. "You'll have to excuse my impatience. Leon and I had a little tiff this morning, is all. I'm having to even out."

Rachel didn't believe for a moment that Gabby and Leon had a tiff. Those two didn't engage in unresolved issues. Gabby was a pit bull when in battle and did not let go until a firm truce issued forth. Rachel didn't know what was going on but it really didn't matter, did it? Someone had done something nice for her.

Besides, the friction had already fizzled. Rachel could no longer hold onto anything cerebral for long—it was, as she was fond of telling Peter, "gone with the wind." In many ways, the inability to stay focused was a blessing.

That became a joke between Peter and her. Their like-lapses.

His incessant, *"What day is this?"* earned a snappy *"You're asking me?"* Followed by laughter. Yep. They were now soul-mates in every sense of the word.

Today, the strawberry cake intrigued Rachel. She'd not been attracted to sweets since the accident but this gift was so colorful and *Southern Homes* perfect she wheeled over to examine it more closely. She inhaled the pleasant strawberry fragrance.

"It looks delicious," Rachel muttered, reaching up to gouge a fingertip of frothy icing and plop it in her mouth. "Mmm, this *is* good." However, the sugary taste sent her stomach a little jolt. "Peter loves strawberry cake. The Gang will have to come over

212 *Emily Sue Harvey*

tonight and help us eat it. You be sure to tell the secret angel 'thank you' for me, will you, sis?"

"Definitely." Gabby turned and smiled. Then she came to lean over and hug Rachel as soundly as she could while invading turtleneck brace province. "I love you, sweet sister. Bunches and bunches."

"Me, too," Rachel whispered, thankful for love and hugs—things now topping her "need" bucket list.

"Did you order the curcumin supplements for Peter?" she asked Gabby, who now waged war on the floor with a dust mop.

"Last night, great sale—Puritan Pride's buy one, get two free." The mop slapped crumbs from beneath the table onto the little pile collecting at the back door. "I actually ended up getting five for the price of two. Around sixty dollars. Not bad. One thousand milligrams, one a day. Should do him for about ten months. I read all the info and they're great for the memory plus some tests show they fight cancer and other ailments. Should boost his memory, along with the pill he's already on."

"That's great." Rachel had not yet been able to sit at her computer desk to do anything beyond a quick email check and occasionally, an abbreviated glance at Facebook. Her elevated, steel-shrouded leg throbbed too much for sit-sessions beyond that.

That's where Gabby took up the slack.

Gabby, God's gift to her.

Gabby was now—in Peter's absence—her right hand, who kept her home going and her nerves from dissipating into a smoldering heap or torpedoing over the moon. Who cared enough to outwit Peter and control his meds and supplements to the tiniest milligram. Who loved above and beyond the call of family duty. Whose strong shoulder was always there for her little sis.

And who searched the Internet for Alzheimer's updates and then ordered the latest available holistic treatments.

"Her name is Dot."

The words floated, disjointed and indistinct. Rachel frowned. "What?"

Gabby scooped debris onto the dustpan and headed for the kitchen garbage container. "The angel who sent the cake. Her name is Dot. And that's all I'm gonna tell you, Miss Nosy."

Rachel sighed. *Great.* A couple thousand members and with a common name like Dot, it was like hunting a four-leaf clover in a verdant pasture.

Curiosity stirring, she squinted, trying to think. But, predictably, her mind rebelled, shutting down until she couldn't remember what she was trying to remember.

She swiveled her chair toward her bedroom.

Rest called her name.

\|/

"I don't feel right about it," Peter told Rachel at the breakfast table.

Rachel chewed on a mouthful of blueberries. She loathed these moments of melancholy contemplations that intermittently struck her husband. In recent days, he obsessed about things he once would've squashed like a blasted mosquito.

"Honey, Gabby's always teased you like this. Why—"

"But does she have to be so mean?" He scowled. "I mean— teasing is okay but it can get to be belittling. You know?" Indignation arose and so did his nose. "My poor yellow coat gets gunned down daily." He crossed his arms. "I happen to love that yellow coat."

Orange! Rachel quickly doused the on-the-tip-of-her-tongue retort.

True, Gabby could get downright nasty in a wit-battle but it was all in fun.

"J.C. doesn't get bent out of joint when Gabby comes at him with claws bared," she reminded him, shrugging, the movement rippling pain throughout her neck region. Why did Peter invite a burr into the seat of his pants? She fought frustration because it only ricocheted back to kick her in her tender hiney.

"Besides," she reminded him. "Yesterday, after you told Gabby you didn't want to argue anymore with her, she backed off and re-focused on J.C. Then, jumping Jehoshaphat, you plunged back into the middle of the fray, knowing good and well how she'd react."

Peter took a sip of his coffee, still surly, ignoring the obvious. "I'm not J.C. and I can't help it if I get overloaded with Gabby's acidosis ways."

"Acidic," Rachel muttered, annoyance sapping her strength. Peter looked at her, puzzled.

"The word is not acidosis, Peter. It's *acidic, Gabby's. Acidic. Ways.*"

Seeing his obsessing kick in, she knocked the brake loose and whirled the chair toward her room, wheeling furiously to her haven. Her fortress. Her cave.

Sometimes, that is.

Not today. Peter followed her, solicitously hovering as she transferred to bed and grabbed her exercise weights from her bedside table and commenced to do her arm lifts.

Peter dragged the glider around to face her. "I'm sorry to bother you, honey. I don't mean to unload on you. Just forget what I said about Gabby. I'll get over it. You just concentrate on getting better. I'm so proud of you. You've come so far."

"Thank you," Rachel said on the twentieth arm-weight lift. "I try."

"You do more than try, honey." He shook his head slowly watching her with a look of pure adoration. "How in the world did I ever get you?"

"Easy." Rachel switched the weight to the other hand. "You just kept coming back." Then she gave him what she hoped was a big smile while pumping her weight.

He laughed out loud. "Best answer yet."

She halted her exercise and said, "Why don't you go on and start your pest control route? Gabby should be here in the next hour or so. I'll be fine here by myself. I can get to anything I need and this way, you'll be through by mid-afternoon." And besides, she wanted to stretch her self-sufficiency muscles. She had to stop being helpless.

Peter looked uncertain. "You sure you'll be okay? I don't like to leave you alone. What if something happens while—"

"Look—what can happen? Huh? I'll most likely stay right here, propped in bed until Gabby gets here. She's only five minutes away and I can call her in case an emergency arises."

She doused the prospect of actually having to flee the house for some unforeseen reason, such as a sudden fire. The steps, without assistance from someone at the ramp, could pose grave problems.

He sighed deeply and stood, walked over, and took her hand, gazing down at her in his indulgent way. "Okay. I just hate to leave you is all." He leaned in and kissed her soundly on the lips then slipped into his neon orange jacket to ward off the day's early February chill. The infamous coat that drew Gabby's merciless teasing.

As soon as he disappeared out the door, Rachel switched on her TV and, for the next hour, tuned in to her morning spiritual teachers. Since she could not yet read the Bible—or for that matter, any text—without her nervous system being battered, she would attempt to soak up some divine provisions via the airwaves. After all, God didn't say you absolutely had to read the Word at all times, did He? No, He did not.

He said in Romans 10:17 "So then faith cometh by hearing and hearing by the word of God."

Hearing.

That's how she was now fed faith. Via her ears.

At the end of Joyce Meyer's daily fare, Rachel heard Gabby's key turning the deadlock.

"*Yoo hoo?* It's me!" Gabby's Reebok footsteps squished to the kitchen where she would check out the needs for today.

Rachel called out, "I didn't feel like putting the dishes in the sink."

To fight the sense of uselessness that gripped her, she'd taken to scraping out the dishes and stacking them on the counter next to the sink. Peter filled the sink with hot soapy water into which went the dishes, awaiting Gabby's full attention.

It was a small gesture but Rachel felt compelled to make the effort, maneuvering the chair around and hefting objects back and forth. With the extra upper body strength, she could cope okay with it. Today, Peter's obsessing about Gabby's irascible ways sapped what little drive she had. She hadn't felt up to the extra struggle.

"Hey, sis, that's what I'm here for." Gabby rinsed the plate and placed it in the drain. "You don't have to lift a finger as far as I'm concerned. You just be a good girl and do your therapy and rest as much as possible. Okay?"

"'Kay." Rachel heard clinking dishes and silverware swishing through water. Tears suddenly burned behind her eyes. Her sweet, giving sister. On the heel of that, she replayed Peter's *"she can be so mean"* comment and it tore into her. She closed her eyes tightly and felt her head begin to spin.

She opened them and took deep, long, calming breaths.

Lord help me. She would simply have to bear up and get over it. Somehow, she must regain a smidgeon of control over her emotions. How?

Time, said that still small voice. Sometimes that silent voice irritated her with its patience.

With its veracity. Time heals all wounds. Wasn't that the famous adage?

Yeah, yeah, she knew that. But in the meantime—she couldn't afford to fall apart every time Peter spun off into ambiguity and insecurity *or whatever.*

When Gabby finally finished up the daily tidying and joined her for a pre-lunch visit, sedately gliding back and forth in the little rocker, Rachel switched the TV to Sirius XM Escape music. Like a divine beacon of light, "Twilight Time" began to play. It wasn't the Platters' version but a soft orchestral arrangement that calmed Rachel as no other music had since the accident.

Suddenly, her mind felt loosened yet attentive—sort of like watching through a turning kaleidoscope cylinder with mirrors containing loose colored beads or bits of glass . . . and light enters from the other end.

The light creates a vibrant pattern due to the reflection off the mirrors.

That's the way Rachel's psyche settled onto a beautiful solution for the latest ill-timed peace hurdle between her sister and husband.

The truth.

"*Here . . . in the afterglow of day . . .*" Gabby warbled along with the orchestra.

"Gabby," Rachel interrupted her. "I need to talk to you."

Gabby blinked, then a wary, "Okaaay."

"Remember how you used to make Drusilla scream and cry when you teased her about being too skinny?"

Gabby mused, and then grinned. "Sure do." She shook her head, still grinning. "But I also remember how she used to sneak in my Barbie clothes collection and stuff them in her pockets to make off with 'em." She pursed her lips. "Yep. It was pretty tit for tat."

"Yeah, but making fun of something she couldn't help was a little mean, don't you think?"

"Oh, I don't know—"

"C'mon Gabby. You know it was mean. Because it was about *her*, not some replaceable thing."

Gabby thought about it for a long moment, rocking back and forth, back and forth in the glider. "Yeah. It was mean. But Drusilla was too thin-skinned, don't you think?"

"She couldn't help how she was wired, sis. Some folks are more sensitive than others. And they can't help it."

"What's this all about, Rachel?" Gabby's perception sharpened, narrowing her eyes.

"Peter's sensitive, too. Like Dru. And he's feeling sad that the two of you aren't always as nice to each other as you used to be. He misses that. I guess it has to do with my being laid up and not as 'there' as I usually am. But he's feeling—"

"Vulnerable," Gabby said gently. She smiled. "Why didn't you say so before now?" She shrugged. "*Jiminy Jack.* He seems to enjoy sparring as much as I do."

"He does. To a point. But lately it's gotten a bit—"

"Out of hand."

"Right."

Gabby arose stiffly from the glider, strode to the bed, and kissed Rachel's cheek. "Thanks for telling me, sis. Openness is the best policy."

Gabby glanced at her watch. "Time to fix us a sandwich." She yawned then stretched soundly before turning toward the kitchen.

"Did you thank Dot for me?" Rachel asked. "For the strawberry cake?"

Gabby turned back. "Sure did."

"I'd like to meet her. It's terribly nice of her to go out of her way to do such a nice thing." But Gabby had already about-faced through the door.

"Ham or chicken?" she called over her shoulder.

And Rachel—curiosity brimming—knew.

The angel subject was closed. Why?

Chapter Ten

\\ / /

"Kind words can be short and easy to speak but their echoes are truly endless."
—*Mother Teresa*

Mark closed his hard-bound journal. He'd just poured out his heart on those lined pages and felt only a smidgeon better. Sometimes the venting relieved him. Seemed lately, however, that the hurt around his heart just plain didn't want to turn loose.

He hid the diary under his mattress and pulled on his jacket to dash outside to do his after school chores, which involved feeding the Hereford sow, Hortense and her rapidly budding piglets. Little Petunia was a beauty, as piglets go, with her plump, rustic red body, white head and feet, and pink snout.

In the barn, fifty-pound bags of Hortense and her babies' meals sat stacked in a corner. He prepared the premixed blend of ground corn, soybeans, oats, and wheat, with added all-natural supplements. His dad was picky about what he fed their farm animals. Everything they used was organic, with no chemicals added. Even the animals' compost served as fertilizer for the fruit orchards and gardens.

As Mark neared the pigpens, he heard the piglets squeal a gleeful welcome at spotting the arriving feast. At least that's how he surmised it. He poured the mixture and stood back to enjoy the exuberant feasting, his eye trained on Little Petunia, who got rooted out, during which he would cheer her on. "Get back in there, Petunia!"

He admired her stubborn attempts to comply and laughed from his belly when she got bumped aside again and took a comical tumble. Nonplussed, she proceeded to reclaim another gap for long moments before the drama played out again.

He deduced that she got her tiny belly full during those brief moments of feeding because when he picked her up, she looked contented.

It was her little snorting sounds that tickled his fancy and made him laugh and forget how messy she was from feeding. Sometimes, he would declare that she laughed with him. Oh, he loved the others in the litter but Petunia looked at him differently, as though she could understand the gibberish he spoke to her.

"Mark! Suppertime!" his mother's voice called from the back door.

He wiped his hands on his pants as he trudged toward the white dwelling. He'd wash up inside.

He wasn't hungry. Hadn't been lately. Too much drama going on around their house. Not home. House. Only place he felt truly at home was outside with the animals. They were his true friends. They loved him unconditionally and, with them, he belonged.

That made him feel he served some purpose here on earth.

Not at school.

Definitely not at school. He wished he didn't ever have to go back there.

Not at church. Especially after Ralph had decided to resign his deacon's post, despite the pastor's objections. And though his stepdad had not in any way blamed him, Mark knew in his bones that the resignation was all because of him and his lies.

So he had no place to call his own, no niche of warmth and security.

Mark did feel that warmth at Gramma's but outside of there, it had gone off somewhere far away.

And he didn't like the feeling.

\|/

The next morning, Mark dragged his feet while getting ready for school. Good thing it was Friday. He could grit his teeth and endure one more day before the weekend break. The bus ride was all too quick.

He entered his classroom with head lowered, looking at the floor, ignoring his teacher's greeting and sliding into his desk, plopping his books on the desktop and stuffing his fists into his pockets. The class seemed interminable, as did the next two.

Lunch time. His second hell on earth.

The trek through the lunch line blurred as he selected indiscriminately, not even thinking about his choices. He headed straight for the very back corner to claim an empty table and turn his back to the room.

There, he was astonished to see that he'd selected two orders of potato entrées and no pizza, his favorite. But he didn't care. The potatoes tasted like sawdust anyway. Only thing tasty was the cold milk.

"Need company?"

Mark's head jerked around and Stinky Dodger stood hesitantly across from him.

Stunned, Mark shrugged. "Suit yourself," he muttered tersely and, determined not to show his unease, took another bite of French fry, more tasty than the mashed variety.

"Say, you didn't get pizza," Stinky commented evenly.

"Nope."

Mark took a big gulp of milk to wash down the fry as Stinky disappeared and then returned with a plate bearing a huge slice of Mark's favorite pepperoni and cheese pizza.

"Thought you might enjoy this," Stinky muttered uncomfortably.

Mark tried to say "thanks," out of habit and training, but just could not force it past his lips. Instead he coolly took a big bite of Stinky's offering. The next few minutes, they ate silently.

As Mark began to gather his tray and leftovers, Stinky said, "Wait."

Mark frowned at him and sat back down. "What?" His voice was cold.

"Look," Stinky wet his lips and his freckled face flushed, at odds with his carrot top head. "I'm sorry, Mark. I've been a real jerk to you."

Mark stared at him. Was this for real? He must have narrowed his eyes because Stinky held out an entreating hand.

"I'm on the level here. I really am. Fact is, I wonder if—" Stinky's eyes dropped as tears welled up.

Mark peered at him, astonished. "Wonder what?"

Stinky blinked and a tear splashed over. He quickly swiped at it, his gaze darting to see if anyone was looking. Apparently safe, he whispered, "I wondered if you could, you know, forgive me?"

Of all the things Stinky Dodger could have said, that was the last Mark expected. He shook his head and continued to gaze, trying to grasp—no, to envision—the olive branch his mortal enemy seemed to be offering.

He crossed his arms and slanted a skeptical gaze. "How do I know you're not—"

"Pulling your chain?" Stinky shook his head so desperately that Mark felt the ice around his heart begin to crack.

"I know I've always been a—bully of sorts," Stinky confessed without bravado. "But I've taken a good look at myself in the past few days." His lip trembled but he swallowed soundly and looked Mark in the eye. "And I don't like what I see. I talked with the pastor about my—" He shrugged and dropped his gaze again. "You know—how mean I was to you about your daddy and all." He looked at Mark again, heart in eyes. "That was totally out of line, man. Fact was, I was jealous of you, Mark.

You're always so happy and you live on that big ol' farm and have such good parents and everybody likes you."

He looked at the floor, face morose. Mark thought how he looked like an old, beaten man and his heart melted a little more.

"Anyway, the pastor helped me see how you can't build yourself up by tearing somebody else down. And that's what I tried to do." He gave a lopsided smile. "And you just wouldn't tear down, Mark. Know that? You're strong, man. You don't have to be top dog."

Mark found himself smiling back.

"I mean it, dude. You're top dog without even trying." The smile vanished. "Do you think—"

"Think what?" Mark asked.

He saw Stinky buck up, chin out and determined. "Do you think we can be friends?" Hesitantly, he held out his hand.

Mark fought back a big ol' Cheshire grin. Rather he smiled pleasantly and gripped the extended hand. "Don't see why not, Stinky."

Stinky couldn't hide his elation as he pumped Mark's hand for long moments.

Mark grew serious. "One more thing?"

"What's that?"

"Do you want me to stop calling you Stinky?"

Stinky's grin grew. "You kiddin'? That's my sole claim to fame!"

They burst into laughter and ventured together to dump their trays as other students gaped speculatively at them, curiosity brimming over the abrupt truce.

\1/

Rachel watched the orthopedic surgeon, Dr. Legett, cut the cast off her leg.

Air kissed the sensitive skin for the first time in months. "Everything looks fine," he decreed as he removed the stitches from each side of her ankle, the surgery sites. The small stings were little to pay for the freedom of movement.

"You're good to go," Dr. Legett said, smiling. "You can bear weight on it now."

Rachel felt like leaping up to touch the clouds. That lasted until Gabby and Drusilla wheeled her back to the car and she stood, trying for the first time to bear weight on the injured member.

"Aiiiaii!" She grabbed onto the car door, dizzy from the shock of pain that imploded out the top of her head and along every nerve ending in her body.

"Here," Drusilla gently helped her regain her balance, after which Rachel pivoted and transferred to the passenger seat of Gabby's car. "You're going to have to take it slowly," she added, then shut the door and got into the back seat.

"No kidding," Rachel grumbled, still reeling. Her heart plunged to an all-time low. She'd thought it would be smooth, instant sailing. She laid her head back against the headrest and closed her eyes, inwardly groaning. She'd taken Shaun's "Do your therapy and when you get on your feet, you'll take off" literally.

It wouldn't be that simple.

"You okay?" Gabby peered at her as she started the car. "Sorry, honey."

"Me, too," she groaned. Then sighed heavily.

"Hey!" Drusilla crowed over her shoulder. "Did you hear what the doc said? He said you could get in the tub, Rachel. You can get that blasted leg wet!"

That got her attention.

"Yeah," Gabby joined in. "No more wrapping your leg in plastic garbage bags and sitting over the water, using that awkward shower hose. Isn't that wonderful?"

Rachel appreciated their efforts to cheer her and pushed herself to blend into the celebratory atmosphere. "It is. Can't wait for bathtub paradise."

And she realized that without the steel brace and cast, her leg felt light and not nearly as tender. But she was still dependent upon the wheelchair. For the time being.

Not for long, however. The overcomer rose up in her and she was determined that she would soon fulfill therapist Shaun's prophesy.

\ı⁄

She'd never appreciated a full bath so much in her entire life.

Peter insisted upon being with Rachel during her first experience the next morning. And Rachel was glad because, despite the extensive daily physical exercises to strengthen both her upper and lower body, the lowering of herself into the tub was difficult. So Peter stood behind her, propped his foot on the back ledge of the tub and the other firmly on the floor, and hoisted her gently down into the water.

With her waterproof neck brace in place, she lay back in the water and shampooed her own hair, sliding down and dipping low to rinse it thoroughly. How marvelous it felt.

After she soaked and scrubbed all over to her heart's content, Peter repeated the transfer process, firmly lifting her to a sitting position on the side of the tub. From there, Rachel could dry off and transfer back to her chair.

How incredible the freedom was. How life affirming. At the same time, Peter suggested that Rachel try dosing again with Meloxicam at bedtime.

"That way, you won't have to fight dizziness but drift off to sleep. And the anti-inflammatory benefits will kick in."

It worked.

Another healing hurdle victory.

\ı⁄

The walker came into serious play again.

This time, Rachel really needed it to get back up on her feet. "I hate sitting in that chair. The world looks different from a standing position—less overpowering," she told Gabby that morning as she pulled up to the kitchen counter to do some of the physical therapy exercises Lizzie had given her.

"Lizzie told me to stand at the counter as much as I can. I'll build strength just by standing. At the same time, I'll be able to wash dishes and cook some, doncha know?" She was on a roll now.

The only thing was, the walker Shaun had prescribed for her at the hospital was too short for her to stand upright while using it to move about. "It was okay when I was bent over and doing the hop-skip but now, I'm really putting some weight on my healing leg. Lizzie says I cannot walk bent over like this on and on."

That afternoon, during PT Lizzie's time at her house, Rachel expressed her concern about the too-short walker. "It's extended out all the way. Will I have to buy another one?"

"No," Lizzie, a strong survivor of a broken back and leg got Rachel's full attention when she spoke because of her own over-comer experience. If Lizzie could do it, by cracky, Rachel could do it. "There's a place in Spartanburg called Spartanburg Shares that loans out PT and hospital equipment."

Rachel sat down in her wheelchair to rest for a minute. "Did you say 'loan'?"

"Loan. I'll give you their phone number before I leave. Tell them I referred you to them."

Rachel scratched her head. Free? Nothing was free any-more. Nah. "What kind of fee is involved?"

"None. You just have to return the equipment in the same condition as you get it, is all."

Could it be true? Oh well, she'd find out soon enough. Rachel collected the information and early Saturday morning she and Peter arrived at Spartanburg Shares Medical Loan Closet, housed in a nondescript building next door to the Epis-copal Church, which, she learned, was one of the sponsors of the ministry.

The program was modeled on similar ministries across the country, which are endorsed and supported by a diverse group of community backers including medical, health, and religious sponsors.

"Seems too good to be true," she muttered as she hoisted herself up from the passenger seat and, gripping the dwarfed walker, began her hop maneuvers to the entrance.

Inside, a meticulously organized hospital equipment smorgasbord presented itself, from beds to commodes to walkers, canes and wheelchairs, in other words, anything needed for convalescence.

Best of all, she discovered that Lizzie was right; no income threshold or insurance requirement was associated with the equipment.

Free.

"I'll trade this walker in on that one," she told the manager.

Fascinated with the generous spirit of the ministry, Rachel and Peter spent over an hour visiting with the volunteer workers, learning Shares' history. "I plan to tell everybody I know about it," she said as she left, feeling as though she'd known her new friends forever.

Wow! This ministry was a godsend to ailing folks with no means of buying or renting such equipment. Rachel had rented her wheelchair and would soon send it back, as soon as she could walk completely unaided.

"It's happening," she told Peter as they drove home. When he raised his brow in question, she said, "Seeing a light at the end of the tunnel."

He reached to grasp and squeeze her hand. "I'm glad." Then he gave her one of his adoring gazes, one that spoke of undying devotion.

It never failed to warm her heart.

The next week, she sat at her computer and wrote a blog about Shares and her publisher posted it on their website. When, weeks later, she went back to return the walker, she carried a copy of the blog piece and presented it to the workers there. Their enthusiasm humbled her.

The new walker was a piece of magic for her. It helped her to begin, in small increments, bearing weight on her injured leg and ankle.

"It still hurts like crazy," she told her doctor during her next visit. "When will the pain leave?"

He smiled. "You'll walk it out."

Aaaarrrgh!

"Oh." *Oh, indeed.*

No pain, no gain.

So *that's* where that came from.

\\\/

Peter felt the world closing in on him today.

Where was he headed? More to the point, *where was he*? He could hear Rachel's voice telling him to slow down and remain calm.

Feeling panic nipping at his heels, he drove aimlessly for a few moments, then whipped into a Lil' Cricket convenience store parking lot. He tugged his aged, cracked five-cent coffee refill cup from beneath his truck seat and headed for the entrance, mind a-spinning.

"Hi, Peter," called the red headed woman behind the register.

She knew him. Good. So he was on course.

"How's it going?" he called to her, trying to remember her name. But he did suddenly recall which store he was in as well as its location. Relief impacted him to the point that his knees felt weak.

Whew.

He filled his relic of a cup and paid the five cents, knowing that when this container broke or disappeared, he would have to fork over seventy-five cents or more for the same purchase.

The worker's name tag rescued him further. "Having a good day, Myrtle?" he asked with a grin, and was rewarded by familiar niceties.

At that precise moment in time, the discount-game wasn't as much fun. But it was something to tether him to himself, to the man he'd always been. Same as knowing where he was and where he was going.

As he walked out into the brisk, sunny day, he took deep breaths before tackling the last part of that thought—where was he going? Again, Rachel's calm counsel helped him to push away fear and regain rationale.

Inside the truck, he shuffled through his portable file of pest control customers and finally found a name that rang the elusive bell. "O'Conner. Yeah." He smiled, restored.

For now.

\ı/

Rachel was determined to burst out of her barricades.

First, she insisted on staying alone for longer periods of time. "You don't need to come every day," she told Gabby. "Leon needs you as much as I do now. And when I'm forced to, I'll get creative about moving from place to place and fill up my time more wisely."

Reluctantly, Gabby agreed to come every other weekday, allowing Rachel private time during the others, but she insisted upon calling regularly to keep tabs on her lil' sister.

In a way, it was a scary step for Rachel. Peter would—she was certain—stay home with her every single day of his life if she didn't object. But he needed—*they* needed—him to work. Her whopping hospital bills now dangled above them like lighted TNT clusters, ready to implode.

Yet—in another way—it was exhilarating. Well, as exhilarating as her numbed out psyche could bear. No, that had not changed a lot. She moved and talked on autopilot. And she confessed daily that God was her copilot and that slanted the dynamics more powerfully in her favor.

Actually, since she could not figure out everything, as she had always been prone to do, she now mechanically *trusted* God with the outcome. Simple. And liberating.

Nothing in the Bible said one must muster up faith and trust.

They just do it. In Rachel's present way of thinking, that settled it.

So with the new freedom at home, once she got Peter out of the house, she felt a new energy. Not a knock down, *Zip-a-Dee-Doo-Dah* one. No, it was a serene force that spurred her determination to escape the dratted wheelchair and ford the gulches that separated her from being who she was going to be.

That confession gave new substance to hour-by-hour resolutions. For instance, after doing her standing exercises, which at first caused tears but grew less painful over time, she moved herself along the counter edge—leaning for support—as long as possible, seeing how tidy she could make the entire length of the sink and counter tops, even putting away all the clean dishes from the dish rack. Time began to pass more swiftly and her mind didn't latch as often onto the pain and depression.

Exhausted, she used the walker to get to her bed for a rest, moving as upright as possible and gradually adding more weight to the injured limb and foot. The pain caused her teeth to clench and her head to throb.

Most days, Peter took time out to collect Rachel for their lunch hour at Eli's Place with The Gang. But some days, the bantering proved too much for Rachel—just as the TV News remained too much. And anything chaotic or high pitched. Peter understood.

So did The Gang.

He found another buffet over the nearby county line, where the atmosphere was quieter.

Quiet to Rachel was now right up there with oxygen.

On days when she especially needed escape, Peter took her to Brandi's Country Buffet, which offered a selection comparable to Eli's. It wasn't the same but, right now, quiet superseded camaraderie and ambience.

Rachel needed healing and not just physically.

\\/

Rachel spotted the boy at church that Sunday.

"There he is," Rachel whispered to Peter as the choir sang and the middle school kids filed into the Manilowe church sanctuary to take seats in their reserved section. They had their own earlier gathering in another building and then joined the adult congregation for the worship hour.

The boy appeared intermittently in the Manilowe church services. Rachel didn't know if she rewarded or punished herself by drinking in the sight of him each time he entered the sanctuary from the front side entrance, near where she now sat. By using the walker to get there, she'd graduated from the chairbound section.

She'd told Peter about the young man who reminded her so much of Jason and how she'd begun to look for him each Sunday.

Peter watched him move past in that loose adolescent gait that reeked of insecurity and budding interest in the opposite sex and a smile slowly grazed his lips. He nodded and Rachel saw a flash of sadness just before he turned his attention once more to the singers.

Did he feel as bereft as she did, missing Jason?

Of course he did.

Or was his sadness a result of an even deeper loss, involving more than Jason?

She cut her gaze to study Peter's solemn features, now more appealing to her than ever. Aging had been kind to him. His salt-and-pepper hair remained full and laid in soft waves that had initially attracted her to him. He cut a fine slender figure of a man and remained attractive, in anybody's book.

How she loved him. *Unconditional*, in that moment in time, took on an entirely new significance. His grief now became her grief.

Strangely, the thought of his ill-gotten *other* son did not do its usual mauling of her spirit. Or was it that her spirit and body were already so battered that they couldn't register anymore? She didn't know exactly how it made her feel. Somehow, the old familiar bitterness did not jive with the *now*-Peter.

The *then*-Peter did not hold sway over her love for this man sitting next to her.

The new sentiment somehow integrated itself into the post-trauma Rachel. And for the life of her, she did not know exactly where or when the old Rachel ended and the new one began. She just knew that, with the emergence of grace and mercy extended to her from the Almighty, all else had flown the proverbial junk-coop.

Her hand made its way to Peter's and she laced their fingers together and squeezed. She felt his return clasp, warm and reassuring, as always.

She rolled her watery eyes heavenward and silently gave thanks to Him for the housecleaning. It was way, way overdue. She still wasn't where she needed to be but thank God, she wasn't where she used to be.

\i/

Peter turned the truck's CD player full blast and warbled along with the Platter's "Twilight Time." He knew exactly which selection button to punch in.

Listening, he remembered his senior prom when Rachel had been his date and they'd danced to this song. From that night, it had become one of their favorites. She'd been a sophomore but just as grownup as she was today and beautiful beyond words.

He could still see her as she was then—slender yet softly rounded and with shoulder length hair the color of wheat overlaid with corn silk, eyes as blue as the sky appeared to his color-blind vision.

He drove through the countryside to the Davis's sprawling brick home. He'd been servicing the elderly couple's dwelling for nigh on fifteen years and had learned to love them as family. And judging from the warm welcome he received each time he entered their door, they felt the same about him.

Peter was having a good day. His mind was clear as crystal. He'd awakened early this a.m. and when he'd eagerly reached for Rachel, she'd welcomed him with open arms. Due to lingering injuries and neck brace hurdles, intimacy now required egg-shell caution, but the affection-connection transformed him as nothing else could.

He felt human again.

Alive.

Why was it that the older they got, the more perfect Rachel looked to him? He grinned at that as more endorphins plunged in to swim alongside the ones who had, since early this morning, been butterfly stroking like crazy, making him feel like the luckiest guy in the world.

He serviced the Davis's account, accepted their cup of coffee, and was regaled with tales of perfect grandchildren—and, in their case, great-grandchildren—then left with a check to deposit on the way home. He must remember to record it. He'd had a fair morning. Would have been better had he gotten out the door by nine, as Rachel had suggested. But, he hated to leave her worse than ever in the afterglow of love . . .

He couldn't get that song out of his mind today.

Couldn't get Rachel off his mind. The pickup seemed to veer, straining toward home. But he could see her pale yet determined face as she urged him to work his routes. "You'll feel so good when you get them done, Peter. You know you will."

His chin lifted and he began to hum along with the words of their song . . . "I fall in love again as I did then."

\1/

The world of reading was slowly opening back up to Rachel.

One of her favorite pastimes during her later phase of healing was reading in short intervals from a hodgepodge collection of old books in her library—ones simple and entertaining that did not require cerebral mastery.

She ran across a May 2010 issue of *Reader's Digest* in which Pulitzer Prize-winning southern writer, Rick Bragg wrote about how reading Harper Lee's classic novel, *To Kill a Mockingbird* had literally changed his life.

"I love Rick Bragg. He's so real," she told Peter after finishing the feature. "Here's a great article of his in the *Reader's Digest*. You want to read it?"

"Sure." Peter usually followed her lead, trusting her judgment. Their tastes ran remarkably similar and, as he read beside her on the bed, she soon heard his chuckles of appreciation.

Rachel had met Rick Bragg at a writers' conference once and found him to be as down to earth and appealing as his writing. His inimitable turn of phrases dazzled her. But, most of all, in the *Reader's Digest* article, she delved beyond style ingenuity and really got his message. Reading that book changed Rick's perception of life and love and fairness in a time of racial turmoil.

And since her accident, Rachel realized more and more that this was also her calling: to write with a passion and truth that changes lives. Suddenly, she couldn't wait to get busy.

\1/

Oh, how she wanted to do it.

"C'mon, Rachel." In-home therapist, Lizzie, stood planted at the bottom of Rachel's front porch steps. "You can do it."

The physical therapist had promised Rachel a "trip" down those sinister steps during the last home session. Rachel believed it possible and knew somewhere deep inside that it was certainly in the future. Was that future now?

A smidgeon of excitement trickled through her as she gripped onto the wrought iron banister and struggled to lower her injured leg down to that first level. Focus! She telegraphed her legs and feet to move down those five steps.

Remember what Lizzie said: up with the good leg, down with the bad. That way, the good limb is doing the work. Simple.

Rachel did the mind-over-matter concentration and then switched to simple I-can-do-this conviction.

The legs refused to cooperate. Pain and weakness prevailed.

"I can't," she moaned, let down to new depths.

"Sure, you can," Lizzie persisted, conviction ablaze.

Maybe I'm not trying hard enough, Rachel again attempted to force her limbs to transfer her down to that blasted, wraithlike level. A mild April breeze brushed and cooled her perspiration-damp face and the spring wildflower bouquet barely registered. Desperation swallowed her whole. *C'mon legs*, her silent voice wailed.

Again, distressed injuries and feeble muscles paralyzed her limbs. Tears stung the back of her eyes. "I can't, Lizzie," she croaked, leaning on the cold banister.

This time, Lizzie absorbed the veracity of Rachel's inability. "Okay, honey. No big deal. You're not ready yet."

Lizzie soon departed and Rachel melted onto her pillowed bed, a mound of smoldering, woebegone matter. She'd never before related quite so closely to disabled souls, whose struggles to overcome remain unrewarded.

"*God help us all*," she muttered, hand flung up over face.

Then she heard Peter's key in the front door. Lizzie had earlier locked it behind her as she left.

She could tell by his fraught features and tight gait that Peter was in crisis mode.

"What?" she asked, already distancing from her own soap opera episode.

Eyes mislaid behind confusion, he muttered, "I've lost a check." His hands slid in and out of each jacket pocket, then pants pockets. "I can't find it. It's a three-month account check. We need it, Rachel." Panic laced the last words.

Bad news.

Rachel took a deep breath and expelled it, pushing up to sit straighter in bed. "Have you looked in your day planner?" That being his constant companion these days. He lived out of it and was lost without its lists. Sometimes he absent-mindedly tucked papers in it until he got them to their permanent home file.

"Yup. Not there." He was having a Richter scale 5.0 meltdown. Rachel knew because this happened daily. Sometimes more than once a day.

"Honey," she said gently, "did you check your visor zip-up pouch in the truck?"

He paused in his pacing, thinking so intently she could almost hear his brain ticking. "No." He pivoted toward the door and slammed through it.

Please, God, she prayed. *Help him to calm down and think. Help him to find it.*

The tension generated by his panic-driven incidents was air-borne viral.

Contagious.

She already felt her insides coiling—like she'd seen her piano tuner struggle to make new strings do when installing them. Peter was the "claw" part of her teacher's improvised tool set used to accomplish the solid coil. One that he said did not work very well but would do till something better came along.

Well, Peter's claw-like anxiety worked very well at helix-ing her insides—sort of like she'd watched her mother wrapping gifts and taking her scissors flat edge to drag the ribbon tightly between her thumb and the metal, producing curlicues, tight little coils to bounce on packages. Her insides tightened, quivered and vibrated and bounced like those ribbons.

Again, she whispered a prayer for the missing check to materialize.

Peter came back a few moments later, holding it up, relief evident. "I found it. In the visor bag."

"Wonderful." The curlicues began to unfurl and float away.

He carefully put the check in his wallet. "I usually put them in here but for some reason, I didn't this time."

He sat on the edge of the bed, looking at her. "How's your day been?"

She hesitated about sharing her own disappointment. But in her fatigue, her resolve flickered then died. "Remember I told you Lizzie was going to help me walk up and down the steps today?"

Peter blinked, his eyes struggling with memory.

"Well, she tried to guide me through it." She spread her palms. "I couldn't do it, Peter. I just couldn't do it."

He took her limp, icy hands in his and gently massaged warmth into them. "You will, honey. You'll do it any day now."

She looked away, feeling as inadequate as she'd ever felt. "I don't know—"

"Listen," one big hand captured her chin, forcing her gaze to meet his. "You're strong, Rachel James. One of the strongest people I've ever known. Just look at all you've already accomplished. Why, you're moving all around the house, holding onto the wall and anything you can reach, balancing yourself and putting up with constant pain. You know?"

He gazed into her eyes, admiration a-glimmer. "This is just another of those one-step-at-a-time challenges that takes a little extra time to beat. But my girl will beat it."

He smiled at her then, that slow, drink-in-Rachel one, confidence shining through like a lighthouse beacon.

It was contagious and Rachel felt her lips curve wide and her heart lighten. "Yeah. You're right. I just get impatient, is all."

She reached up to pull him down for an awkward hug and kiss. They'd gotten used to neck-blockage to the point that now the armor-like brace seemed almost normal.

Almost. She could not complain, however. Getting rid of the leg ironworks felt uncommonly blessed and gave them the kind of access to each other that took them to the galaxy and back.

Yup. Despite the stairs-span set back, she was a blessed woman.

Part Three

\|/

"I count the moments, darling, (while) you're here with me,
Together at last at Twilight Time."

Chapter Eleven

\│/

"Faith is why I'm here today and faith is how I made it through."
—*Jonathan Anthony Burkett,* Neglected But Undefeated

Mark had just finished his afternoon chores when he spied his stepdad heading to the barn where more eggs were close to hatching. He turned away and loped in the opposite direction, toward the house.

He still kept his distance.

The betrayal of lying about his real dad had not stopped stinging. He didn't think it ever would. Knowing Ralph followed him, he hastened his pace and slammed in the back door and raced through the kitchen and past his mother, who was having a cup of tea at the dining room table, soaking up warm sunshine spilling through the windows.

"Mark!" she called to him. Reluctantly, he skidded to a halt, hearing the tremor in her weak voice. He was still angry at her but on a deeper level, he loved her with all his heart.

"Yeah?" he muttered, avoiding eye contact, shuffling his antsy feet and struggling out of his lined jacket, suddenly too warm for indoors.

"What's got you all in a frenzy?" she asked quietly. Mark heard the dread in her voice. But he knew she was strong. Wasn't she?

He shrugged. "Can't a person just want to be alone?"

"Look at me, Mark." It was not a request. It was an order, so he turned to look her square in the eye. She looked so sad it was like a knife pierced him. She shook her head. "We've both apologized to you over and over and we are both truly sorry that we didn't tell you the truth sooner but—"

"But?" He huffed a brittle laugh and looked away. "But why? You can't expect somebody to turn on a dime with a thing like that, Mama. Ralph should have—"

"Don't," she stood and put forth a trembling hand. "Please, Mark. Don't blame Ralph. He wanted to tell you all along but I was too stubborn—thinking I was protecting you . . ."

"Protecting me?" He peered at her, emotions roiling inside him that he could not begin to decipher. "From what?" He paced away, leaving her standing there, hand outstretched. He pivoted and felt a tear spill over and quickly swiped it away. "I still don't know who my real father is. And you know what? I probably never will." He felt another tear and angrily wiped it away with his shirt sleeve.

"Mark," his mama moved closer but did not crowd him. "You must forgive Ralph. He's never been anything but good to you. And to me. He's made a home for us when we didn't have one and—"

At that moment, Ralph stepped from the kitchen and Mark knew he'd heard everything. "I wasn't intentionally eavesdropping," said the man Mark had always called Dad. "It's true, son. I wanted to tell you from the get-go that your father wasn't dead. But for her own reasons, your mother wouldn't have it. I respected her wishes because she birthed you, you see. And that cops any of my own opinions in this case."

He walked right up to Mark and put a big hand on the boy's shoulder, not allowing him to step back. "I never lied to you, Mark. I just didn't tell you everything. If you think on it, you'll see that I'm telling the truth. Why, I wouldn't harm a hair on your head."

Mark saw tears well up in the aging eyes and felt his heart soften. And he realized in that heartbeat that his dad was telling the truth. He'd never lied. Only his mother, when pressed, had declared his biological father dead.

"Dad—" he croaked.

"It's okay," the big hand pulled him against the strong chest and Mark felt the strength of arms that had always held him when he needed them. "You just know that I love you as my own. Always have. Always will."

Mark's arms slid around the solid torso and he squeezed back, blinking against tears. When he finally stepped back, he shook his head. "Dad, I'm so sorry about the church thing—you being deacon and all. I feel responsible—"

"Naw," Ralph shook his white mane and chuckled, ruffling Mark's hair, restoring a spark of normalcy thereabouts. "The pastor called me just this morning, begging me to reconsider about resigning. Said Steven—Stinky—had confessed to trouble making, absolving you of anything and everything, and really did a turnabout in his life. That was a real answer to prayer." He grew somber. "What do you think, Mark? Should I reconsider about remaining on the deacon board?"

Mark stared at him. He was asking him? The man's humility and strength smote him anew. And he remembered what his dad had always taught him about all things working together. And he thought of his new friendship with Stinky. It brought a warm rush of gratitude that something which had started so bad had turned out so good.

"Yeah, Dad. I think you should reconsider."

His dad's laugh rumbled as he threw his arm around Mark's shoulder. "Put your jacket on. We got some new chicks a-hatchin' in the barn. Can't miss that, now, can we?"

"No, Dad. We can't miss that for sure."

As he turned to retrieve the jacket from the dining room chair, he caught a glimpse of his mother's tears of joy. And the sun suddenly seemed brighter.

Several weeks later, the neurologist removed Rachel's neck brace.

Space ambushed her.

Only then did she realize just how much she'd tuned out its claustrophobic effect. Too, to suddenly rely upon her still sore, battered neck muscles and tendons to support her head was a bit daunting.

Unabashed delight, on the other hand, filled Peter, who took blatant advantage of the new accessibility when nuzzling her neck and cheeks.

"Hey, we fit together again," he enjoyed pointing out during amorous bear-hugs.

Those pleasure doses soon drove away Rachel's trepidation.

Sudden twists of her head were slow in coming, due to months of forced restriction. Seemed everything Rachel did took concentration and deliberate forethought, from rising from a chair, to walker-pacing, to a small turn of head—no wonder fatigue overtook her so often.

But she was making progress, thank the good Lord!

Along about that time, Peter saw a heading in the news-paper, *Alzheimer's Buddy Program Pairs Patients, Med Students.* "Here," he said, handing the paper to Rachel. "See what you think of this."

Rachel read about the eighty-year-old retired Chicago phy-sician and educator, Dan Winship, getting a last bittersweet chance to teach about medicine—"Only this time he's the sub-ject," Rachel read aloud. "In his early stages of Alzheimer's, he's giving a young medical student a close-up look at a devastating illness affecting millions of patients worldwide."

Peter's interest rose. "They're part of a 'buddy' program pairing med students with dementia patients?"

Rachel nodded and summed it up for him. "It was pioneered at NW University and adopted by a handful of other medical schools. The idea is to expose the med students to a disease they will encounter during their careers as well as giving the patients a sense of purpose and a chance to stay socially engaged before their illness eventually robs them of their minds. Sounds like a great plan."

Peter remained silent.

"What do you think?" Rachel asked him, sensing fear raising its ugly head.

He shrugged tightly. "I don't know."

Time for reassurance. "Well, the way I see it, the purpose is to make the future doctors take a closer look at the patients, get to know the disease beyond what they learned in a classroom. They learn that people during stages of any dementia still need to live and enjoy life."

Peter crossed his arms and looked into the faraway. Rachel could see alarm inserting itself—soon it would control his thinking, or lack thereof. But she gave him space to work it out in his own way. It was, after all, the only way.

Finally, he responded. "I don't know—I just don't know how much I want to be studied like a bug under a microscope."

"You're referring to the stigma?"

"I am. There is one, you know."

"There is. But the article says that the objective of these 'buddy' programs is to erase the stigma attached to Alzheimer's and help the doctors treat the patients with more compassion and understanding. One good side note—about seventy-five per cent of NW University med students who participate in the program become doctors in fields that deal with Alzheimer's patients. Interest is growing, and hopefully more studies and advancing treatments will emerge."

She reached across the kitchen table and took his hand. "Someday soon—a cure will be found." She had to keep that before him.

She had to keep that before them both.

Peter pulled his hand loose, arose, and headed for the front door, muttering, "They'd better hurry."

"Play me a song, Ms. Piano Girl," Gabby sang out from the kitchen.

She still came to do "purging" service once a week and right now she was swabbing as though the kitchen floor was infested with e-coli.

Rachel could still only manage piddly tasks—dishes, light cooking, general wipe down or dusting of easy-to-reach surfaces—things that she could accomplish on one foot, leaning against the counter. Floors and bathrooms were Peter and Gabby assignments.

Rachel insisted—over Gabby's strident objections—upon paying Gabby for her time, an expenditure that strained their budget, but Rachel's perfectionist leanings could not survive chaos and dust. No way José. Her mind's groping for sanity was sufficient unto the day, thank you very much. It needed no further taxing.

Rachel walker-shifted to the upright piano bench she'd occupied since girlhood days and began to play "Mr. Piano Man," a pathetic, slower version, yet the concentration made her head spin.

"Gabby, it's so out of tune you'd think you were in the Rusty Spur Saloon. I might just see about hiring this thing out to a B-western honky-tonk."

But God bless John Wayne, how did it get so tinny sounding?

Rachel knew.

She'd not played in months and months and even then, for only a song or two. And having it tuned was costly, as was replacing her car's broken CD player and fixing their own leaky roof and weak utility room floor, and restoring the village's historical Scout Building that was now in their possession and falling in upon itself . . . The list went on and on.

She ambled through the song and then walker-hop-skipped into the kitchen, now mopped dry.

"Why'd you stop?" Gabby frowned over her shoulder while emptying the mop bucket down the utility sink.

"My ears were turning in on themselves. My head can only stand so much clamor these days."

"You need to have the piano tuned, sis. You shouldn't be deprived of your music, doncha know?"

"This is not something I need to be concerned about right now."

"True. When you're up to it, I can help find someone and set it up."

Rachel heard the rattle of the mop bucket sliding into its resting place beneath the utility sink. She refrained from poor-mouthing over the cost of piano tuning because she knew the result would be Gabby refusing payment for her cleaning services. And Rachel wouldn't have that. She felt useless as it was.

Even worse than that was to be a user.

Rachel appeared fine if nobody looked too closely at her dull, lifeless eyes and dark circles beneath. Makeup hid much of lingering trauma tell-tales. She just wished the invisible emotional wounds were as easy to escape.

She could not move out of her head, however.

She still had not regained one iota of chattiness.

Silence fit too well these days. Oh, she'd answer and act engaged enough to remain personable and polite. But the former easy conversational flow still hibernated somewhere far and away.

Would it ever return?

The thought fizzled and drifted off.

Gabby joined Rachel in the bedroom, still Rachel's fortress, her haven, as she propped herself up to rest on the pillowed bed, her body still screaming for respite several times a day.

"Gabby, do you think I'm a selfish person?" she asked.

Gabby's brow rose. "What brought this on?"

"I miss Amber. My own daughter fled from me." She shrugged, not angry, not weepy, just cheerless. "She once told me 'it's always all about you, Mama.'" She peered dully at her sister. "Is that true?"

"Huh." Gabby rocked a little harder, chin in air. "You can't pay any attention to that girl of yours. Seems to me she's the one who's all into herself—"

"Please don't, Gabby. That's not why I brought that up. I just feel so useless and defeated lately and—"

The glider stopped. "*Heaven help us*, sis. Listen to yourself. Look at all you've overcome." Rachel watched moisture gather in her sister's eyes, a rare thing. "You're a saint, Rachel. If anybody ever was, you are. And you're not useless just because you're still physically and emotionally fragile. You're still healing! *Banana shenanigans, girl*! Give yourself time."

"It'll be a year soon. How long does it take to heal? Lately, the years stretch out before me like the Mojave . . . vast and empty. Too, too challenging." Rachel stopped just short of revealing suicidal feelings.

"Was Amber right?" Rachel murmured, mostly to herself.

"Psshaw!" Gabby crossed her arms and picked up her cadence. "Don't let that possibility light in your head for one second. Amber was unforgiving and selfish herself. A case of the pot calling the kettle black. And no, you are not selfish, no more than any other good mother."

In that moment, Rachel wasn't so sure of that.

\i/

Rachel heard the front door unlock. Peter was home.

His arrival always lifted her heart. Today was no exception. As Gabby took her leave, he kicked off his shoes and joined Rachel on the bed, propped by his own pillows, half watching the ever-playing TV. Today, he halfheartedly flicked it to the Golf Channel, a game he could no longer play due to arthritis.

Quickly, he apologized. "Sorry, honey." He turned it back to where she had it. When home, he never veered far from her side. Rachel played Sirius XM Escape—easy listening music to level her out—reflecting that months ago, the same music had not helped. She had, she acknowledged, made some progress.

Compromising, she switched it to family programs, mostly for Peter's benefit.

They held hands and she felt him watching her closely as Dr. Quinn's beauty filled the TV screen. "You okay? You look like you're down."

"I'm okay." She slid him a smile that she hoped looked genuine. "Just tired. Gabby and I did one of the recipes out of Jan Karon's *Mitford Cook Book*, the gift given to me in the hospital. 'Mama's Ice Cream in a Tray.'"

Mostly Gabby's efforts but she had coaxed some participation from Rachel, even if it was just the piddly measuring of ingredients. "We both knew how much you love homemade ice cream. This really is good. It's made from sweetened condensed milk, a little water, vanilla extract, and heavy cream."

He grinned. "If you ever think I'm dead, just put a little ice cream on my lips to make sure."

She playfully swatted at him. "You doofus."

His face lit up and they watched more of the *Medicine Woman* episode, with Rachel wheel-chairing her way to the kitchen for tiny samples of rich, smooth vanilla ice cream during commercial breaks. The chair enabled her to carry the bowls in her lap. She'd become resourceful in that way.

Peter protested, "I'll go get that."

"Nope," she called over her shoulder, wheeling away. "I need the exercise."

"Do you know how much I love you?" he asked later, turning toward her.

"Mm hmm. Like I love you." Oh, how she wished her emotions were not so flat.

Within moments, he turned restless. "I need to do the bills early in the morning."

Rachel's antennae rose. "We did them this morning."

He frowned, eyes struggling. "You sure?"

"I helped. Yes, I'm positive."

He slid off the bed and padded into the office where she could hear him rattling open the file drawers and shuffling paper.

"What are you looking for?" she called, feeling a knot beginning in her stomach.

"I'm looking for the bills. I don't think I paid them all. In fact, I don't remember paying any of them."

She was dealing with the take-charge man who trusted only in his own perception of responsibility and facts. The drive and focus remained intact. The points of reference were deleted from the equation. Peter moved in the *now*.

This moment.

Rachel arose and wheeled into the office. "Look," she pulled up the PAYMENTS file on her computer. "I started this file just last month where I record the date, name, and account number, as well as the check number. It's all here, honey."

But the dragon had surfaced, the monster that siphoned his memory and plummeted him into panic.

He sank into his desk chair with a thud and gazed at her, eyes bleak.

"It's okay," she said gently, swiveling to face him. "We're in this together, all the way."

He shook his head. "Fear is the worst. It scatters my mind in every direction. When I can't remember, the fear rises up until—"

"You panic."

"Yeah." He nodded and she could see that her understanding eased him in some way.

Respect was the word.

Rachel shrugged. "If it's any comfort, fear and panic do that to me—they scatter my mind."

She felt it, his relaxing and it did her heart good. She clarified once more. "So, we're all caught up with the bills, except the AT&T bill that hasn't come yet. We'll send it as soon as it comes in."

His mood shifted from gloom to delight.

"Let's find a good movie on TV," he suggested as they detoured to the kitchen and piled dishes high with Eli's great chicken salad for a nighttime snack.

"Sounds like a plan." Rachel wedged a glass of iced tea between her knees and tucked a bag of chips in her lap as she wheeled her way to the bedroom. Peter carried the plates and napkins, where they spread the picnic fare across the bed and began flipping through movie channels.

Holey Moly! *Dumb and Dumber* was playing. One of their favorites.

And all was right in their world again.

\I/

The sunny afternoon was unseasonably warm when they left Eli's Place.

"Let's go visit Jason's grave," Rachel suggested. "I hate that we haven't bought a fresh silk arrangement in recent months. I just haven't been able to focus on anything." This one wooly thing really bothered her.

Peter chuckled. "I know that feeling. We'll have to order a nice winter arrangement right away."

Rachel grabbed his ever-present day planner and scribbled down the reminder.

The drive was refreshing and mind clearing as the country landscape flowed past in constantly evolving earth tones. When they finally reached the turn off to the family cemetery that served generations of the West family, a sense of home swathed Rachel.

Peter parked his pickup, grabbed Rachel's walker, and their footsteps squished over winter-buff sod to where Jason rested at the feet of Hampton West, his grandfather. The stroll proved awkward for Rachel's unsteady walker-gait and Peter hovered to steady her along. Both of them remained reverently quiet and reflective as they approached the burial site.

Rachel stopped abruptly. "Who put those flowers there?" she asked Peter, who looked equally mystified.

"I have no idea." He shook his head.

She moved closer and reached to touch the lovely silk fall flowers, perfect for the season. "Am I going crazy?" she muttered. She turned to Peter. "Did you put these here?"

"You're asking me?" He shrugged, clueless, and Rachel knew that had he done so, she would have known, wouldn't she? Peter didn't have the connected thoughts to follow through on many projects like this. He lived in the now. He could not connect the dots much anymore.

She snapped open her cell phone and punched in her sister's number.

"Gabby, did you put flowers on Jason's grave? No? Do you think Drusilla would have?"

She hung up. "She couldn't speak for Drusilla but she didn't put them here."

Rachel shrugged and frowned. "Well, whoever did this is an angel. The last flowers were a year old and in terrible shape. The cemetery caretakers even disposed of them." For the first years following their son's death, she and Peter had been faithful in placing seasonal memorial silk arrangements on his grave.

With Amber's leave-taking and then this past year's trauma experience—plus Peter's dilemma—their devotion had become flawed. Not good. More guilt heaped atop the mounting pile. But Rachel knew there was no solution.

Her perfectionism was taking a real hiney-kicking.

When they pulled away, Rachel watched the riot of color in her rearview side mirror. Until it was out of sight.

Who?

\\/

Gabby snapped her phone closed. Then called Drusilla.

"Did you put flowers on Jason's grave lately?"

"No. Why?"

A nervous sigh. "At least I didn't lie about that."

She told Drusilla about Rachel's call and her confusion about the mysterious fresh flowers. "She's sniffing around more. I'm afraid she's gonna—"

"You worry too much, Gabby. Anyway, we don't know if our friend put those flowers there or not, now do we?"

"No. But it sounds like something she'd do. Rachel doesn't suspect, though."

A long silence. "Maybe. But don't underestimate that sharp little writer's mind. If she finds out I know something and am keeping it from her, she'll never speak to me again."

"Aww, Gabby! Don't be such a drama queen."

"Dru, you know how hurt she's been over—things. And if she finds out I'm involved with—"

"Well, I'm involved, too."

"Then that makes two of us she'd never speak to again."

"You know better'n that, Gabby. Why, Rachel's always been one of the most forgiving people I know."

"Was. I'm not so sure about now. That accident has left her—different. Not as predictable as she once was. Her emotions aren't really stable at times, you know? I just don't want her getting hurt."

"Me neither. It could really set her back."

"So mum's the word. Right?"

"Right."

"I-I feel so torn, you know? I feel like a traitor—sort of." Gabby sighed. "Y'know, I really don't want to like Ms. Dot but I just can't help myself."

"I know what you mean. She's such a sweetie. But—"

"But Rachel might not understand. Might disown us."

"Yup."

A moment of contemplation stretched out. Then Drusilla said, "Yeah. I feel torn, too. Not wanting to hurt Rachel but at the same time, I don't want to hurt—"

"Exactly. We'll just have to put it in a package and mail it First Class to the Almighty."

"Love you, Gabby."

"Me, too. Bye."

They rang off. Gabby stood there for long moments with the phone in her hand, trying to shake off the niggling guilt.

Chapter Twelve

\|/

"The greatest minds are like film, they take the negatives and develop themselves in darkness."
—*Brandi L. Bates, Remains To Be Seen*

The sunny, mild Carolina day offered no warning.

Rachel enjoyed her early morning agenda of a light breakfast, then primping with TV Bible teaching for background. She'd seen Peter off by nine. A perfect start.

Mind fresh, she went to her computer to check email and respond. After that, she got busy writing a new Facebook fan page blog, reminiscing about how far she'd come in her recovery from trauma.

Needing to move around by now, she walker-hobbled to the kitchen and began to look for something to do.

Rachel's phone rang. It was Peter and he sounded agitated.

"What's wrong, honey?" she asked, standing at the kitchen sink washing a couple of cups, an unnecessary thing but it kept her on her feet and busy, working her muscles and building endurance.

"Amber called," he stated in a flat tone.

Rachel had to hold onto the counter ledge, emotions pummeling her. "What did she say?"

Peter gave a harsh laugh, causing her insides to tighten. *Oh no. Collision.*

"She wanted to come here and stay for a while," he relayed. "Demanded it, in fact. Said she lost her job and didn't have anywhere to go. Needed some money for gas and food and *yada yada yada.*" Another harsh laugh.

"What did you tell her?" Heart in throat, Rachel closed her eyes and slid into the nearest chair.

"I told her no, that she'd made her bed. Now she can lie in it."

"How do you know she's not really in need?"

"Rachel, *Rachel*," he said, as in *moron*. "She left us. Abandoned us in our darkest hours." His accusation was so vehement that it slapped Rachel upside the head.

"But you don't know for certain." Her insides coiled, then headed for cover because she smelled an avalanche of resentment on its way.

That bark of a laugh. "Look. If you want her to come here, I can leave."

"Say what?" Rachel felt herself drowning. "Why does Amber's situation have anything to do with us?"

"Well, you seem to want to have her come here and live—after she made the decision to abandon us years ago. I can't forgive her for that." He sucked in a furious breath and blew it out. "So, if you want her here, I'll have to leave because I can't live with her. I spent my childhood years in hell because of a raging drunk father who had—in essence—abandoned his family and at my age and in my condition, I cannot live through it again. Amber's hot headed and so am I. We cannot coexist."

Rachel's insides shriveled and her head sank to the table. "Okay." The word was reedy.

"Okay what?" Peter demanded. Decision time for Rachel.

"Okay. You come first." It had to be.

Was it right? On that, she was clueless.

Yes, it was emotional blackmail. But she could not live without Peter. And further, he could not live without her. She really had no choice.

They rang off. The rest of the afternoon, Rachel felt drained and vacant. Thoughts popped into her mind and lingered . . . scripture saying "fathers, provoke not your children to anger" . . . Amber had been a mere teen when she'd seen her father's flaws and her mother's obsession with grief . . . what if Amber really needed just a boost to the next job . . . what if Peter's cold rejection had pushed Amber too far and into desperation—and as a result drove her to say those vile things to him?

'Course, as her daddy always said, circumstances cannot force you to do anything against your own will. Amber certainly had a choice in the matter. She could have mended fences somewhere along the way.

Rachel realized anew that she couldn't escape her soul-searching, intuitive self, one who sniffed out each nuance of an issue, refusing to allow sentiments alone to guide her. She knew that this knack to explore the "what ifs" sprang from her writer's mindset.

What if Rachel's own father had rejected her so coldly in her time of need? When she had nothing left to fight with? Yes, she probably would be angry and desperate.

But to call Hamp West vile names? Rachel could not imagine that scenario. In the first place, her father would never have given up on her because he'd not had the dire, alcohol-fueled past that was Peter's. Hamp would have been hands-on daddy through any valley and over the craggiest, highest mountain. Not in an enabling way, but solidly *there* with spiritual and emotional support.

Peter, on the other hand, could not help his fight-or-flight response when a perceived challenge presented itself. He'd not been blessed with nurturing parents and was forced to forge his own fortification. Security continued to evade him, even into his twilight years.

Bottom line: Rachel conceded that she had more to give than Peter.

\\//

Night fell and peace eluded Rachel.

She felt it pending, something reckoning and disturbing—even more than what the day had already heaped upon her.

Her phone rang. She sat up and looked at the ID.

Amber.

Fear struck Rachel and she detested it, hated it being linked to their mother/daughter bond, like some foul smelling hyena chasing her down. But her collateral damage from the fall forced her to endure it yet again. She willed her voice to behave.

"Hello, Amber."

"Mama, I need help. Can I please come there tonight and stay? I lost my job and can't—"

"Daddy says no, Amber. He feels so strongly he threatens to leave if you come here." The words tore her heart in two.

Rachel heard screaming on the other end of the line—a tormented, furious scramble of words and phrases. *I hate him! . . . wish him dead . . . you're a*—followed by choice profanity to describe her traitorous mother who was no longer her mother, someone she hoped would die.

Shocked, Rachel clicked off the tirade. It hurt, but on some deep, primal level, she understood Amber's hurt and sense of abandonment.

Peter came in later and Rachel gave him a mild version, knowing that to divulge more would be like tossing gasoline on a bonfire. Even so, the watered down version cast his face into a stone-dark drama mask but he managed to whistle his way to the bedroom, where he soon stretched out on the bed and fell into a deep sleep.

Rachel didn't know where his tuning-out came from. It was alien to her. So she went to her computer and began working on her novel.

Writing always helped her to shuck off current disturbances, ushering her into peaceful regions of the soul.

BAM!

Rachel swiveled from her desk. Was that something falling somewhere in the house? She heard Peter turn over, mumbling, "What was that?"

"I think something fell somewhere in the house," she said, but after long moments of silence, she returned to her writing.

Minutes later, another crash brought her to her feet. She grabbed her walker and met Peter coming out of the bedroom, scowling. "Amber's car's outside," he said. "She's doing something."

He strode upstairs. Away from IT. In a way, she was glad. She didn't want to face a confrontation between the two. On the other hand, one more primal, she felt like the captain on a sinking ship.

Alone.

Rachel set aside her walker and flung open the front door. Amber's car sat parked on the lawn's grass. A disheveled Amber stalked toward the house, a cup of Starbuck's coffee grasped in one hand and an empty soft drink bottle in the other. In that instant, Rachel sighted another bottle lying on the porch and it dawned that the bottle was the weapon of harassment, one thrown against the house to get their attention.

Oh, yes. When Amber couldn't get her parent's attention any other way, she resorted to childish waywardness.

Rachel wished in that moment that she could see the real Amber for just a moment behind those furious features.

Profanity spewed from Amber's mouth as she flounced up the porch steps, to the top, where she halted and dashed her entire cup of coffee against the white porch wall, splashing it in all directions.

"What's wrong with you?" Rachel demanded, flummoxed. "Why are you doing this?"

Amber was like her dad in that she was fierce in battle.

Amber's finger pointed like a revolver at Rachel as she tearfully and furiously enunciated, "You let me down. I always thought that you believed in me—that you'd be there for me in a crisis. But guess what, *Mommy Dearest*? You weren't!"

She strode away, arms flinging back and forth, body rigid with rage and desperation, shouting over her shoulder, "I have nowhere to go!" She pivoted and glared, hatred spilling from those green, green eyes and Rachel realized that had she not known, she'd not have recognized those enraged features as Amber's. "I'm going to Aunt Gabby's. She won't turn me away."

A dozen memories flooded Rachel's brain. In that swift moment she remembered . . .

"Amber—" she whispered, seeing the little girl Amber, who crawled up in a chair to help bake cookies and who reached up to hug her mommy's neck with a big, "I love you, Mama!" Sixth grade Amber excited that Daddy agreed to be her date for the Valentine's Day Father/Daughter Banquet and the two of them dressed formally, leaving the house arm-in-arm on their "date" . . . Daddy crying with relief when his little six-year-old girl's bicycle accident proved not to be life threatening . . . the video replays all crowded in on Rachel.

"Aahh, Amber," she groaned, tears spilling over.

But the woman-Amber's seen-better-days car was already backing from the driveway, spitting gravel.

Rachel felt a torment she'd only imagined, but in reality, was much, much worse.

Why oh, why did God give her a mother's heart and then allow pandemonium such as this . . . when her emotions were already strained to their limit?

Peter came into the den where she sprawled, limp and spent.

"She gone?" he asked scratching his head.

"She's gone." And she felt a frisson of irritation that he'd abandoned not only Amber, but her as well. He knew her emotions were beyond raw.

But in the next instant, she acknowledged that even at her worst, she didn't face the challenges that Peter encountered every hour of his life.

Dear God, help us both.

He slid into his shoes and went outdoors to check, Rachel was certain, for any Amber-induced damages to property. Rachel wearily grabbed some big towels to do clean up. Awkwardly, she parked her walker and, leaning against the wall, went to work on the front porch, washing away Starbuck's stigmata as well as her limitations allowed.

Peter came back into view. "She let the air out of my truck tire."

Rachel was not surprised. The damage was minimal, considering Amber's righteous anger-index reading. Again, Rachel could only imagine the frustration of a girl needing her father and being rejected by him. Genuine no-holds-barred dismissals, consistently.

Murders had been committed for less than that.

Was Peter guilty of the scriptural provoking his child to anger? Or was she, Rachel, guilty of being too compliant and trusting when it came to Amber?

Or was Amber the culprit by virtue of her role as the Prodigal Daughter?

For the life of her, she did not know for certain. So she did the only thing she knew to be right—she released it to the Almighty to fix.

The next morning, Peter used his portable tank to put air in the flat tire and took it to the mechanic for inspection. He came back, face engulfed in resentment. "It didn't have a nail or puncture or anything that would've caused the air to escape. Amber did it. She deliberately did it to hurt me."

He looked at Rachel, heart in eyes. "I can't believe she would purposely do something to upset me. I've always been a good dad, haven't I?"

Rachel felt stunned by the vast perception gap between them. "Yes," she replied, not daring to set off that terrible explosive anger again. And yet, conscience forced her to add, "But—I think Amber feels rejected. And that's hard—"

"Rejected? So I *am* the villain again, huh?"

"Nobody's calling you a villain, Peter. Amber's just desperate because she's down and out."

"She's down and out because of her own stupid decisions. I wouldn't help her if she was on the side of the road begging. She's chosen her course and she's going to have to live with it. She's not a kid anymore, Rachel. She's nearly thirty. When we talked on the phone this afternoon, I told her that I'm not giving her money to flush down the toilet. She's not making anything of her life."

"Did you tell her that?" Rachel's voice trembled as badly as her entire body at that moment.

"I certainly did. She proceeded to call me every depraved name in the book. No, I'm not giving her refuge. No way."

Rachel watched him stride out the door, whistling.

The whistling got to her.

It was getting more hairy, the memory defect.

She wished his forgetter would limit itself to the crappy bad memories and leave most of the good ones intact.

\\/

Rachel had already waded into her current book project, one loosely based on her trauma experience the previous year.

She found that her stamina was not always up to the task. Neither were her emotions. So the story's skeleton came in sporadic jerks, halts, and starts, at first ostensibly a confused stick figure. Now, adding meat to the structured bones involved even more focus and fortitude—neither of which was always plentiful.

Today was one of those days.

She'd learned that Amber, after a couple of days at Gabby and Leon's house, had departed again for parts unknown. This leave-taking overrode her Aunt Gabby's objections and selfless support. *Thank God*, Rachel thought today, for her sister's good heart. And she had to credit Leon as well, who armed Amber with enough cash to carry her over until she hit job-pay-dirt.

Rachel insisted upon paying it back, without Peter's knowledge, of course. She was so not ready for another civil skirmish. At the same time, she admired Amber's adventurous spirit. She didn't know if—faced with identical circumstances—she could launch out into the proverbial cold, cruel world on her own.

"Honey?" Peter called from the adjoining bedroom.

She swiveled from her desk. "Yes?"

"I'm lonely."

Rachel closed her eyes and took deep breaths. She wasn't ready to stop. She'd just sunk her teeth into an idea and needed to go with it or lose it. "I'll be caught up in about another thirty minutes. That okay?"

A long pause. "Okay."

She'd learned to ask Peter's permission to interrupt their togetherness. That way, his noble side emerged and her writing time became stress free. Nevertheless, guilt nibbled during longer computer sessions because she knew he needed her more deeply than he ever had before.

She finished the scene and checked email messages for anything from her publisher.

Peter quietly entered her office and pulled up a chair to peer over her shoulder as she checked Facebook for replies to her fan page blog she'd posted the previous day. Sure enough, several comments appeared that lifted her sagging morale.

Despite his long ago computer course for beginners, Peter had not gained one iota of computer savvy. "Everybody in that class already had some knowledge of the computer, Rachel. I was the only dummy there who didn't even know how to get online, much less navigate. I was so embarrassed I just dropped the course."

So, here he sat, riding shotgun on Rachel's daily sprees that he perceived as her social jaunts. Rachel knew he felt left out. *Deprived* was the word and Rachel tried to tune him in to funny videos and warm messages from long-time mutual friends in an effort to make him feel like a participant.

She clicked on her Facebook timeline and was checking messages when Peter asked, "Where's my picture?"

She looked at him, puzzled. "What do you mean? On the sidebar section?" She pointed.

He was as sober as she'd ever seen him. "Why isn't there a picture of me there? There are Gabby's and Drusilla's, even Leon's and J.C.'s pictures. So where's mine?" Rachel mentally shook her head to clear it. *Reassurance time.*

"Facebook's staff assembles those from profiles of my Facebook "friends," Peter. I have nothing to do with the display here. They do it. It rotates at times."

The green depths still swam with hurt but he said no more. He stood. "You ready to go to lunch?"

"Sure." She was relieved that he'd dropped the subject.

On the way to Eli's Place, Rachel doubled up efforts to navigate the day to more upbeat places. She forced herself to be more chatty—difficult since the trauma—in hopes of lifting Peter's morale. To reach an upward level of calm spelled blessed relief and she was determined to enjoy it as she kept the conversation afloat for a while—until she noticed Peter's lack of response.

"You okay?" she asked, concerned. "You don't have much to say." Which was unusual.

"No. I'm not okay," Peter replied. "That really hurt me earlier. I think you should know that."

It caught her off guard. She peered at him, shocked at his abrupt declaration of misery.

Peter's features sat galvanized in stone.

"*Heavens to Betsy*, what hurt you?" Dread slithered through her, stifling cheer and tightening nerves.

"It hurt me that my picture wasn't on Facebook. Everybody else's was."

Rachel's mouth dropped open. Had his reasoning always been this blemished? She didn't think so—but not only was his memory faulty, he was getting older and more needy.

Not unlike her own state of affairs, she was quick to remind herself.

"Peter, I told you I had nothing to do with those picture groupings. Facebook does that automatically. I had nothing to do—"

"Well, I have something to do with paying for the computer services. I'm the one who pays utilities and keeps things going—like a roof over our heads and—"

"Peter—you're not listening to me." His insecurity and paranoia chewed into Rachel "It's not my fault that your picture isn't on Facebook. I—"

"Well, I'll fix that. I'll just stop paying the bills and see what happens." He grew quiet for long moments, during which Rachel decided to stop trying to reason. No use at this stage.

Then he spoke again. "When I'm planted below ground, you'll see just how much I do for you, Rachel. Then—"

"Peter! Stop and listen—I do know how much you do. I love and appreciate you more than—"

"Not enough to put my picture on your Facebook page." His statement was flat and resolute.

They were pulling into Eli's Place. "Let's leave and just get some burgers and go home," Rachel proposed, reluctant to expose herself to The Gang's scrutiny today.

"Suits me," Peter said, jaw set.

Wordless, they detoured by Hardee's for burgers. At home, they sat at the table in pregnant silence. She could tell that he ruminated over dark perceptions of life according to Peter. Rachel found that if she didn't engage in Peter's pity parties, he usually dropped them.

Today, however, he kept tossing the invisible streamers and confetti in her face. Rachel felt the dam-burst building.

It erupted.

"I'm still that little boy inside, Rachel, the one who couldn't afford lunch at school and had to sit in the classroom while others enjoyed good meals. Alcohol stole my childhood."

"I understand that, Peter," Rachel replied, feeling tears of frustration burning. "And I'm still the little girl inside who was treated like an outcast because she wasn't 'cool' like the other girls, because she wasn't permitted to go to movies and dance and wear much makeup. Who was so bashful she wanted to hide when she walked across the church auditorium to the piano bench." She paused for breath.

"At least you had your music," he stubbornly persisted.

"Try sleeping next to that or getting hugs from it. Everybody has their insecurities, Peter. That's no reason to try to make the whole world pay you back for your childhood losses."

She stood. "C'mon. I want to show you something."

He followed her to the office and sat beside her at the computer, where she clicked the link to his own Facebook page, one he never visited anymore. Too much for his tech-challenged mind, was his justification.

"Look, Peter," Rachel pointed to the "friends" names grouped there. Did you put these here?"

He shook his head. "No."

"Well, neither did I put those photos on my page, the ones you're so upset about."

She clicked back on her own page. "Here, watch as I scroll down to earlier posts. See here, there you are with me last Christmas and here at the hospital during my stay there and here with Leon and J.C. at Eli's Place. You're all over my Facebook pages, just not in the one you saw this morning."

He looked at her. Understanding dawned on his face.

"Peter," she took his hands in hers. "Please try to trust me when I clarify things for you. You come first with me. Always."

His eyes began to twinkle. "I don't deserve you, Rachel"

She sighed. "Oh, Peter, we are so blessed."

"Huh uh, that's not the right answer. I don't deserve you," he repeated.

"Yes you do, Peter James," she sassed, grinning, "*You got everything you deserved.*"

He burst into laughter and kissed her.

\I/

Gabby visited Rachel one afternoon and soon, Drusilla dropped by, too. Peter was out working his pest control route. The girls munched on some fresh gingerbread cookies Dru had brought with her.

"Mmm," Rachel groaned. "These are good."

"Yeah," Gabby said, washing down a bite with cold fat-free milk. "Almost as good as your cinnamon coffee cake."

"Actually, cinnamon is good for many ailments," Drusilla informed them, wiping her hands on a napkin.

Rachel laughed and shook her head.

"What?" her two companions asked simultaneously.

"I was just thinking about the last time I went to Dr. Fanning's office, our primary care physician before he moved away. He'd written me out a prescription for a statin drug for cholesterol on my previous visit. Well, this time, he asked me if I was taking it."

"You aren't, are you?" Gabby said.

"Nope. Too many side effects. And with fibromyalgia riding shotgun, how was I to know if the side effects were the statin ones, huh? Same identical symptoms! So I'll take my chances with diet and exercise for cholesterol control." She nodded for emphasis.

"Anyway, when I told him I wasn't taking it, his face turned red. Didn't, however, intimidate me a'tall. I make my own health care decisions. Later, I mentioned that during Peter's next checkup, to please gauge his short-term memory loss."

Neither Gabby nor Drusilla commented on the ailment, as Rachel knew they would not.

"Then I mentioned to Dr. Fanning that I'd put Peter on the coconut and MCT oil regimen and he nearly went ballistic."

Gabby snorted. "I'll bet. The medical profession doesn't like anything that doesn't go through their office, prescription pad, and computer payment file."

"I told him that the person who made the video, extolling the benefits of pure coconut oil and MCT oil on Alzheimer's, was a lady doctor who'd studied long and hard and treated her husband with it, reaping miraculous results."

Drusilla cut another piece of gingerbread. "I'll bet he loved that, huh?"

"He snapped that it didn't matter if it *was* a doctor, it hadn't been through clinical trials and been proven effective. He was extremely irritated with me. Know what he said?"

"What?" Gabby asked, mesmerized.

"He said 'How can you believe in something you find on the Internet while you refuse to take a medication that went through clinical trials and has been approved?'"

"What did you say?" Drusilla asked.

"I said that I refused to take the statin drug because of the serious side effects. Period. And he left the room shaking his head."

"Huh." Gabby's brow drew into a frown. "Closed mind."

"Yup. I've seen a leveling off with Peter's memory since he's been on the oil and other supplements. The loss has not progressed noticeably."

"Me, too," Drusilla said.

"He's definitely doing great, in my estimation, sis," Gabby added, looking as sincere as Rachel had ever seen her.

"Well"—she stood and began running dish water for the dishes—"we've got absolutely nothing to lose by exploring homeopathic remedies."

"Got that right," Gabby retorted as she gathered the glasses and lowered them into lemony, soapy warm water. "The medical profession isn't offering much by way of a cure at this point."

Rachel began washing the utensils, "But it's on its way. I've got a new article I want to show you that says the medical profession has discovered a system that drains waste products from the brain. The finding may reveal new ways to treat neurodegenerative disorders like Alzheimer's disease."

"Wow." Drusilla wrapped up the remaining gingerbread for the guys to eat later. "That sounds amazing."

Rachel smiled. "Yes, it does, doesn't it? Let's just pray they'll perfect it and find a cure in the end product."

\\|/

Rachel's mind, she discovered, still produced as clearly as ever.

Thanks be to the Almighty.

Month's earlier, Rachel had begun going to her computer for short intervals to create blogs for her readership. When called for, she sent them to her publisher during book promotions.

A story already germinated inside her brain's creative niche.

With distance, her trauma experience no longer creeped her out.

Rachel discovered her writer-self subconsciously outlining her trauma experience. And at the same time, Peter's decline into Alzheimer's intertwined and inserted itself into the drama. But would Peter allow her to use his personal battle in the book?

At first, her suggestion met with hesitance and a touch of cynicism. "I'm not sure I want the world to know I'm losing my memory," Peter balked. "Everybody would start looking at me differently. I don't want that. Life's too short as it is, you know?"

"Yes, I do know. I won't use it then." She reached for his hand as he drove them to Eli's Place for lunch. "You're the most important thing in life to me. I wouldn't ever do anything to betray your love and trust."

Lunch at Eli's Place with Leon, Gabby, J.C., and Drusilla ended on a pleasant note. When they dispersed in the parking lot, Leon yelled, "J.C. might need help finding his car, Peter!"

Peter solicitously took J.C.'s car keys and said, "Right here, J.C., now look close—you mash this button and your horn will honk." His grin was road kill. "That way you won't get lost."

J.C. took off his Army cap and scratched his bald head, looking amazed. "Well, I'll be a monkey's uncle, Drusilla. Would you look at that." He demonstrated the button-horn honk.

She giggled and playfully swatted him. "Go get in the car, J.C."

They were all laughing as each of their cars pulled out of Eli's parking lot.

"What day is it?" Peter asked as he pulled their pickup out into traffic.

Rachel silently counted to five, the exact number of times she'd already told him today. "It's Monday, November third." *I am winning the war on patience,* she silently recited.

"Anywhere you want to go before we head home?" he asked.

"The dry cleaners. Remember that bedspread we took back to be redone? The one you took to Speedy Cleaners, actually, right after my accident?"

Peter looked blank.

"Anyway, something sticky—I suspect syrup—somehow got broken and spilled on it. It happened when everyone came in—while I was in the hospital—and moved furniture around and stored some of it. This bedspread got stained and needed cleaning."

"So it was dry cleaned?" Peter asked.

"It was, but the goop stain was still on it. We paid thirty dollars for the cleaning. I took it back last week to see if the cleaner would do a do-over. The employee said that she would call the manager-owner and see if he would honor it, but he might not because it was done so long ago."

"When?"

She could see Peter was having difficulty grasping the flow of information. It was confusing even to her.

"It was taken to the cleaners after my accident, cleaned, and picked up. But it was stored in the plastic bag until last week, when I opened it and found it unusable because of the sticky stain. It had to be washed."

She repeated the rest of the info. "I signed a waiver in case it shrinks. So I'll stop by there now and see if he agreed to honor that."

At the cleaners, a young African-American male employee laid the plastic-packaged bedspread on the counter. "That will be twenty-one dollars."

Rachel peered at him, disbelieving. "Did the owner consider that I was nearly killed in an accident that has left me wheelchair bound for months? I'm still using a walker, as you can see. The manager on duty when I brought it back seemed to understand and said he might consider a redo."

"He knows but he says he wouldn't honor a redo that's gone this long. Nearly ten months since we cleaned it. Folks could use an article and bring it back and make false claims so he has an iron-clad rule."

"Oh." Rachel's heart sank. The trust issue. Oh, well, the man didn't really know the two of them. Too bad more professional folks weren't merciful. She looked at Peter. "He's not going to make it right for us. Do we have cash with us?'

"I don't think so," Peter reached for his checkbook. "Why won't they clean it?" She saw his eyes grow confused. Then begin to glint.

Rachel hastened to explain. "They did. But we have to pay for it again."

Peter still looked baffled.

"Because," the male employee clarified. "Too much time passed before your wife made the claim."

Rachel felt pressure building in her head. "I was sick for months," she repeated, irritated at his blunt appraisal. "Does that not count? I couldn't even walk up my stairs, much less check on a bedspread in storage." *Dear Lord, what's happened to human kindness?*

"I'm sorry, ma'am," the young man said without conviction. "Rules are rules. I don't make 'em. I just have to enforce 'em."

Disappointment ambushed Rachel and she leaned against the counter, fighting dizziness. She took a deep breath and looked the employee in the eye. "I won't be back. I can't believe the owner can't understand my extenuating circumstances and have a little mercy. Do you realize I'm paying over fifty dollars to have one aging bedspread clean enough to use?"

The employee shrugged. No sympathy there.

"Do you have a pen?" Peter addressed the young male, who looked like he was maybe nineteen or twenty. She saw Peter reach over the spread and succinctly extract the pen from the man's extended hand. Peter signed the check and handed it to him.

"We've worked with the public for many years," no-nonsense Peter addressed him. "And when our renters or pest control clients complain and are not satisfied, we always, without charge, make things right. This is not right."

During Peter's diatribe, another neatly dressed African-American male entered, arms loaded with laundry.

Rachel smiled apologetically at him—realizing he'd overheard some of the dialogue—and briefly explained to him that the bedspread had not been cleaned properly and she'd tried to get a redo and failed. The man smiled sympathetically.

"Peter," she interrupted him. "It's not this young man's fault. He's just following orders. Let's please leave."

"Boy, oh, boy," Peter shook his head. Rachel tensed, recognizing that he was now on a roll and not likely to stop until he'd had his say. "I tell you, this is not how business is done with the public."

Rachel regretted having troubled Peter about this. She could see his control slipping more by the moment. Much of it was because his protectiveness sprang into action when he'd seen her upset.

Peter was still wound up, however. "I'm going to tell everybody I know about this. Boy! What bad service. And when you see my back as I go out, that's the last you'll see of me."

"C'mon, honey," Rachel touched his arm and he followed her briskly to the car, opened the hatch and tossed the sealed spread into the back.

They got into the vehicle and Rachel said, "I feel badly about that scene."

Peter's jaw remained set. "We didn't do anything wrong."

"Not legally. But—the man has a right to his business policies."

Peter cranked up the engine. "Not when he does business that way."

Silence settled in during the drive home.

Peter broke the silence. "My nerves are shot. I'm trembling all over." His anger had gone off somewhere and Rachel was glad.

"Mine, too. That was so *not good* back there."

"We didn't do anything wrong. We live in America, you know, the land of free speech? We have a right to complain when we feel we haven't been treated right." But his declarations now were half-hearted.

"Yes. But—I still feel like apologizing to those folks back there."

Peter's emotions turned on a dime. "Do you want to go back?" He slowed the truck, gauging her for a signal.

Rachel closed her eyes. Her head whirled like Hula Hoop champion Tootsie Avis's hip rotations. "No. I couldn't handle any more emotion right this minute. I'll call them later."

"Why wouldn't they clean the spread?"

Back to square one.

Rachel willed the trembling inside her to stop. "Because it had been too long before I complained."

"So, they didn't clean it?"

\\//

A half hour later, after lying down, Rachel felt her nerves beginning to mend a bit and moved into her study to her computer and began to check Facebook. Peter joined her, pulling up a chair to enjoy their friends' fun tidbits.

Her cell phone jangled. "Hello."

"Rachel James?"

"Yes."

"This is Michael Nixon, owner of Speedy Cleaners. I'd like to speak to your husband."

Good. She could apologize. "I'd rather you talk to me, Mr. Nixon." No way could Peter handle any sort of confrontation. He wouldn't be able to keep the issue clear in his mind.

"I want to talk to your husband." The voice grew agitated.

"I'm sorry but that's impossible. I'm glad you called because I want to—"

"You and your husband came into my business today and disrupted the peace. You upset my employees and harassed them, demanding and in general being a nuisance—"

"Please, let me say—"

"No. I haven't finished. If you ever come into my business again—"

Icy shock spliced through her. "I already said I wouldn't—"

"No. You let me talk. You've said all you wanted to in—"

His angry voice was like a wrecking ball crashing into Rachel. She was again that tall building crumbling to the ground as her head thrummed and swooshed.

The voice continued the vivid clattering.

CLICK. She snapped the phone shut.

"What a rude, bitter person," she murmured, voice quivering.

"I know." Peter hovered nearby. "I heard."

"Holey Moly!" She took deep breaths to slow her pulse and reduce the head pressure. "That man is one angry dude!"

"You okay?" Peter moved to put his arms around her.

"I'm okay," she lied, with her head on his shoulder. "I'm gonna let him calm down and call him back to apologize." After all, everybody cooled down after a while, didn't they?

Twenty minutes later, she pushed redial.

"Hello."

"Mr. Nixon, Rachel James. I want to tell you—"

Again, like on a paused video restarted, the man's tirade recommenced, not allowing Rachel a word, though she tried several times.

"I've called the police. They have your names and we have a video of the incident and the harassment—"

"Harassment? What are you talking about? We didn't harass anyone."

"Your husband did. He actually touched my employee and called him 'boy' more than once. The man is married with two kids."

"You can't be serious. *Boy*? A southern preface to 'Boy, I don't do things like that'—we use that idiom as emphasis, not to address anyone. And as for touching your employee? He reached for the pen in order to sign the check. That's all."

"It *was harassment* when he practically hit the man. It's all on video. And the police have your names on file. If you ever set foot on this property again, I'll have you arrested. You can—"

CLICK. Rachel had taken all she could. Her trust in human nature plunged to an all-time low. Even *lower* than a sidewinder's belly.

So much for apologies. And mercy. And grace.

Peter was growing exceedingly agitated, pacing back and forth. "Do you think I should leave for a while?" He looked at her with trust shimmering in the green depths.

He'd overheard the loud ranting. "What do you mean, *leave?*"

"The police might come looking for me."

"Oh, Peter." Rachel's heart sank lower. "No, honey. They won't."

He peered at her, worry in his eyes. "You don't think so?"

"No. We haven't done anything wrong." *Except run our mouths.*

Oh, well. Like Peter said. It's a free country. Folks got a right to complain.

Peter pulled her into his arms and spoke quietly. "You know, Rachel—folks can look at a video and interpret it any way they want to. But fact is—we know who we are. God knows who we are. And that's what's important."

Wow. In moments like that, he amazed Rachel.

How she loved him.

Chapter Thirteen

\|/

"You need to spend time crawling alone through shadows to
truly appreciate what it is to stand in the sun."
—Shaun Hicks

"What you doing?" Mark heard his dad yell from a distance
where he'd been checking on the chickens. Mark set down the
bucket of mixed feed in order to turn and firmly close the barn
door.

"Going to feed the hogs," Mark yelled, dusting his hands on
his pants. The weather was mild today and the fleece pullover
with the farm logo was plenty warm without a jacket over it. The
spring-like weather sat well with the boy.

"Naw," his dad called emphatically, wiping his face with
a red bandanna and replacing his Sugar Hills Farm cap on his
white crop of hair before stuffing it back in his overalls' hind
pocket. "Don't go there today. I traded boars with our neighbor
and I don't trust this one. I'll feed 'em so I can keep an eye on
'im. He looks like a mean cuss."

"Okay." Mark understood his dad's protectiveness of him
when it came to bulls and boars. Sometimes they used domestic
boars to breed for new strong blood from their sows and at that
precise time, some of the sows were in heat, an especially risky
time to get in the way of a boar's instincts.

His dad had educated him well as to the dangers of the
razor sharp tusks and aggressiveness of the species so Mark was
happy to keep his distance.

Anyway, his mom was going to take him to meet Stinky at school for the spring festival. She would visit under a shade tree with Alice Dodger, Stinky's mom, while the boys enjoyed the rides and refreshments. The two women had reconnected recently, developing a warm camaraderie, following their sons' newly blossomed friendship. This was the farm's helpers' day off so Mark's dad could enjoy some solitude and leisure after he finished his chores.

Mark hastened to feed the other animals, then went into the house to clean up and change clothes. And soon he and his mom were on their way to town and an afternoon of fun. He felt a little guilty when he thought of leaving his dad before the chores were done. But hadn't his dad insisted he go on?

Mark relaxed when, as the car angled into one of the school's few vacant spaces, he spotted a carrot-topped grin as Stinky raced toward them. In the background, rides beckoned and friends scrambled about like startled chickens, laughing and yelling in a cacophony of glee.

"C'mon!" Stinky screeched and tore off toward the amusement area.

Boy! Mark joined him. *He was ready for some action!*

\I/

Dusk was falling when their white BMW purred up the long drive to its niche behind the farmhouse. Mark's mother looked exhausted and his heart lurched with emotion. He'd stayed and stayed, squeezing every drop of enjoyment he could out of the uncustomary time off from farm chores and such.

He didn't mind the chores because they took him all over the wonderland of life and beauty that spelled home to him. But he'd ignored his mother's silent appeals to cease the celebrating so she could go home—

"I'm sorry, Mama. I didn't mean—" His words jelled at the look on her face as she stood frozen at the back door stoop.

"What is it?" he croaked, thinking she might be having a stroke or something.

"It's dark," she murmured. "No lights. No sound. Where is your father?"

Mark looked about. "His truck's here. And so is the red car."

"Exactly." The word was a mere whisper.

"Don't worry, Mama. I'll go look for 'im. You know Dad. He's probably watching some eggs hatch or something. You go on and lie down. You look like you're ready to topple."

Reluctance showing, she compromised by stretching out on the living room sofa.

As Mark's feet ate up the pavement to the barns, his mind raced . . . no eggs were scheduled to hatch right now. No calf birthing due. Feedings would have taken place a while ago, considering his dad's propensity for keeping tight schedules. He treated the animals as kindly as he did his family.

His family. Mark felt the impact of that truth and tears sprang to his eyes.

Desperately, Mark rushed from one building to the other, crying, "Dad? Where are you?"

The silence battered him.

There was one other place he hadn't checked. The hog pen area. He ran around the fence and nearly stumbled over something. He looked down.

His dad lay face up on the grass, eyes half closed. The gate was shut tight—so he'd locked it behind him. But what was wrong? Zooming in, he noticed that blood covered his lower body, soaking his overalls and pooling in the grass beneath him. Slowly, Mark dropped to his knees and touched the beloved face.

The eyes cracked and Mark's heart jumped with hope. "Dad? What happened?"

His dad's lips moved slightly and Mark leaned in to hear. "Boar."

"I'll get you help, Dad," he started to gently lay the white head down onto the grass and tug out his cell phone. But the mouth was working again as the eyes fought to remain open.

"Go . . . find . . . him." The whispered words puzzled the boy.
"The boar?"

The head moved slightly from side to side. "Your . . . dad."

Mark blinked and heard one last gasp. And then nothing.

"Dad?" he cried. "Dad! Come back. Don't leave me!
Please . . ." He sobbed for long moments before he felt anger cut
through the grief and bubble up.

It wasn't right.

It was not right!

He heard the snorting and saw the boar's beady eyes casing
him out from a distance, turning his blood to ice.

And he knew. The boar attack could have involved him. His
dad had made it out of the pen before blood loss had rendered
him unconscious. He'd been bleeding all this time.

"Oh, Dad," he groaned, tears flowing. "Dad! I love you!"

All this time while Mark had been having fun, his dad lay
there dying.

He gathered his father to his chest and rocked back and
forth, weeping for the only father he'd ever known. If only he
could tell him again how much he loved him.

But that generous, loving heart would never again be there
for him.

Mark wanted to die.

But first, he must go tell his mother the bad news.

\|/

Walking is falling forward.

Rachel learned this from Pulitzer Prize-winning journalist
Paul Salopek, who goes on to say that each step we take is an
arrested plunge, a collapse averted, a disaster braked. In this
way, to walk becomes an act of faith. We perform it daily: a two-
beat miracle—an iambic teetering, a holding on and letting go.

One day Peter said, "I live in the now, mostly. There's not
much yesterday anymore."

It somehow reminded her of the walking quote. Peter felt The Box closing in, shutting off the past, even, at times, the asides.

"I live in the now," he said calmly. "Much of the confusion and anger comes when I realize I've forgotten something important. I do crazy things, like going to check my oil in the pickup, and something steals my attention away, then later I see the hood raised and don't even remember why." He moved to the study window and looked out into the faraway.

"Imagine!" He snorted a humorless laugh. "When I'm reading, that happens. I forget the back plot at times. If I lay the book down for a couple of days and then go back and try to pick up where I left off, I'm lost. My mind hasn't stacked the memory of what I read before. So that's what I mean by living in the now."

He turned and gave a sad smile. "I don't even remember if I've been to the post office this morning. Nor whether I picked up nails at the hardware store." He shrugged. "I think as you progress, you'll lose the ability to recognize faces—like my mother did. And my siblings."

Another withering introspection emerged. "You ask why I'm hiding things all the time. I'm not hiding them. It's just that I put things away and forget where I put them. I no longer have control over that part of my mind."

"I know," Rachel said, understanding. "I do that, too, Peter. You're not alone."

He gave her a sad smile. "But I know that things will only get worse with time, should a cure not show up. You need to write about how desperately we need Alzheimer's research bumped up to the forefront."

Peter sat down in the extra desk chair, hooked an ankle over his leg, then steepled his fingers. "The fact that I do as well as I do is because of your attention to seeing that I regularly take the coconut and MCT oil and other supplements that delay the progress of Alzheimer's. I know that."

"Hey," Rachel said, smiling encouragement at him. "We're a-gonna lick this hellacious ailment once and for all!"

Rachel went to him, crawled on his lap and hugged him, feeling the warm clasp of his arms around her in response. She wanted to say to him, "You are so brave, my noble warrior," but she didn't want to add her perception to his and perhaps cause him to veer off into depression and despair. As long as he voluntarily opened up, it was his.

Instead, she said, "I understand and I love you more than words can say."

Peter's courage was in walking and falling forward. The act of faith.

Never had there been—to her—a more beautiful specimen of manhood than Peter James.

\\//

Eli's Place was, more and more, The Gang's home away from home.

Today, Peter studied Rachel as they slid into jackets, preparing to embark on their lunch time journey. "You okay? You're kinda quiet. Would you rather go eat at Brandi's Buffet?" He referred to the alternate eatery they'd used during Rachel's more difficult recovery season, when she'd needed to escape into silence.

"No. Remember? I don't go there anymore." *Oops.* She'd mentioned the R word. Not good.

She saw Peter's befuddlement. "I just don't want to talk about it, honey," she clarified. "Too painful." One incident there still haunted her. Memories of it spelled *overload* to her battered mind and thrust her into meltdown.

His eyes lit with recall. "Oh." Then he shook his head firmly. "No. I don't want to go there, either."

Eli's Place was home, from which she would not roam.

"I don't cook anymore," Rachel told an old school friend who later stopped by their table to say hello.

"Must be nice," replied Marlene Brown, a still-beautiful woman who'd marched with her in the Manilowe High School Band color guard many years back. "I don't eat here more than once a week. Carl loves home cooking," she said, rolling her eyes.

Rachel laughed. "So does Peter but the three hours a day I would spend in the kitchen preparing, cooking, and cleaning can be utilized for writing my current project." She didn't add that the culinary/cleanup process would drain her.

Housework? Impossible beyond light tasks, like dishes, dusting, and laundry—without melting into an exhausted heap by midday. Peter hired Gabby or Drusilla once or twice a month to do "maid purging" with the heavier mopping and bathrooms. Actually, Peter had taken to scrubbing the bathrooms himself between the scheduled cleaning services.

Thus, respite from cooking via Eli's was monumental in Rachel's writing enablement and right up there with—well, H2O, soap, deodorant, and makeup.

It made sense to everybody, especially to their close Gang, who'd arrived at the same conclusion regarding their own twilight years' dining sentiments.

Now, with Christmas approaching, Rachel began to feel a hint of that old tradition-pressure to over-achieve with décor and food. Today, Eli's lunch crowd overflowed and The Gang seasoned their meal with greetings and hugs with other regulars, all of whom had become family through the years.

Rachel sighed during a conversational lull. Newly plumbed candor colored her revelations and loosened her tongue. "I don't feel like doing the usual cooking for Christmas. Nor to decorating a tree. Besides, I don't even know where you guys put my artificial pre-lit tree last year when you took it down after the accident."

Somewhere along the way during the years since Amber went away, Rachel had begun using artificial, pre-lit trees. The absence of her two children eliminated the traditional tree trimming and decorating. It brought with it too much heartache to conquer. So Rachel improvised.

It had worked. Until now. This year was different. Her vulnerability had mushroomed. So had Peter's—strong, stalwart Peter. Much of hers had to do with PTSD, aka lingering effects of trauma.

At the same time, Peter's dilemma wove into the equation, complicating further the dynamics of survival. Of overcoming.

Amber's last civil skirmish did not help, either. Would Rachel ever see her daughter again?

"Look in the upstairs guest room closet for the tree, Peter," Gabby said, disrupting Rachel's angst. "Rachel's still not doing steps without her walker, which can be hazardous." She cut Rachel a bossy look. "And as for cooking, you're still not up to that much stress. You know that even in the best of times you go bonkers, cooking and working yourself silly trying to get everything just right."

Peter spoke up. "Gabby's right, honey. You don't have to do anything to make Christmas special for me. Just being with you is enough."

"*Woo hoo!*" rang the grinning chorus-ers.

Rachel shot him a grateful look, then fell silent, daintily chewing fresh chicken salad.

"Besides, "Gabby added. "Leon and I aren't going to be home. We're taking our two grandkids to Disney World for the entire week of Christmas."

"And we're going to Atlanta for Christmas to visit our son," Drusilla chimed in. "The rest of the family is traveling there to be with us."

Rachel's heart plunged. "You're going away, too, Dru?"

"Uh huh," Drusilla said, tucking into meatloaf and mashed potatoes. "So you don't have to worry about feeding or entertaining us."

Rachel's mouthful of chicken salad turned to sawdust. She washed it down with iced tea and pushed away her half-devoured plate. The apprehension of holiday overload was replaced by a melancholy so heavy as to crush her like an uninvited cockroach.

Alone for Christmas. Just the two of them.

No Amber.

No Jason.

No family.

Sudden tears burned her eyes and she blinked them back.

"What's the matter, baby?" Peter leaned to stage whisper. "You okay?"

She nodded but her attempt to smile fell flat. By now, Gabby noticed, then the others.

"Say, Rachel, why don't you and Peter come with us to Atlanta to celebrate Christmas?" sensitive J.C. asked, as sincere as Rachel had ever seen him. "We'd love to have you along."

Tears did fill her eyes then. "Thanks, J.C. I appreciate your offer. I really do. It's just—with Amber gone and all, not to mention Jason's empty space, I just get a little emotional. I'll be okay."

"Hey," Gabby reached across the narrow table to take Rachel's hand, "I can come over and help you decorate if you like. And get you jump started with your cooking."

Drusilla brightened, "I'll bake that carrot cake you love so much. Freeze it and it'll be fresh as dew when you take it out for Christmas."

Rachel dabbed away tears and forced a smile. "Thanks, both of you. Honestly? I don't feel like messing with a tree. As for cooking some goodies, I'll let you know."

Gabby's eyes remained worried. "Okay."

"Know what I think?" Gabby added. "I think you're still not one hundred percent recovered from the accident. I want you to chill out and not worry about a thing. Especially a tree."

Rachel felt a little pinch to her heart. She'd never in her life not decorated a tree. But her heart just wasn't in it.

On the drive home, the sky was overcast but the temperature was a crazy southern December sixty-eight degrees, and Rachel couldn't snuff the nostalgia of happy years gone by.

Nor could she shake the grief of what no longer was.

"Sure you don't want me to help you cook and decorate the tree?" Peter asked.

She shrugged, with slight despair. "Nobody's going to see it, anyway. Why bother?"

"You and I would." His declaration was half-hearted. He'd never been a Christmas person because his family had not. Not at all. That had all been hers. From November through December, Christmas had defined Rachel.

"What day is it?" Peter hiked up his wrist and peered at his watch. "This watch isn't correct."

"Today is Friday, December six."

"Oh."

"Now, be honest," she insisted. "Would you be bothered if we don't have a tree?"

"No."

"That's what I thought. And you know what?"

"What?"

"I don't really feel up to the task of decorating anyway."

"Then don't do it."

She measured him with a look. "You really don't mind?"

He glanced from the road. "Hah! What do you think?"

She laughed then. "Ol' KISS, Peter James."

"What does kiss mean?"

"Keep it simple stupid."

He grinned. "That's me."

"Yup. And you know what?"

"What?"

"That's one of the things I love about you."

He reached to take her hand and squeezed it gently. "I'm so lucky."

"Me, too."

"What's tomorrow?"

\\/

Rachel's novel, *Deepening Shadows*, grew day by day.

Once reached, that illustrious moment all writers seek— finding their voice—propelled her forward and the story kept rolling.

Her germinating trauma-tale quickly morphed into fiction. Re-establishing her author-footing had proved more taxing than she'd ever imagined. It wasn't that she couldn't produce, it was that physically and emotionally, she wasn't always up to the task. So she compensated by writing in short-to-moderate time increments.

Bottom line?

Writing the book sometimes felt like a case of combat fatigue. Inside her mind, she felt that excavating the buried trauma memories was like continually taking a jackhammer to her psyche. She entered weird and perilous waters each time she wrote a page. Still she wrote and wrote, struggling through the assault of guilt at her crime of full disclosure.

Not about her own trauma experience—that, other than the sheer horror of recall, was no longer threatening. No, what bothered her were disclosures of Peter's vulnerability. Because even though he'd given full permission and cooperated in sharing his odyssey, there was always the chance that he would forget the negotiations and later feel betrayed. So all along, Rachel made it a point to give him the option to withdraw his concurrence.

She coped daily with the threat of culpability. And repeatedly, Peter declared that his story should be told to encourage others who struggled with forms of dementia that there is life after Alzheimer's.

"You know, Rachel," he said one day on a sunny, peaceful drive through the countryside. "God made each of us unique."

"Absolutely."

"Even down to our fingerprints."

"Amazing."

"Just think, no two people in the entire universe have exactly the same fingerprints. Even identical twins, who have the same genetic blue print and, to a standard DNA test, they're indistinguishable. But any forensic expert will tell you that there's one sure way to tell them apart."

"You go, ID expert." Rachel grinned at him. Nightly, they watched ID—the TV Investigative Detective channel.

He laughed. "Yup. Identical twins do not have matching fingerprints. So God even gave identical twins individuality. I'd say that's pretty significant in the scope of time and the universe. So He gave me a distinct imprint with which to impact the world."

Rachel absorbed his wisdom. "That's an awesome reflection, Peter. And so on target."

"So I've got to make the most of the time He's allotted for me to make my mark."

She looked at him, tears burning behind her eyes and wanted to record his image in that moment—head held high, eyes full of hope.

Oozing courage.

And she knew that image of him would forever remain indelible.

Chapter Fourteen

\|/

"They think I don't know what I'm thinking, but I do."
—Ron Mayes

Peter strode into the kitchen, where Rachel was doing a half-hearted tidy up.

He stopped at the sink, where she wiped down the counter. "Can I talk to you?"

"Sure." She wiped her hands on a dry towel and sat at the small round maple table. "Sit down and relax, honey." She saw that he was keyed up. Almost frantic.

He slid into a chair facing her and she watched him struggle for control before speaking. "It's hard to live in the now."

He looked so sad, Rachel felt her heart splinter. "Talk to me about it."

"When you're experiencing depression and anxiety *now*, you don't have those past pleasant memories to draw from to balance things out. Like 'I've whipped this before and I can do it again.' Nor do you have a recall cache of helpful things from which to garner."

"I'm so sorry," she said from her heart.

"Me, too. If I could just play golf like I used to with the guys, it would help. But old Arthur beats up on me for days afterward. If I just had *something* to keep me connected."

"I know." And Rachel did know and her heart hurt for him in moments like these, when he met it head on and acknowledged the limitations of his shrinking world.

She arose and rounded the table, arms outstretched. "C'mere."

He stood and stepped into her embrace. She held him closely, never wanting to let him go. His phone jangled in his hip holster.

Peter stepped back and answered. "Yeah, I called, Gary. Did you check on number ten and their leaky faucet?"

Rachel finished up the cleaning as he walked from the room, phone to ear.

She'd decided to take Gabby up on her offer of jump-starting her on the holiday cooking.

Drusilla's moist, three-layer carrot cake with cream cheese icing appeared and after sealing it in a Tupperware cake holder, Dru carefully stored it in Rachel's big freezer.

"Maybe that'll cheer you up at Christmas time," she said and kissed Rachel on both cheeks. Then she instructed, "Just thaw it out a day ahead and then keep it cooled in the fridge because I beat the daylights out of that cream cheese frosting and if it gets warm them layers will slide right off."

Rachel gave her a big hug, laughing. "I'll definitely use TLC on that cake, Dru. You went to a lot of trouble to do that for us. Thanks again."

"Pshaw! It was nothing." she waved a dismissive hand as she departed. "Love you, Rachel! You, too, Gabby."

That first day, the sisters put their heads and hands together—along with Peter's kindhearted help with chopping onions—and prepared sage dressing and giblet gravy for the freezer.

"That's some of the heaviest cooking," Gabby said as she left that evening. "I won't be able to come tomorrow—Leon has a doctor's appointment. But I'll come the day after if you need me."

The next day, gaining emotional momentum, with a spark of *you-can-do-it-baby*, Rachel tackled sweet potato soufflés on her own, with Peter helping to measure and chop nuts for the crust topping.

Each day, she'd gotten up with a little more confidence and stamina. She had to sit to do most of the preparations but leaned on the counter to stand and get down and dirty with the final touches. By afternoon and their break-time to dine at Eli's Buffet, she ached as if she'd been tackled by the entire Manilowe High football varsity team.

Seeing the freezer stocked with holiday entrées poised to be pulled out and popped in the oven almost made her want to dance a Piney Mountain jig. Almost. If she could just get rid of the walker now—to span the steps unaided—she'd be over-the-moon happy.

Thank the good Lord, the wretched neck brace was long gone. She still battled constant fatigue, inflammation, depression, and intermittent headaches that clanged like Big Ben at midnight.

But there was something about seeing the freezer stash that made all that fade away until exhaustion took over and she maneuvered to her bed. *But God bless America!* She had food to serve for the holidays. Her tradition had survived after all, minus the Yuletide tree. She had much for which to be thankful.

After all, The Gang would come together for their own little celebration the week before Christmas, before scattering to the four winds.

The Christmas spirit was taking hold.

Not nearly as intensely as in the past but something sweet and familiar began to stir.

Peter, too, seemed to share the exhilaration. "Let's do something fun today."

It caught her unaware. "Okay. What?"

"Oh, anything you want to."

"No, no, adventuresome one. You name it and we'll do it."

"The Flea Market on 101. Let's go strolling there. I'll get one of the wheelchairs for you and we'll make an afternoon of it." How she loved his spontaneity. But there was only one problem here.

Rachel hesitated. "It's not open today, sweetheart."

"Isn't this Saturday?"

"Huh uh." She saw his face fall and hastened to add, "But we can go to Wally World, can't we?"

"Yeah." He still looked crestfallen.

"But first we'll meet The Gang at Eli's for lunch."

That instantly brightened him. "If you're waiting on me, you're backing up."

\1/

Peter's appetite was slowly dying.

Rachel watched it diminishing by the day and felt helpless to stop its decline.

Eli's bustled about when they arrived, unusual for a Thursday. "I suppose the cold, rainy snap drove folks here," Rachel surmised after Peter asked the blessing.

Drusilla shivered. "It's cold as a well diggers' hiney out there. I hope the snow prediction doesn't come to pass."

Leon laughed. "That rarely happens here. We get snowed in, Gabby might have to cook up something at home."

"You mean she can cook?" Peter asked, his eyes alight with mischief.

"Ah ah," Rachel warned, kicking his foot under the table, then whispered, "You're starting it."

"Yep." Gabby shrugged, ignoring Peter's baiting, to Rachel's relief. She didn't want a repeat of his jabbing at Gabby and then getting offended when she bit back.

Gabby added, "I just don't *like* to cook anymore. I did enough when the boys were still at home. Made enough buttermilk biscuits over the years to fill a transfer truck. Besides, Leon invested wisely years ago and eatin' out is a luxury we can enjoy."

J.C. piped up. "I don't want Drusilla slaving away over a hot stove anymore. Don't want her too tired at the end of the day, doncha know?"

"*Woo hoo!*" Chorused hoots rang out at the hint of romance.

"You don't say, J.C.?" Drusilla's raised eyebrows and droll challenge always brought on more guffaws.

Besides, the thing Rachel didn't shout from the housetop was that she just plain didn't have the stamina and drive that she'd had before the accident. Occasionally, during his financial crunch-anxiety, Peter would suggest that they put a little food in the house and try staying at home and eating.

A little food. Really? Even chicken quarters and ground beef prices, the olden days' standbys, had shot out of sight. Peter had not priced grocery stock lately. She had. Rachel hated his monthly combat with the checkbook and credit card bills. Witnessing any outward cash flow really tripped out her hubby, unlike the old tiger-by-the-tail Peter.

"The last few times I bought groceries," she addressed Peter, "I ended up throwing away more fresh produce than we ate because you don't do leftovers or repeat-fares more than a couple of days in a row. You like to eat healthy but with variety. That doesn't jive with frugal. Trust me. It's cheaper for two to eat out—at least at Eli's Place, what with the senior lunch discount with free drinks."

The bottom-line concern—one she didn't feel free to advertise—was Peter's increasingly finicky appetite. Without the enticement of a buffet smorgasbord, she doubted he'd ingest enough to keep a hummingbird above ground.

So their little group continued convening at Eli's cozy, family-friendly buffet.

Today, J.C., a Clemson Tiger fan, was on the receiving end of much good-natured ribbing from Gabby, a dyed-in-the-wool Carolina Gamecock rooster. "I didn't see you yesterday at church, J.C." She leaned across Peter to continue her harassment of J.C., who sat on his other side. "You know you've been avoiding me."

J.C. did his folded hands, angelic smile, and rolled his eyes upward. "I reckon I was."

"You've got to get tougher than that."

"I reckon I do."

She held up her spread fingers. "Count 'em."

J.C. counted them aloud. "Five."

Gabby grinned triumphantly. "That's how many games the Tigers lost to the Gamecocks."

J.C. rolled his eyes and then looked at Drusilla. "Isn't my wife gonna help me out a little bit here?"

"I'm eating." She scarfed down a big bite of pecan pie.

"And I'm *her husband*." J.C. lamented to Rachel, slowly shaking his head. "See how they treat me?" Rachel burst into laughter. J.C. wrote the book of Woe.

"Okay c'mere," Rachel motioned him over to her side of the table for a big consoling hug. "I'll be your champion, J.C., seeing as you're surrounded by Gamecocks. I'm so sports challenged, I can celebrate with any moment's underdog."

As was the custom, J.C. removed his Army cap and leaned over for Rachel to plant a lipstick print on the top of his bald head, a ritual shared by Tammy, their regular waitress, as well as all of Eli's other waitresses.

Gabby let out a hoot. "Underdog. That's J.C. all right!"

"Oh stop picking on poor J.C." Rachel pouted, scraping her leftover chicken salad into a takeout box.

"He's poor alright," Leon guffawed.

Peter laughed and joined in the "picking on J.C." fun, something they'd all honed and refined through the years, each enjoying his or her role, none more than J.C., who had been, in his younger day, the most robust and feisty of The Gang.

Rachel watched Peter exchange droll rejoinders with the others and felt moved that her husband's wit was as sharp as ever.

That was a good sign, wasn't it? Of course it was.

Eli, the proprietor, visited their table for a few minutes and made sure everything was kosher with his regulars. "They giving you a hard time again, J.C.?" he asked, grinning.

J.C. put on his poor-me face. "Everybody but Rachel."

"Hey!" Drusilla paused in eating her ice cream to scowl. "How about me?"

J.C. turned up his nose. "You're too busy eatin'. I'm just a nobody to you."

More whoops of laughter as Eli patted his shoulder consolingly and moved away, shaking in laughter. Even patrons at other tables tuned in to the trash talk.

Rachel didn't know what she'd do without this time of fun and validation with loved ones whom she trusted with her life. And Peter's. They knew of Peter's lapses but deftly danced around them and treated him as they always had.

Peter appreciated that.

So did Rachel. Oh, how she appreciated that.

In the meantime, she must do all she could to keep Peter functioning normally. And that meant to keep him eating, even if she had to force-feed him.

\1/

Mark River's world had come to a crashing halt following his stepfather's tragic death. His dad had been such a huge hunk of his life that now, the vacuum threatened to devour Mark.

"Man, I'm sorry," Stinky Dodger patted Mark's shoulder following the funeral service. They'd come back to the farm for friends to gather in the Event Barn for dinner served by their church. "This is a tough happening," he shook his head and pushed into motion the barn's white porch swing in which they sat.

Mark sighed and fought back a fresh swell of sorrow and wondered when tears would know when to dry up. "Yeah. Thing is—I have to be strong for Mama. She's all broken up over everything and what with her health and all, it just plain sucks."

Stinky gave a dismal snort. "That's a good way of putting it. I know God doesn't put more on people than they can stand but—" He shrugged elaborately and fell silent. Then he stood, gave Mark's shoulder a good squeeze and said, "Anyway, I know God will help you, pal. He's sure helped me a lot lately. See you later."

When his friend departed, Mark was impressed that the boy didn't wait for his reaction to the spiritual jargon he was tossing about as though he'd always used it. Fact was, coming from Stinky's mouth, it impacted him more than it would from any adult's mouth because he knew the old Stinky and this new version was—

Impressive. That's what it was—Stinky's conviction in his words rang a new bell with Mark—it was extraordinary.

He watched Stinky join his mother at the open gate near their car, she was hugging Mark's mama and no doubt whispering encouragement in her ear. Mark pushed the swing into motion for long moments, reflecting on the recent changes in Stinky, changes he'd never have imagined possible. Amazing. In the midst of it all, he'd gained a great friend.

His stomach's rumbling reminded him that he'd barely eaten anything all day. Oh, Maybelle and Sam had set food before him at home but he'd barely touched it. He was certain his mother hadn't eaten enough, either. But he saw Maybelle nearly force-feeding her, muttering that her diabetes did not take time off for funerals and such.

He halted the swing and went back inside the building to find it emptied of condolence bearers. When had all those folks left? He'd not even noticed. He meandered aimlessly toward the food area. Maybelle spotted him as she was gathering leftovers from the counters to refrigerate for later meals.

"You hungry?" she asked, hope lighting her eyes.

Mark shrugged and scratched his dark head. "Stomach's growling."

"A pretty good sign. Here, sit and I'll fix you a plate. I already done your mama one. You need to go get her and make her sit and eat some more. She's a walking zombie, she is. And I'm afraid her blood sugar's a-gonna crash."

Fear struck like lightening and Mark took off out the door. He saw Stinky sitting in their car playing some game as Mark approached Mama and Frances Dodger, still in intimate conversation. Remembering his manners in the nick of time, he paused and cleared his throat. "Mama, sorry to interrupt but Maybelle's fixed you some food and wants you to come and eat up. I'm— she's worried about your blood sugar."

His mother nodded. "She's right. I'd better go, Frances. Thanks for everything."

Frances gave his mama one more quick hug and departed with "I'm here for you twenty-four seven now."

They waved until the car was out of sight.

The two walked slowly back to the building, arms around each other.

"What we gonna do now?" His mother's words barely registered. And when they did, Mark gulped back a surge of panic.

He groped for something inside him that would encourage her. On some level, he knew that he must be strong for her. She was so fragile. His dad had always known it and protected her. Now, that mantle had been passed to him and it was overwhelming.

He now knew what courage meant—doing and saying things in spite of your fear.

His bravado was strained. But he forced the words out. "We'll be okay, Mama. You'll see." He sure hoped that was true. And then he remembered Stinky's words and grabbed them like a lifeline. "God will take care of us."

Mama's arm tightened around his waist. "I hope you're right, son."

Mark didn't say it out loud but the words echoed in his spirit . . . *"I hope so, too."*

\\|/

On Friday at Eli's, Tammy, their waitress friend, passed by, eyes red and swollen from crying.

All three females were on their feet, rushing to her. "What's wrong, honey?" Rachel asked, putting her arms around the girl's shaking shoulders.

"My sister's boy, Tony, was found dead today." Her voice cracked. "He was only t-twenty-three."

"Oh my goodness," Gabby groaned and all three of them encircled their friend and wrapped arms all around, crying with her. The men, too, stood and offered condolences.

Rachel was so thankful for the family closeness here at Eli's. It was more than a restaurant.

To her, it was a refuge.

\|/

Two evenings later, The Gang journeyed to the funeral home, where Tammy's clan was gathered to spend the last precious hours with their beloved Tony. Tammy met them at the door, walking into Rachel's arms for a long weeping embrace before turning to each of the others for more tearful hugs.

"Thank y'all for coming." She blinked back tears and led them into the viewing room, now filled with dozens of young folks whose stunned faces spoke of their grief and of death striking too, too close, flaunting their mortality. How could they comprehend something like this happening? Yet, how could they stay away?

Looking at the beautiful young man—dressed in casual attire—lying so peacefully in the casket, so surrendered to his fate, tore Rachel's heart in two. Tears burned and in her mind's eye she saw another young man, one she'd birthed, one she'd loved more than life itself and who had left far too soon.

Then her gaze connected with the tortured one of the boy's mother, who was Tammy's sister. Rachel embraced and comforted the distraught mother as best she could. She could only encourage her in that she, too, had stood where this mother now stood. "You *will* get through this," she whispered in her ear. "Just take it one minute at a time."

Then she embraced the boy's father and repeated to him the hard-earned expression of wisdom. The grief-battered father sobbed and hugged Rachel as one would a buoy in a raging sea.

Finally, Rachel moved back for Peter to step up and say a few words of consolation—father to father. To Rachel's surprise, Peter did not take the weeping man in his arms but instead, shook his hand and spoke the proper sentiments. At once removed.

Not the way the old Peter would have responded to this need.

Rachel couldn't help but compare then and now. Not being judgmental. Just sad. Because Peter, when on all cylinders, still had so much to offer. At times, like now, he seemed to step outside himself and observe rather than engage, like an onlooker to life.

Rachel spent considerable time going to each family member to offer support. Peter followed along saying little, yet appropriately sympathetic.

On the drive home, Rachel wrestled with the thoughts. Finally, she said, "I thought you might have offered to embrace the heartbroken father."

Driving, Peter never took his eyes off the road. "I can't help who I am, Rachel."

"Honey, I'm not criticizing. I just wondered why—having gone through the loss of Jason—you couldn't empathize more with what he was feeling."

Peter was quiet for a while and Rachel regretted having brought it up. As always, she felt torn between treating him as normal and cutting him slack. Then he spoke.

"Know why I didn't take charge like I used to do?"

"Tell me."

"Because today, my box has been rattled. My mind's scattered. Nervous as all get out. Back there at the funeral home, I couldn't wrap my head around how the boy was related to Tammy or who was who at the wake. If I'd started asking questions, I'd have made a fool of myself. I don't want everybody knowing I have memory lapses. They start staring at you when they know and begin thinking you're loony."

"Ah, honey." Rachel reached out and took his hand. "I understand. I really do. And Peter James, you are not and will never be loony." She decided to dump the whole load. "You still have so much to offer, darling. You're special, you know."

"Think so?" That brought a trace of a smile to his lips. "Thanks."

Another long silence. Then he asked, "Will you do me a favor?"

"Of course."

"When we're in a situation like this, in a social setting, please just take charge. Let me stay close to you, yet on the fringe of conversation so I won't put my foot in my mouth asking stupid questions."

"I will. Of course I will."

"Cover for me."

"I'll have your back."

"Thank you." He smiled at her then. "How did I ever get you?"

"Easy." She grinned and shrugged. "You just kept coming back."

\I/

Later that night, after they were in bed, Peter snuggled up to Rachel's side and asked again, "What was it that caused the young man's death?"

Propped beside him, watching a Hallmark movie, Rachel sighed and replied, "A blood clot, I already told you." Oops! Shouldn't have said that. He'd asked the same question for—how many times now? She strained to hear the dialogue of the movie she'd been watching for over an hour.

"It went to his heart," she added more gently.

The evening had been disturbing for Rachel, and her nerves, too, were rattled. Tuning into the movie was an attempt to relax and leave darkness behind for a spell, to settle her emotions.

"So he was Tammy's son?"

"No, her nephew."

"What causes a blood clot?"

"I don't know," she said more sharply than she meant to, then softly backpedaled. "Different things. Not sure in this case."

Peter rolled away from her to lie flat of his back. Eyes closed. And she knew.

He was hurt. Slighted. She'd spurned his attempts at conversation and lost patience with his confusion. Again. Frustration chewed on her. How many times can one repeat the same information without irritation setting in?

Trauma aftershocks still disturbed her and she didn't know if they would ever completely leave. Sometimes, like now, she needed time out to simply *be*. Watching a movie or reading a book helped level her out but being interrupted during crucial scenes aborted pleasure.

But Peter was not just anyone. He was the love of her life.

She looked at him. His eyes were closed, a sure sign. "What's wrong?" she asked in a gentle voice, hoping against hope that he would snap out of it on his own, which he sometimes did. But he only shook his head, eyes still shut against her. His face looked so pinched. So defeated. It jerked her back to who she was.

She was his champion.

"Did I hurt your feelings," she asked.

"You just spoke kinda sharply to me when I asked that question. I can't help that I can't remember."

He looked and sounded so despondent that her heart broke anew.

His next words tore at what was left of her heart. "I guess that's why folks like me stop talking. That way, they don't get hurt."

Folks like me.

She twisted around to peer at him. "Peter James, you'd better never stop talking to me. You can ask me the same question a gazillion times and I'll answer you. Just every once in a while, give me some space to mess up, as well. Like just now. Okay?"

He opened his eyes and returned her gaze. He got it. Then he gave a crooked smile. "Okay." He snuggled to her side again as she returned to her movie.

And the thought flitted through her bruised brain: *What else can happen? Surely I deserve some calm, don't I?*

Rachel sighed and relaxed.

Sure I do.

\I/

But she soon learned that her life held no place for complacency.

Drama seemed determined to deluge her existence and rattle loose any rogue buds of tranquility.

Today's Spartanburg Herald Journal headlines screamed *UPSTATE BRACES FOR IMPACT. MAJOR STORM EXPECTED TODAY.* A massive winter storm now targeted the Southeast and would, according to the forecast, move from Atlanta into the Carolinas, the usual tempest route.

Snowfall in South Carolina, as a rule, briefly flirted, promised a great deal, then delivered little—only to disappear within a day beneath an erratic sun. Just that week, temperatures had risen to near seventy degrees.

Now this.

Just when she'd learned to barely survive normalcy.

Rachel recalled the last major storm, in 2005, when their power went out for three days. "Do we still have that gas generator we used to have?" she asked Peter, apprehension trickling along her nerves.

He shook his head. "I haven't seen it in some time."

"Ask Gary if he's borrowed it." Peter could easily have loaned it to someone in need and forgotten about it. Handyman helper friend, Gary, usually knew where Peter left things.

Gloomy weather forecasts jam-packed the day and Rachel prayed that the storm would magically pass over. That had happened before, many times, in fact. But as they left Eli's Place that afternoon, the temperature had dropped a good twenty degrees, and as the low-hanging cloud bellies grew grayer, her optimism fizzled.

By nightfall, she saw the first snowflakes. "It's started." Apprehension again gnawed at her. "Honey, did you call Gary?"

Peter stood gazing out the door. "No."

"Why not? Look, do you want me to call him and ask if he's seen the generator?"

"No." He closed the door and cold air gusted through the den. "Because I don't want Gary to know that I'm having memory problems."

Rachel knew that with Gary's close working relationship with Peter, he had to be aware of Peter's bleeps but she held her tongue.

Irritation threatened to overtake her. "We bought a lantern to use. But if there's a power outage, we have no heat backup."

"I'll look in storage tomorrow for the generator."

By morning, pristine white blanketed the landscape. The roads remained clear, their wet gray in stark contrast to the snow. That was a relief. Peter took the pickup out to check out the local highways and found them all clear.

They lunched at Eli's Place.

"There's another storm coming in tomorrow night," Gabby informed them. "It's the major one, doncha know? They're calling it a historical one."

"Look," Rachel interjected, nerves jumping, "Do any of you have our generator?"

Everyone looked at each other, shaking their heads. And no one had a spare kerosene or gas space heater, either. Rachel's heart fluttered with anxiety and then slithered down to floor level.

"You can always come pile up with us in our den." Drusilla offered. "We have gas logs, in case of electricity failure. We can pitch pallets to sleep on."

Rachel knew Peter would not go for that. He was funny about sleeping in his own bed. Actually, so was she. "Thanks. I'll keep that in mind," she replied graciously.

That night, icy wind gusts and deepening shadows echoed Rachel's mood. A sense of gloom settled inside her and refused to budge. She read until the Conroy novel dropped from her fingers and she slid into exhausted slumber.

The next morning, Rachel arose and peeked out through the blinds. Nothing had changed. Maybe the monster storm would overlook them. She breathed a sigh of relief. But by mid-morning, large flakes began to fall. Soon, the white turned into blizzard drifts.

She was beside herself.

How much longer before power lines would snap under the weight of ice? No way could she face freezing weather with no heat. Topping every weather forecast "things needed" list was backup heat.

The white stuff continued to fall and within two hours the roads disappeared into a world completely colorless, save spotty, shadowy reliefs.

Throughout the day, she prompted Peter to search again for the generator. Peter would comply, then return from outside, feet caked with muddy ice, which made tracks until he thought to remove his corrugated work shoes inside the door.

Rachel's manic-obsessive mood now switched into high gear. She silently lamented the mud-stained hardwood floors. They intensified her fears of more chaos in an already messy reality.

Unable to contain herself, she got in her wheelchair and, using the long-handled grabber to push the towel, slowly swabbed the stains up. Not easy but she persevered. Amazing how the clean floors sustained her, made her feel less helpless. And she recognized anew what a complex creature God had created in her.

Please Lord . . . please don't let our power fail. And if you will, please protect us from the elements. I praise you for all you've already done for me . . . for us. Thank you.

The thick falling flakes and wind gusts grew eerie and increasingly threatening and Rachel migrated to her computer, checking Facebook posts for upbeat news from local friends in the same crisis as she. Peter shadowed her and seemed as at loose ends as she felt.

Tiny *pings* against her study window told her it was sleeting.

She checked the weather again, propped on her walker, opening the door. Frigid gusts seized and shook her to her bones.

"Peter," she called, slamming the door. "We have some burners with propane tanks. Remember?" How she hoped the R word wouldn't offend him and that he would recall said tanks.

He looked blankly at her, shaking his head. "I don't—"

"Ah, honey, you used them to cook the big black pots of chicken bog."

His eyes lit up. "Yeah." Then his features fell. "But I don't remember where they are."

"Look in storage. With them—if the power fails—we could at least light them for short periods of time to keep the extreme chill away—with adequate ventilation, of course." She sighed nervously, fighting the urge to wring her hands. "I wish I was able to go search—"

"Whoa!" Peter's face creased in astonishment. "Honey bun, I wouldn't let you go out in this weather for all the rice in China—even if you could walk well enough. You don't need another fall."

He left and was back twenty minutes later. "They weren't there. Reckon I should try to make it to the other storage, the old Scout Building?"

"Probably. We simply must have backup heat. I feel an urgency about it." Actually, she felt tied in all the Eagle Scout rope knots Jason used to practice. She recognized lingering PTSD symptoms and tried her best to shake them. But the uptightness remained dug in.

Rachel wondered in that moment if she should simply trust more in Providence.

But didn't the Bible teach about the ten virgins, some prepared by having oil in their lamps and the others who did not were turned away from the wedding feast? So God meant for her to be prepared, even if He chose to favor their home with light and warmth. That settled it in her heart.

Peter's pickup did make it to the old building but to no avail. He came back empty handed. Rachel's ire was building in that she'd tried to get him to act upon this for four days, as soon as she heard the forecast. But he had not.

Still . . . he disappeared outside again and reappeared within minutes.

"I found them!" he called out and proudly presented two propane burners that could, in case of emergency, provide heat. "They were behind the storage building, out of sight."

Rachel felt ashamed of her impatience, realizing he'd done his best in staying focused enough to simply function in the everyday demands on his life. And now, in time of emergency, he'd persevered until he'd found solutions to each challenge.

He remained her hero—in the words of their song . . . "Here in the sweet and same old way . . . I fall in love again as I did then." Yes, she did. Over and over again.

Still . . . the stress inside her stubbornly refused to leave.

Rachel felt herself becoming increasingly obsessive. Her frenzied focus on details tightened her insides until her stomach cramped. She finally gave up on diverting her mind via Facebook and crawled into bed.

Peter, already stretched out and waking from a nap, asked, "You okay? You look pale."

"I'm cramping underneath my rib."

"What do you think it's from?"

"I don't know. I'm stressed out, I know. Probably that. But I'm also chilled to the bone."

Sometime during the day, the cold from outside had crept inside her and took up abode, whether by osmosis or in ghostly form, she didn't know but she'd not been aware of it until now. And it threatened to pitch her into teeth-clattering spasms, much like the shock of trauma after her accident.

Truth was, something about the monster storm was resurrecting those trauma ghosts—ones that didn't need awakening.

She groaned and pulled the cover up under her chin, frigid chills rippling over her.

She felt Peter nudge something against her. "It's the heating pad," he said, adjusting the heat. Soon, the warmth began to seep into her. Her body slowly relaxed, along with the stomach cramp, and she felt her lids grow heavy.

Next thing she knew, the clock said 7:45 a.m. Peter already had the coffeepot going.

The house was warm. She flicked on the TV and it sprang to life with weather reports.

Rachel shook her head in wonder. Snow still peppered down outside but the worst was over. Even the DISH signal had persevered, a miracle in itself when just a heavy rain could wash it away. She tuned in her TV Bible teachers and arose to begin her morning routine, which was, this morning, to simply be thankful.

Seemed her prayers had been heard. No, He hadn't excused her from doing all she could to weather the latest tempest. She smiled as she spread the covers on the bed and de-cluttered her bedside table, digesting that it simply was not His way of dealing with her.

The message was loud and clear. The Almighty loved her too much to allow her to become a lazy wimp.

\|/

Snowed in.

Peter felt trapped. Suffocated.

Another challenge as he surveyed roads buried beneath ten inches of snow and ice. The day spread out before them, with little hope of getting out.

Another challenge on the heels of worrying about Rachel's emotional fragility that had persisted throughout the storm—a worry that had left his mind as scattered as bowling pins during a perfect strike.

But this morning, Rachel seemed sprung from the anxiety that had gripped her for the past three or four days, especially bad last night when pain had bent her double. But the heating pad had done the trick. Today, she seemed different. Relaxed. Her blue, blue eyes cleared.

From the den window, Peter saw Sam, his next-door neighbor and leasee outside, digging his way out of his yard at the bottom of the hill.

"Know where my shovel is?" Peter asked Rachel, tugging on heavy socks and brogans.

"I think you put it in the storage building," she called from the kitchen.

Happy for a physical diversion, he retrieved the tool and, for the next hour, heaved and dug alongside his friend until the long driveway displayed naked tire routes, which promised passage to the outside world.

When he re-entered the house, heavenly smells from the kitchen made his mouth water. Just in time, he remembered to slide off his muddy brogans. He'd felt terrible earlier that he'd tracked muck all over the house without even thinking. Rachel had almost cried and ended up washing up the tracks with wet towels pushed by the grabber. But she never said a word to him.

Such an angel, Rachel.

Made him feel crappy. On second thought—he should've cleaned up the mess himself. Too late now but he stored that away for later opportunities to vindicate himself.

"Hungry?" she called out.

"Starved!"

She leaned against the counter near the stove, turning lean sausage patties and stirring cheesy grits. From the oven, she pulled out a small covered Pyrex. "I found this sage dressing from my frozen Christmas stash and baked it. Also"—she moved to the microwave—"a treat for you," she extracted another glass bowl. "Sweet potato soufflé with the nut-crunchy crust. Another from my frozen cache."

"Wow!" He washed up and sat down at the table.

"I'm going to have a once-over-lightly egg with mine," she said. "Want one?"

"Sure. Make mine a little more done, please?"

"Quite a weird assortment of entrées, huh?" She chuckled. "Oh, well. It's a brunch menu. So anything goes."

"Looks like a feast to me," he said with gusto. To him, she was the greatest cook on earth. Bar none.

"Did you get Sam out of the hole?" She finished filling their plates, poured hot, aromatic coffee, and sat down to join him.

"Yup. I think he can drive out now. But the secondary roads still don't look promising. The sun is coming out, however. That'll melt some of it. But if the temperature drops again this evening, it'll refreeze. Not a great forecast. But if the snowplows get the main roads cleared, there's a chance we'll be more mobile by tomorrow."

Peter asked the blessing and felt better than he had in days. And he knew that Rachel felt the same contentment as he did. He could see it in her eyes as they exchanged tender smiles during this intermezzo that bridged past and coming challenges.

Yeah. The big IT intruded at times.

But out of the night Rachel's sweet voice called him back, time and time again.

All else but today's sunshine faded.

For this moment in time, he felt that he, Peter James, was the luckiest man alive.

Chapter Fifteen

\\\\/

"Find joy in your journey."
—Alzheimer's Association

"Would you please give Rachel and Peter this for me?"

The little white-haired church lady handed Gabby a red-foil wrapped box. "They're leftover Christmas goodies. And here's one for you and Leon."

"Oh my goodness," Gabby exclaimed, her heart thumping fast as a marching band snare drum. "How sweet. I'll share ours with Drusilla and J.C. Looks like there's enough here to feed the entire church choir."

Guilt nibbled at Gabby as she stacked the two boxes on one arm.

"Thanks again, Ms. Dot. You're an angel." She hugged the stooped shoulders and blew an air kiss. Then she reared back and angled a discerning look. "What's wrong? You look like something's not quite right."

With obvious reluctance, Ms. Dot said, "My son-in-law just passed away."

Tears sprang to the aged blue eyes.

"He was a wonderful Christian man who loved my daughter and her son through the years." She touched Gabby's arm. "Please pray for them—" She seemed about to say more but then to decide against it. "God bless, honey." And she was off.

Gabby blinked back tears—sensing the enormity of the loss—watching her move away through the church vestibule, disappearing into the throng of worshippers greeting one another with the warmth that had kept The Gang tethered here since—well, as far back as Gabby could remember. To when the simpler church structure was a fraction the size of this more grand architectural design and sported only four hundred members.

Young Gabby, Rachel, and cousin Drusilla occupied the very front pew, to enable her pastor dad, Hamp West, to keep an eye on them. Later, Gabby and Drusilla graduated further back. Only Rachel continued to sit up front, this time on the piano bench. This continued until Gabby went away to college and Rachel later married Peter and the two of them finished college. Hamp later delighted in his grandchildren and soon, before he knew it, proclaimed they'd grown up faster'n any weed he'd ever seen.

Losing Jason had been difficult for him, Gabby recalled while standing there in the vestibule. The loss had devastated both the entire biological and church families.

That was when Hamp stepped down and surrendered his pulpit to a younger man. "It's time," he decreed matter-of-factly. By then widowed, he'd retired.

Gabby missed him. Oh, how she missed him. If he were here, she'd ask his advice on how to handle this double-cross-limned situation she found herself in. And now, with today's news from Ms. Dot, the load intensified. Gabby knew too much not to figure out that the boy she'd spoken of had to be Peter's son, the one he was forbidden to acknowledge.

Her sister's nemesis situation.

And now, the boy's father-image had been taken away. Gabby couldn't forestall the pain that settled around her heart.

She looked down at the goodie boxes, her mouth already moistened in anticipation, feeling like the Judas Iscariot she was. What would Rachel say?

She headed for the exit, catching one more glimpse of the little white-haired woman with the adolescent boy and her gaze lingered on him for long moments.

How her heart went out to him today, with his wan, grief-emptied features. It took great effort not to go and wrap him in her arms. But that would really be crossing a line of no return.

Yup. What would Rachel say?

She sighed and, when she did, she whiffed the heavenly bouquet of spiced goodies and her mouth watered. She couldn't help but grin in expectation. What Rachel didn't know wouldn't hurt her, now, would it?

Nope, it wouldn't.

\\|/

Today was a good day.

Peter drove to his next pest control appointment with the CD player going.

He played "Twilight Time" over and over again. Remembering.

Today, The Box was a little bigger, giving him breathing and thinking space. Today, yesteryear was touchable. Sun painted the Carolina foothills golden with dappled earthen tones of dried leaves, lending them rich dimensions.

The client there on Hogback Mountain had taken a bad fall from a horse three years earlier. Ginny had made a remarkable recovery, considering she was now quadriplegic and required around-the-clock nursing care.

Her husband, Carol, had died suddenly of a heart attack not long after Ginny's accident, leaving her even more vulnerable since her family lived out of state. But she chose to reside at the home where she and Carol had lived and loved through the years.

Peter's heart bled for her. How easily Rachel's destiny could have paralleled Ginny's, who chatted with him from her special bed today as he moved about, lightly treating cracks and crevices in her lovely home. Most of his chemical applications were on the outdoor perimeter of the dwellings. Peter only did indoors when a maverick insect found its way inside.

"I read your wife's latest book," Ginny informed him, smiling her upbeat smile beneath her short, spiky nutmeg-colored hair. "I really enjoyed it."

Peter felt himself preening. He couldn't help it. *Goodness gracious to Betsy*, his pride in Rachel's success was as unstoppable as his love for her. "Thanks, Ginny. I'll be sure and tell her."

"You do that!"

"Rachel may come visit next time I'm up here. She's busy writing today."

"Tell her I'd love that," Ginny called after him.

When he left, he decided to forego charging her for the quarterly visit. Ginny's situation always reminded him of how merciful God had been with Rachel.

With him.

How would he manage without Rachel? Life wouldn't be worth living. He told her as much daily when his mind veered off into that crazy empty zone. When he couldn't think his way out of a paper bag. When nothing looked familiar and his reasoning went on the lam. This didn't happen too often but when it did, it turned his insides to jelly.

He'd taken to sharing the intervals with Rachel because she always soothed his alarm and offered him hope. "You'll feel better tomorrow," was her usual reassurance. And it was true. A good night's sleep helped. That is, when he was able to snooze without waking up in a cold sweat, encountering the restlessness of a wartime, front-line soldier. Only thing, the enemy that came at him from the four corners was not flesh and blood.

It was financial.

Peter's Alpha strength had cast him as the main provider in charge of keeping all their plates spinning smoothly. Holding it all together in the past had never given him problems. Fact was, he thrived on it. Now—he hated this menacing entity hovering, stalking him, ready to pounce.

Rachel could put those fears to rest with her quiet reasoning.

Most of the time.

Last night, he awoke to an old recurring pain.

He'd dreamed about his son. The one he'd never met. He wanted to approach Rachel once more about seeing his boy, who would be thirteen now, the age of Jason when he died.

Sometimes he felt he would die from longing to hold the boy.

His.

But not Rachel's. That "but" spoke volumes.

He shook his head. How could he hurt Rachel all over again? She was just beginning to regain a small measure of her pre-accident mobility and endurance. Not a total restoration but it was a start. How could he ask her to accept the child when she'd said over and over that it would kill her?

No. He wouldn't.

Couldn't.

He loved her too much.

This was one thing Rachel couldn't help him with.

It was his punishment.

\\\//

Dot Rivers' cell phone jangled and she snatched it from her apron pocket, anxious to hear from her daughter. "Hello?"

"Mom, I'm sorry it took so long to get back with you. I had a dialysis treatment yesterday and felt really exhausted afterward. Before yesterday's treatment, I did talk with Bill Winston, the executor of Ralph's estate. Unfortunately, Ralph didn't complete the changes to his will that he intended, which would have provided for Mark and me to live out my life on the farm. He did, thank God, manage to get a trust fund set up for Mark's college and expenses."

"But why didn't he change—"

"Mom—he didn't plan on dying suddenly. He thought that he would live to be an old man and felt no urgency to—"

Dot heard silent weeping. "Ahh, sweetie. I'm so sorry. He was such a *good* man. What will happen with the farm and all? There's so much to be done there."

Mary snuffled and cleared her throat. "His son, Chris, has applied for an early military retirement on grounds of hardship. He wants to carry on the organic farm tradition his dad has worked so hard to accomplish. It's a success and I understand his son wanting to step into his shoes. Mark and I could never do that. I hate to leave the farm but Chris and his family deserve this legacy from his dad."

"Oh my," Dot murmured, hand to throat. "So where—"

"Mom, the farm transition will take from three to four weeks. Chris has already lined up fill-ins for the farm work until he is officially able to move here. Maybelle and Sam will stay on in their positions. Chris has known them all his life so it's only natural that he'd keep them on."

"So—"

"So, Mom, if it's okay, Mark and I will move in with you. I'm getting weaker by the day. I don't like to talk about it, but there it is. I'm slowly dying. And I need my mama." Her voice broke on that.

Now was Dot's turn to silently weep. After long moments, she snuffled and said, "Of course. You know my home is your home, honey. For now and always."

"Thanks, Mom. I love you bunches."

"I know. And you are my heart. How's Mark doing today? He looked really shredded inside over the weekend but he didn't seem to want to talk about it."

"He's a little soldier. He's being so brave for me. I'm letting him. He needs it to keep going. It's going to be like death all over again for him to leave the farm. You know how much he loves those critters—as Ralph always called them. They're like his family. And though Chris wants Mark to feel free to come visit as often as he wishes—it just won't be the same."

"I know. We'll have to get him a dog from the local animal shelter—and a cat and a gerbil and fish and whatever else he wants."

"Great idea." A long pause. "Thanks, Mom."

"For what?"

"For being there—and loving me so much."

"What's not to love? I'm getting your rooms ready. So just say when and we'll get you moved in."

After they rang off, Dot finished her Bible reading. She couldn't get Mark off her mind. She kept hearing what he'd said to her on the way home from church last Sunday.

"Y'know, Gramma—just when I get a really good friend, I'm having to leave him. Stinky's become a real pal. He's there when I need to talk about Dad and about Mama's sickness and all. It's gonna be real hard to move here. Not that I won't like being with you," he hastened to add, ever the considerate one.

"I understand, darlin'," Dot replied. And she did. Then she brightened. "There are always your cell phones. You can keep in touch all you want, doncha know? And he can visit on weekends, holidays, and during summer vacation. He'll be welcome at my house any time. And you can visit him—and you two can visit Sugar Hills too. You won't be totally cut off."

"Yeah." That had seemed to make him feel somewhat better. Dot drove the long way home, the more scenic route just along the village outskirts, wanting to capture and preserve the intimacy of the moments. "Y'know, Gramma, there's this sick feeling inside me. Like—I'm empty. It hurts kinda but it's not an ordinary pain?" He shook his head. "It's hard to explain it."

"Grief probably. It feels that way sometimes."

"I suppose." He shrugged limply, eyes straight ahead, like he was seeing something way off down the road.

Her heart had ached for him. And then he said the thing that broke it.

"I think it's because now—" He cut those green eyes at her and she glimpsed behind them a vast desert. "Now, I really, really don't have a daddy."

\ı/

Rachel felt something simmering.

What? She couldn't say, but she knew it was something vital she'd been searching for, something that would turn her life around in a heartbeat. Today, she was silent on the ride home from church. Thank God, Christmas was past. Finally.

She'd seen him again today, the boy who reminded her of Jason.

He'd been talking with another boy as they marched into the sanctuary from the side door, following their youth service in another building. All the church, from middle school up, came together for the main worship service.

Again, she'd had to tear her gaze from him. Something about him today had pierced her heart—a vulnerability. He looked somehow gaunt. Depleted. How she'd wanted to go to him and gather him in her arms. She'd wiped tears from her eyes and tore her mind loose from memories.

Two days loomed before the turn of another year. This anniversary represented a mammoth chunk of her life skidding to a halt. Peter, too, seemed in a pensive mood, not engaging or teasing her as he usually did. Something about him today—a defenselessness—tugged at her heart in unparalleled ways. He was so good to her . . . beyond neither rhyme nor reason.

Beyond duty.

Once home, they ate burgers they'd picked up on the way in and then when Peter lay down to nap, she went to her study and found her father's file of old sermon notes, one he'd left to her in his will. They sang out her name today, in four-part harmony. Actually, seemed she heard a fifth today, a dreamy second soprano.

Reverently, she sat back in his worn easy chair, another bequest, and ran her hands over the folder's leather cover, feeling a certainty that these journals of wisdom would provide the guidance she so desperately needed.

She closed her eyes and reached inside. Her fingers gripped and tugged out one paper-clipped copy. She took a deep breath and opened her eyes. The topic zoomed in: *"HOW TO LIVE ABOVE THE DRAMA OF LIFE."*

Drama of life. Timely?

Wow. Ya think, Rachel ol' girl?

No soap opera held a flicker to what hers had been in recent months.

Her eyes burned and moistened. "Thanks, Daddy," she whispered, then sniffed and blinked away tears.

The first of Pastor Hamp's steps was to *"KEEP ONESELF SPIRITUALLY HUNGRY TO SEE GOD'S GLORY CONTINU-ALLY REVEALED."*

It was somewhat wordy to her writer's editorial eye, but try as she might she could not edit it down without altering its heart or losing her daddy's sweet, rich voice.

This one was easy, seeing as how the first layer of scales had fallen from Rachel's eyes at the time of her accident. Every day had presented infinite examples of heavenly glories, from her a.m. rising to the settling of her feet upon the floor; from the movement of her limbs—albeit with the aid of her walker—to the ability to speak and think coherently. All wonders.

Gathered splendor.

Around her, things once mundane had taken on the shim-mer of grace and mercy, like an unemployed bread winner, one day struggling to make ends meet and the next, receiving an unexpected job offer with great benefits . . . or her faith-ar-mored friend who defied all odds by beating cancer, even when the doctors said there was no hope. The examples were endless and exhilarating.

She moved on to the next "how."

This one said *"TAKE SERIOUS THE SMALLEST SINS IN YOUR LIFE."*

This one was a gen-u-ine Hamp-ism. Her father's face flashed before her . . . a mixture, during preaching, of Efrem Zimbalist Jr.'s dignity and grace with Billy Graham's passion and conviction. She remembered Pastor Hamp's devotion to this topic, always guiding his little girls to never, ever allow the little foxes into their lives, ones that spoiled the vine.

"Be careful," he gravely admonished Rachel and the older Gabby, "not to drift away from God's peace. Never allow yourselves to grow comfortable with small wrongs, things that you don't feel quite right about, you know? It can open the door to bigger wrongs."

Both the PKs got it.

The "drifting away" had been simple yet on target in Daddy's sermon truths and ranked high up on the totem. Broken down, the imploration spotlighted her own astonishing post-trauma metamorphosis.

Rachel now saw the world through different eyes—especially in respect to her own contributions. Behind each word and action she'd felt an extraordinary accountability that would not be ignored.

Yet . . .

She closed her eyes and recalled—with shame—the day she'd been seen Ziploc-ing and discreetly sliding into her purse leftovers from her meal at Brandi's Buffet.

Jumping Jellybeans, Eli would have brought Rachel a carry-out box for her leftover chicken salad, a tasty entrée that suited her sagging appetite. Eli's equated home to her and Peter and The Gang. And she'd grown accustomed to that.

Following the accident, however, after she'd become ambulatory, Rachel had needed a different itinerary to battle the post-traumatic stress disorder that rode shotgun to her every thought and move. So occasionally, she and Peter played hooky from The Gang to visit another buffet, a little "getaway" time. Her tolerance for gabbing and joking wore thin at times and— love The Gang as she may—she'd needed silence.

And solitude.

She'd needed to survive the persistent assault on her mind and body.

She needed to heal.

The perfect retreat was another buffet restaurant in a neighboring area managed by Agnes, a church friend. Many days when Rachel and Peter dined there, Agnes would take her own lunch break and eat with them. Their conversations were light and engaging and the change relaxed Rachel.

Agnes made it feel like home.

Like Eli's Place.

Rachel's appetite, most days, was poor and she ate only portions of her chicken or wings or whatever bar-featured entrée. She missed Eli's tasty chicken salad, one not available at Brandi's bar menu. Rachel had been raised to believe it a sin to waste food.

Post-trauma, her reasoning was still not the sharpest, either.

Though she later steadfastly refused to use that as an excuse.

Along the way, Rachel noticed that Agnes stopped joining them at their table but thought little of it since the woman was a hard worker and stayed constantly busy. Rachel did note that her friend now took her meal break with other patrons.

One day during their getaway, unexpectedly, Agnes marched to Rachel and Peter's table, sat down, and in no uncertain terms told Rachel that she'd been under surveillance and reported for taking food from the restaurant.

"What you're doing is wrong," she stated coldly. The declaration vibrated with condemnation.

Rachel nearly passed out from shock. It was her worst nightmare. Ever. Her carefully constructed emotional fortification came crashing in on her.

Agnes went on, "This is embarrassing to me because my servers know that you go to my church." It got worse as the dressing down continued. "I didn't want to believe that it was true. I'm terribly disappointed in both of you."

It hit Rachel like an unmanned drone: *She'd been spied on?* How demoralizing. How humiliating! Couldn't her friend have come to her long ago and voiced the suspicions, giving Rachel some compassionate warning? A dignified way out? That's what she would have done.

Suddenly the place felt anything but her home away from home.

Agnes, cheeks magenta with indignation and disillusionment, dismissed them with a curt, "Don't ever do it again."

She left as abruptly as she'd arrived.

Stunned, Rachel looked at an equally staggered Peter. "I'm sorry," she whispered, because Peter was never involved in her prudent leftovers-bagging. And Agnes had included him in her reprimand. Poor, innocent Peter. Now, she understood why Agnes had stopped dining with them, why she'd avoided them . . . distanced herself.

Suddenly, Rachel felt like a fugitive from justice, a murderer on the lam, the thief on the cross, the worst of the worst . . .

She'd failed God.

She'd failed her friend and all the servers. And Peter.

Rachel had failed her father.

She wanted to slither through the floor.

If only she could.

Oh, dear Lord, she was tagged a *thief.*

How deep the valley into which she plunged! How dark!

She landed with a resounding *crash!* One equivalent to her atomic-impact head-smash into the wall.

With Peter supporting her and with the aid of her walker, Rachel made her way out of the establishment, pausing only to offer a heartfelt apology to her friend, Agnes, for letting her down, offering no excuses. She took it full on the chin.

She asked forgiveness and received an embrace and an "I love you." But Rachel knew—Agnes may love her but she couldn't like her. A big, big difference.

She left, with head down and spirit dragging.

Simultaneously, Peter kept up a constant stream of encouragement. "You are not a bad person, darling. To you, it was no big deal to take the leftovers. After all, you hate to waste food. It's been ingrained into you. Agnes could have come to you earlier and let you know you were being spied on. A real friend would do that, Rachel. I can't believe she didn't give you a chance to cease and correct it all without humiliating you."

"It's not her fault. I was wrong. She's just doing her job." Rachel's case was as limp and desiccated as her morale.

"Yes, but she accused me, too. I'm considered guilty as well. I still think she could have handled it better, with a little more tact and earlier on."

"That's what I hate the most," Rachel said as Peter helped her into the car. "You've never taken a crumb out of the place." She shrugged flaccidly, numb inside but the outside doing a Richter scale 7.3 quake. "I can't believe this is happening," she muttered, her teeth beginning to clatter.

"You okay, honey?" He leaned over to kiss her cheek. She nodded, too frozen to cry.

"I still say she could have done it with more kindness." He slammed the car door. Dear, sweet Peter, ever her champion.

The incident proved pivotal in Rachel's life.

That was the time Rachel faced up to the fact that she had a ways to go before she was OK in God's eyes. And honestly? In her own eyes. After she'd apologized to Agnes, Rachel did not go back to Agnes' store because she didn't want to further embarrass her friend nor be reminded of the humiliation.

"I can't think about it," she told Peter when he would begin commiserating, which he was prone to do these days. "Dad always said to let go of disappointment quickly. After all, he always reminded me, things happen for a divine reason. The good ones encourage us. The bad ones teach us valuable life lessons.

"I was wrong," she reminded Peter. "I sinned."

Peter would shake his head and kiss her, "If you don't make it into the pearly gates, nobody will."

That always brought a smile to her face, his confidence in her character.

"Thanks, darling. But He's not through with me yet. Painful though it was, He apparently needed to teach me this character-building lesson. Daddy was right. Small sins should be taken seriously or they can land you in hot water."

After the incident, Rachel had written a public Facebook confession/apology. And she prayed, and prayed, and prayed. Despite Peter's glowing support, she lost many nights' sleep regretting her lousy judgment and realized how seemingly small lapses could taint one's good name, a thing to be treasured above all riches. She learned what the Apostle Paul meant when he said he must be all things to all people. Eli gave her leftovers to take home. It was not a sin. But to Agnes, Rachel's taking leftovers definitely fell under "betrayal."

So betrayal was relative to situational ethics.

A hard-earned lesson.

Tonight, with hindsight, she had to admit that the valley experience was not without merit. She learned many lessons plodding the difficult terrain, one being that not everybody will love you, or for that matter, even like you.

She'd told Peter as much one day as they went for a sunny ride in the country.

"Friends come and go in life. Some stick through the darkest of times, not thinking less of you when you screw up."

"Like The Gang," Peter inserted, listening closely.

"Yes. Others, like Agnes, walk away. And that's okay because they have their own valleys—disappointments like me—and have their own miles to run."

"If I ever see Agnes again, I'm going to tell her that she should have—"

"No, Peter." Rachel held out an imploring hand. "Please let it go, honey. For some folks, it's difficult to let go of grievances, to not judge. After all, she forgave me. Remem—" She cut off the R word.

"You're the most forgiving person I know, Rachel."

"But not all folks are wired to easily turn loose offenses. Even *spiritual* people can be like pit bulls when it comes to betrayals. They may *forgive* but they won't forget. So, unfortunately, friendships are often trashed over seeming imprudence."

He looked at her. "What's imprudence?"

Rachel laughed. "It's actually lack of judgment. Foolish blindness to consequences. That sort of thing."

"You are not foolish, honey."

She hugged him and remained silent. No use trying to change his view of her. She was kind of glad she couldn't. It helped her stay in contact with who she really was deep inside.

Tonight, Rachel blinked away the image of his trusting face, one that adored her.

The memory gave Rachel pause for long seconds . . . but her overloaded mind slid forward, leaving it behind in a mist.

Fact was, Rachel had immediately stopped judging others following that buffet fiasco. Who was she to referee anybody's behavior? There were always underlying variables that only the Creator Himself could know in each person's life.

The bottom line? Her *Rachel-image* was no longer rose-colored. Another truth emerged: we alone determine who we are. Nothing can destroy one's name *or* life's mission as long as one learns from mistakes, repents, and moves forward.

Best of all, today, Rachel realized that she *could* live above life's dramas by following her pastor-father's old sermon treasures. She could make peace with the past so it wouldn't disturb her present.

Rachel went down the list of wisdom-nuggets and checked them off as "done."

She should have been marinating in sheer serenity.

Yet . . .

Something else hovered in the wings. Something disturbing.

It was time she found out *what*.

\\/

How did he get himself into this?

Peter had been so certain this was the right decision.

Then why had this excursion become his worst nightmare?

He gazed about him at the dormitory walls and paced about the Clemson University quarters now emptied because of semester break. He'd insisted upon signing up for the five-day pest control seminar—at a belt-tightening expense—feeling an urgency to acquire some of his required continuing education hours.

Everything these days seemed imperative and life threatening. Keeping his pest control license headed the militant combat march.

For the moment. Tomorrow another drum major might strut into the lead.

"You don't have to do it," Rachel had insisted, worry spilling from her blue eyes. "You can select more local, day-long workshops along the way. The drive to Clemson takes about an hour and a half—you'll have to stay on campus for the duration. Anyway, the classes run late and start early a.m., so commuting isn't logical."

She angled him a doubtful look. "Sure you want to pursue this?"

"Yup. This way, I'll get ten hours—fast—for the classes."

She'd still not looked convinced. "Are you confident you can handle such an intensive agenda?" She had kindly omitted the R word.

"Sure I can," he'd blustered. His bravado was sporadic, alternating between denial and terror. But he had something to prove to himself and *by cracky*, he was going to do this if it killed him. He was not ready to give up on normalcy yet.

So Rachel had driven him up in their only operating vehicle at that precise time, her Honda van. His truck was being serviced and needed some serious repairs, so he reasoned it was the perfect time to get 'er done. He could walk to the classes, couldn't he? Sure he could. He was still sprightly. Students did it all the time.

Too, there should be a whole passel of other pest control attendees to catch rides with, shouldn't there? Maybe he'd form some new friendships there. Rachel agreed.

Rachel still used her walker for difficult maneuvers but she was gaining ambulatory speed, and soon she'd helped him get registered and settled into this dorm space, actually a two-bedroom unit with central bath, den, and kitchen. Of course, all the den furniture was gone until the next students arrived with new furnishings.

"Two of the four beds are made up," Rachel voiced her observation. "You may get a roommate, honey. We're a little early."

On the kitchen bar, Rachel arranged their spread of lunch she'd brought from home. Chicken salad and slaw, compliments of Eli's Buffet. He'd offered more but they'd politely declined. As it was, Rachel recapped the leftovers for Peter to eat later and put it in the refrigerator, making the strange quarters feel a little more like home.

In a moment of boldness, Peter said, "You can leave any time, honey. Others will be coming in soon. It's already near three o'clock and I don't want you having to drive after dark."

Rachel had looked at him, concern bleeding through. "You sure you'll be okay?"

He huffed a weak laugh. "Of course." Would he? He sure hoped so.

Then, as she did her transfer from ground to car seat, he'd felt a frisson of fear. "Sure you don't want to stay with me?" he heard himself blurt, because he knew that she'd packed an overnight bag. "Just in case."

"Do you want me to?" Then, she'd shaken her head. "You will most likely have a roommate later today. I can't stay under those circumstances."

"Yeah." He'd understood her reasoning. But *holey moly*, he hated to see her go.

Then daring seeped through the fear. "I'll be okay, honey." He kissed her again and closed her door.

"Call me if you need me?"

"I will."

He watched her drive off and felt as though he stood on an iceberg in the middle of Antarctica, except the temperature was at least a mild, unseasonable seventy degrees, even with trees shading him.

His heart seemed to burst from his chest and trail Rachel as she disappeared from sight, leaving an emptiness in him that immediately filled with terror.

He turned on his heel, clenched his teeth together, and marched back to the dormitory.

He would lick this wimpy dread if it was the last thing he did.

\|/

Rachel cried most of the way home, replaying the sight of Peter, so desolate and alone, watching her leave. Somehow, she could read him like the back of her hand and feel what he felt.

Terror.

She prayed that he would get it together enough to attend classes—to get his required hours and rid himself of that pressure for months to come. It was now a matter of the lesser of the evils.

The drive home—aided by their newly purchased GPS—took less than the hour and a half she'd figured on. At home, she felt at loose ends. How was Peter coping? Perhaps he had a roommate by now. Peter's affability would automatically ensure a new friendship.

She punched in Peter's cell number. No answer.

Of course—they were having orientation tonight. He would be busy.

Good. She could relax. After a light snack, she turned in and read until the novel fell from her hand.

Her phone jangled. She awoke with a start. A glimpse of the clock revealed it was twelve ten. "Hey, darlin'," she croaked.

"Hey." Flat.

Her antennae shot up and her heart dropped. "You okay?"

"No. I'm not okay. Whatever made me do something this crazy? I'm here alone in a virtual jungle. Trees everywhere. And I don't know how I'll ever face those tests. We're having *exams,* Rachel!"

Rachel remembered the beautiful wooded campus and was disappointed that Peter now saw it differently.

"Peter, do you have a roommate?"

"No. Some young guys moved into the dorm unit next to me but I don't have a roommate."

Regret slapped her upside the head. There went the hopes of him acquiring a supportive pal. "Are they friendly?"

"Oh, yeah. They're nice. But we have homework and—all of them brought computers with them and I think most of the research will have to be done online and—what am I going to do, Rachel?" This ended on a note of despair.

Poor Peter, who was the most computer challenged person she knew. Who knew they would have homework requiring computers?

But hey! We're now in the twenty-first century.

"Honey, maybe they'll help you. Just ask and explain that you aren't tech savvy. Surely they'll help you."

"I don't know."

A long moment's silence. "Rachel. Come and get me. I can't do this."

Rachel felt his desperation but she knew he needed to hang in there. She believed he could tackle it all, just as he did his daily work. "Peter, let's see how you feel after a night's rest."

A despondent "Okay."

Beyond tired, Rachel rang off and fell into deep sleep.

\\//

And Peter did tackle it all with aplomb. For the first day. He checked in with Rachel in the evening. "We walk everywhere here. Seems miles to the meal destination and by the time I get there, I'm not even hungry."

"I hope you're eating enough. Look in the dorm fridge for leftover chicken salad that I left for you, in case you get hungry at night."

"I already ate it. Came in handy."

"Good. Take good care of my man."

A long silence, then a soft, "Thanks, honey. I'm gonna be okay."

She was happy that the younger pest control technicians had included Peter in their circle. That way, he could keep up with much of the curriculum via osmosis—keeping his ears open. His memory was something else.

For that, she prayed nonstop.

\\/

Peter struggled minute by minute to keep up. At times, the classes sped by and at others, crept like drugged snails. Those younger pest control guys huddled, discussing and studying together. They were sharp-minded, tossing ideas back and forth. And Peter was too proud to intrude—no, actually, he was too embarrassed to reveal his ineptness.

Peter began to despair. If only he had one real buddy—ideally a roommate, to confide in and share with. Basically, someone to study with for the exams.

Exams.

The word itself rang terror and rattled his bones.

He struggled through the day, trudging wearily to lunch, picking at his food, and later, to dinner—through the blasted woods, across a creek bed, and up a hill. Again, appetite eluded him. The left-out feeling flooded him. On an average, five or six technician-peers represented each company, as opposed to Peter, who single-handedly owned and operated his own business.

He felt alone. Insignificant. Incompetent.

That evening, he called Rachel. "I'd rather walk away from this than fail, Rachel."

"I understand, honey. But I still think you can get some credits from this. I rather doubt that they'll give you a refund since you've already attended classes."

"Probably not. And I hate to lose nearly a thousand dollars."

"Nope. Try to hang in there, honey."

"I'm tired, Rachel. I didn't sleep much last night."

"Maybe your tiredness will make you sleep more tonight."

"Maybe."

"Peter—have you been taking your oil, pills, and supplements? I put each day's meds in a separate Ziploc and labeled them for that day."

"I don't remember."

"Then check the labeling and if you missed this morning's dosage, take it tonight then get back on schedule tomorrow. Okay?"

"Okay."

"Your meds are important, honey. I'll call you again later to check with you."

He checked and sure enough, he'd missed his day's dosage. He took it and soon, fell into deep sleep.

\I/

Peter awoke to a sunny day and felt he could tackle whatever the day handed him. The walk to breakfast tired him but the classes were easier. One thing his teacher said excited him. He called Rachel with the upbeat news.

"The teacher said that if we did our best, regardless of the test scores, he would give us our hours."

"That's wonderful, darling! You can relax now and just put in the time."

"Yeah. One of the guys offered to help me with a report. He's going to look up references for me on his computer."

"An answer to prayer! Ah, honey, you're gonna make it. Just you wait and see."

"Love you."

"Me, too. Stay in touch. The week will be gone before you know it."

And Peter headed for his neighbor's room to study and finish that report.

\\//

Rachel felt it gaining momentum, snapping at her heels.

Trepidation.

Peter's circumstances began to manhandle her in a brutal, stealthy manner. Her original optimism that Peter's reservoir of pure strength would get him through this week took stunning blows in the next twenty-four hours.

His moods pogo-ed up one moment and down the next. With each climb, she tensed and braced herself for the certain plunge.

Cell phone calls permeated time.

"I got an A on my report."

"Wonderful!"

The next call groaned of hope dashed against the rocks. "Exams are scheduled at the end of the course—for each class. I'll never be able to do it, Rachel."

"Darling, surely if you're honest with them about your memory lapses, they'll give you some extra consideration. Anyway, the teacher promised to give you your hours, regardless of the tests, didn't he?"

"Yeah. But he may not be counting on me not remembering anything at all."

"Just share with him your memory problem, Peter."

But transparency could not find its place in Peter at that time.

From then on, distress escalated hourly.

One call offered Rachel a small reprieve. "I'm going to try to finish out the week. Hang the grades. I'll just see what happens."

"That's the idea. You can do it." But despite her pep talks, she was no longer certain of that.

That night, each time she dozed, the phone jangled on the hour.

"I can't stay here in this jungle another minute," Peter's anguished cry woke her yet again. "I've never felt like this in my life. I nearly jumped out the window. I'm that desperate. *Please come and get me, Rachel!*"

Rachel heard in Peter's plea that he had reached a point of no return. She also knew she could not keep her eyes open and focused. She rubbed them and tried to make out the time on the quartz clock. Three a.m. "Honey, I couldn't drive there even if I tried. I've had no sleep. I'd fall asleep at the wheel. You don't want that to happen."

"No. But I can't stand it any longer, Rachel."

"Peter, if you'll just lie down and try to turn it all off and know that it's over—let me sleep a couple of hours, until daylight, and I'll come get you."

"You promise?"

"Yes, darling. I promise."

She would keep that promise. But first, she fell into a dead sleep.

\|/

Rachel arrived on campus by eight thirty the next morning.

On the drive, she'd prayerfully donned boxing gloves to defend Peter.

Peter had his belongings packed and lined up at the front door, ready to haul to the car. After loading, they met with one of Peter's teachers, who'd grown worried about him when he missed class that morning, after learning from the younger pest control students that he'd also failed to connect with them for the breakfast trek.

Rachel parked her walker within reach and took a seat in the conference room. And when Mrs. Wise expressed doubts as to Peter receiving any credits for the course, Rachel briefly explained to the woman about Peter's short-term memory lapses and his test anxiety escalating that memory loss.

Peter, in anxiety's grip, for once didn't object to the candor and Rachel was glad because she was determined to champion Peter's cause today.

"Listen," she reasoned with the instructor, "Peter has put in three *entire difficult* days here. He's done his very best to cope. One instructor was willing to give him hours if he could hold out. But, in spite of all his efforts, he cannot finish the last two days. Don't you think you could give him credit for the three days here?"

"I'll talk with the board, Rachel. I'll explain that Peter was an exceptional student and he participated in so many help-ful ways. Everybody loved him. I'm sorry to see him go but I understand. I can't promise anything, but I'll do my best on his behalf."

On the way out to the car, Mrs. Wise whispered to Rachel that one of the young pest control guys had really liked Peter and had tried to take him under his wing as much as possible.

Rachel was grateful. But she knew that the effort had not been enough.

Because Rachel was not there for him.

On the drive home, Peter said, "I'm sorry, Rachel. I tried so hard but I failed—"

"Peter, you have nothing to apologize for. You *did not* fail. I'm so proud of you I could burst. It took courage to stay three long days and nights, considering the nightmare it was."

"I wasn't kidding about wanting to jump out that third-story window, Rachel. I felt those trees and darkness closing in on me. I couldn't sleep or eat. It was the worst nightmare of my life."

"I'll never allow that to happen to you again, honey. I promise."

In coming days, the haunted look slowly left Peter's green eyes as he gained distance from the seminar washout. Then one morning, Peter came running in from the post office.

"They gave me six hours!" he exulted, waving the letter at Rachel.

"That's great, Peter!" She grinned at him. "That's fair, don't you think?"

"I think it's more than fair. So that money didn't all go to waste."

"Nope. It didn't."

"I don't ever want to be away from you again, Rachel."

"You won't. I promise."

That was one promise she would keep.

Chapter Sixteen

\|/

"To care for those who once cared for us is one of the highest honors."
—*Tia Walker*, The Inspired Caregiver

She had no idea it was going to happen when it did.

It was an ordinary day, one she spent alone.

Actually, Peter's recovery from the trauma week at the pest control seminar was a gradual one. He still showed signs of PTSD but he'd picked himself up, dusted off the seat of his pants, and departed for work early that morning.

Rachel's failure to walk up and down steps without the aid of a walker merely fueled her determination.

She'd continued her physical therapy on her own, spending less time sitting and more standing and doing whatever chores she could manage during the day. She began putting added amounts of pressure on the injured foot and leg.

Now, in the aftermath of Peter's courageous battle to overcome fear, she was filled with more grit and determination than ever to surmount her limitations.

The main reason being, Peter needed her.

That morning she resolutely retired her walker.

Most of the time she barely bore weight before limping to the good limb. But, *leapin' lizards*, it was a start. On that particular morning, she held onto the counter and reached the door between the kitchen and the utility room. She'd been eyeing the sunken quarters for weeks now, dying to span that drop on her own. The reward would be to walk, unaided, to open the back door—to stand on her own and feel sunshine and fresh air kiss her face. She wanted to span the back steps into the outdoors.

On her own.

The unattainable beckoned like a panorama of paradise.

The only thing was, the step down onto the lower level measured a steep twelve inches. To her anxious scrutiny, it was Mt. Everest.

She closed her eyes. *Lord, I really need your help with this. Thank you. Amen.*

Inside her, conviction burgeoned and she reached both hands to take hold of one side of the door frame for balance. *Down with the bad*, she lowered the tender foot to the next level and quickly followed with her good foot to take the weight's brunt.

Her perception changed in a flash.

She no longer looked down at the washer and dryer. She was on a level with them. What a difference those few inches made in her view of life. How marvelous to have moved up by stepping down.

On her own, *glory hallelujah!*

Then she had second thoughts. Would she be able to pull up with her good leg? What if she got stranded here?

The walker was out of reach. No help there.

She could always call Gabby to rush over and help.

Nah.

He'd helped her get down and He would help her back up.

Without hesitating, she again grasped the door frame, gritted her teeth together and hoisted up with her good leg.

Suddenly, she stood on the upper level. She blinked in wonder. Wow! She did it! The entire transfer.

Rachel was so over the moon she immediately did it again and, holding onto the washer, did her awkward hobble—actually a Frankenstein shuffle—over to open the back door and breathe in crisp air and see, up close and personal, the deepening green of the back lawn framed by crepe myrtles that, come springtime, would sprout crimson blossoms.

She snapped her cell phone from her holster and punched in Peter's number.

"Guess what I did?" she asked before he had a chance to speak.

"Hmm, I don't know. What?"

"I'm. Standing. In. The. Utility room! Looking out the back door! Without. The. Walker!"

A cautious, "Is Gabby there with you?"

"Nope. Did it all on my own." Then she added, "With a little help from above."

"That's wonderful, babe!" Excitement limned his breathless response. "I knew you could do it. Didn't I tell you?"

"You did. And you were right. Ahh, Peter, I feel so *free*. Like all the world's gates are springing open right this minute." She chuckled. "'Course, I know from past experience that nothing happens instantaneously. You know? I mean, I've been doing therapy for months now to get to this moment and after just a short prayer this morning—" Emotion choked her words as tears gathered.

"I know," Peter said softly, reverently. "He does things in His own time and way. Isn't that what Hamp always said? It's true, honey. Lordy, I miss that man. He was like my own daddy. I miss him every day."

"Me, too," Rachel sniffled. "Look, I've gotta ring off and go for some tissue to blow my nose. Love you, darlin'."

"Love you back. Be careful, now."

Rachel sniffled again, then hoisted herself back up onto the kitchen level, feeling quite jubilant by now about the conquest, and slowly made her way to the bathroom for some tissue.

Sitting at the kitchen table, she snapped her phone open again, exulting in victory as much as her dulled senses tolerated. She couldn't wait to tell Gabby.

She wanted to shout it to the whole wide world.

She knew that The Gang and Eli's entire crowd would celebrate with her. And how exciting it would be to soon march down the church aisle to her seat without any aid. That way, her church friends would see the result of prayer.

Ahh, she felt brand new, washed inside out with joy and triumph. Fresh tears rushed to her eyes. She looked up.

Thank you, God!

She couldn't jump high but she felt like reaching up and high five-ing all the angels watching over her. They were there. She could feel them. Not in a warm fuzzy way but factually.

Finally.

She believed that she would be completely restored physically.

She punched in the number. "Gabby, guess what I did?"

\\\/

Peter inhaled the brisk winter air, now flavored with distant smoke of burning dried leaves. New Year's Eve sported a mild forty-four degrees, South Carolina light jacket weather. He enjoyed the crispness against his face as he worked on the deck banisters for rental number eighteen.

He'd come a long way these weeks since his seminar meltdown. *Caesar's ghost!* What a nightmare. He didn't even want to think about it, much less discuss it. Now he more fully understood Rachel's former reluctance to re-visit her accident.

When his phone rang, Peter laid down his power drill, tugged his cell from his belt holster, and peered at the screen. He didn't recognize the number. Probably one of the lame-brained utility companies again. They'd gotten to where they pestered him for payments, claiming he was late or hadn't paid at all.

Usually, it was Rachel who called and set them straight or immediately issued credit card payment via phone.

Annoyed, he shoved the phone back into its holster, snatched up the tool, and recommended tightening the banister screws. Gary, his helper, was down with the flu so Peter was fly-ing solo on repairs today. This being the last one.

Peter was doing his best to keep up with the bills' due dates but they remained burrs in the seat of his britches. His mem-ory glitches ticked him off to no end. But he was determined to function as long as possible.

"I don't know how long I can keep doing this," he kept tell-ing Rachel. Oh, how he hated to see her features morph into creased worry. He didn't want to cause her stress. Lord knew she had enough just regaining her health after that fall . . .

He paused and looked up into the sky's infinite blue.

Thank you, Lord, for sparing her. For leaving her here with me.

He blinked back sudden tears that always sprang up when he recalled the close call, then bent once more to the task at hand. Rachel bragged on his great work ethics. Something inside him swelled pleasantly at the thought.

Rachel kept insisting he involve her more in their finances but he was so accustomed to doing it all, that after all these years, it wasn't easy to relinquish control. Rachel's forte was not numbers and he had to teach her each step of banking and such. But she was a fast learner, he was happy to discover.

The plate-spinning was growing increasingly exasperating. Where did all the money go? For the life of him, he couldn't figure it out. They didn't waste money but there never seemed to be enough.

Thank God for Rachel's calm assurances each month that they would make it. She offered marvelous suggestions for cut-ting corners, insisting they would make a difference. And mirac-ulously, they did.

He tested the banisters for solid hold. Satisfied, he put away his tools and headed for his pickup. The cell phone jangled again as he climbed into the driver's seat. His teeth clamped together in aggravation. The clattering continued until he yanked out the cell again and barked, "Hello."

Silence. "Hello!" he roared. When silence lengthened he started to click off.

Just as he lowered it, he heard a barely audible, "Dad?"

He grew still. "Amber?"

Soft throat clearing. "Yes. It is."

Emotions spun into a turmoil . . . relief, confusion, hurt, the last being anger. "What do you want?" The moment the words left his mouth, Peter regretted them. Something deep inside him *heard* the unkindness and he recoiled.

"Where are you?" he added more gently.

"Ah . . . in Manilowe. I'm here—at Eli's." A sniffle.

In a heartbeat, his mind switched twenty years back in time.

Peter's breath hitched. "You okay, funny face?" All he could see was a sweet little apple-cheeked girl gazing adoringly into her daddy's face.

A sob, then more throat clearing. "Yeah." A nervous little laugh. "Eli's feeding me. I'm okay."

Eli's feeding me.

His little girl. Hungry . . . possibly homeless. The picture tore at his heart, destroying all his defenses.

Tears burned behind his eyes.

"Daddy'll be right there."

\\/

Rachel put the final touches on her makeup and smoothed her hair.

The New Year's Eve church service was going to be one of prayer and music and she didn't want to miss it. That unsettling *something*, latched onto her mind's fringe, demanded she march in the search for peace tonight.

How excited she was to be walking completely on her own. She was whole again!

Peter, already dressed in blazer and crisp pleated slacks, watched a news program in progress. He looked neat, as handsome as ever with his thick head of dark salt and pepper, which, she often told him, gave him a distinguished look.

She grinned, remembering J.C.s corny counter that the gray made Peter look "extinguished." The past couple of hours, since he'd finished his chores, Peter had seemed different—*preoccupied* best described it.

"You okay?" she asked, rubbing Sugar Vanilla lotion into her hands. "Anything I should know?"

He looked up, a startled look on his face, which he quickly banked and shook his head. "I'm fine as can be. Any better, I'd be twins."

She chuckled, relaxing. "We'd better hustle."

"Where we going?"

"Church." Still he looked blankly at her. "New Year's Eve Service," she clarified.

"Oh." Then his features morphed through kaleidoscopic changes before settling into one unreadable to Rachel.

The bleeps no longer startled her. Nor did his unpredictable moods.

The drive to church was silent and she kept sliding glances Peter's way, wondering what was transpiring in that mind of his. Could her unease have some connection to his silence—to his drifting away?

Rachel's unaided entrance into the church foyer filled her with unparalleled emotions, ones mingled with joy, contentment, and a sense of something like pride, but not.

Never had she felt so humbled by yet another miracle that was hers.

She clamped her teeth together and smiled, determined not to limp.

Inside Manilowe Community Church, most seats were filled but Peter took her by the arm and guided her to the front, peering about as if searching. He stopped abruptly and nudged her toward two empty spaces. She saw that the lady sitting there had laid a couple of programs beside her to reserve the spaces.

"But, she's saving those seats," Rachel whispered to Peter, preventing his claiming them.

"Honey," he whispered back. "Look who's sitting there."

For the first time, Rachel's gaze swept to the seat occupant's face.

She felt the blood drain from her face. Peter had to hold onto her to prevent her from sliding to the floor in a heap.

"Amber," Rachel moaned, reaching out a trembling hand while steadying herself by anchoring against the forward pew.

"Hey, Mama," Amber croaked, arose, and slid into her mother's arms. They both sobbed, oblivious to others around who wept knowingly at the reunion. Few secrets endured in the seat sections claimed by regulars.

Rachel's legs gave way—Peter's hands supported her as she sank to the seat. "You okay?" Amber asked Rachel, pale and worried looking. "Mama, I didn't know about your accident until Daddy told me today." Tears puddled in her sea-green eyes. "I would never have stayed away had I known."

Rachel turned her still-tender neck to peer at Peter, who wiped tears from his eyes, snuffling. "Today? And you didn't say a word?" There was no reproach in her voice, simply wonder.

Peter's smile wobbled and his eyes filled again. "I wanted to surprise you, honey."

She felt Amber's hand slip into hers and squeeze.

Rachel gave a huff of a laugh, one that ended on a soft sob. "Surprise me, you did!"

She looked at Amber then, really looked at the beautiful woman she'd become. A little gaunt maybe, but lovely. Womanly. No longer girlish. "Both of you. There's so much time we've missed. I want to know all about—"

"Later, Mama." Amber leaned to kiss her cheek soundly. "I've got lots to share with you, but for now let's enjoy seeing the New Year in together."

Rachel felt Peter's large, warm fingers lace with hers and she squeezed both hands on either side of her, gratitude swelling her heart to bursting.

The music began. As they stood and sang old familiar hymns and contemporary choruses of praise, their hands remained clasped in love and belonging.

Still, Rachel felt something hovering, something unsettling. She should be the happiest woman in the world. Her family was with her.

Yet . . .

What, Lord? She prayed . . . *tell me what.*

\\1/

"The service was great, Mom," Amber hugged Rachel and kissed her after they both changed into warm flannel granny night gowns. Then they squeezed into Rachel's cramped but charming little bathroom and washed their faces, a girl ritual of theirs not lost through the years.

"Um hmm," Rachel agreed as she patted her face dry and applied cold cream to her skin. "Where did your thoughts travel during the evening?" She'd missed out on so much of Amber's life. She didn't want to lose another moment or morsel.

They moved into the den and sat on opposite ends of the cream-toned, plush sofa. "I enjoyed going back to the church of my childhood and reliving those days when Papa Hamp preached such sweet sermons. I loved singing the old hymns and of course, I liked the contemporary ones, too. We sang lots of those at the little mission I attended last."

She sighed contentedly and smiled at her mother. "Glad to see our church here growing with the times."

"Yes." Rachel smiled, drinking in the mature beauty of her daughter. "I feel like I'm in a dream," she murmured. "Seeing you, after all this time." Her gaze lowered. "Except for that last time."

Amber's features morphed into sadness. "I'm sorry, Mama, for that ugly scene. And for all the grief I've caused you and Daddy. I've been so selfish and—" Her eyes filled and she shrugged as tears spilled over. "I'm so s-sorry." Her head dropped into her hands as she burst into turbulent sobs.

Rachel moved over and slid her arms around Amber. "Shh." She held her until the weeping subsided and then held the icy hands in hers like she'd always done during both her offspring's childhood angst. "Honey, we all do things we regret. The real tragedy is in not learning from our mistakes. The important thing is that you're here now. And you've apologized. I forgive you. How can I not?" Her finger tipped Amber's chin up and their eyes met. "You need to apologize to Daddy, too."

"I did," Amber croaked and snuffled. "And he forgave me." She reached for a Kleenex on the end table. "Though I don't deserve it."

"Your daddy's a wonderful man." And Rachel felt like doing a do-si-do spin for his stunning turnaround.

Amber nodded as she blotted her eyes and blew her nose. "He's—losing it, isn't he?"

Rachel's heart skipped a beat and she narrowed her gaze. "What do you mean?" But she knew.

"He's repeating himself a lot. Does that mean—"

Rachel squeezed her hand. "That means he has short-term memory bleeps. For the time being, that's all. We live in the moment, honey, and so should you. We're doing all we can do to preserve what he has left and making the most of the time we have together."

New tears gathered. "I've missed so much time with him."

"Yes." Rachel nodded, then hurried to say, "But you're here now. That's what counts."

Amber seemed to relax a little and smiled. Then yawned. "I've got to turn in. My eyes feel crossed from tiredness." She arose and leaned down to kiss Rachel's cheek again. "We'll do more catching up tomorrow. G'night, Mama"

"Night, sweetie." After another fervent hug and kiss, she watched her daughter climb the stairs to her old room, still exactly like she'd left it eleven years earlier, and softly shut the door.

\\\/\/

Wow. What a day it had been.

Rachel's emotions were on overload. She knew she wouldn't be able to sleep much so she returned to her office desk where she'd earlier left her father's sermon notes spread out. She'd highlighted and studied all except the last: *HOW TO LIVE ABOVE THE DRAMA OF LIFE.*

The last point was the most simple of all. *IN EVERY SITUATION PURSUE THE PATH OF LOVE.* Her dad's scriptural reference was I Corinthians 14:1, "Pursue Love."

Simple concept? Yes.

And no.

Rachel moved to the old navy blue sofa she'd reassigned to her cozy little writing/work room when she and Peter bought new den furniture. She couldn't bear to part with the chintzy thing. It was soft and welcoming, like outstretched, warm arms that wrapped her when she folded herself onto it. Like family, it was.

Tonight she sighed and closed her eyes. How far she'd come these past months since she'd faced near death, just feet away from where she now lay. She'd managed, via celestial aid, to ford the rapids and span the mountains. The valleys were thornier. Those, she still had to muddle through until God got good and ready to give her an outside pass.

She began to silently pray. *Show me, Lord.*

What hovers there?

Her eyes opened and she stared at the ceiling, wondering why she still didn't feel peace. Her mind ambled about, searching out all the tests she could have failed. *Show me, please?*

Like a video, the words of her father's sermon outline danced across her mind's screen. *IN EVERY SITUATION PURSUE THE PATH OF LOVE.*

Now why did that replay?

Suddenly restless, she sat up and tucked one bare foot up under her.

Those words were meant for her. *In every situation pursue the path of love.*

But where had she *not* pursued the path of love? Oh, she knew she wasn't perfect but she didn't know of a soul she didn't love.

She and Peter had a wonderful marriage, didn't they?

Peter absolutely adored her. He would do anything in his power to make her happy—to the point of denying himself.

But what about her? Did she love Peter the same selfless way?

A torched arrow of despair struck. It blindsided her and stung like a swarm of hornets.

The unease spread and tightened her chest until her lungs felt choked and she began to struggle for air. She sprang to her feet and moved aimlessly about, seeing Peter's pleading face.

Pleading. And she knew the source. Her pace picked up and she felt a lingering tenderness in her foot—but she could not walk away from what she'd seen in Peter's eyes. Desolation. No, she could no longer outrun it.

Give it to me.

It stopped Rachel dead in her tracks. "What?" she whispered, looking about to see if someone had joined her. No one was there. But she felt a presence, felt it in her bones.

Give it to me.

This time, she knew its source and collapsed onto the sofa. She began to weep. "I don't know how," she moaned.

Just listen and trust. Remember how you felt when you were judged for taking food?

Of course she did. She would never forget it. "Yes."

Well, I showed you mercy by forgiving you and giving you peace. Afterward, you talked to Peter about how some folks might 'forgive' yet not 'forget' a betrayal. Is that you, Rachel? You say you forgive Peter for that long ago betrayal but have you really? He's pleaded with you to allow his son into his life and you refuse. Is that love?

Remember, in every situation to pursue love.

This time, Rachel would have avowed she'd heard her daddy's Efrem Zimbalist Jr. voice but looking around through her tears, she saw that she was alone.

At the same time, she knew that she was not alone.

The same one who had borne her up during that horrible fall now bore her up again. And in that heartbeat, Rachel knew beyond doubt that she could trust Him.

Forgive and let love take over. Give the hurt to me, Rachel. See in your mind a box, then put the offense in it.

Rachel did as she was told. Picturing herself placing the betrayal and anger into the box.

Now, hand it to me.

Rachel did as she was told.

Don't ever pick it up again. Never. You're now free.

Rachel felt the weight of a freight car lifted from her, both inside and out. Her eyes popped open at the change and she began to weep from relief. She felt as though she'd suddenly sprouted wings.

How marvelous it was to forgive! Joy bubbled up in her and she paced from sheer happiness, gazing upward to its source, laughing.

She brushed the tears from her eyes, still gazing heavenward, and smiled. "Thank you for being patient with me."

Rachel suddenly yawned and felt drowsiness ooze over and into her. On the way to her room, she felt light as down and calm as a lamb. Then she climbed into bed beside a softly snoring Peter, spooning against his back and smiling. "I get it," she whispered dreamily. "So simple."

And as she slid into sleep, she repeated, "I finally . . . get . . . it. Simple."

\|/

Mark and Gramma ate one last slice of the strawberry cake before turning in.

"It was a great New Year's service, wasn't it?" Gramma asked as she carried the plates to the sink and rinsed them.

Mark wasn't really listening. He felt torn as he labored listlessly through the transition journey from the only life he'd ever known.

"I miss Dad," Mark mumbled, elbows on table, chin burrowed into palms. "And I miss the farm."

"Didn't Chris say you could visit any time you want to?" Gramma turned to look at him, worry niggling her brow. "In fact, he said you could live with them if you want to."

Mark slouched back and sighed. "It's not the same, Gramma. You know that. It'll never be the same, with Dad gone. And Mama's here with you. She needs you. And I don't want to leave her." He shrugged limply. "Or you."

Gramma chuckled. "I would be sorely disappointed if you did."

Mark sighed heavily and his hands dropped into his lap. His emotions felt mushed up.

"Stinky's coming to visit next weekend," Gramma offered, and he knew she wanted to cheer him.

"Yeah. I'm looking forward to seeing him. But—" His gaze dropped to study his hands lying motionless in his lap. All the energy seemed drained from him. Life was so different.

Gramma came to sit across the table from him. "But what, sweetie?"

He looked at her then. "I want more than ever to know my real father. The last words Dad said to me before he took his last breath were, 'go find him.'"

"What? Really?" Shock flashed over her face. She slowly shook her head. "I didn't know. What a good man he was. Does your mom know that?"

"I didn't tell her. It seemed—sacred. You know? I was afraid she'd ruin it again by refusing to tell me who he is." Tears rushed to his eyes and he angrily swiped them away.

Gramma's wrinkled hand reached across the table and after a moment's hesitation, Mark reached to grasp it. "You need to tell her, son. She needs to know."

"You really think so?" He gazed trustingly at her.

"Yes, I absolutely do." She angled him a resolute look. "And I think she'll feel differently now."

That settled it for Mark. Gramma's judgment went a long way with him.

"Do you think it's okay to wake her up and tell her?"

Gramma smiled. "She's not asleep. She's reading. Go on. The time is right."

\ı∕

Later that night, Rachel's cell phone roused her from slumber. She slid from bed so as not to disturb Peter and tiptoed to her study.

"Hello."

Wonder dawned and then tears ran down her cheeks as she listened to the woman on the other end of the connection. Then a smile spread over her features and she said, "Thanks for calling. The timing is wonderful. No—more than that. It's divine." She laughed, then spelled out a plan.

She ended the call with "I can hardly wait!"

\ı∕

"Happy New Year," Peter mumbled against the nape of Rachel's neck, softly nuzzling and kissing it as he lay spooned against her back.

Rachel awakened with a sense of something good about to happen.

"Mmm," she arched and received his warm embrace and words of love. "Back atcha, darling."

"Let's go cook a great breakfast to celebrate Amber's homecoming." Peter rolled over and off the bed, stretching and driving away leftover slumber.

Rachel was so happy that Peter's memory had not gone back to the dark times that reignited his anger toward Amber. But then, she had put the matter where it was supposed to be, hadn't she?

Simple trust.

"Sounds like a winner." Rachel slowly got to her feet, struggling with stiffness and stubborn muscles after a night's inactivity. "Nnuuh," she groaned. "One of my resolutions is to double up on my physical therapy exercises. The old gray mare just ain't what she used to be."

Peter rushed to her and gave her a big hug. "You look wonderful to me. I wouldn't change a thing about you."

"I feel the same about you," Rachel murmured in his ear, then gently bit it.

He leered at her. "Do that again."

She angled him a saucy look. "Huh uh. Think I'm crazy? We'd never get anything done today."

He refused to turn her loose. "What's more important than this?"

"Amber's home." She refrained from adding "Remember?" Besides, she had lots of other matters on her mind.

Awareness dawned in his eyes. "That's right." He reluctantly released her.

Breakfast was a fun time, featuring everyone's favorite entrées.

Peter's phone jangled and it turned out to be an emergency—a broken water pipe in rental number twenty-two. "Gary and I will both go and try to finish as quickly as possible." He grabbed his work jacket. "I want to be here to eat some of those black-eyed peas and collards while they're hot." He winked. "Need a good financial launching into next year."

"I got out the best ham to celebrate Amber's homecoming. The food won't be ready before late afternoon," Rachel reminded him. "So take your time."

When he'd left, Rachel pulled Amber into her study and sat her down. First thing she did was to present a gold ring that her mother had given her long ago. "I want you to have it, honey."

Amber swallowed back tears, gazing at her. "I feel like the Prodigal, Mama. First the big ham roast and now the gold ring. Thank you so much. What an honor to wear this ring that I don't deserve. You won't be sorry. I promise."

Rachel hugged her. "Of course I won't be sorry. I'm so happy to have you back I don't know what to do with myself." They sat for long moments, side by side, hands clasped together.

Rachel suddenly angled herself on the sofa to face Amber. "I've got something I want to run by you, honey. Something you need to know."

Then Rachel poured out the entire story of her life since Amber had left—the good and the bad, the failures and the triumphs, all of it. Of course, Amber knew all about her father's indiscretion and the result of that. It had precipitated her leaving home.

"I'm different, honey," Rachel concluded, eyes moist. "I'm not the same mother or wife I was thirteen years ago. And I want the chance to demonstrate it to each of my loved ones."

Amber embraced her, eyes puddled with tears. "I know, Mom. I already feel the difference."

Then she settled back on the sofa. And Rachel discerned that disclosures were not finished.

"I've changed, too, Mom," Amber said, looking to Rachel like a wise old soul with her green eyes that shifted shades as she emoted. "I don't have all the answers and I certainly don't have a corner on decency." She gave a sad little snort. "Not by a long shot. But I've learned enough to know that I had a good upbringing with great parents."

Rachel's eyes stung and she blinked. "I'm sorry I ever let you down."

"I was the one with a stinking attitude. Criticizing you for grieving." She rolled watery eyes and threw up her hands. "How could I have been so mean?"

"I think you felt abandoned," Rachel said softly. "And, in a sense, you were."

Amber shook her head and gave another heart-wrenching smile that didn't quite reach her eyes. "It wasn't that. I—"

She paused and picked a nonexistent piece of lint from her fleece pullover, eyes downcast. "I—it should have been me who died that day." She looked at Rachel then, sea mist depths shimmering ongoing torment.

"I usually rode in the front seat with Dad. That day—I didn't go to school. I could have—my throat felt better but the warm bed felt so warm and comfortable that I just kept dozing until I heard Dad and Jason leave. I just smiled, turned over, and went back to sleep."

Then she caved in before Rachel's eyes, burying her face in her hands and bawling like she had at age three. "Jason, poor Jason had so much to live for, Mama!"

Her mouth formed a grief rictus. "He was so sweet and I was so—so selfish . . . why did he have to die? I—I should have been the one." The sobbing revved up for long moments before Rachel's mind caught up.

She gathered Amber in her arms. "Shh, baby. You had as much to live for as Jason. You are every bit as valued as your brother, in both our hearts and in God's. And you mustn't ever blame yourself for what happened to your brother. Yes, it was tragic, but Jason wouldn't want us to spend the rest of our lives agonizing over this. He's in a much better place and for that, we can have peace and go on. And then, when this life is over, we'll see Jason again."

She held Amber until the gale subsided and they poured hot tea and settled down on the den sofa, sipping peacefully.

Rachel sat up straighter. "Honey—I want to share something that's transpiring. And I hope you approve."

And she spelled out to Amber what she felt her next step of spiritual and emotional healing would be.

Over an hour later, eyes brimming with tears, Amber said, "I think it's marvelous, Mama. Go for it."

\|/

The glazed ham baked to golden perfection. Black-eyed peas simmered in their own brown gravy, while Rachel had stewed collards to tender, tasty southern excellence. Amber added baked sweet potatoes to the menu, a nice touch, in Rachel's opinion.

Amber was setting the table with their finest china when the doorbell rang.

A look passed between mother and daughter as Rachel dried her hands and removed her work apron. On the way to the front door, she paused to pat her hair in place. She noticed Amber hovering in the kitchen doorway.

Rachel's heart raced with what she at first thought was nervousness. But as her hand reached for and connected with the brass knob, she recognized it as excitement.

She opened the door.

And her mouth dropped open.

Standing outside the door was the boy from church, the one who reminded her of Jason.

The one she'd been in love with since first sight.

The Almighty *did* work in mysterious ways!

The adolescent boy stood awkwardly on her porch, like a buck caught in headlights. She feared he would bolt any second. She noted his mother's SUV pulling away from their curb. As agreed upon in their earlier phone conversation, Mary would return later to pick up her son. Their phone conversation last night had given Rachel the opportunity to fill Mary in on her transformation of the past year.

And to ask her forgiveness.

She now was forgiven for years of stiff-necked stubbornness and bitterness. At least the boy's mother had shown compassion; more than she deserved. She still needed another act of mercy from this innocent youngster.

Rachel smiled and offered the boy her hand. "I'm Rachel."

He hesitated, then took her hand in his. "I'm Mark Rivers."

His voice sounded so much like Jason's that it tore into her heart.

Rachel blinked back tears and managed to maintain her smile. Her maudlin' could come later.

This time belonged to this young man.

"Come on in," she ushered him inside and nearly bumped noses with Amber, who looked like she did the time they vacationed in Disney World inside the Magic Kingdom. "This is Amber."

Rachel saw Amber's arms start to reach for the boy, then relax as she clasped her hands together and smiled a big old smile Rachel hadn't seen for so long it stunned her. "Hi, Mark. It's good to meet you."

"Dinner's almost ready, Mark. I hope you brought your appetite with you. Here, let me take your jacket."

As the gangly thirteen-year-old slid skinny arms from the coat, Rachel's breath hitched. He not only had Jason's dark hair and olive complexion, his features were strikingly classic like Jason's had been, down to the beautiful, thick-lashed green eyes.

So like Peter's.

No wonder it had been love at first sight when she'd seen him at church. Rachel had already fallen so hard—months ago—that she wanted to take the boy into her arms and never let go.

He was Jason's brother. Jason's blood ran through him.

And Peter's.

Dear God. Why hadn't she seen this before?

A glimpse at Amber showed Rachel that she, too, was deeply impacted by the resemblance. Tears shimmered in Amber's eyes as she held out her arms and boldly said, "I'm your sister, Mark. C'mere and give me a hug."

Rachel held her breath. Would he be open . . . ?

He rushed into Amber's arms and squeezed her rib cage until she began laughing through her tears. "Wow! What a strong fellow you are!" They rocked back and forth, laughing and crying together.

"I can't believe it!" Mark crowed, a little shyness bleeding through as he wiped tears from his cheeks. "I've got a sister."

"And don't you forget it!" Amber gave him some tissues and seated him on the sofa with offers of iced tea before dinner.

Rachel noticed his eyes roaming each door and cranny and she realized why.

"Your father will be coming in for supper soon." She was amazed that the words slid so easily from her mouth. He brightened and accepted the beverage offer. Rachel iced the glass and poured sweet, golden tea, listening to Amber and Mark's curious questions and replies, filling in the puzzles of each other. She smiled, warmed by it all.

The front door opened and closed. "*I love you, home!*" Peter called out his usual homage, sliding from his lined work jacket. "Man, does it smell good in here. I could eat a—" He stopped abruptly and stared at the boy standing hesitantly before the sofa, with a half-empty tea glass gripped in both hands.

"Peter,"

"Dad . . ."

Amber and Rachel spoke simultaneously. Rachel stepped up to catch his hand in hers. She looked him in the eye and said, "Peter, this is Mark Rivers. I invited him to dinner tonight."

Peter shot a glance at Mark and appeared confused. He cleared his throat and looked questioningly at Rachel.

Oh no. She realized that he didn't get the connection and cast a glance at Mark and saw his face fall into disappointment. Amber quickly moved to the boy's side and slid her arm around his shoulder, then took the dangling tea glass from his hand and placed it on the coffee table.

"Honey." Rachel caught Peter's eye and said more slowly, "This is your son, Mark."

She saw the flicker in his eyes and watched the blood drain from his face and felt his hand grip hers as his legs began to fail him. "My . . . son?" His voice was a whisper.

Rachel ushered him to his easy chair and lowered him into it. Then she smiled at him. "Yes, darling. This is Mark, your son. I invited him to dinner and his mother was kind enough to bring him."

Alarm flickered and he gazed furtively about the room. Rachel spoke up gently, "She couldn't stay, although I invited her to. She wanted to give Mark time to get acquainted with his father because he's wanted to meet you for a long, long time. Just as you've wanted to meet him."

"You did?" Mark spoke up as he lowered himself down beside Amber, who reached to take his hand in hers. "You wanted to meet me, too?" At once, he appeared fascinated and bewildered. Then his brow furrowed. "Why didn't you?"

Rachel sat down in a chair across from Mark. She took it full on the chin.

"Honey, it wasn't your father's fault. It was mine and mine alone. You see, I didn't realize how much he loved and needed you." She choked up and had to swallow several times before she could go on. "Many things happened during the time your mother conceived you. We—your father and I—had a son, Jason, who was killed in a car accident. Because of my grief and insensitivity, I blamed your dad for the accident. This hurt him very, very much."

"How old was he?" Mark asked, pulled into the story.

Rachel smiled sadly. "He was thirteen, just your age."

"Why did you blame—him?" He stumbled short of calling Peter "Dad" and looked at Peter, obviously confused.

"It was wrong," Rachel said. "I was wrong to blame your father for Jason's death. I was selfish and angry for many years and refused to let your father include you in our lives."

Mark looked as though he wanted to cry. "But—*why?*" His young face creased into grief.

"Ah, honey," Rachel shook her head, "I wish I knew the whys. I'm so sorry and I hope you can someday find it in your heart to forgive me. But I drove him into your mother's arms with my anger and—"

"Now, honey," Peter sat on the edge of his chair now, ready to defend her. "You—"

"Indirectly, I did. Anyway, that's all water under the bridge now." What a liberating thing to be able to say that with all sincerity. She observed Peter's features as he peered at her, wary, gauging, and weighing.

She was aware that this was the boy's time—but it was also Peter's time. She only hoped she could balance it all with no further injuries to either of them. She'd inflicted too many already.

Rachel looked directly into her husband's eyes and smiled, liberating all vestiges of love into the gesture. The question clouded his gaze. *Are you sure? Are you certain this won't be more than you can handle?* His humility and sensitivity smote her, tapping even deeper into her soul's reservoir, stirring and spilling over and filling her.

It astonished even her, the enthrallment of her love for Peter.

She saw exactly when he believed her because something in those marvelous sea mist green eyes cleared and filled with such gratitude and devotion she almost burst into tears. Instead, she laughed . . . a rich bubbly sound of joy.

How could she have punished him for so long for something to which he'd fallen prey during the darkest period of his life? A thing to which everyone is susceptible.

Again, to forgive brought with it the greatest sensation she'd ever felt. It made her feel like spinning and twirling and floating up to the clouds and basking in golden sunlight.

She stood and motioned to Mark. "C'mon, son. We've got a big fat ham and all the trimmings." Seeing the tamped down expression on his young face, she added, "And we've got a lot of catching up to do."

Mark's freckled face seemed older suddenly and he didn't reply. Her heart felt squeezed. *Please, God, help him to not feel so sad over the past.*

Then instantly, she felt ashamed. He's lived with rejection an entire lifetime.

He needs time.

"Boy," she heard him murmur to himself. "That ham sure looks good."

And she felt thankful for the resilience of youth to surmount emotional flip flops.

"So you like ham, huh?" Rachel asked.

"I love ham." The statement was matter-of-fact, not as exuberant as she'd hoped. But it was a start.

And she thought, *maybe there's hope.*

Chapter Seventeen

"To love a person is to learn the song that is in their heart and to sing it to them when they have forgotten."
—Arne Garborg

Peter felt as though he'd been given a reprieve from the guillotine.

He'd never, in all his imaginings, seen this coming.

He watched the boy eat with gusto. He'd not lied when he said he loved ham. Seemed he loved all the entrées set before him, from thick, creamy black-eyes, to baked sweet potatoes oozing butter and topped with brown sugar and cinnamon— even collards, for heaven's sake.

What kid loves collards?

Then Peter remembered that Jason had smacked his lips on the rare treat—usually on New Year's Day, the good luck charm for the year's financial prosperity.

"May I have a piece of onion to eat with my food, please?" Mark politely enquired after Amber sliced herself some and began to crunch into it, an echo of Jason's hero-worship of his big sister.

And yet—Mark was not Jason's replacement. No one could ever take his place.

But the Almighty did things in His own way, didn't He?

Yes, He surely did.

Memories of Jason corked to the surface and Peter could hear him asking for a chunk of sweet onion to eat along with the cornbread that accompanied the southern soul food.

Tears suddenly burned his eyes and he quickly blinked them back, fearing he would somehow rattle loose the newly found truce. He quickly glanced at Rachel, whom he knew remembered, too. She was watching Peter closely.

Oh no. He didn't want her to see how affected he was by the boy's likeness to their son. *Please, God.* He gulped back a sob poised on the back side of his throat and swallowed hard.

Rachel's mouth began curving up into a smile. "Remember how Jason loved collards, cornbread, and onions, honey?" she asked quietly, slowly shaking her head.

Peter nodded and felt his insides unfurl and begin to relax.

The meal ended and they moved into the den to lounge before the open fireplace. Mark sat beside Amber on the sofa, facing Rachel and Peter's easy chairs. He was too subdued for his age and Peter wanted desperately to draw him out—help him feel that he belonged here.

Rachel, bless her kind heart, began filling in a bit more of the family history.

She addressed Mark. "It was a difficult time for us when Jason, your brother, went to be with the Lord thirteen years ago."

Mark's eyes grew even sadder and he lowered his gaze. "I know. Gramma told me about him. She says I look a lot like 'im." He looked up at her then. "Do I?"

She chuckled. "Boy! Do you ever!"

Amber joined in. "Like two peas in a pod." Then she stuck her nose in the air. "'Course I'm the one who got all the beauty in the gene pool."

Mark looked uncertain until Rachel burst out laughing,

"You also got all the haughtiness." Mark quipped and gave a weak, lopsided "You got a big ol' dose of big head, sis"

She reared back and peered at him. "Know what, bro? You're gonna do just fine in this crazy family."

Peter felt a lump the size of California seize his throat when he saw the appreciative look spring into the boy's eyes—and then just as suddenly, he watched the light extinguished, replaced by a rush of tears.

The boy's hands clenched into fists at his sides as he abruptly stood and faced off with Peter, who remained slouched in his easy chair.

"Why did you have to shut me out?" He snuffled and wiped his nose on his shirt sleeve.

The shock of Mark's abrupt change left Peter at a loss for adequate words.

"I'm so sorry—" he began.

"This was a mistake," Mark raised his palms up and rolled his eyes upward. "Being here only shows me how much I've missed out on!" Mark looked at Peter with a mixture of sorrow and challenge. "Why didn't you ever call me or visit me? Am I some freak or something?" His passionate entreaty ended on a sob.

But as Peter stood at the same time Rachel did, the boy threw up his palm. "No. I don't need you anymore. I'm going home. You're not really my family." He stalked away, then pivoted to fling one more spear into Peter's heart. "You're not my father. My dad's dead. He's the one who really loved me."

Rachel shook her head at Peter and Amber as they made as though to entreat him. Peter understood her unspoken message. *"Back off. Give him space. This is too much, too quickly."*

Within five minutes Mark had called his mom to collect him and stood at the door, watching for her when she drove up.

Rachel moved to him before he could bolt. "Mark. We understand how you feel. And we want to give you all the time you want to get used to the idea of—having us as family."

Mark didn't turn to face her. He remained stiff and unyielding, watching for his rescue vehicle.

Peter moved to stand beside Rachel, joined by Amber. He started to put his hand on Mark's arm, then decided against it. "Son, there's not been a day since you were born that I didn't think about you and—"

He turned a wary glance Rachel's way, wondering how transparent he could be now. She nodded and then began to speak. "Mark, he's telling you the truth. I've seen his pain all along. If you need to blame someone, blame me."

Mark remained frozen and unbending, eyes riveted to the darkness outside—a lone tear rolled down his cheek and he angrily swiped it away.

Peter swallowed back tears. "If—when—you're ready to join our family, son, just say the word. We're here for you."

"Don't hold your breath." The near inaudible words floated hatefully to Peter's ears.

Car lights appeared outside and Mark burst through the doorway and down the walk to the curb, where he threw his things in the SUV and without a backward glance, hauled himself inside, and disappeared into the night.

Peter felt shredded as Rachel gathered him into her arms. "He'll be back, Peter."

"I don't know," he shook his head.

Had he lost his son for always?

\\l/

Gramma was there for Mark in those following days. She held him as he sobbed out his frustration over all those lost years.

"Why couldn't I have had my family all along?" he wailed and tossed on his bed while Gramma sat quietly in the little glider chair in which she always rocked while visiting with him during their long talks about life, love, and anything else on their moment's menu.

Today was no exception. Two days had passed since the disastrous reunion with Mark's biological father and he was still distraught over the rejection issue. In his estimation, nothing hurt quite like being tossed aside like garbage.

Nothing.

Except his dad's death and Mama's sickness. But those hurts were different. They were things one couldn't help. Being *eliminated* was a result of someone's choices.

Rejection *reeked.*

Gramma arose and patted his shoulder during a lull in his dramatics. Yeah, he knew he was probably over the moon but also felt that he deserved to scream and holler if he wanted to.

Gramma had told him as much.

"Stinky will be here in a little while," Gramma said softly. "His mother called and said they were on their way about an hour ago. We'll have a nice lunch of ham and baked beans when they get here."

"Oh no," Mark put his hands over his face. "You didn't, Gramma! You know how Stinky got his name—"

"Just kidding!" Gramma burst into laughter as she left. "Actually, I do know. And I did potato salad instead." The amused words floated over her retreating stooped shoulder and *man*! Was Mark thankful!

Stinky's arrival was noisy and blissful, lifting Mark briefly from his gloomy pit. They lunched and afterward adjourned to the front porch swing to catch up on news while the boys' moms and Gramma had girly talk in the den.

Mark shared with Stinky his reunion with his other family. He told him how catastrophic it had been, really spreading it on thick.

"Wow!" Stinky shook his head. "Why didn't you tell me? I tried to call you all week and couldn't get you."

Mark pushed the swing harder with his foot. "I didn't feel like talking about it. Fact is, it still bothers me to think about it. Why did they wait so long to want me?" He shrugged, feeling the pain re-settle around his heart.

"You said his wife—Rachel?—said it was her fault, didn't you? In that case, Mark, your dad couldn't help it. And you also told me a while back that even your mom wouldn't tell you who your dad was. Seems the fault lies with more than your real dad. He seems to be a victim as much as you." He shrugged elaborately. "Anyway, that's the way I see it."

Mark didn't respond. Stinky had a way of getting right to the heart of matters. The idea swam around for long moments and then settled into a logical niche of his brain. "I guess. But . . ."

Stinky was now cranked up and when he got going, his mind threw out some profound stuff. In the past, some of the stuff had been bad but lately, all of it was good. So Mark listened.

"And you said your dad's last words to you when he was dying were to go find 'him,' and you knew he was referring to your real father, didn't you? And we know how wise Ralph was, don't we?" Without waiting for a response, Stinky plowed on.

"Now, he loved you like his own son, didn't he, Mark?"

"Yeah." No doubt there.

"He wouldn't have ever told you to do anything that would have hurt you, would he?"

A no-brainer. "No. I reckon not."

This time, Stinky's feet propelled the swing faster. "Then you can assume that he knew your dad would be good for you."

Mark remained silent but the thoughts swirled, fighting to attach themselves to the mind's logical niche.

Abruptly, Stinky's feet aborted the swing's motion and he stood. "You've got some things to think about, huh? Let's go ride bikes."

They unhitched Stinky's ten-speed from the car hitch and they rode off into the sun-filled day.

\|/

Those following days of the New Year offered Rachel another chance to get to know the adult Amber.

"It still seems unreal, your being here," Rachel said that cold, rainy morning after Peter left for work. Rachel joined Amber in the den, where, still in sleep shirts, they lolled on the sofa, feet propped on the humongous ottoman.

They sipped steaming green tea sweetened with Stevia and Splenda because Rachel had accumulated ten pounds of extra fluff in the past year of near sedentary existence.

But *fiddlesticks*, now they were saying Splenda was bad for her. "What's a soul to do?" she asked Amber. "Next thing, they'll be ridiculing Santa Claus 'cause he's fat."

Amber chortled. "Those grand, ominous *theys*, the party poopers of the world."

"Anyway," Rachel muttered. "Any time I complain of my fluffiness, your dad always replies, 'I love everything about you, Rachel. You're still the most beautiful girl in the world to me.'"

He really helped her resolve to lose that cellulite, *by jiminy*!

"So much has happened to me since I left, Mama." Amber's abrupt change of subject surprised Rachel.

"Do you want to talk about it, honey?" Rachel didn't push Amber. She knew her independent daughter too, too well to do that. She could only guess at the dark gaps left in their conversations and they were not pleasant.

"You don't want to know, Mama," Amber muttered, her little chortle dry. "Trust me. You. Do. Not. Want. To. Know."

Rachel sighed. "Okay." Then she said, "What could I have done differently?"

Amber looked at her. "Mama, it wasn't anything you did. It was me. My choices. I own my bad decisions. Even the one with Zac—" She abruptly shut down.

"Zac?" Once open, the can of worms worked away in Rachel's imagination.

Amber waved her hand. "Forget it. He was—*nothing*, when it came right down to it."

"Did you love him?"

Amber rolled her eyes. "I sure thought I did. But—"

"But?"

"Mama, it was a disaster. I thought he was God's gift to humanity—the most gorgeous hunk of man I'd ever seen." She stared off into space, remembering. "Then he started offering me these great 'trips' into ecstasy. When that happened, he took my innocence, my health, my virginity—that thing I'd always held sacred—I ended up pregnant."

Rachel's intake of breath jerked Amber's head around, her eyes piercing. "See? I told you that you wouldn't want to know." Tears sprang into the green eyes.

"Ah, honey," Rachel leaned forward and extended her hand. "I'm only sorry I wasn't with you, to help you."

Amber slowly shook her head, snatching a Kleenex from the end table. "I wouldn't have listened to you, Mama." She snuffled and blew her nose. "I was so hard-headed. When Zac insisted I get an abortion, I didn't want to. But he kept hacking away at my resolve to protect my baby, using every ploy known to man. It wasn't the right time. He couldn't marry me until he got his divorce and—"

"He was married?" Rachel felt a burst of mama-bear rage she'd not felt in a long time.

Amber smiled sadly at her. "'Fraid so. He was married but I didn't know for a long time. Anyway, to make a long story short, he finally wore me down and I got the—" Her voice choked off for long moments. "I've regretted from the moment I lay on that cold sterile table and felt them—"

"Ah, sweetheart," Rachel moved over to sit beside and put her arm around her. "I'm so sorry you had to go through that. And I'm sorry I wasn't there—"

"No, no, read my lips," Amber said softly. "It. Was. Not. Your. Fault. I'm sorry I gave in and aborted that precious life in me. I didn't have to listen to that jerk. I was so deceived, Mama. I really thought he wanted what was best for me, you know? That he cared—like Daddy always cared for you."

She turned her tearful face and looked her mother in the eye. "Yeah. I realized how judgmental I was toward Daddy and how messed up things were after Jason died. Everybody was fighting their own wars." Tears coursed down her cheeks. "I'm so sorry I ran out when all of you needed me."

"Shhh. We all made mistakes, honey." Rachel held her while she wept. "John 10:10," Rachel said gently. "The thief comes to kill, steal, and destroy. And he does it most of the time by deceiving folks. You're certainly not the only one this has happened to, sweetheart."

Amber lifted her head and looked at her, tear-streaked cheeks pale. "Mama, is there a chance I can be forgiven? I mean—I'm not telling you the half of it, all the places I've been and the things I've done for drugs. You couldn't handle it."

"Ahh, precious," Rachel laughed then, a full belly laugh. "You have no idea at all of what I've learned to handle in my lifetime. And yes, you can be forgiven. I know that for a fact. And you can reclaim who you once were. With just a slight alteration."

Amber blinked and snuffled. "What's that?"

"Once you've been through the valley, you'll be even better."

"You think?" Hope began to dawn in her face.

"I know. Been there, done that. And believe me, sweetie, it gave me spiritual muscles."

\\//

Peter's phone rang. He'd just finished his last route of the day—a chilly one.

"Hi, Gary."

"It's Betty. Gary's in the hospital again with the same urinary tract infection he had over a week ago. He wanted me to call and let you know."

"Wow. I'm sorry, Betty. Is there anything we can do to help?"

"No, but thanks. I'm sure he's in a lot of pain. He's in the ER right now. They're going to keep him. When he calls back and is in a room, I'll let you know."

"Thanks, Betty. Do that. And call me if you need anything." He knew his friends' car was out of commission at that moment and Gary wasn't able to get it fixed right away. He wished he could pay to get it repaired but he was bicycling uphill as hard as he could with keeping his own finances afloat. And while his friend was without wheels, Peter cheerfully shuttled him to the grocery store, doctor's office, or any other place he needed to go.

He rang off and drove on home, where Rachel greeted him with a big hug and kiss. *Whoa*, that could cheer a man up quick.

"Cold out, isn't it?" Rachel commented as she pulled out dishes for a light supper.

"*Whooee.* Is it! Glad for a good warm house to thaw in."

Rachel studied him across the table after he said the blessing. She said, "You look tired, honey."

"I am. I feel so exhausted sometimes, I can't take a deep breath."

"I wish you could retire completely," she said and he knew she meant it.

If only.

"There's no way we can make it without the extra pest control accounts."

"Somehow—we'll find a way, Peter. You'll see. And soon." She could always soothe him. Make it all seem possible.

He and Rachel ate Eli's chilled chicken salad with some fruit. Then, as Peter stretched out on the bed, Rachel put on her warm flannel gown to ward off the night's chill, cleansed her face of makeup, and put a few rollers in her hair.

Beyond tired, Peter dozed. When he awoke, he arose and padded to the bathroom, spying Rachel working away at her computer. How he admired her determination and focus. He thought her pretty brilliant at the keyboard, in fact, though she always blew it off, insisting that her skills were vastly inferior to those of the younger generation.

Somewhere along the way back to the bedroom, an overpowering compulsion hit him to visit Gary at the hospital.

"Let's go to the hospital," he said to Rachel.

She peered at him. "I can't."

"What do you mean, you can't?"

"Peter. Look at me. I'm already dressed for bed and my hair is damp and in rollers."

"So?"

"So, I'm not going. You can go without me."

He recognized Rachel's stubbornness in her set features. But he couldn't go by himself. He just knew it.

"Besides, it's icy cold and raining," Rachel threw in for good measure as she crawled into bed and clicked on an old movie with Esther Williams and Van Johnson. "We can go in the morning."

"I have to work in the morning." Peter lay back down and tried to get into the movie. But the uneasiness inside him wouldn't let up. He got up and slid his feet into his shoes.

"Where you going?" Rachel asked, obviously disappointed that he wasn't going to enjoy the Technicolor forties flick with her.

"I feel I ought to go see Gary."

"Okay." She remained transfixed by the swim scene.

"Aren't you going with me?"

"No." She looked him in the eye. Dug in. "I told you I wasn't going out looking like this."

Peter felt his temper rising. "You mean you won't go with me?" Hurt slithered through him. "Can't you at least ride down there with me?" It was a twenty-minute drive to the hospital and he was not even close to feeling secure about finding his way. Daylight driving was different and he'd not had any problems. It was the twilight time that gave him visual perception problems.

Rachel hesitated and he saw her frustration. Then she arose. "Okay. I'll ride down with you but I'll sit in the car while you visit. I've got a book to read."

He felt a little guilty forcing her to get out of a warm bed and redress. Not counting insisting that she go out into the cold, wet night with him. But he felt a revving in his gut to trek to the hospital tonight. He watched her patiently tug on jeans and pullover, socks and Reeboks. She peered in the mirror and succinctly tied a scarf over her curlers, making a face at the full image.

"Ready?" she asked, sliding her arms into a fleece jacket and snatching up her purse.

Outside, the icy air stung and Peter had trouble with night vision. But he knew that Rachel had always struggled with nocturnal blindness as well. Rain-drenched surfaces made it worse.

On the twenty-minute drive to their destination, Rachel recited the directions into the hospital. "We'll park in the building parking and you'll only have to cross the street and enter the revolving door and go to the desk, Peter. They'll direct you to Gary's room."

Peter's mind began to balk. "You're going in with me, aren't you?"

"No. I told you I couldn't be seen like this."

His stomach began to knot and his head tossed out everything she'd told him on the way. Parking was simple with Rachel navigating. The parking place gave him full view of the crossing as well as the entrance door. Still, his head swam.

"You're going in with me, aren't you?" he asked, growing desperate.

"No, Peter," her voice sounded sharper than usual. He knew how she hated to be seen without makeup, much less with curlers in her hair. "Honey, I told you I would only ride here with you. You can get directions at the information desk."

"But I don't feel good about you sitting in the car out here. It's not safe." This was partly true, but not the whole story. Fear was taking a fierce hold.

"I'll be okay, Peter." This was a bit sharper.

He shut his door then heard Rachel click the automatic door lock. The walk across the street was like entering the twilight zone. He did spot the revolving entrance and entered the lobby.

The information desk sat empty. He gazed about him and everything appeared otherworldly. Nobody looked like hospital personnel. Who could he ask for help?

After wandering about for five minutes, he felt even more disoriented. Even if someone gave directions, he wouldn't be able to follow them through. He was too nervous. And with that thought came anger.

Rachel could have come in with him.

By the time he retraced his steps to the pickup, he was furious.

"You couldn't find him?" Rachel asked after clicking and unlocking the car door for him, laying her novel aside.

Peter climbed into the truck, slammed the door and snapped. "No. I couldn't find him."

Remorse engulfed Rachel's face. "I'll go in with you, honey. I'm sorry. I didn't realize—"

"I'm too upset now to visit with Gary. You should know by now that I need you. I don't know why you couldn't have gone in with me to start with. I do everything in my power to make life easier and better for you and you can't do one thing you know I need you to do to help me?" He turned the key in the ignition.

"Oh, Peter, I'm so sorry. You're right. I should have gone in with you and sat in the lobby if nothing else. I will never abandon you like that again."

Anger and disappointment did not want to release Peter. He was silent for a while as he drove. He knew Rachel regretted her decision, thinking he was more capable than he was. And that was what really ticked him off.

"Know what makes me so angry, Rachel?"

"No. What?" The question was wary.

"The fact that I'm not capable. You cannot imagine how that affects me. I've always had such a good sense of direction and now, something like this happens."

"Well, you have no problems navigating your pest control route. You're still functioning well, Peter. I think you get panicky and your mind scatters. It happens to all of us to some degree."

He absorbed that. Leave it to Rachel to help him gain perspective. "Yeah. You're right. I get embarrassed to ask folks directions because I feel it will reveal my weakness. Then I get panicky and my mind scatters even more. A vicious cycle." He reflected on that for long moments.

"But you're right. I don't ever get lost when I'm driving in familiar territory. It's only the unchartered territory that challenges me and sends me into a tailspin."

Rachel reached to hold his hand. "I love you Peter James. And I promise you, I will never leave you stranded again. You have my word."

He looked at her and smiled. "Thanks, honey. How did I ever get you?"

She rolled her eyes upward as though thinking about it. Then she looked at him and shrugged. "You just kept coming back."

Lordy, that woman was something else.

\\I/

Rachel knew she had to do something.

Mark had not responded to her calls. She'd talked to his mother, Mary, several times and the two of them had not managed to budge the boy from his dug-in resistance to joining the James family.

Even Gramma Dot had not had any success.

"I have little influence on his decision at this point," Mary insisted today when Rachel called to invite him over for strawberry cake. It was a suggestion from Gramma Dot and Rachel had gone all out following the time-honored recipe.

"Seriously," Mary continued, sounding sincere. "I've talked until I'm blue in the face and he just cuts his eyes accusingly at me—no doubt remembering all those years that I wouldn't hear his pleas to guide him to his father. So, you see, I'm amongst the condemned, too."

"But he doesn't cut you out of his life." Rachel's reply sounded as dismal as she felt. "I really do love him, Mary. We all do. And we want more than anything to include him in our lives. I know that sounds presumptuous after the way I've acted through the years. But God's really spanked me for my hateful ways and turned me around."

"Seems He's doing that with all of us." Mary chuckled. "Stinky, Mark's best friend? Well, he's recently undergone a phenomenal change. He was once Mark's worst nightmare and then—well, along the way, God got hold of him and he's a different kid. He's really there for Mark now. They talk daily on their cell phones. Mark's birthday is next weekend and I hate for him to be so unhappy at this time of the year."

They were silent for long moments, then Mary spoke, "You know, Rachel. That may be the key to Mark opening up to your family. "If we could just come up with something—"

"Something to chew on."

"And pray about," Mary added.

"Yup. Let's do that and see what develops."

\\/

Mark was excited.

Mama had suggested he needed some time away and maybe spending time with Stinky would be a great birthday treat. Mark agreed.

This weekend at Stinky's included a visit to Sugar Hills Farm! His ol' buddy had set it all up and he couldn't wait to see his entire farm "family." Hortense the hog would be glad to see him, he was certain, as would little Petunia, who was no longer so little—and Honey, the half-grown calf—and all the other animals he'd grown to love. He knew the nature of each species and could forecast the reception from each.

Only thing, all that Saturday morning, Stinky kept putting off going to the farm, insisting on riding bikes around the Dodger family property. Mark had to admit, the scenery and the near spring-like day was refreshing and pulled his mind from the shadowy niche that had become too comfortable in recent days.

Finally, Stinky suggested they go back to the house, freshen up and head out to Mark's old home place. As they boarded the Dodger SUV, Mark noted that Mary was loading covered dishes in the back hutch.

"May I help you?" Mark ventured, remembering his manners and wondering where the food destination would be.

"It's covered," Stinky quickly replied. "I helped carry most of it while you showered and dressed. That's why I showered first."

"Thanks, anyway." Frances slid into the driver's seat. "Jim will be on in a little while."

Jim, Stinky's dad, rode a tractor in their distant field. He was the iconic farmer who never wasted daylight hours, reminding Mark of his own late dad. The memory sparked a moment's sorrow that grew as they reached the familiar crepe myrtle-lined drive that led to the place he would forever call home.

Frances parked the vehicle in the driveway. Mark noticed a few other cars parked in random locations of the sprawling parking area and he had to succumb to the changes there. New workers, no doubt, as well as Chris's family vehicles.

"C'mon!" Stinky captured Mark's arm and steered him away to the pastures, where his ol' buddies greeted him with snorts, lowing, chirping, gobbling, and even crowing. He laughed and nuzzled and scratched bellies until he was exhausted.

The sun seemed to grow brighter by the minute as cooling breezes kissed his skin and Mark felt peace settle around his heart as it had not in a long time. "I love it," he said to Stinky, chuckling. "No place like home."

"Yup. So right." Stinky's arm snaked across his shoulders, turning and guiding him back toward the house, where more cars were pulling in. But suddenly, Stinky veered Mark around to the back of the red barn complex.

"Wonder why so many cars are here?" Mark asked, curiosity rustling.

"Probably folks buying eggs," Stinky suggested, propelling Mark to the back of the Event Barn. "Let's swing by here for a drink of water."

"I'm not thirsty," Mark replied.

"I am," Stinky insisted and tugged him inside. He slammed the door loudly and went to draw a glass of water from the kitchen faucet. He drank greedily and ended on a burp.

Mark rolled his eyes. Some things never change.

"Let's go out the front," Stinky again grasped Mark's arm and propelled him toward the reception area.

"Hey," Mark skidded to a halt when he saw the assemblage of folks gathered in the room. "There's a party going on here, Stinky," he hissed.

He spotted Chris, held out an entreating palm and muttered, "Sorry!" And started to back out.

"SURPRISE!" A chorus rang out, startling Mark so that his knees went weak.

"Happy birthday!" Stinky crowed, chortling.

Then Mark remembered that today was his birthday. He'd been so sad lately that the prospect of celebrating his birth had leaked out the bottom of his bucket list. Fact was, sometimes lately, he mourned the day he was born.

Then faces began to emerge from the crowd.

Faces shining with love.

Acceptance.

Mama, Gramma, Chris and his family, Amber—

His heart picked up. Amber . . .

Then Rachel's smiling features surfaced . . . beside her, his birth father's face materialized and the green eyes shone with pride. Mark's heart seemed to be doing a weird tap dance but it couldn't be from joy, could it?

He was still angry with them. Wasn't he?

"Let's sing!" Stinky called out, at his best being in control. They all burst into a cheerful if dissonant chorale of "Happy Birthday" and Mark found himself touched by the display of affection.

At its end, Stinky ceremoniously demanded, "Speech, birthday boy!"

Mark gulped and managed a wobbly, "Thank you all for—" He shrugged awkwardly. "For coming."

Applause and whistles made him smile and feel less tongue-tied.

Out of the group a male voice rang out. "I want to propose a toast."

Mark was stunned. It was Peter James. Head high and eyes focused on Mark, he stepped forward and held up a glass of Coke, "I want to propose a toast to my son, Mark, who has always been in my heart, from the day he was born. I didn't get to share that birthday—"

He stopped and swallowed audibly, and was silent for long moments, visibly pulling himself together. "But I want to share this one. Mark, my son, I wish for you the best life has to offer and I hope—*I pray*—that you will allow me the honor of being a part of that life. Rachel, Amber, and I—and all our clan—all want you to be in our lives forever more. I toast you today, on this beautiful celebration of your life—one that means much to me."

"Hear, hear!" arose a chorus of assents and tea glasses clinked all over the room.

"Let's party!" Stinky cried out and bear-hugged a dazed Mark as folks began to rush to him, hugging and extending best wishes as music wafted from wall speakers.

Stinky pulled him aside. "Mark," he looked into his eyes, searching. "I hope this is okay with you. If not, I'll do penance until Jesus comes back."

Mark felt confused. But he also felt—good. He realized he was nodding.

"What?" Stinky asked, probing. "Yes . . . good or no?"

Mark cleared his throat. "Good, Stinky, you rattlesnake!"

Stinky cackled loudly. "Did I get you or what?"

Mark grinned and lightly fisted his shoulder. "You got me. And you know what?"

Stinky slanted a wary look at him. "What?"

"I'm glad."

Then Peter, Rachel, and Amber began introducing him to his Aunt Gabby and Uncle Leon, cousins Drusilla and J.C., friends Tammy and Eli—who catered much of the food, with a few additions from the family—and a host of others who would become as family to the boy who just yesterday seemed alone.

For the first time ever, Mark knew who his real father was. And he knew his father wanted him—had always wanted him. And now, Peter James had confessed before the world that Mark was his son and not only that, that he loved him.

When Peter James held out his arms to his son, this time, he ran into them.

\\/

"Mark's coming over for the weekend," Rachel called out to Peter as he came in the door from his pest control route and slid out of his work jacket. "He should be here any minute"

He lit up, as he always did when he knew their son was coming.

Not just his son, *theirs*.

Rachel felt so lucky to have another chance. Not everyone had the opportunity to right terrible wrongs. And Rachel's deep love for Mark made it a fantastic prospect.

And that was fine with Mary, Mark's blood mother. During visits, she'd shared with Rachel and Peter that her time on earth was limited and, like Rachel, her priorities had done a major shift as she faced her mortality.

Mary and Peter had regained—if not their former friend-ship—a newer, deeper respect that had them all working together to help Mark find his comfort zone while being shut-tled back and forth.

Today, Mark arrived in time to accompany them to Eli's Place for lunch. Amber passed on it, reconnecting with some old friends who had some job leads for her to check out. As soon as possible, she would get her own place nearby. And Peter expressed that he was glad. He wanted his family close by.

Time was swiftly passing. Too swiftly.

Oh, how Rachel counted her blessings these days.

Mark's welcome at Eli's Place was exuberant.

"Whoa!" Gabby jumped up to meet them, grabbing Mark in a big ol' bear hug. "Give Aunt Gabby a hug!"

Mark was a great sport and seemed to abide being embraced and bussed by two old broads and a younger, pretty waitress. Too, the men's hugs and shoulders slaps appeared to make his chest swell.

'Course, he'd already been initiated weeks earlier, during his fourteenth birthday celebration at Sugar Hills.

Later that week, Gabby and Drusilla stopped by Rachel's to deliver another pie from Gramma Dot, this one being southern pecan, a favorite of Rachel's—a fact Ms. Dot had gleaned from Gabby.

Gabby and Drusilla had looked sorta sheepish at first that day, the first time they'd linked up one on one with Rachel since the birthday reunion.

"What's wrong with you two," Rachel asked as she poured them iced tea. "Sit down, for the love of *Neil Diamond*. You act like something's stuck in your craw or something."

"Something," Drusilla muttered, cutting her eyes at Gabby, who sat stiffly in the kitchen chair across from Rachel, not quite meeting her eyes.

"C'mon," Rachel sipped her chilled drink. "What's going on?"

"Are you mad at us?" Gabby's voice was as close to timid as Rachel had ever heard it.

"About what?" She was truly mystified.

Gabby cut an appealing glance at Drusilla, who picked up the mantle. "About us cohort-ing with the enemy."

"*Lands sakes alive!*" Gabby slapped her palm against the table in exasperation. "I wouldn't exactly call it *that*, Drusilla!" She rolled her eyes to the ceiling, muttering under her breath.

"Well, I would," Drusilla insisted, features stricken with guilt and indignation at Gabby's dressing down.

Suddenly, Rachel got it. And her lips began to twitch at the corners.

But she figured it would be entertaining to let them go at it for a bit. She straightened her mouth and asked, "What enemies?"

The two women peered at each other, for once at a loss for words.

Rachel affected a frown. "You mean—you two have gone behind my back and . . ." She let the words trail off and watched bald guilt engulf her two best friends in the whole wide world.

She couldn't help but burst into laughter. "If you could only see your faces," she gasped, unable to stop the giggles.

"What's so funny?" Gabby's face morphed into thunderclouds, reflected by Drusilla's.

"You two," Rachel said, wiping tears from her eyes. "Look, I know you two have good hearts and felt you were doing the right thing, aiding Gramma Dot in aiding me. And you know what? It's okay."

"It is?" Gabby slid her a sideways look of skepticism.

"No hard feelings?" Drusilla asked, eyes wide with surprise and doubt.

"None whatsoever," Rachel stood and held out her arms. They both rushed around the table to do a big group hug, laughing with joy.

\\|/

Today at Eli's Place, Mark reaped the bliss of an extended family, warts and all. Conversation flowed in a more polite direction and the information they gathered from Mark filled in the puzzle of the lost years.

Likewise, the information filled in lots of whys, wheres, and whats for him.

Dot Rivers, his gramma, was still going strong in her eightieth year and continued in her role as caregiver to her daughter, whose dialysis treatments rendered her more fragile by the week. And his newly acquired family of aunts, uncles, and friends spoke of his gramma's behind-the-scenes good deeds.

"She's so depressed," Gramma, according to Rachel, had said of his mama. "The anxiety gets to her at times. So Mark's finding his daddy is a blessing to her. Frees her up from the guilt she's carried all these years."

Mary realized that Mark was learning that the situation was not his alone. Many were affected.

And oh, yes! Rachel had since connected the dots. She'd learned that Mark's grandmother was the Angel Dot who'd baked the strawberry cake and left flowers on Jason's, his half-brother's, grave.

His gramma had also loaned all the hospital equipment—used by Mark's late grandpa, an invalid—to The Gang to use for Rachel. He liked that tag, "The Gang," because they now included him. Gramma had later shared with Rachel how expensive and financially burdensome the original purchase of the hospital equipment had been, and at the worst time imaginable.

Gramma was the angel who, when Rachel's need for the equipment ended, had donated it all to Spartanburg Shares Medical Loan Closet—falling in love with Jerry Toth, the lead volunteer coordinator, and all the volunteers there and wishing she were younger so she could become a volunteer herself.

"We're all praying for your Gramma, Mark," Rachel told him, reaching to take his hand. "And your mother."

"Yeah," J.C. said. "We're here for you, son."

"Thanks, Uncle J.C.," Mark said solemnly. "I appreciate all of you." He grinned then. "I always wanted a family like this one."

"You mean like crazy?" Gabby winked at him.

"Yeah." The grin grew even wider. "Like crazy."

He read L-O-V-E in everybody's eyes and it made him want to shout and holler, like cheering at school ball games. But he was now old enough to restrain himself.

Just barely.

"Hey," Tammy swept past and poured fresh tea and coffee, "I've got a niece I want you to meet, Mark. She's real cute."

Mark's grin vanished and he felt that disgusting blush began to creep up his neck.

To everyone's credit, they looked everywhere but at Mark for a few minutes, ribbing each other with nonsense.

Whew. He was glad.

\|/

"How'd the day go?"

Peter didn't answer right away and Rachel knew something was amiss. He'd just come in from his pest control routes. Actually, he came in earlier than usual, a sure sign of distress.

He took a deep, weary breath and blew it out. "Property taxes are due." He lifted his shoulders. "I don't know how I'm going to pay them. I woke up at four this morning worrying about where the money's gonna come from."

Rachel frowned. "But honey—we already paid them."

He cut her a sharp look. "We did?"

"Yes, don't you rem—" She clamped her jaw shut.

Obviously he did not.

"Two weeks ago, we mailed the payment off."

She saw the struggle in him, the lax jaw, the confusion in the green depths. "How did we manage it?"

She sat down beside him on the sofa and took his limp hand. "Thank God there was enough in several of our different bank accounts."

He gazed at her, still baffled. "But there couldn't have been enough to—"

"Shhh." She squeezed his big hand that now gripped hers as though it were a buoy to a drowning man. "We took the rest from my inheritance fund—the one from Daddy's estate."

He scowled and sat up straighter. "I didn't want to use—" He peered at her, eyes stricken. "Aww, honey. We'll put that back right away, starting next month. Within a year, it'll all be right there where it's supposed to be."

Rachel smiled and placed a finger to his lips. "That's a plan. So stop worrying about it. We're covered, honey."

He seemed to drift off for long moments and then appeared to come to some decision. "Rachel, there's something I want to talk about. It's a revelation to me."

"Okay, honey."

"Well, for some time now, it's like this third person is inside me, inserting himself into my life. He's a person I don't like. In fact, I can't stand him. He's hateful and vicious. He makes me say things that the real Peter just doesn't say. For instance, I told Amber that I didn't love her during that argument a while back."

His eyes pleaded for understanding. "I'm her daddy. How can I *not love her*? But this person doesn't. I'm dealing with this terrible person who wants to control me, who wants to erupt at inappropriate times. I'm afraid that I'll lose control. When he shows up, it ties my nerves in knots and makes my mind scatter. Can you understand that?"

"Of course, I do, Peter. I sense this battle going on inside you most of the time."

"It's like I'm bipolar, as I've heard it explained, y'know? Or a split personality. The thing that sets it off is when I lose my centered state. Like trying to do more than one thing at a time. I can only stay centered on one thing or else my mind scatters and I can't accomplish anything."

"Ah, darling," Rachel reached for his hand and laced their fingers. "How difficult it is for you."

"If I stay centered, I do fine. But once I lose my perspective or goal, it's like an eclipse in my head—or a delete button is pushed on the entire goal. The real me is calm and in charge but when my memory bleeps, fear enters in and this provokes this angry entity."

He sighed. "I have to stay single minded. I can't carry but one thought and goal—not like I used to pack three or four goals in at once."

Rachel squeezed his hand. "And you did it all with aplomb."

He shot her a questioning look. "What's ap—"

She smiled. "Aplomb means you've always been confident and skilled."

"Oh." His eyes lit up, then settled back into sobriety. "You never know what that entity is going to do. And the fact that your memory doesn't stack those memories, you fear you'll do embarrassing things that you won't remember. You do things that don't register or compute in the brain. Does that make sense?"

"Absolutely."

"It's like a fog over my brain—one I can feel through my eyes. When the fog lifts, my mind is clear as a bell. What brings that fog on is that I try too hard to work my memory, and it shuts down. Worry is the same as fear—it provokes anger, which provokes the stranger. This guy is unpredictable and I fear him.

It's like the real me stands back and watches in horror at him ruining my life. As long as I stay calm and don't allow fear into me, I do fine. I carry a day planner at all times to record everything I need to do. That really helps me to function within the scope of normalcy."

"You do an amazing job, darling."

"Do I make sense?" he asked, worry hovering in the green depths.

"Yes," she said in all honesty. "You make perfect sense."

"Thank you, honey, for understanding and—treating me with respect. That makes a world of difference in the quality of life while fighting this crazy disease. And it is a battle. A difficult one. Just when we need love and encouragement, so many people turn away from us."

Then his brow furrowed. "Do you think Mark will turn away when he realizes I'm—"

"No, no. He won't. He'll want to make the most of the time he has with you. You can take that to the bank."

"It's not fair, is it? He just finds me and then this stupid—" He stopped, took a deep breath, and visibly slid into acceptance. "I hope you're right. I've seen so many turn away that it's hard to believe anything different will happen."

"I'd like to change that, Peter. You and I can make a difference by being transparent and exposing that stranger inside you for whom he really is, one who seems like a roaring lion but in all reality—when exposed—is really a toothless old tomcat. I'm going to find a good support group. We'll invest ourselves there and then expand our efforts to declaw him and kill Alzheimer's and dementia's stigma."

"I'm in favor of that," Peter said. "Another thing, in case I haven't done so, I want to thank you for making sure I take my meds and supplements. I really believe they're making a difference. As long as an Alzheimer's patient has one person who believes in them and respects them, they can have quality in their life. Never before do we need love and consideration more than now."

He leaned to kiss her on the lips. "Thank you, darling," he murmured.

"My pleasure," she smiled and kissed him again. "You're my delight."

He relaxed and sank back into the cushions, tugging her with him. They melded together like they had as teenagers and Rachel began to softly hum "Twilight Time." She heard Peter sigh with contentment.

"Honey?" he gazed into her eyes. "Use my experience in your book. Maybe, just maybe it will help somebody who's going through what I am."

She looked back at him, reading his features and body language. "Are you sure, Peter? I don't have to, you know."

He smiled. "I'm sure. The fight against Alzheimer's is bigger than me. We all have to team up to get results, don't you think?"

Trust shimmered in his gaze.

"Yes," she whispered. "You're right."

Then he whispered, "I don't deserve you?"

She blinked back tears, thrust her nose in the air, and drawled with sass, "You got *everything you deserved*, Peter James!" They burst into laughter and he nuzzled her neck as she resumed singing in her rich contralto.

"Deepening shadows gather splendor as day is done . . . Fingers of night will soon surrender the setting sun . . . *I count the moments, darling, while you're here with me* . . . Together, at last, at Twilight Time."

Notes From the Author

This book is especially close to my heart because I've seen up close and personal how Alzheimer's slowly steals loved ones from us. Like my character, Peter, and his siblings and mother, members of my husband's own family have succumbed to this disease. So I've done extensive research on the subject because the genetics are passed on to my progeny. Like Rachel, I fervently pray for a cure. And soon. Time is of the essence. In the meantime, I keep my eyes open and my ear to the ground, searching out every promising nugget of help available to the afflicted and their caregivers.

The following excerpts from Alzheimer's newsletters and such offer hope and encouragement. I want to share the ones that stand out to me and that I trust will reach out to you, too, who share in this challenging struggle.

I urge everyone to read the book, *Alzheimer's Disease: What If There Was a Cure? The Story of Ketones by* Mary T. Newport, M.D.

Changing the View Of Alzheimer's Disease:

From our first breath to our last, the stories we hear and the stories we tell define who we are and how we perceive our world.

Stories connect us by revealing universal truths. They create patterns of thought and behavior that become indelibly ingrained into our subconscious.

It is the power of personal stories (and the memories they make) that gives the specter of Alzheimer's disease such strength, regardless of an individual's location, ethnicity, or philosophical leanings.

The disease is viewed as a story-stealer—one of the few ailments powerful enough to strike at that which makes us uniquely human. By pilfering our personal narratives, Alzheimer's threatens to disintegrate our humanity, one recollection at a time.

Who are we, if not an accumulation of a lifetime of experiences?

A shell, a husk, a hollow container—this is how the world views men and women with Alzheimer's disease.

So influential is this perception that those who are diagnosed are soon written off as a tragically lost cause, incapable of learning, growing, or forming relationships. Everyone buys into this image. The person with the disease believes it, their family believes it, society believes it, and the notion of hope becomes just another shattered memory.

The stigma of Alzheimer's tends to silence those touched by the disease. But with no medical antidote to the epidemic appearing on the horizon, some are fashioning a different kind of remedy, spun from their very own real-life stories of tragedy and triumph.

By sharing their experiences, these inspiring individuals support and educate one another in a collective display of human empathy unmatched by any benefit concert, fundraiser or government initiative. They exist as living proof that people whose realities have been forever altered by Alzheimer's still have stories to tell.

These are the tales that inspired the Fade to Blank project, an account of six separate lives, united by one deadly disease.

These men and women have offered up their candid accounts, agreeing to let you into some of the most private aspects of their lives.

Their offering will enable you to gain a truer understanding of what life is really like for those faced with the reality of a mind slowly fading to blank.

All they ask is that you listen, you learn and you grow.

I encourage each of you to go to the link below and check out these courageous stories first hand.

\\//

To find out more about fighting the Alzheimer's stigma, read "Fade to Blank: Life Inside Alzheimer's" by Anne Marie Botek. You can find it at www.fadetoblank.org/about.htm.

The article was contributed by AgingCare.com. AgingCare connects family caregivers, shares informative articles, provides answers and support through an interactive Caregiver Forum, and offers search capabilities for senior living options for elderly loved ones.

\\//

So in the meantime, dear readers, keep the faith, live each day in the now, and get involved. HAPPY READING!

About the Author

Emily Sue Harvey is a past president of the Southeastern Writers Association. She has contributed to several volumes in the bestselling *Chicken Soup* and *Chocolate for Women* series and has published articles in multiple venues. She is the author of the national bestseller *Unto these Hills*, along with the novels *Song of Renewal*, *Homefires*, *Space*, and *Cocoon*, and the novella *Flavors*. She is the mother of grown children and lives with her husband in Startex, SC.